The phrase "it's a classic" is much abused. Still there may be some appeal in the slant of the cap Overlook sets in publishing a list of books the editors at Overlook feel have continuing value, books usually dropped by other publishers because of "the realities of the marketplace." Overlook's Tusk Ivories aim to give these books a new life, recognizing that tastes, even in the area of so-called classics, are often time-bound and variable. The wheel comes around. Tusk Ivories begin with the hope that modest printings together with caring booksellers and reviewers will reestablish the books' presence and engender new interest.

As, almost certainly, American publishing has not been generous in offering readers books from the rest of the world, for the most part, Tusk Ivories will more than just a little represent fiction from European, Asian, and Latin American sources, but there will be of course some "lost" books from our own shores, too, books we think deserve new recognition and, with it, readers.

The Process

Brion Gysin

"I will a round, unvarnished tale deliver."
OTHELLO: I iii 90

TVƧK●IVORIES

Published by The Overlook Press

This Tusk Ivories edition first published in the United States in 2005 by
The Overlook Press, Peter Mayer Publishers, Inc.
Woodstock & New York

WOODSTOCK:
One Overlook Drive
Woodstock, NY 12498
www.overlookpress.com
[For individual orders, bulk and special sales, contact our Woodstock office]

NEW YORK:
141 Wooster Street
New York, NY 10012

Catalog Card Number Library of Congress

Gysin, Brion.
The process.
p. cm.
I. Title.
PS 3557.Y8P76 1987   813'.54   86-43064

Manufactured in the United States of America
1-58567-711-6
1 3 5 7 9 8 6 4 2

Wherein of antres vast and deserts idle,
Rough quarries, rocks and hills whose heads touch heaven,
It was my hint to speak, such was the process;
And of the Cannibals that each other eat,
The Anthropophagi, and men whose heads
Do grow beneath their shoulders.

OTHELLO: I iii 140–145

BRION GYSIN 1916–1986
by Robert Palmer

A philosophy that does not culminate in a metaphysic of ecstasy
is vain speculation; a mystical experience that is not grounded
on a sound philosophical education is in danger of degenerating
and going astray.
——Henry Corbin, *Creative Imagination in the Sufism of
Ibn 'rabi.*

[T]he past remains present to the future . . . the future is already present to the past, just as the notes of a musical phrase,
though played successively, nevertheless persist all together in
the present and thus form a phrase.
——Ibid.

I understand that the late Henry Corbin was, in recent years,
given access to books in Bombay belonging to the present Aga
Khan, whose position as head of the Ismaili sect of Islam
derives from his presumed descent from Mohammed's daughter
Fatima through the last Old Man of the Mountain. . . . Corbin
and many others know infinitely more than I do about the
Ismailis. I know next to nothing: read Marco Polo in my childhood, became a hashishin in Greece at 19, read my Baudelaire,
got syphilis like he did long before penicillin, smoked a lot in
the Algerian Sahara and Morocco where I spent what is still
more than a third of my lifetime. I did not become an Assassin.
——Brion Gysin, Points of Order, in *Here To Go: Planet
R-101*, Brion Gysin interviewed by Terry Wilson.

I rub out the word. . . . I the Man from Nowhere negotiated
like a Tangier Space Draft on a Swiss bank.
——Brion Gysin, *Minutes To Go*

"But, Hamid," I laughed, "I am not an Assassin at all!"
"We are Assassins, all of us," he gravely replied.
——*The Process*

The Process is a funny, picaresque, provocative magic carpet ride, a careening good read. Like its central character, a pot-smoking professor who has forsworn teaching in order to learn, it ranges widely, and travels light: "No baggage. This is the way I came and—Inch'Allah! (God willing)—this is the way I shall return."

It may be of interest that the city of Tanja (Tangier), the village of Jajouka with its Master Musicians, the desert outposts, the trance rituals of the dervish brotherhoods, and many of the characters of this novel are drawn directly from life. Though timeless in mood (or transtemporal, in the Corbin/Ismaili sense), the book is also time-specific to a sixties Gysin knew from the inside, the sixties defined by the good doctors Hoffman (inventor of LSD) and Fanon, who figure herein.

But as equipment for appreciating *The Process*, information like this is probably marginal. My suggestion is that you abandon this preface and read the book. By the time you have finished it and doubled back here, you will probably want to read the novel all again anyway. For as William Burroughs observed, "You will find that it reads itself."

The Process comes bracketed between Shakespeare's pledge to deliver "a round, unvarnished tale" and a thirteenth-century Persian mystic's insistence that "from the book alone, nothing emerges." The book is an entertainment, an education, and an enigma, and in this respect getting to know it can be a little like getting to know the author himself. "He who seeks the mysteries and the realities, must seek out someone who knows"—words quoted at the end of *The Process*—and Gysin's offer in *Minutes To Go*: "If you want to disappear, come around for private lessons" were all the encouragement I needed to seek him out in Tangier in the early seventies. The recent publication of *The Process* in America had generated little media attention; my admiring review in *Rolling Stone* had been a singular exception and was more than sufficient to get me in the door.

Before leaving New York, I had managed to hear tapes of Gysin's beloved Pan music from the Moroccan village of Jajouka, recorded by Brian Jones of the Rolling Stones, when Gysin took him there. I was enthralled; Moroccan music, especially the "music as psychic hygiene" of the dervish brotherhoods, provided the common ground for my first encounters with Gysin's adventuring spirit and formidable intelligence. Accidentally ("as if there were any accidents," Brion would have said), I had begun at the beginning.

"I never was much immersed truly into Islam. . . . It was most particularly the music that interested me," Gysin told interviewer Terry Wilson. "I went with Paul Bowles, who was a composer long before he was a writer, and . . . had very, very extraordinary ears, and, uh, he taught me a lot of things. I owe him a tremendous amount, I owe him my years in Morocco really."

When I met him, Brion was in his mid-fifties. He lived in a European-style apartment building in Tangier's "new town," in a balconied flat from which he feasted his painterly eye on the patterned light and shade of the city's whitewashed buildings, spread out across a series of low, gently rounded hills on the shore of the indigo blue Mediterranean. On a clear day, and most days were, he could examine through his powerful binoculars the pitted detail of the rock of Gibraltar, facing Tangier across the Pillars of Hercules.

Photographs of Brion as a youth reveal an almost arrogantly handsome young Adonis, the happy result of his mixed Celtic and Swiss genes. In his fifties he was still striking and trim, keeping in shape with the help of regular visits from a Moroccan master of exercise and massage. He went striding through Tangier as if he owned it, finding time for everyone from the expatriate crowd at Lily the Lion-tamer's Parade bar to the budding Moroccan painters he enthusiastically and generously encouraged, from visiting hipsters to the Casbah's canniest con men to the monied exiles who surveyed Tangier from their elegant walled villas on the higher outlying hills. He even found a renegade European audio technician down by the port to make a patch cord linking our two Uher tape recorders, so that he was able to download onto my bagfull of blank tapes some of the hours of recordings of dervish ceremonies he had made over the years. While the reels turned, conversation flowed. At times, it raged.

Brion was a living reproach to the sort of thinking that confuses category with reality and demands, "Yes, but what is it that you *do*?" It is easy enough to compile a laundry list of *some* of the things he did. He painted, for example. There were astonishing panoramas of the Sahara's "wordless wastes," and studies of the D'jemaa el F'na, or Great Square, of Marrakesh, crowded with hundreds of shadowy yet indisputably alive figures playing music, buying and selling, riding bicycles, and, always, hustling. Other canvases overlaid calligraphy, "as if one took a page and wrote Japanese from top to bottom and Arabic across it from right to left," in a pictorial space suggested by the cabalistic gridwork of Moroccan magic squares.

The writing Gysin left us includes, in addition to *The Process*, a second novel called *The Last Museum*; he was working on it when I first met him in Tangier (but not finally published until shortly after his death in 1986). This second book is a re-imagining of the period in Brion's life when he accomplished his most influential work with words, the early sixties, when he was living in a rundown Paris hotel that William Burroughs, Allen Ginsberg, and other seminal Beat figures also called home at the time—thus the nameless hotel's nickname, the Beat Hotel. When Maurice Girodias agreed to publish a volume of Burroughs' visionary written "routines," it was Gysin who collected the scattered pages and independent episodes, intuited a larger pattern, and was primarily responsible for assembling the manuscript published as *Naked Lunch*.

While at the Beat Hotel, Gysin was working on a collage when he "accidentally" sliced through some pages of newspaper with his Stanley blade. He typed out the cut-up prose, read the results, and found himself rolling on the floor, convulsed in laughter like a man high on nitrous oxide. A period of extensive experimentation with the cutting-up and random reassembly of diverse combinations of texts followed, involving Gregory Corso, Sinclair Beiles, and others in addition to Gysin and Burroughs. Some early results were published in the seminal small-press chapbooks *Minutes To Go* and *Exterminator!* "We began to find out a whole lot of things about the real nature of words and writing," Brion recalled one night when I had my Uher running. "What are words and what are they doing? Where are they going? The cut-up method treats words as the painter treats his paint, raw material with rules and reasons of its own. . . . Painters and writers of the kind I respect want to be heroes, challenging fate in their lives and in their art. What is fate? Fate is written: *Mektoub*, in the Arab world, where art has always been nothing but abstract. *Mektoub* means 'It is written.' So . . . if you want to challenge and change fate . . . , cut up words. Make them a new world.''

Burroughs' extensive use of cut-ups in *Nova Express*, *The Ticket That Exploded*, and other books made the method highly controversial in the literary world. There was some talk to the effect that Brion was a bad influence, a keef-crazed, razor-wielding, dada-spouting anarchist whose high-art theorizing was corrupting an authentic American voice. In time, cut-ups became enshrined as an alternative strategy for dealing with words, studied and employed by poets and novelists and even playing a part in pop music, as a lyric-writing aid or inspiration for, among others, David Bowie, Iggy Pop, Mick Jagger, and Keith Richards. But Brion wanted no part of any movement or school. From the beginning, he privately urged Burroughs to make more use of his gift for narrative or ''representational'' prose writing, and while the cut-up experiments form part of the context from which *The Process* and *The Last Museum* emerged, neither of Gysin's novels is a work of abstract or experimental fiction: ''I will a round, unvarnished tale deliver.''

What else did Brion do? He was, he liked to point out with amused irony, one of the fathers of sound poetry, among the first artists doing serious work with the tape recorder and the human voice. But Brion did much more with his Uher than that. For him, the tape recorder was as much an artistic medium as painting and writing. He used it to overlay and orchestrate, as a musical composer would, a series of works utilizing the spoken word and permutative techniques, a method of word-manipulation quite distinct from cut-ups. From ''I Am that I Am'' came ''I Am That Am I? Am I That? I Am!'' and so on. ''Junk is no good baby. No junk is good baby. Is baby good? No junk! No junk baby is good. Junk is goooood, baby . . . No!'' Invited by the BBC to realize these and other works on audio tape, using their studios, he turned his ''permutated poems'' into symphonies. Another work in this series used as its source material pistol shots recorded at several volume levels and distances from the microphone. Permutating his pistol shot readings like the words in a sentence, using his acute musical ear to divine an appropriate rhythmic context, he came up with a piece that sounds uncannily like the precisely percussive drumming and handclapping of Berbers from the High Atlas of Southern Morocco.

This ''Pistol Poem,'' far from being an intriguing anomaly, has more to say about who Brion Gysin was, and what it was he did, than any laundry list, however extensive. Looking back over my list, I find that it somehow misses the point. My description of his magic square paintings, for example, omits perhaps the most important detail: the genesis of the idea. Brion's study of Japanese while in the U.S. Army during World War II, his later study and appreciation of Arabic calligraphy, and his lifelong interest in magic as the ''Other Method'' for exercising control of matter and knowing space were contributing factors. But here is what happened.

In 1950 Gysin was present at a religious festival outside Tangier, held in what had been in Phoenician times a sacred grove, and very probably a cult center. There he heard strangely riveting music, related to the ecstatic trance music of the Sufi brotherhoods but different; it had a luminous, hieratic quality all its own.

"You know your music when you hear it, one day," he later wrote of the experience. "You fall into line and dance until you pay the piper." Later, with the help of the Moroccan painter Hamri, he traced this music back to the village of Jajouka, which perches high on a hilltop in the Rif, just as *The Process* describes it. What he heard there confirmed his initial impression: "I knew I wanted to hear that music every day for the rest of my life." What he saw, as the first "foreigner" to visit the village since anyone could remember, utterly astonished him.

In Jajouka, rites and myths from the dawn of Western civilization are preserved, not as faintly remembered traditions, but as a living, integral reality. There Gysin witnessed a ritual he immediately recognized as the Lupercalia, the Rites of Pan, which in Jajouka are not celebrated as folklore but employed as a technology if you will, for bringing the male and female forces in nature into a positive and fruitful equilibrium. In *The Process* Hansen persuades Hamid to pronounce words from the village's ritual language and discovers that they are Punic in origin. "Jajouka," Gysin would say with a gleam in his eye, "that's a very old scene."

If the village astonished Gysin, so did the circumstance of its "discovery" by someone so well-equipped to understand what was going on there. Gysin was passionately immerged in the literature and lore of antiquity, and particularly fascinated by the esoteric traditions and Gnosis of early times. He was well-versed in original Greek, Latin and Arabic sources, having built on a first rate education at the Sorbonne and other European universities with a lifetime of reading and study. The fact that he had found a place where the Old Gods still walked the hills and music and magic were still synonymous was, for him, a magical event in itself.

Brion insisted that cut-ups actually cut through the word lines and association lines that moor us in present time, and that sometimes the future leaked through. Sentences formed by cut-ups often prove to be about future events, he said—or perhaps in some cases to *determine* future events, a rather unsettling proposition, which led Burroughs to postulate that "Writing, when it's successful, is Making Things Happen." Well, Jajouka was a similar proposition, though in reverse: the past leaking through into the present. For Jajouka, which has no electricity or running water, is on no map and at the end of no road, exists somehow in its own time, not in our media-saturated century. It constitutes living proof that what we call reality is a perceptual and, socially speaking, a *consensual* phenomenon. Jajouka's reality is the magical reality of antiquity. Whether the visitor "believes in" magic or not, in Jajouka he sees magic as method, magic that works.

And here we return to the genesis of Gysin's magic square paintings. At the urging of Jajouka's Master Musicians, Brion opened a lavish restaurant in Tangier, with a troupe from Jajouka providing the music. This was in the days before Moroccan independence, when Tangier was a free port, an International Zone—the Interzone of *Naked Lunch* and of Joy Division's rock classic *Unknown Pleasures*. "There were a hundred banks on the Boulevard," Brion recalled; the restaurant did well. Living in such proximity to the Jajouka musicians, Brion was inevitably curious about their magical practices.

"I kept some notes and drawings," he wrote in *Brion Gysin Let The Mice In*, "meaning to write a recipe book of magic. My Pan people were furious when they found this out." There was also a minor falling out over money.

The result was that one day in the restaurant, Brion discovered "a magic object, which was an amulet of sorts, a rather elaborate one with seeds, pebbles, shards of broken mirror, seven of each, and a little package in which there was a piece of writing, and the writing when deciphered by friends who didn't even want to *handle* it, because of its magic qualities, which even educated Moroccans were not anxious to get in touch with, but it said something like, an appeal to one of the devils of fire, the devil of smoke—to take Brion away from this house: as the smoke leaves this chimney may Brion leave this house and never return . . . . And within a very short time I indeed lost the restaurant and everything else. But I realized that this was a very interesting traditional example . . . of a cabalistic square, which I then began to apply . . . to my own painting when I returned to Paris in 1958." (from *Here to Go: Planet R-101*)

Perhaps this snatching of an artistic victory from the jaws of a magical defeat was the sort of thing Gysin had in mind when he talked about artists as heroes "challenging fate in their lives and in their art." For me, he was precisely that. Painter, writer, sound poet, scholar, philosopher, traveler, explorer, metaphysician—the labels are so many words. Cut up, isolated, each word cutting *away* from the big picture, they bounce off Brion the Irreducible like so many rubber bullets. No painting without the magic. No magic without the words. No words without the sound. No sound without the music.

"If you want to disappear, come around for private lessons."
He was slippery, Brion. You had to learn to see him whole
before you could see him at all.

If there is a "key" to *The Process*, this is it. By no means
should one confuse Brion Gysin with his central character, the
fun-loving black pothead professor. Not that there isn't a lot
of the one in the other. The work that won Gysin one of the
first Fulbright Fellowships included two books: *To Master A
Long Goodnight*, (the biography of Josiah Henson, whose life
was the inspiration for *Uncle Tom's Cabin*) and *The History
of Slavery in Canada*. Like Hanson, Gysin used his Fulbright
as a one-way ticket out. As for Hanson's Blackness, "I was
slipped into the wrong colored package and delivered to the
wrong address," Brion wrote in a piece included in the "Brion
Gysin Special" issue of *Soft Need*. "Just look at all this lousy
oatmealy skin. Not enough melanin. I've lived the best years
of my life in Morocco and it can't take the sun. When I'm
with Africans, I forget that I'm white. But they can't forget
it. I stick out like a sore thumb." Nevertheless, Ulysses O.
Hanson isn't Brion Gysin. *The Process* itself is Brion Gysin.

When Hamid tells what it's like to experience the Rites of
Pan in Jajouka, it's Brion talking. Then there's Thay Himmer,
on his family's mystical inclinations: "All the women in my
family, for the last three generations . . . at least, have been
ardent Theosophists, followers of Madame Blavatsky and Annie Besant, in close contact with Swami Vivekenanda and
Krishnamurti; aunts, great-aunts, always talking about Gurdjieff, *pranna*, and the hallucinatory effects of superaeration—
and all that sort of thing—or trailing around in trances at
home." That's Brion, talking about his own family. When

Maya Himmer remembers a childhood spent partly in Canada's open spaces, when the Himmers' lawyer talks about what it means to be Swiss, it's Brion again, with more fractured autobiography. Similarly, the evocations of Sufi ceremonies, from the marvelous *Zikr* in a desert compound early on to the almost unbearably vivid descent into the collective unconscious of the massed Hamadcha near the book's halfway point, are either reportage or composites, transformed, in any case, into poetry. By the time I met him, Brion had infiltrated the ceremonies and recorded the trance rhythms of every major dervish brotherhood in North Africa. Often he went incognito, his Uher hanging on a strap under his flapping jellaba; if he'd been discovered, he would probably have been torn apart. The artist as hero, challenging fate again, living to the hilt in his chosen milieu, "the wild west of the spirit."

Hassan i Sabbah, Old Man of the Mountain, Ismaili Gnostic, founder of the Order of Assassins—is he Brion Gysin too? Not to hear Brion tell it, but doesn't he protest rather strenuously? Certainly the Old Man of the Mountain, who reportedly used hashish to vouchsafe his Adepts their visions of Paradise, intrigued Brion greatly, for a long time. His first reference to the subject in print was in *Minutes To Go*:

> Yesterday a thousand years ago, Hassan i Sabbah, a Persian by birth and school chum of Omar Khayyam, walked by accident (as if there were any accidents) into the studios of Radio Cairo to find all the cats bombed. He realized like a flash that *he* could SEND, TOO. He took the mike to an unheathed (sic) pent-house called Alamut near the Caspian. . . . His original station nearly a thousand years ago could broadcast from Alamut to Paris with Charlemagne on the house phone and as far

as Xanadu East. Today the same lines have been proliferating machine-wise and a stray wire into the room I am in. . . .

Apparently able to dispatch his Assassins (a word from the same root as hashish) from Alamut and then direct them at a distance, Hassan i Sabbah forged a monastic order and some practical applications of a venerable mystical tradition into an organization, feared throughout the Christian and Islamic worlds. The comparison to present-day organizations like the CIA, which use science and pervert enlightenment in the service of a sinisterly shadowy Grand Design, was for Brion an obvious one. Yet he felt such a compelling connection to the Old Man and to Alamut that finally, some years after that first reference in *Minutes To Go*, he made a special trip in order to climb up to the ruins of the fortress, which had been leveled by Mongol invaders in 1256.

"I found it very disturbing when I was at Alamut to . . . find myself under strong psychic attack," he told Terry Wilson. "I suddenly was attacked with vertigo, which I hadn't ever experienced before in my life, and altitude fever. . . . But I also felt psychically attached to the place as I have never felt before in any other spot in my travels. . . . I felt that I was somebody that'd been pushed over the precipice, and I wasn't certain that I wanted to be a victim to such an old scene. . . ."

The only weapon that ever proved effective against Hassan i Sabbah, according to Gysin, was cut-ups. Before he founded his Order, the story goes, Hassan was director of finances at a Persian court. From the Wilson interviews: "He found when he came to deliver his speech on the exchequer that his manuscripts had been cut in such a way that he didn't at first realize that they had been sliced right down the middle and re-pasted. . . . All of his material had been cut up by some unknown enemy and his speech from the Woolsack was greeted with howls of laughter and utter disgrace and he was thrown out of the administration.''

For Brion, the Old Man of the Mountain represented Control, a principle now embodied by other Old Men who sit in their electronic Alamuts with their long, bony fingers on the nuclear detonator button. Cut-ups were a useful tool because they sprung the trap of language, enabling the spirit to soar free from Control's prison of words. Getting Out—out of that prison, out of the body, and ultimately out of this world entirely and into space—was for Brion the Great Work. The purpose of his art, from paintings to *The Process*, was Liberation.

Sometimes his preoccupation with this purpose can leave an unpleasant aftertaste. In particular, there is an apparent misogyny in *The Process* and in Gysin's other writings that shouldn't be glossed over. His tendency, shaped both by sexual preference and by years spent in the sexually-segregated Arab world, was to be with the boys. Yet women were always among his closest friends. ''There are no Brothers,'' he would say; yet he called his lifelong chum Felicity Mason his pseudo-sister.

''Don't go calling *me* a misogynist . . . a mere misogynist,'' he railed in *Here To Go: Planet R-101*. ''I am a monumental misanthropist. Man is a bad animal, maybe the only bad animal. . . . No one but man threatens the survival of the planet. Space Man may well blow up the planet Earth behind him. When ya gotta go. . . . Now we know what we are here for. We are not here to love fear and serve any old bearded but invisible thunder god. We are here to go.''

Pardon me if I snicker just a bit at the idea of a self-styled misanthropist who had uncountable hordes of friends and was gregarious and giving in his personal relationships, a philosophical posthumanist who seemed to want to know all there was to know about the whole history and thought and experience and dreams of humankind. But don't get the idea that I'm not taking the man seriously. He was Here to Go, all right. He streaked across Present Time like a runaway rocket, and then he was Gone. And I don't think I'll ever get over missing him.

New York City
March 1987

1

I

I am out in the Sahara heading due south with each day of travel less sure of just who I am, where I am going or why. There must be some easier way to do it but this is the only one I know so, like a man drowning in a sea of sand, I struggle back into this body which has been given me for my trip across the Great Desert. "This desert," my celebrated colleague, Ibn Khaldoun the Historian, has written, "This desert is so long it can take a lifetime to go from one end to the other and a childhood to cross at its narrowest point." I made that narrow childhood crossing on another continent; out through hazardous tenement hallways and stickball games in the busy street, down American asphalt alleys to paved playgrounds; shuffling along Welfare waiting-lines into a maze of chain-store and subway turnstiles and, through them, out onto a concrete campus in a cold gray city whose skyscrapers stood up to stamp on me. It has been a long trail a-winding down here into this sunny but sandy Middle Passage of my life in Africa, along with the present party. Here, too, I may well lose my way for I can see that I am, whoever I am, out in the middle of Nowhere when I slip back into this awakening flesh which fits me, of course, like a glove.

I know this body as if it were a third party whose skin I put on as a mask to wear through their "Land of Fear" and I do go in a sort of disguise for, like everyone else out here in this blazing desert where a man is a fool to show his face naked by day, I have learned to wrap five or six yards of fine white muslin around my head to protect the mucus of my nose and throat against the hot, dry wind. All you can see of me is my eyes. For once, I look just like everyone else. No need for me to open these eyes. I know what is out there—nothing but the very barest stripped illusion of a world; almost nothing, nothing at all.

Bundled up like a mummy, I huddle here under my great black burnous, a cape as big as a bag for an animal my size, shape and color. It also serves as a portable tent smelling of woodsmoke and lanolin, under which I fumble for the two pencil-thin sections of my *sebsi,* my slim wooden keef-pipe from Morocco, to fit them together. A fine flesh-pink clay pipe head, no bigger than the last joint of my little finger, snuggles up over a well-fitted paper collar shaped wet with spit. I try it like a trumpet; airtight, good. My keef-pouch from Morocco is the skin of a horned viper sewn into a *metoui* and stuffed with great grass. I check with my thumb the tide of fine-chopped green leaf which rolls down its long leather tongue, milking most of the keef back into the pouch. What remains, I coax into the head of my pipe with the beckoning crook of my right forefinger.

A masterpiece matchbox the size of a big postage stamp leaps into the overturned bowl of my left hand, riding light but tight between the ball of my thumb and my third finger.

2

I make all these moves not just out of habit but with a certain conscious cunning through which I ever-so slowly reconstruct myself in the middle of your continuum; inserting myself, as it were, back into this flesh which is the visible pattern of Me. Yet, I know this whole business is a trap which may well be woven of nothing but words, so I joggle the miniature matchbox I hold in my hand and these masterpiece matches in here chuckle back what always has sounded to me like a word but a word which I cannot quite catch. It could be a rattling Arabic word but my grasp of Arabic is not all that good and no one, not even Hamid, will tell me what the matches say to the box. I hold the box up to my ear as I shake it again, trying to hear what the box stutters back. If I remember correctly, Basilides in his "Game" reduced all the Names proposed by the Gnostics to one single rolling, cacophonic, cyclical word which he thought might well prove to be a Key to the heavens: *"Kaulakaula-kaulakaulakau . . ."* Can the matches match that?

I love these little matches bought back in Tanja. Each match is a neat twist of brown paper like a stick dipped in wax, with a helmet-shaped turquoise-blue head made to strike on the miniature Sahara of sandpaper slapped onto one side of the box. Matchbox is clamped into the claw of left thumb and middle finger. This indifferent caliper proves suddenly sadist as it rams poor matchbox back onto himself, with little-finger of right hand clear up his ass. Little-finger holds him impaled; proffering a drawerful of identical matches to caliper, who solemnly selects one little brother, pinching him tight. Matchbox is closed with a small, scraping sigh against the heel of right hand. Little-finger withdraws from the rape to help snub poor match against the backslide of his box; striking and exploding his head.

3

I elbow my way out of this cocoon of felted camel-hair smelling of woodsmoke to thrust forward this pipe, pouch and matches just as we go over a bump and I open my eyes. I am not alone. We are five passengers in here, where we should be only four in the blistering metal cabin of this truck whose red-hot diesel is housed in with us, too. Two seats on either side of it are called First-Class Transportation, while Third-Class is out on the back on top of the cargo of sacks beneath a cracking tarpaulin. In the front seat, Driver, who looks like a chipmunk with the toothache because of the way his sloppy turban hangs under his chin, crouches over the wheel like a real desert rat. Black Greaser, his number-two man, has been playing a long windy tune on a flute made out of a bicycle-pump and the bump nearly rams the flute down his throat. An anonymous vomiting man, like a doll leaking wet sawdust and slime, flops out the far window carsick while, here right beside me, crammed into my seat with me when we are not up in the air, is Middleman; Stowaway. We rise shoulder to shoulder and I hope he lands back on the diesel and burns.

He has risen up in the air without losing his cross-legged Sufi saint pose, as if to show me he knows how to levitate. I shoot up my own dusty eyebrows at him as much as to say: *So can I!* because he glares at my pipe with all the baleful ferocity of a carnivorous bird. He feels I pollute him with my keef-smoke—too bad! We both drop back into my seat. I paid First-Class Transportation for these broken springs; no need to share them with him. Yesterday, or the day before, or one of those days back along our trail, he suddenly jumped up from behind a bare dune in the middle of nowhere, flagging us down. I had spotted him up there ahead of us and was just saying to myself: "Is that a man or a bush?" when he started up, skipping and waving his arms. Driver changed gear without daring to stop in the sand from which this little old stick of a man hopped up quick as a bird when Black Greaser threw open the door, grandly waving him into my seat with me. He is a Hadj, just back from the pilgrimage to Mecca; a new little saint. Black Greaser let his whole ugly face fall apart in a welcoming grin: "No baggage, Father?"

The little old man twitched aside the yards of gray-green muslin piled on top of his head and swathing his bearded face: "No baggage. This is the way I came and—*Inch'Allah!*—this is the way I shall return."

I push back the window of opalescent glass frosted by the blasting of sand, to thrust the whole length of my slender pipe out like a periscope into the bouncing air of the dazzling desert through which we churn night and day no faster than a funeral. When I lean out the window, the light out there hits me like a blow. Shading my eyes, I look down into the granular shallows of flowing sand on whose current we ride until I am dizzy and sick. Everything visibly crawls; even the cloth of my sleeve when I look at it close. I glance up and out with my eyes clenched against the all but intolerable brightness of the blazing desert where the mirage sizzles across the horizon like a sweep of glittering marshes, thickly grown with tall rushes whipped by the wind. Air ignites and flames up around the truck like the billowing breath of a blast furnace searing my lungs. The water should lie not more than a half hour's distance away— or so you might think. Hour after hour, day after day, we bore on through the sands without reaching those marshes.

All this ululating emptiness aches in my ears like the echo of a shell. Now and again, I swear I can hear the lowing and bellowing of invisible herds of longhorn cattle but, of course, there are none. When I listen even further down into myself, I contact something else which shakes my whole intimate contact with Me. When I try to tune out the constant moaning roar of the wind, my whole being vibrates to a sound down below the threshold of hearing. My sinuses, antrums, the cords of my throat and the cavities of my chest, the very hollows of my bones hum in a register too low for my ear but, for no known reason, I tremble, I quake. This, so they tell me, is the voice of Ghoul and Ghoul is the Djinn of the Desert, Keeper of the Land of Fear. Grains of sand in their incalculable billions of billions are grinding, grinding together, rolling and sliding abrasively in dunes as big as New York and as high, vibrating this ocean of air through which we paddle like sick fish on their flight from some distant dynamite blast. At that, a very American thought suddenly strikes me: they do have an atomic center out here in the Sahara. Could this air be radioactive, perhaps? Or, is that just the black breath of Ghoul?

Far away back up north in the green hills of Morocco, which I call home since I began to merge almost against my will into this scene with Hamid my Moroccan mock-guru, everyone around the keef cafés is always talking and singing of the Sahara but not one man in ten knows where it begins or ends or how to get into this desert. "It lies down that way, many days marching," they say, swinging their long slim keef-pipes around vaguely south. Yet, every last man sitting there on a straw mat on the floor feels he owns the whole sweep of the Sahara desert, personally, inside his own Muslim head. Let some paleface tourist appear on the scene and they will all proclaim themselves competent "guides," if you please; when not one of them can read even a map. In my forlorn

American way, I thought to teach Hamid the lay of the land and, to this end, I pulled my poor self together to make an expedition up out of the damp grotto in which Hamid and I were living in the native quarter of Tanja, in the impasse of a narrow alley in a section of the Medina below even the tight-packed little pedestrian square of cafés called the Socco Chico; in other words, lost.

I adjusted my shades and smoked one last pipe for the road before I stepped cautiously out into the mainstream of mankind in the swarming alley as narrow as a corridor that is our street. At first, the entire Medina of Tanja feels like one mysteriously rambling mansion packed full of maniacs but, eventually, what looks like a terrifying trap to a tripper gets to feel like your very own house. I cut into the traffic and kept my head down as I whipped around corners with my eyes glued to the ground; so as not to be noticed, I hoped. I slid through alleys so wide I could touch the walls on both sides with my elbows and I had to flatten myself into doorways to let heavily-laden donkeys and porters push past. The whole point of this game, best known to Old Tanja Hands, is to get from one side of the Socco Chico to the other without crossing it; invisible to all traders and touts. My own cunning route, first shown me by Hamid of course, is a turnoff between the old *Hotel Satan* and the *Casa Delerium,* once a whorehouse in better days. This way, you can bypass not only the Socco Chico but also steep Siaghine Street running up out of it; lined as it is with neon-lit bazaars, swarming with tourists and tramps.

I meant to drop by the American Library on my way up to the Boulevard in the New Town of Tanja but, when I caught sight of myself in a mirror in a shop window, I thought: Uh-uh, better not! I managed to make myself look a little more human before I got to the Café de Paris on the Place de France. I drew up in front of a raggedy man who sells raggedy books in the street. On an earlier trip, I had spotted his stock of old dog-eared French guidebooks and road maps of North Africa, put out by Michelin, the makers of tires. As I bent over his wares, I picked up on the fact that I was getting scanned from behind their newspapers by the whole row of white American and British operatives seated, as always, out on the terrace of the Café de Paris. They had their telepathic finders out feeling all over me as I bought, for one dirham, a map which is now out of print. I scuttled back down to the Socco and called Hamid out of his cavernous keef café to drag him home for a bout of instruction in the map.

#151 Morocco, Algeria and Tunisia (1 centimeter for 20 kilometers or 1/2,000,000). On this map, one handspan to the right along the Mediterranean shore lies Woran. With your thumb on Woran, your little-finger lands on Algut. If you pivot due south from that white city on the cliffs, your thumb will fall on Ghardaïa, the mysterious desert capital of the Dissident Mozabites. All that can take at least three or four days of travel from the bright blue Straits of Gibraltar, along the lush coastal valleys, over green hills and mountains so high they are covered with snow. On the far side of these are plains marked in brown to denote almost no annual rainfall at all and they must be crossed before you get to even the fringe of the bright golden Sahara. The trouble with this map is that it has two big insets of Woran and Algut, shown in some detail at a scale of 1/500,000, and these effectively obscure the desert trails to the south.

I trundled myself back up to the Boulevard again next day, or was it next week? Anyway, one fine day when I could tear myself away from the great smells of Hamid's cooking and manage to part the curtain of keef which hung over our door, I fell out into the street and worked my way back to the Boulevard bookstall, where I bought, unobserved, an old guide to Algeria and the Michelin map #152—a great prize. This pretty, pictorial map was printed to illustrate the glorious exploit of General Leclerc, who marched a Free French army from Dakar all the way north to Tunis across the Sahara by way of Lake Chad. Not even the Romans could have brought off such a feat but Hamid shows little interest in anything done by the French or the Roumis, in general. Being Black, I am not a real Roumi to Hamid. On the other hand, Hamid looks down on all Blacks as the natural slaves of the Arabs; even though his own hair is curly enough to give him trouble finding a barber, back in the States. Hamid shuts me up when I tell him I am Black. "You're not Black, you're American! *Safi!* Enough!"

Hamid suddenly became fascinated by the form he began to see in my map. He pointed out that the Great Desert is in the shape of a camel stretching its neck right across Africa, from the Atlantic to the Red Sea. He laughed like a lunatic to see that the western butt-end of his camel was dropping its Mauretanian crud on the Black Senegalese—"Charcoal Charlies," Hamid calls them, having picked up the term in the port. The head of Hamid's camel drinks its fill in the sweet waters of the Nile. The eye of the camel, naturally enough, is that fabled city of Masr, where the Arab movies are made and all the radios ring out over streets paved with gold. Us poor Nazarenes call the place Cairo, for short. Suddenly, somewhere down on the lower middle belly of Hamid's camel, about four knuckles north of Kano in northern Nigeria, I dowsed

9

out a big carbuncle. With no more warning than that, my whole heart rushed out to this place which was pictured as an out-cropping of extinct ash-blue volcanoes jutting up out of the bright yellow sands. I noted that the whole area was called the Hoggar and it seemed to boast only one constantly inhabited place, whose name I made out to be Tam. I was truly surprised to hear myself calmly boasting to Hamid, as if I were AMER-ICAN EXPRESS: "I'll be in this place, here, this time next year."

"*Inch'Allah!* if God wills," Hamid corected me automat-ically and then, as if he were indeed the Consul of Keef, who was sending me out on this mission, he went on: "I'll get them to cut you a green passport of keef to see you through everything. I'll see that you get the best of the crop from Ketama and I'll bring it down from the mountain myself with the blessings of Hassan-i-Sabbah, the Father of Grass. On your way, you're bound to run into some other Assassins."

"But, Hamid," I laughed: "I am not an Assassin at all!"

"We are Assassins, all of us," he gravely replied.

When the time came, I found myself settling back in the train leaving Tanja, gliding slowly along by our magnificent deserted beach on the Straits of Gibraltar. "So, I'm off," I sighed to myself in my cold First-Class compartment. Just then, Hamid, whom I had not seen for more than a week, swung aboard with all the fine acrobatic ease of an old *contra-bandista*. With a big golden grin, he waved my "passport" under my nose; a parchment sheep's bladder as big as two fists, packed hard as a rock with the pick of the crop from Ketama, high in the hills of the Rif. We tried a few pipes of the pot as the green winter landscape of northern Morocco picked up and flowed past the window of our train. A few happy hours later, Hamid dove off the train outside of Kebir, before we got into the station. "No money, no ticket: I travel free!" He was going on up into the hills to his village— Jajouka, Mount of Owls—to stay with his uncles the Master Musicians, who practice their Pan music all day on their pipes as they amble out of their little whitewashed thatched houses in their white woolen homespun jellabas and their white turbans to wander over their green Little Hills after their goats. I gave Hamid the money to have a sheep killed in my honor for a feast up there; to bring me luck on my journey, I said. He waved once and blew me a mischievous kiss as he slid through a hedge of giant blue cactus and was gone.

We just sat in Kebir for a long hour in the rain, which I spent fending off children in steaming wet rags who lounged through the train selling green oranges, used razor blades and, for all I know, reclaimed chewing gum and their not very appetizing selves; anything. At long last, the train started up again with a jerk and we soon slid off into the night, but it was hours past dinnertime when we finally staggered into the junction at Sidi Karim, where I learned to my horror that I would have to wait several bleak hours in the dingy station which the stationmaster was even then shutting up, turning off all the lights but one feeble bulb outside in the rain. As he got onto his bicycle to pedal off through the downpour, he regretted that there was no café or restaurant where I could find food in the forlorn village of Sidi Karim. I took out my pipe and managed to light up in the lee of the wind. Quite quickly, I felt very much better, indeed. As soon as I was turned-on again, I caught my breath with a gasp of fearful delight; one single step outside the murky circle of artificial light and I was back in Africa. East wind tore great silver rents in the night sky and slashed an occasional sharp sluice of rain across the shining railroad tracks alongside which ranked choruses of bullfrogs recited the interminable Word they were set a long time ago, now, as their *zikr: "Kaulakaulakaulkaulakaulakau . . ."* it sounded like. Sky-diving bats looped about the lamps they lit along the track, presently: *"Train coming!"* The bats squealed up into their ultra-sonic radar frequencies like the brakes on distant steel wheels. When the train did come, it came in an orgasmic rush of hot diesel-oil odor, trailing a veil of orange blossom like a bride; as a charming excuse for its lateness, no doubt.

The train was strangely empty, almost like a ghost train with only a few sleeping Moroccans huddled under their hoods. Carrying no baggage, ever, I made my way to the bar, where a group of French colonials eyed me coldly, taking me for a Moroccan I rather suspect. I adjusted my shades, forgetting for the moment just how much more Moroccan they make me look. At the bar, the Moroccan barman refused to serve me, at first, pointing to a fly-blown text on the wall which said in several languages: "No Alcohol May Be Served to Muslims," followed by the text in very small print of a *dahir* or order-in-council promulgated before the last war. I settled down at a table and got something both to eat and to drink when I showed the barman my U.S. passport but he went on speaking to me in Arabic, nevertheless. The French people got off at Fez, where we barely stopped. The train rocketed on through the night, up to the pass at Taza, and then it ran on to the frontier at Oujda, where trouble had been reported on the outskirts of town but, despite this, no one even asked to look at my passport.

On the other side of the border, I found they had put on

a sleeping-car so I paid a supplement on my ticket and got some sleep. In the morning, I lit my first pipe and looked out on a new landscape. The stainless-steel sun glittered through clouds onto the coastal plains where the red tiles on the rooftops of the houses and barns make it look more like Alsace than Africa, giving the tiny robed figures of Arabs in the background an air of people flying past in a dream. I took out my journal and wrote: *As no two people see the same view along the Way, all trips from here to there are imaginary: all truth is a tale I am telling myself.*

When we got to Algut, late at night, I realized that I was the sole passenger to get off that train. The station, awash in shallow neon illumination, was ghostly and cold. There was no one about but me and the exhausted, panting train breathing heavily beside me in the empty echoing station. I abandoned the train and made for a public telephone to call up the hotel but the phone was dead. Somewhere, I had heard there was a curfew; perhaps that was why no one was about, not even a sentry to challenge me at the gate. I walked out into the street, where there was one single taxi, waiting just for me. I ordered the driver, in my almost impeccable French, to take me swiftly to the *Hotel Saint Georges,* on the heights of the city, where the suites of rooms in that old Turkish palace are named after the commanders of World War Two, who once stopped there amidst the luxuriant gardens which some long-dead pacha long ago ordered to be laid out and planted with one thousand and one varieties of palm. My driver glanced at me oddly in his rearview mirror, but he may have realized I was merely quoting the old pre-war guidebooks I fancy so much. When I am high enough, I quote almost anything from Aesop to Zarethustra. I judged from the back of my man's neck that he was, probably,

13

a very white Corsican Blackfoot; a colonial leftover. Never-theless, I leaned over the front seat to ask him politely what *that* was—pointing down to a sawn-off shotgun lying beside him. He replied: there were hoodlums about.

The streets we flashed through were shining with rain on the tram tracks along which we skidded as we climbed. Patrols of sodden soldiers huddled here and there under the trees in public gardens; their firearms and the whites of their eyes glinted sharply in our headlights, which the driver blinked only for military jeeps. High above the harbor of Algut, sentinels stood guard at the gates of the *Saint Georges;* not for the first time in its history, I judge. The hotel itself was locked up like a fortress. From inside, one man opened the door very cau-tiously to my knock as another man covered the crack in the door with a gun. They had a message for me at the desk to say that two American gentlemen were waiting for me in the Churchill suite. I replied rather grandly that I wanted my room and my bath and a good hot dinner with a bottle of French wine in front of an open fire before I saw anybody. Sponsors be damned, I thought; I was going to be very grand. Positively, I was not about to go crawling up to them, right off the beastly train, on my hands and knees like a suppliant. They had the Foundation money for me; I meant to look good when I ac-cepted it. They probably thought I was being arrogant but I was nothing but tired; and more than a little bit stoned.

As I lay back in my hot bath, I giggled. It was awesome, the matter of fact way Hamid had taken my magical flight. I laughed aloud at the confusion of terms, for what is magical, Hamid considers normal and, besides, he expects nothing less out of an American—*his* American, at that! Of course, he is right: I have done a very American thing. I've forgotten, now, where I first picked up on the Foundation for Fundamental Findings; with an address in Basel, oddly enough. I am not about to explain Foundations to Hamid. Besides, what could I tell him—that a Foundation gives you money if you know how to beg for it and I do? I have taught: I have published. Hamid is not likely to read my *History of Slavery in Canada,* which served to get me out of the States on my first Fulbright, years ago. My book could have made me a full professor; with tenure, what is more, in almost any good school in the East, and would have, I think, if I had only been white. As I ponder on this, I play with myself in the suds and stand up, creaming my body all over with soap in front of the full-length mirror they have opposite the bathtub in this luxurious bathroom of the General Alexander suite. When I applied for my Fulbright fellowship, I sent them this very white photograph of myself. When we all passed muster at a cocktail party before sailing, I thought some members of the board were surprised to see me in the old flesh, as we call it. It was not a nude photograph; of course not! I laughed and saluted my white sponsors in the mirror, waving my cock at them all, before I rinsed off and became my black self again.

I have been told that Fulbrights are already a legend in the grim groves of American Academe since so many of us are still drifting around the world instead of returning to teach. What could I possibly teach anybody since I have found out how little I know? Why, my first trip to a hammam with Hamid taught me that Americans do not even know how to take a bath! I remember him saying: "It's a good thing you're circumcised, anyway; so I'll not be ashamed to show you to Muslims, at least." I try to follow the ritual he showed me as I kneel in the spacious tub of the hotel and rinse my mouth out, using only my right hand, which serves me, also, to eat. My left hand, I use only to swab myself after toilet and I never put it in the common dish, no matter how carefully washed. I step out of the tub to drape myself in a giant-size white towel, posing in front of the mirror as Alexander the Great. I figure all these old generals must be regular narcissists if they need these big mirrors to try on their armor. I wonder what kind of bathroom my sponsors must have in the Churchill suite and I wonder if they are busy bathing each other as Muslims would do; or are they just sitting around dressed, listening to the radio, waiting for me?

Then, I struck a very grand Roman pose in front of the pier glass: I am the Great Benefactor endowing poor scholars. Playing both parts, I throw off my toga to grovel naked at the Great Benefactor's feet. I am the newly manumitted slave who has worked out his indenture to the Great Library of Alexandria. I slobber ecstatically over the Benefactor's invisible hands and feet, nearly pissing myself on the floor out of sheer gratitude. At that very moment, I heard the hotel servants moving about in my room, so I jumped up to make sure I had locked the bathroom door. A very nice terry-towel bathrobe was hanging on the back of the door, so I slipped into it. I tied up my towel into a towering turban around my head and strode back to the mirror. I felt much more like the pacha ordering his slaves about than the poor stoned wandering scholar I am, waiting for a handout from a Foundation such as the one to which I have, obviously, just sold myself; as they like to say. In my application, I sold them on the idea that it would be of interest for someone with my background to cross the Sahara, taking advantage of commercial transport as far as the village of Tam in Tuareg country. From there, I will strike out back down the old slave trails of the Sahara, which are still being used by the nomads. I will continue right down to the Slave Coast, as it used to be marked on all the maps printed in Europe; because all of Europe was engaged in the slave trade. I intend to find coastal steamers to take me around the big bulge of the continent, stopping along the way at all the old slave markets as far around the hump of Africa as St. Louis in Senegal, north of Dakar. One thing I neglected to tell the Foundation when I applied is that I have left not one foot back in their world, as they think, but a mere fading footprint. This foot I put forward into the Sahara is already firmly implanted in this African world, where my guide so far has been Hamid. I wonder where Hamid is, now?

One Arab hotel servant was on his knees lighting the fire in my drawing room, while another assisted him. Two slightly grumpy young waiters, who looked as if they had been booted out of bed, wheeled in my meal under the direction of a head waiter, while a wine waiter followed him in, nursing the wine, which he set to warm in front of my fire. A fat Arab chambermaid, looking like an animated sack of potatoes wrapped in an old lace curtain, waddled around aimlessly, looking for my bags to unpack my clothes. "This is the way I came: no baggage!" I barked this out in my best imitation of Hamid's crude country Arabic. They all looked rather horrified and incredulous, as they speak a quite different Arabic here, but they snapped to attention, all right. You can't treat me like a tourist, is all I was telling them. I settled down to eat my shrimp-salad cocktail and was revolted to find, under the spicy pink sauce, mostly wet lettuce and nameless white fish. I waved without words for my partridge and my bottle of Chateau

Latour 1952. Finding it corked and gone a bit thin, I waved it away and back to the cellars for another bottle. I thought to myself: Man, oh, man, if I could only show this to Hamid, he would *know* it was all an illusion! After all, he and I were living in a leaky two-room house without inside water in the Medina of Tanja, only last week.

A tall, dead-black Sudanese waiter came in with the coffee, all dressed up like the head eunuch of the late pacha's harem. I had him bring me back the sommelier with a big snifter of *poire* and asked them to turn out the lights as they went. I sank back in my chair to look at the firelight through my colorless *poire* in the belly of the glass. What I saw made my hand tremble, for I was thinking of my journey, of course, and there I was in a bright red movie of fire which was being shown like a miniature TV on the convex side of my glass. I peered into the fire where I saw myself like an ant in a torrent of ants, being whirled along by the wind on a burning leaf like a litter or palanquin all in flames, carried on the shoulders of a streaming throng of naked people, themselves all in flames, who ran me along through a country on fire, in which trees, grass and the very sky were blazing around me. We rushed through a river of fire, down which we paddled to an ocean of flames, where I ran up the red-hot iron ladders of a fire-boat under whose grated decks burned a seething, white-hot caldron of Whites. In the flaming red wind, we sailed like an arrow from one burning port to the next fiery town on which we swept down to stoke up our ship's boilers with a sizzling stream of white Colonials, who flared up and burned like a gem or the core of an atom exploding. I rubbed my eyes, shivering. It was cold in my chair as the fire died away. A second later, I shot up almost out of my skin, utterly startled by the sudden preternatural racket of wakening birds, all screeching at once in the palm trees outside my window. When I looked out it was morning.

Two days later, when I had bought a rucksack and a little gasoline Primus stove, I said thanks and good-by to my sponsors with my hand over my heart. That is where, along with my U.S. passport, I always carry my money. I caught a very early train out of Algut, up country to Blida, and that afternoon I rattled through the high mountain passes to Boghari on the rim of the Sahara where the train track ends. There, I caught a bus to Djelfa in the bare metallic mountains of the Ouled Naïl; a tribe of tinkers whose women are prostitutes, loitering around like painted idols, suggestively clinking with lucky gold coins. Long after dark, I changed to the back of a Berliet truck in a rising sandstorm. In the hours after midnight, we passed through Laghouat, where the French painter Fromentin was the first White to spend a summer, more than a hundred years ago, now. He mistook that one idyllic oasis for all of the Sahara, while we barely stopped there at a filling station, under some palms whose ragged heads were whipped down into the driving sand. The yellow headlights of our truck drilled out a sandy tunnel through the roaring streets of the town as we bored our way back out into the thick of the Sahara. The wind scoured the track we followed, tacking across a vast howling plain until, several hours later, we landed in the lee of the long walls of a desert caravanserai. We charged through a banging, broken gate, stampeding the hundred camels of several caravans which had taken shelter in the vast open court-yard. On the far side of this harbor, light streamed out from the tiny windows of one small room, like a cabin built to huddle against the far wall. Someone in there, on the floor,

19

was making tea by the light of a hurricane lamp. Inside, I came across an old Visitors' Book without a cover in which there were signatures and comments dating back into the last century. I added my name: Ulys O. Hanson, III, of Ithaca, N.Y. Moroccans tend to pronounce my name like Hassan, so that is what they all call me back in Tanger: Hassan Merikani. I signed that as best I can in Arabic. I had no comment to make.

The following day, we got to the sly and secret city of Ghardaïa, the outlaw capital of the Mozabite Dissident tribes who were driven out into these desert potholes where they found water many centuries ago. From this stronghold, the Mozabites have always ventured back into the orthodox community as small grocers who live in their shops which are real family affairs, crawling with children like mice. They are rapacious, good-looking, inbred people whose tiny children can do sums in their heads, running whole shops before they are ten years of age: experts at false-weight and short-change. For several hundreds of years, at least, they have sent every last penny of the money they amass back to their isolated city guarded all around by the Sahara where it is buried, they say, under their windowless houses. The Mozabite treasure of gold is greater than that of Fort Knox; gold goes in there and never comes out again. A Mozabite woman, on the other hand, may go out of her house twice in a lifetime; once to her wedding and once to her funeral. From the better homes, a woman never goes out: she marries a resident cousin and, when she dies, she is buried in the garden.

I tossed all night in an Arab hotel on a bed so hard it may have been made of gold. An odor of drains came gliding through the room, so strong it glowed in the dark like a ghost

20

and left a faintly luminous trail of iridescent slime where it passed. Black Greaser, down in the narrow court of the cara-vanserai guarding our truck like a treasure, whimpered away all night on his flute made out of an old bicycle-pump; playing over and over the only windy tune that he could play:

> *Oh, I got a gazelle in Ghardaïa*
> *She's rich and loaded with gold*
> *I want to marry but her father says: No!*
> *Oh, we'll buy a diesel, my love, I swear*
> *They hung three millions in gold on your neck*
> *But you can't move out of that room!*
> *We'll purchase a diesel, my love, with the gold*
> *Oh, we'll cross the Sahara and never come back!*

In the morning, I went out in the cool bright air just after dawn to find the whole city already afoot, doing business. In their handsome open-air marketplace, half as big as San Marco in Venice but with whitewashed arcades, I bartered my GI boots, field jacket and worn Levis for sandals, baggy *sarouel* pants with embroidered pockets and this fine black burnous which has made me feel invisible, here, since it first dropped over my shoulders. Shyly, I bought veiling; five yards or so of fine muslin to wrap my head and face against the dry desert air and the bite of the sun. Since then I go, automatically, more and more deeply disguised through their Country of Fear.

The silky surreptitious silence of the Sahara starts in Ghar-daïa, where every soft footfall is shod in sand. A hush hovers over everything like the beating of invisible wings beneath which one hears the incessant hissing of the desert. Men, and even women, speak softly, knowing they will be heard. When

21

desert-dwellers meet, they stand off a few paces to whisper sibilant litanies of ritual greeting, almost indistinguishable in sound from the rustling of stiff cloth, as they bare a long arm to reach out and softly stroke palms. They exchange long litanies of names interwoven with news and blessings until a spell of loosely knit identity is thrown over all the generations of the Faithful like a cloak:

> . . . *and ye shall drink no wine, neither shall your sons forever. Neither shall ye build houses nor sow seed nor plant vineyards but all your days ye shall live under tents that ye may live many years in the land where ye sojourn* . . .

Everything crackles with static electricity as if one were shuffling over a great rug. Everyone in the Sahara is very aware; tuned-in to the great humming silence through which drones the sound of an approaching diesel from hours away.

Previously assured transportation suddenly became precarious. We all sat or lay around in the shade of the truck which stood becalmed in the shallows of some new Time-Barrier. Departure was indefinitely delayed while the truck throbbed gently, as if poised like a porpoise ready to take off. Travelers must show their identity papers to the captains of Saharan Security in the Bordj or fort, before leaving; likewise, trucks. Officially timed departures are said to be relayed anead to the next Bordj or fort where the captains are supposed to follow your progress across the floor of the desert, like a cockroach crawling across a carpet in broad daylight. A conspiracy of silence on the part of the Arab truck drivers seemed to oppose this occult power of the captains. Restless and bored and just about ready to take a last turn around the marketplace, I was lucky enough to be still there when the truck suddenly began to take off, unannounced. I scrambled up into the vibrating cabin, screaming like an American tourist, waving the proof of my right to First-Class Transportation under the nose of the new driver, who had simply strolled over to the truck, jumped into the cabin, thrown in the clutch and started to leave. Even now, I sit here looking at the back of his head, wondering if he is not stealing the truck, the cargo and me.

Later that afternoon—no, the next afternoon, we picked up the Hadj back from the pilgrimage; the little old man I had taken, at first for a bush. I recollect, El Hallaj was skinned alive in Baghdad for proclaiming: "If a bush can say: *I am the Truth,* so can a man." I have not been comfortable since. We grind along, hour after hour, like a metallic dung-beetle pushing its nose through the sand, probing the Great Howling Waste. Only sand dunes move more slowly than we do. Schools of golden dunes, which vary in size from ones you could ride astride to some twice as big as this truck, cavort like dolphins across the trail. They were not here when the trail was laid and they may be gone on the next big blow or they may grow into a dune as big as a city, they tell me. We break a new trail over the hard black *reg* in which the dunes seem to lie half-submerged, for we are skirting a giant paw of the Great Sandy Erg which lies athwart the Sahara like a vast rosy-golden sphinx as big as a country, Guardian of the Sandy Wastes.

At times, we roll down steep corridors of rotting stone which take us from one geological layer to another of this spot where Earth looks like a peeling onion. Torrents of water can sweep down these canyons without warning when rains have fallen miles away, gathering on vast impervious plains to rush through here faster than a locomotive. Many a slow caravan has been overtaken and drowned under a wall of water beneath a cloudless sky. An hour or so back, we stopped on a ridge of this giant washboard to exchange news with a group of wild-looking road-workers who turn trails around moving dunes or can lay down such marvels as a hundred miles of flattened-out jerricans pointing like an arrow at the horizon, across quicksands. I suspect them to be forced labor of sorts, for not even a starving nomad would work in such conditions, but they seemed jolly enough for such a pack of jackals bound up in their rags. Their official name is the Genie of the Sahara, but everyone calls them, more simply, the Broken Boys.

We entered and passed through a string of oases called Algol without stopping for anything but water and fuel because Driver wanted to climb onto the high plateau of the Tademait, the Table of Stone, before nightfall. I barely looked out from under my burnous at the monotonous horror of the landscape up there. Long after sunset, we halted in our tracks and, while the others fell out to sleep beside the truck, I stretched out in the cabin where I was glad of the cooling diesel beside me, for the night turned very cold. Late the next afternoon, we rolled down the great military ramp called the Akba, which was built long ago by somebody's army. The trail ahead looped like a slack fire-hose over an immense charred plain on whose far side crouched distant dunes at whose rosy paws lay the ancient city of Salah. Salan was once a market town known to the caravans of Solomon with whom the inhabitants dealt in gold, ivory, ostrich plumes and, of course, Black slaves: some say they still do.

24

I went directly to the military fort and, there, I read a notice posted in French on the red mud wall:

EVERY TRAVELER
WITHOUT ANY EXCEPTION
MUST ALREADY HAVE POSTED A BOND
IN ORDER TO ENTER
THE COUNTRY OF THE GARAMANTIANS.

I entered the fort to ask for the officer in command. These men have no particular names of their own but, when the sun rises high in the sky, the natives call them Captain, loading them with reproaches because they burn and lay waste the surrounding country and themselves. Herodotus is my authority for this. I radioed back to the American consul in Algut asking for a letter of guarantee to be sent in my name to the next post south, the red village of Tam. Now, there is a mountain called Atlas, so high the top of it never is seen, clouds not quitting it summer or winter and the natives take their name from it; being the veiled Atlantes of legend. I radioed ahead to the Atlantes to say I was coming, bond or no bond. These people are reported to eat the rock dragon, a species of giant lizard whose meat they scoop out with a big wooden spoon as he roasts on his back over a fire. They call this lizard their "maternal uncle" and they are said not to have any dreams. I am still quoting the first historian, Herodotus, but only by memory of course.

When we debarked in Tam long after midnight, Greaser, who had never spoken directly to me before in all the miles

25

we had spun out together, drew me aside in the dark. "An Assassin," he murmured, presenting me with a slim Broken Boy in rags, who dropped silently from the back of the truck onto the sand between us. After all, the same word Assassin or Hashishin can be used to denote those who smoke keef, so I took it in this sense, glad enough to have a guide in the dark. My young guide picked up my sack, drawing me off into the night after him as he moved silently ahead of me over the cool, silky sand. We walked down an avenue of feathery tamarisk trees beneath which we sat for a while smoking my pipe without saying a word. Then, he led me to a ruined hut whose cracked mud walls threatened to cave in on us. The goats of the wild wandering people came to glare with yellow eyes at us from the fringe of outer darkness, beyond the square white patch of light thrown by my gasoline Primus stove on which we made tea. We fell asleep in there, wrapped up in my big black burnous, but, in the middle of the night, knee-hobbled camels stumbled into our ruined hut, nearly bringing the walls down on us. I insisted on moving out to a place in the open where, just before dawn, we were almost run over by a pack of tiny wild asses, who pulled up short a few unshod hooves from our heads, like inquisitive schoolboys, scampering away when I clapped my hands at them.

In the morning, my Broken Boy wanted to draw me along his way through the quiet sandy alleys of Tam but I insisted on going straight to the fort where I found a letter addressed to me by Mr. Knoblock, U. S. Vice-Consul in Algut, stating:

The Consulate General has been informed by the Government General that, as far as the Atlantes, the names of the nations inhabiting the Sandy Wastes are known but, beyond them, all knowledge fails.

A bond ought not be required of an American traveler intending to visit the Sandy Ridge as far west as the Pillars of Hercules.

I surmised the vice-consul had been dipping into his Herodotus, too, so I asked for the officer in command. I was taken in to an adjutant, who informed me that the Captain of the Southern Wastes could not see me but, until he would, I was not to leave Tam. I wanted to visit Murmur, said to be a city of silence about two days' journey from Tam. The adjutant said no. Murmur is said to be built entirely out of slabs of purple and greenish-white gem salt and, therefore, so dazzling it cannot be approached or even easily seen in the daytime: its inhabitants come out only by night. The salt is quarried from an ancient crystalline flow which spills over a broken rim of the Hoggar, on the far side from Tam. The Hoggar is an immense volcanic cup of basalt, brimming with sand. Its jagged rim rises nearly ten thousand feet into the milky sky against which it can look peacock-blue or viridian green. It stands on an eternity of absolute desert, infinitely attractive to those who know those glittering wastes.

Far, far to the south lie the broad savannahs, the shimmering grasslands where naked Black men of infinite beauty and dignity herd their lyre-horned cattle. Beyond, begins the bush and the forest throbbing with drums; the jungle through which broad, calm, dangerous rivers can float you right down to the sea.

I walked out in the bright morning through the silent village of Tam, whose one broad avenue of white sand is bordered by gray-green tamarisk trees from the red mud fort to the red mud marketplace built by the captains in Sudanese Flamboyant style. No wheeled traffic moves except by direct order of the fort. Down by the waterless *oued,* blue-veiled men were barracking camels; Black men were loading them. I asked for the master of the caravan, intending to go with them when I heard they meant to leave before nightfall. At that moment, a uniformed runner from the fort came up silently over the sand with a coiled whip in his hand to inform me that I was to speak to no one in Tam and that I must move into the hotel before noon under pain of the captains' displeasure: all Americans of whatever color must sleep under roofs. I shrugged, thinking I could shake him off, but he fell into step behind me, dogging my footsteps so that no one would speak to me or sell me anything to eat in the market. I allowed him to herd me to the hotel, which turned out to be a one-story building of red mud, splashed around the doors and windows with whitewash.

I brushed through a curtain of big wooden beads, stepping directly into a dark room where, behind a primitive bar, the Syrian manager lay drunk on the mud floor in a puddle of urine. Several sullen Black ''boys'' were skulking about, so I ordered them loudly to wake the white man, who opened his eyes and struggled up on one elbow, staring at me dully. I bent down to help him but, when he saw the color of my face in front of him, he suddenly hurled at me a hunting knife with a six-inch blade. The knife struck me flatly and clattered harmlessly to the beaten-mud floor. Startled, I asked him: ''Do you know me?'' involuntarily speaking in English. He sat up and demanded my papers. When I handed him my American passport, he looked through it dubiously for quite a long time, trying to run a dirty thumbnail under my photograph; flicking at it for several minutes before he barked to one of the "boys" to show me a room.

My room had mud walls and a mud floor, a split-palm ceiling which dribbled sand onto a gray sheet thrown over a bare iron bedstead: the only other furniture was a battered tin pail of water. Barred windows looked into an open-air kitchen court where food of a sort was being prepared by three ragged old women with tattooed faces who sat on the ground, screaming back and forth at each other over their pots at the top of their lungs, for hours on end. Meals were served by the scarecrow "boys," who shuffled back and forth between kitchen and dining room, stuffing into their mouths whatever rejected food guests had left on their plates.

There were flies: the "boys" were covered with flies like a living garment. Flies swarmed around them like a veil, supping on the juices of their big, empty eyes, which they rimmed like animated mascara. Flies landed to drink at the trough of their loose lips or got pushed into their mouths along with the food. Naked puff-bellied children begged for scraps outside the dining-room window or just lay there listlessly in the dust, like sick iguanas covered with flies, cramming red earth into their mouths. Flies swarmed so thick on the dining-room tables that I took them for a furry tablecloth until a "boy" made a lazy swipe at them with a filthy rag. Then, they rose for a second into the air only to settle back again in precisely the same order. Flies in the Sahara ride in squadrons on everyone's back. They show a decided preference for khaki and their remarkable discipline is most clearly observed on a khaki field. They ride around on everyone, nose in the wind in glittering chevrons, flight patterns which lift into the air to shift and reform as their field moves.

29

I might have been welcome at the hotel, for the Syrian, too, was at war with the captains but, when night fell like ink dropping into water and he called me to drink anisette with him and some other palefaces at the bar, I had to refuse him and so lost a possible ally. I slipped out of the hotel to where my young guide, the Broken Boy, was waiting for me in the threadbare shadow of a tamarisk tree.

Somewhere out there in the dark, someone is singing in a husky quavering voice like the wind:

Oh, we'll cross the Sahara and never turn back!

Eternity flows all about us as we pull at my pipe, utterly silent under the stars. Our feet make no sound as we pass through the shallows of starlight beneath the ghostly tamarisk trees and over the last sandbar on the edge of the village. Where are we going? "To the Sahara," he whispers in my ear with one arm about my neck. I can hear the pulse jump in his wrist. Suddenly and inexplicably, there is a rough mud wall under our outstretched palms as we feel our way to the door of this compound out on the outskirts of town. Somewhere within, somebody plucks at the strings of an instrument. The player runs up a shivering chromatic scale and, as our lips break apart, a quick fire of aromatic thorns bursts up snapping, on the other side of the door. Through the cracks between the boards we can see into an African compound glowing red in the firelight. When my little friend softly raps out a rattling code on the door with his knuckles, I hear with a smile the same chuckling word the masterpiece matches say to the box. Animals are stirring in there. Someone is shuffling across to the door. My companion is gone. *"Eshkoon?"* Who are you? they ask, from

30

inside the door, and I hardly know what to reply. Who am I, indeed?

Someone I think I must know and who surely knows me has opened the door and stands there with the firelight behind her, inviting me in. This black witch-shape against an orange background of fire is familiar to me since the dreams of my childhood, and the sensation becomes more and more overwhelming as she flaps up and down, bowing me into the compound, dancing in front of the flames. I step into an adobe courtyard of sculptured mud the color of a burning rose, glowing like African flesh. Dear little donkeys and a baby camel turn to blink at me from under a palm-thatched manger. Mothers and grandmothers sit smiling around the fire. Everyone who ever has loved me is there: I am in Africa, home.

I bow and we softly stroke palms, murmuring greetings and blessings from the distant hills and plains. A door is flung open to my right, making me blink in the sudden diamond-white glare so many times brighter than firelight which streams out from that room. Holiness shines out from a chamber as bare as a Saharan shrine. Singer is there; sitting cross-legged on a golden straw mat with his big, full-bellied *gimbri,* a lute he cradles like a murmuring child in his lap. A tiny carbide *kinki* lamp whistles and flares, illuminating the room less than his smile. Where he sits the ground is a throne.

Singer's giant shadow leaps up the red walls behind him, overwhelming the light in the room as he stretches out his arms, bending over the lamp on the floor, to welcome me, drawing me in. The wings of his cloak extinguish the lamp for a second; just the time to whisper in my ear as he embraces me: "*Dar tariki tariqat:* In darkness, the Path." I set my sandals neatly on the smooth floor of white sand at the foot

31

of an iron army cot with its sheet drawn tight for inspection
—the only furniture in the room. Hanging high on the wall
over an empty monumental fireplace sculpted in red mud is a
rifle; no other objects in sight. My place is beside Singer; on
the woven straw mat to his right, facing the door. I throw
back my burnous to pull out my parchment bladder, hard-
packed and as big as two fists. With some little ceremony, I
slowly unwind the thong at its neck to show him the emerald
grass of Ketama—my "passport." His eyes and smile widen:
"Ul-lah!" he breathes in a voice almost as deep as Ghoul's
own.

From the depths of the unlit fireplace, he drew out a span
of bamboo as thick as a cane and half as long, onto which he
fitted a clay bowl as big as a briar pipe for tobacco, packing
it full of my keef. We smoked the first pipe together in absolute
silence. Hearing the Brothers arrive in the courtyard, Singer
clapped for them to come stumbling in, slipping off their sandals in the sand, murmuring greetings and blessings as they
shuffled up one by one to snatch kisses from my lucky hand
before settling down in a ring. The big pipe was stoked and
lit by Singer, who passed it around the full circle, instead of
letting each man finish his much smaller pipe as we do in our
chapter at home. I was only mildly surprised. Some of those
present had come three and four weeks by camel across the
Sahara to be with us that night. In such scattered communities
as these, small divergencies creep in.

The pipe passed and passed again. I knew they had never
smoked any keef like this before. Without thinking, some of
the Brothers began to recite. With a smile, because I am
not really one of them, I drew slightly out of the circle to let
Singer lead them into more intricate patterns of words but he

32

arrested them all with a great clap of his hands before anyone could start to profess. Abruptly, they stopped and rose to
their feet as two latecomers slipped into place. Singer, their
master, stepped into the center of the circle as the Brothers
joined hands. I remained in my corner, seated in their leaping
shadows. They stamped and swung hands in order to catch up
the rhythm and, then, they began jumping and shouting in
unison:

AL-*lah* . . . AL-*lah* . . . AL-*lah* . . .

Exhale on the first syllable, inhale on the second. It becomes:

HA-*ha* . . . HA-*ha* . . . HA-*ha* . . .

And then:

A-*a* . . . A-*a* . . . A-*a* . . .

And, at last, the cyclical, rattling word of our *zikr,* a pair
of unvoiced aspirates, our Key and our Link: what the matches
say to the box.

When the master raps out a command, they all go into
reverse. The dancers stop jumping; exhale, knees bend; inhale,
straighten up. Then, they stand still while they jump with only
their chests. Inhale a sharp gasp on the *"AL"* and exhale at
great length on the *"lah."* From sixty paired strokes to the
minute, they drop to about forty-five. Eight minutes for each.
It is always advisable to have one Brother outside the circle

to act as an *assas* or guardian who can pick people up if they fall too soon and put them back in their place.

Singer moved about the inside of the circle, looking sharply into the eyes of each Brother as he strummed rapidly on his *gimbri*. When he bent down to where I was sitting, I gave him a quick lift of my chin to indicate two Brothers who were faltering and he jumped back to switch them in line. Outside the circle again, I began clapping my hands as Hamid instructed me back in Morocco but Singer shot me a flash of distress for, suddenly, one after another the Brothers stepped forward with eyes completely revulsed, crying out in rapturous tones; bliss and exquisite pain thrilling along on one nerve. I left off as he caught them up to pull them along as he knows them best, on the strings of his *gimbri* with hands strumming too fast to be seen.

Beyond that, when the word of our *zikr* has opened them up, they enter into a state where they bark or grunt from the very depths of their entrails. It is a very curious animal sound brought up from the solar plexus. I have heard something like it made by ecstatic women worshipers in storefront churches back in the States. Here, only male voices are used and this is more frightening, for the voice of Ghoul bubbles up from the pool of their depths; a truly subterranean sound in which the Voice, singing throat and the song are all one! At this, the Brothers all drop to their knees, still jumping their chests until they fall in convulsions, flat on their faces in a star formation; beating their heads on the ground in a ring about the feet of Sweet Singer, their *shekh*.

In this close place, their youngest Brother fell over my knees, so I kissed him on top of the head. He got up at once to take his place tightly wedged in beside me. Singer went on twanging his *gimbri* over the heads of the others in the orthodox way, making the strings say:

*Allahu ak*BAR . . . *Allahu ak*BAR . . . *Allahu ak*BAR . . .
God is Great . . . *God is* Great . . . *God is* Great . . .

over and over again until they began to sit up, wiping the sweat out of their eyes, the foam from their lips. Singer started them swaying to a new lilting tune as I refilled the pipe with my excellent Ketama to send it passing around the re-formed circle on the mat. I told Youngest Brother I had come further across the Great Waste of the World than he—from beyond a great river of salt called the Atlantic, which runs away in the sands to the west. For the River, I quoth, hath more need of the Fountain than the Fountain hath need of the River. I am that River, running away on your Afrique shore where, from your lips tonight, dear Brother, I have heard the Fountain well up; bubbling up from the great fossil underground river where the blind crocodile of our Master, Hassan-i-Sabbah, Old Man of the Mountain and Great Sandy Waste, has lurked for centuries in darkness. Youngest Brother nodded eagerly: "Yes, one day he will break out to devour our Enemy the Sun!"

"Ah, so he will, indeed!" I thought: "Mister Ugly Spirit himself, disguised as a hydro-helium bomb."

Yet, oh, the strange relaxation of it! I alone of all these Assassins had ever been foolish enough to conceive of happiness. The staggering assumptions in my young companion's calm eyes would make my white American compatriots collapse with a whimper or run screaming for the police. There is no friendship: there is no love. The desert knows only allies and accomplices. The heart, here, is all in the very moment.

Everything is bump and flow; meet and good-by. Only the Brotherhood of Assassins ensures ritual continuity, if that is what you want and some do; for the lesson our *zikr* teaches is this: *There are no Brothers*.

Sun just crashed over the other side of the *oued*, trailing no dusk. A copper-green disk rimmed with magenta burned on the back of my closed lids for a minute or two and, when I opened my eyes again, the stars were out. Sunset hit me like this twenty-four times in Tam. There was no way I could go on further south. The man with the whip had summoned me, early one morning, to the fort, where a drunken Arab civilian employee advised me in bad French to go back to America; my visa was cancelled. It turned out to be true. Day after day, the captains remained adamant. I had consorted with undesirable elements: there was no appeal. When I protested too loudly, I was put under "hotel arrest" in my room. I was not to leave Tam until a military convoy was ready to go north. All other carriers were warned not to take me.

As a Black man, a so-called American Negro, I know the meaning of perpetual quarantine: I have been under some sort of arrest all of my life. I ought to be used to it but I am and I am not. Just to breathe is to flaunt authority in some states, so I know how to flaunt authority really quite well. I walked out in the village like a tourist, learning to ride a camel a little further each day. I rented the beast from one of the tall Tuareg slave-owning gangsters who drift around veiled, looking for tourists to "guide." This one spoke little Arabic and almost no French but, by drawing easily erased maps in the sand, I learned a few things from him about the lay of the land. The village doctor came up on us silently during one of our geography lessons. He was a bit of a cynic and thought, I believe,

36

that the captains were treating me badly. I am sure it was he who persuaded the Tuareg to take me north on his camels to Salah so that, from there, I could strike west to the other trail leading back south. As it turned out, I had to go back all the way to Algol before I could strike west again and south.

My Michelin map showed Salah some six hundred and forty kilometers north by the road. A Tuareg racing camel was said to cover sixty kilometers a day but the doctor assured me this was a legend left over from the days when Tuareg prowess was exaggerated by a universal dread of the bloodthirsty desert pirates. Even so, that made more than ten days to Salah by camel. We had covered the same distance in about thirty hours of continuous driving. An ordinary caravan cannot do more than twenty-five kilometers a day, for camels amble and stray, eating whatever they can as they go. On the road to Tam, we had, luckily for them, overtaken just such a caravan of straggling, badly ballasted animals foundering under the blows of thirst-maddened men who slogged along beside them on foot, day after day. In any case, no such caravan would dare take me with them for fear of running into a desert patrol sent out by the captains. Besides, said the doctor, who understood where I wanted to go, the trail west from Salah to Reggan was closed to all traffic. I would have to go four hundred and fifty kilometers further north to Algol from where I might be able to strike west through Timoun to Hadrar on the other trans-Saharan route, south to Reggan and then over the worst of the worst of the desert, the infamous Tanezrouft, through Bidon Five down to Gao on the Niger. It would be just a short side trip, or so it looked on the map, from Gao to Timbuctoo. From there, perhaps, I could drift down the Niger on a paddle-wheeler or even a raft, for the winter season should provide

37

enough water in the Niger to float river traffic. The Niger rises from torrential rainfalls in the mountains near the Atlantic, from where the waters flow back in a great buckling loop, inland through desert country. Many a raft-load of slaves must have perished on its sandbars.

I crept away to Singer's compound, becoming each night less and less welcome there as my bladder of keef was burned up in smoke and collapsed. No doubt, my presence may have compromised the Assassins but the worst was an evening cut short by the sudden arrival of a man dressed entirely in white, bound up in yards of turban, veils and flowing robes. From out of this big bundle of laundry stared two black eyes; the most hateful I ever have seen this side of the Klan when they told him I was black but a Christian. I understood what he meant later, when I saw twenty-five or thirty sooty-gray and putty-colored children slither past in a long crocodile through the sandy streets of Algol. The Brother from Aoulef had taken me for one of these Harratin children of abandoned slaves whom their Tuareg masters deem utterly worthless and drive away to be "taken in" by the Christians, where there still are any such creatures about.

The following night, when the blue tide of darkness had raced across the Sahara, bowling over the giant purple shadows of the amethyst mountains like ninepins, I was off and away without taking leave of the captains. In the Sahara, you are supposed to check in and out of each fort, showing your identity papers, stating your purpose and time of departure for what destination, as if you were leaving one island for another under semi-independent authority. I skirted the airstrip in a sandstorm on foot, beating my way back to a black basalt cave where my Tuareg guide was to meet me. I would almost as soon trust my life to the Klan as to these ex-convoyers and hijackers of slave caravans but there was no other way. A group of about twenty Tuareg was sheltering in there from the storm; among them, one hugely fat man, their king, the Amenokal, with whom I spoke through an interpreter. In his presence, they stripped me of my gold class ring and my watch and the old-fashioned straight razor I carry, as "presents" even before we discussed their terms, which were cutthroat. When the storm died down a bit, some of them went out in search of their camels and, as I lay on my back on the sandy floor, I noticed a fine prehistoric fresco on the ceiling. Its ochers and blacks were still lively under a glacis which looked so like a recent varnish that I was foolish enough to ask the fat king if they knew who had painted it. Too disgusted to translate the stupid question, the Arab interpreter snapped: "Women's work!" I laughed to myself for a while but the hours dragged on so that I had begun to wonder if they had already sold me to the fort when my man came up in the night with the camels. I mounted and rode away behind him in the dark.

The next days went by so quickly I can hardly remember them. We were mounted on two giant camels, more like yachts under sail than four-footed beasts. The first part of the trail was all downhill through volcanic moon-surface landscape which fled past like painted stage sets or, as I rarely looked up for fatigue, a nightmare series of absurdly old-fashioned surrealist lantern-slide pictures projected on the curtains of air, almost solid with wind-borne sand. We paused to catch our breath in a circular valley like a tar barrel five hundred feet deep into which we led our balky, protesting camels through a bung-hole in the stone drilled by the wind. We stopped for a moment to admire the white sand floor of the basalt barrel set out with thorn trees which had been so clipped by passing generations of camels that they look like a topiary garden designed around the gigantic chunks of black stone, some as big as a truncated skyscraper, which have fallen from the cliffs to be sculpted by the blasting of sand into statues of monsters a hundred times bigger and more astonishing than those of Bomarzo. The valley looked and felt old and evil.

As we mounted our camels, my guide pointed with his whip down to the odd arrangement of white boulders, about twice as big as a man's head, on which we had been sitting. The stones looked whitened, as if they might have been bitten by the acid from a car battery, perhaps. From the height of our saddles, they formed a pattern of letters to be read from the air: *S O S*. "Seven Roumis," said my guide. "Seven Romans?" I asked in surprise. "Roumi Merikani," he assured me with a cruel laugh from behind his veil. "Americans?" He pointed again with his whip to a message spelled out in stones on the ground. I could believe it was in English for I was able to make out the letters forming the word: T H E Y. The word, if it was a word, occupied my imagination many hours and many days for if anyone was to leave his last message in the Sahara, surely he would begin by I, or even We. Why *"They"*?

From the last high black gate of the Hoggar, we looked out over the Great Seas of Sand across which, I understood, we were to run with our sagging waterskins banging away at our knees, tied to the pommels of our excruciatingly uncomfortable wooden saddles. We would have to make a big circle around most wells for fear of running into a desert patrol; darting in quickly to fill our skins with water, leaving as little trace as possible of our passage. I realized how hopeless this was when the Tuareg read tracks which he claimed were twenty years old near a well which is rarely visited because it yields, in the best years, only a trickle of bitter water the color of urine. It must have been already dry when this last caravan before us got there to find no life-saving water for their valuable merchandise, which they had abandoned in chains to perish at the brink of the deep dry well. Nearby, the wind had uncovered a mass grave dug shallow by a desert patrol sent out by the captains, presumably; almost certainly not by the Arab traders who left their slaves here to die while they ran for the next well. The skin of a Black child had been dried, tanned and mummified; abandoned there in the hot dry sand by its young owner, like a broken doll. My tall Tuareg, laughing behind his veil, played a quick game of football with some dried heads still covered by enough parchment-like skin to make them grimace abominably. He dropped several of them neatly into the dry well. It was a long time before they hit rock bottom: luckily, we still had some water.

Most monuments in the desert are flat on the ground: laid out, stone beside stone, in a place where the wind is least likely to cover them. We came across graves of the Faithful who had dropped from some caravan and, even, whole little camps of Muslim graves marked by stones all pointing to Mecca, showing where an entire caravan had gone down. We came on a mosque which is famous in all the Sahara. It is said to be composed of exactly one thousand and one big stones, laboriously carried to the spot to be laid out in the dotted pattern of a mosque. We halted our camels nearby but neither of us entered this impressive "building."

I began to have a little trouble with my mind when it started playing about like a mind in the parallel mirrors of a barber-

shop. At times, I had sharp visual hallucinations in which I
thought I saw myself from about twenty paces behind. As my
Tuareg rode on another twenty paces in front of my visionary
self, that made three of us out in the Sahara and all three of
us seemed to be singing. I could tell which one I was only
when *he* would stop singing. Then, I knew I must be the one
who mumbled old Hit Parade songs to drown out the monotonous horror of my own thoughts. I hated the song the Tuareg
sang so much that at times I found myself imitating him until
my throat ached. He forced a reedy falsetto out of his throat
or his head which sounded so much like the wind that I could
not tell where his voice left off and the wind went on crying
and sobbing. His treacherous tune was nothing like Singer's
black music, which still warms my blood. I could feel this
cold, windy air in my bones and I knew I had heard it before.
Horror suddenly gripped me like a big monkey jumping up on
my camel behind me, growing bigger by the hour until Fear
rode my camel, onto whose hard saddle I clung as best I could.
Someone kept singing, over and over again, inside of my head:
*"He is going to sell you. When we get to Salah, he is going
to sell you!"*

When we did get to Salah, I had lost count of the days.
All I wanted was to get into that town where, I hoped, I could
give my guide the slip in the marketplace. My most rational
fear was that he would denounce me to the fort. We left our
camels hobbled out in the Sahara on the outskirts of town and
walked together into the market. As we passed a tiny sandal-
maker's shop as big as a telephone booth, I stepped up to the
low wooden counter across his door because I knew I had
come to the place. This man was a Brother, I can always tell
by the signs, and he recognized me. As I gave him my sandals

to cobble, he invited me into his shop smelling of leather and feet to sit on a pile of tanned hides in a corner. My Tuareg, sure of me, strode grandly off to visit the town. I slumped down on the skins, pulling out my withered bag of Ketama to fill us a pipe. My Brother let down his shutter, closing me up in his shop while he went to get strong green tea, bread and a plate of beans, which we ate by the light of a *kinki* lamp, both putting our right hands in the same dish. While he poured out the tea, he told me the Brothers were dancing that night in the dunes far outside the oasis where their drums would not be heard by the fort.

We found the dancers in a big, rolling dimple of sand. They were already in trance; sometimes a dangerous state. We jumped in and joined them, loudly professing and naming the *zikr*. When the Brothers took me by the hand, I became a Link: I found it pleasurable enough to indulge myself all night. We switched rhythms back and forth faster than ever I heard them called in Morocco where I first fell into a dance of this sort with Hamid. Here, no one knew who I was and, very soon, neither did I.

Our bare feet drumming on the hard, hollow sands made the dunes rumble and thunder beneath us. We may well have been dancing over a *foggara;* one of those many thousands of miles of underground waterways which the sedentary people of the Sahara have dug, throughout the long centuries of their survival since greener days, to bring water from miles away under the sand. Many thousands of specialized slaves died digging them and, even now, many are lost when the *foggara* they seek to repair caves in on them. The *foggara* are deep but, of course, not nearly as deep as the artesian wells sunk by the captains. From their artesian borings more than a thou-

43

sand feet deep in the earth have spurted congenitally blind fish who lost their eyes during eons of waiting in the dark. From a well of this sort once came a fossil crocodile which has given the drillers of oil wells to think.

As we danced all night with the Sahara vibrating beneath us, I felt through the chain of Brothers in the usual manner, following the usual procedure, but, finding none as inviting as Youngest Brother in Tam, I ventured outside of the circle. This is something I rarely permit myself because it means leaving the body untended. Once out there, I thought: Perhaps, I can get into the network of the *foggaras?* I was feeling foolhardy that night, almost relishing an encounter with Ghoul. I knew he was out there; no doubt of that, and along the way I must go. The moon rose, rode high and away. Some Brothers began falling to the ground in fits of possession. Two Guardians, called *assas,* strode about the leaping gaggle of dancers, having made themselves deaf to the *zikr.* When anyone fell, they ran up to thrust a stick like a bit between his teeth while they reached into his head with their slim, indigo-dyed fingers to fish out his tongue before they dragged him up close to the drum. This must have happened to me for I thought I was out under the sands on a long, eerie chase after Ghoul through endless, whirling tunnels when, abruptly, I heard the drum again as a drum. That finished the *zikr* for me.

I found myself laid out on the sands under my burnous, not at all sure where I was for a time. My Brother the sandal-maker came up with my Tuareg guide, finding me tongue-tied; afraid to admit I was afraid. They bundled me forcibly back into the tall saddle. As my Brother helped me up, he whispered: "There are no Brothers!" thus revealing his rank. He added: "You will find the Old Man of Buffalo Bordj in Algol." At that, he slashed at my camel with a whip which suddenly leaped into his hand like a snake. Clinging desperately to my saddle, I was swept along after my inscrutable guide.

For the next eleven days, he rode on before me at that same constant distance; perched high on the top of his giant racing camel like a bundle of indigo rags whipped by the wind. We pushed on all that first night without stopping, over a vast beach as hard as cement glowing blue in the faltering starlight. When day broke, it was not rosy dawn which hung across the horizon but a smooth wall of black basalt seven hundred feet high; the Table of Stone. My truck had crossed the Tademait in a night and a day but my guide counted a day for each finger; ten blazing suns for those who must cross it by camel and stay out of sight of the trucks. We rested "in hiding" that day; flat as stones on the desert near our camels, who lay trussed up beside us like boulders swinging their swan necks as they ruminated. I lay there under my burnous thinking how ridiculous this was but, apparently, nobody came by to see us. There is only one way to get up onto the Table, along the ramp called the Akba at whose foot we waited until night covered our quick dash up the ten miles or more of zigzagging incline which no truck would dare navigate after dark. Just at dawn, we stepped onto the slick surface of the Tademait, burned black as an elevated parking lot in hell. A dusty trail for trucks took the easy way across; we had to take the other.

I had caught the trick of the saddle by then so I could ride all day, reading the only book I carried in the hood of my black burnous; that odd *"Report"* of our Brother, Ibn Khaldoun the Historian. The Great Desert, according to him, is Life. No one can tell which way he has come into it, for the wind covers his tracks as he moves and the prospect looks, in

45

all directions, as if no man had ever traversed it safely before. There are almost no animals but that winsome rodent, the dancing jerboa or gerbil, and the foxlike fennec who hunts him. No birdsong is heard. This land consists of shattered mountains, rotted valleys and shifting bare plains in an infinite variety of desolations. There is nothing at all to eat and travelers are not allowed their own dreams. Ghoul is Master of the Sahara and his abrasive voice moves the traveler in the very fiber of his being, for Ghoul's voice roars out like an endless pasture of camels but it is only the hollow and disembodied wind, grinding together the infinite and never-to-be-numbered grains of sand.

When a man rides by night through the desert, he often hears voices, and, sometimes, they may even call him by name. (Hassan is an easy name for the wind.) Calling upon him, the voices may make him stray from his path so he never can find it again. Many, many travelers have been lost and so perished. Even by daylight, a man in the desert may hear these siren voices or the strains of musical instruments; the fainting, dancing voice of a flute or the rattle of drums in a sandy defile, as if some army was coming over the crest to fall upon him and his camels. Many a traveler has been led away or has fled only to die of thirst. Through the endless, echoing silence comes, like the song of an ant, the faraway grinding clatter and throb of a diesel or, sounding more like the swarming of wasps, the whine of an oil driller's rig—but that is only illusion. Many, many have fallen victim to this last illusion for it, too, is part of the mirage of which all travelers speak but few can explain.

All day long under the white-hot silvery tenting of the sky we advance through the Country of Fear. We march in the eye of the mirage with the dancing and swooning horizon a full wavering circle closing us in. Heat billows up out of the ground like the breath of a glass factory rolling out the mirage. Mirage is that quicksilver stuff you run through with your car on the rise of a macadam road in midsummer but, here on the desert as out on the sea, the round swell of planet Earth is your rise in the road. You and your guide and your camel, or you in your diesel, are shrunk down to the size of an ant dragging a straw—only smaller. The watering eye of the mirage is the great Show of the World. On its dazzling round screen you assist at the creation and destruction of the world in flames. This overwhelmingly present act of erosion, scouring and pulverizing the landscape under your eyes, throws up a demoniacal vision of glittering marshes forever just out of reach. But, this is neither water nor fire. Perhaps, it is a vision through eons of time, back into the unthinkable past hundreds of millions of years, into that long Mesozoic afternoon when protoplasm fumbled with blind fingers through boiling-hot shallows on the baking shores of a planet which cooled. Your camel suddenly lets out a terrible bellow and roars off to take a deep gulp of the stuff.

When you get your camel in hand again, there all of a sudden, are more of those piled-up stones. Who can be piling them up? A black disk neatly balanced on a big white stone carries two red blocks topped by another white stone, round as a ball, on which stands a blade of basalt to twist into a spire—and it does! Mirage bends the air, throwing out long veils to catch up these stones into one little show. While you look, the stones swell into a fortress seen from a distance; a citadel with turrets and towers. No, it is a gaudy temple of Shiva somewhere in Hind and, now, it falls back again into a pile of stones as you approach.

47

The Sahara is a place of running shadows but no shade. Other white stones are scattered about. Out of the corners of your eyes, you catch them jumping up quick as snipers to drop down again, changing place. White turbans and burnouses the color of sand; yes, of course, these are snipers and wherever you look there is one who has you in his sights and, at sunset, they fire off a shattering volley as day is done. The stones burn all day in the sun and, when night falls, they are so seized by the sudden cold they crack and scale off razor-thin shards of basalt which have become this endless, fathomless heap of broken black bottles we cross.

So end the terrors of the day and, now, the terrors of the night begin. Contrary to what may be true elsewhere, the terrors of night in the Sahara are easier to bear. All day long, I can hold the snipers at bay only by being totally aware of each one. My being is drawn up tight as a bow; the terrors of the day are the terrors of the mind. At night, I know the stones cannot shoot me for they are not my Assassins. It is Ghoul who is putting me out of his desert at the point of a stone.

Another nightfall, with its by now familiar rattle of gunfire, reassures me. I lie in the lee of my camel to unstring the bow of Me; chuckling a little in sympathy with the animal's ever-so justified moans and complaints. The desert fires off a last broken volley of exploding stones and I laugh. Do they think they are chasing the sun? I shiver under my stiff black burnous, scratching the itch of the sun from my skin. Sun collapsed down in the west like a blazing balloon and is gone. The black rack of night, frosty with stars, clamps down on the Great Desert and me. Now is the Good Time; so, I pull out my pipe and rattle the matches. Night and I settle down to the perilous pleasures we know. Yet, even here, many travelers have been lost and have perished, for they may not have their own dreams to guide them and they hear the voice of Ghoul like the bellowing of a legion of camels, as numerous as the grains of sand. Travelers start up and run off without knowing whither they run and are so lost before sun seeks them out in the morning.

I wake to the greasy glitter of stars mirrored back by the slick, sand-polished basalt sea all about me. My evil-tempered camel bucks and bellows to find his hobbled knees buried in the drifting sand. I seem to be floating above him and a bundle which well may be me; if that can really be my body half-buried there like the dried carcass of some mythological bird. The drape and fold of my woolen burnous is sculpted in sandstone. The lunar Sahara about me is cindered over with a fine blue ash of frost. Time has stopped. A familiar indigo rag flutters out of the sand where I look for my guide to find him, too, buried in moondust. I think we both may be dead. I glance up to see it is six o'clock by the winter stars and a light like a comet comes soaring up from the south. The night plane out of Black Africa, I think first, and, when I realize it must be a cosmonaut, I put that out of my head. My mind boggles at the idea that someone like me could be up there, locked into an Iron Lung of that sort. I struggle back into the ruin of my half-buried body to waken my guide with my voice. A bundle of indigo rags breaks out of the sand-crust, over there by our other camel, and sits up to stretch. From somewhere back in the folds of his *tagelmoust,* the yards of fine muslin with which we both wrap our faces day and night, I see the light of his eyes and in them I see what I know. I have never seen more than this of his face, for we both go disguised through the

Country of Fear. We reach out to stroke palms in the briefest of greetings. It is enough; we can go on together another day.

Early on the eleventh day, we came to the northern edge of the Table of Stone. We crawled up cautiously to peer over, being whipped by the wind; suddenly awed and fearful lest we plunge down hundreds of feet onto the celebrated oases of Algol, lying directly below us like a pool of mirage. On the bottom of a bright sea of air, tapestried patches of feathery palm-garden lay stitched out in green on the rosy-golden sands; pinned down by the silver threads of water which run through them in elaborate patterns of irrigation. The various oases are strung out like a broken necklace of emerald along the former course of a fossil underground river. I could make out the military fort by its flag hoisted over the richest cluster of palms and I plotted my course to avoid it. Some miles up the valley lay a last thinly-planted satellite oasis; a mere handful of palms standing around a group of domed adobe buildings dominated by a squat tower. I took that to be Buffalo Bordj and, starting to speak to my guide, found he had silently turned back with the camels and gone.

I swung my field glasses around again to catch a glint from the sun on another glass which someone on the tower of Buffalo Bordj had trained on me. Trust any Old Man to catch me in his sights! I worked my way down a stone chimney in the side of the table of rock; tobogganed down a long col of scree and struck out across country. I could make out a tiny speck moving out of the oasis across the bare plain; someone running to meet me. Within the hour, Sudanese Mr. Barigou came up babbling officiously, ambassador-wise. He wore a brightly flowered Hawaiian shirt over baggy black *sarouel* pants and he smelled of sour red wine even at that hour of the morning. He was still pretty glossy but already the plump side of thirty; a bit shifty-eyed, he had obviously taken to drink. His Old Man— *"Mon Colonel,"* he called him—was already delighted to see me, he said. Even as we walked over the desert, the colonel lay on his iron army cot on the top of his tower following us closely through his telescope, every foot of the way. We could feel him out there with us, while we were still some miles from the house. "He can walk in the *souk* of my head," Mr. Barigou gravely assured me; regretting that, therefore, he could not hold my hand as we walked.

We came to some rain-ruined outbuildings and then the imposing main portal of Buffalo Bordj; a handsome gateway of red desert-cement in Sudanese Flamboyant style. "No woman pass here," said Barigou proudly. "Museum," he waved grandly at some small buildings like bunkers on either side of the big outer court. At the far end was an arch big enough to drive a truck into a smaller whitewashed court at the foot of the tower. In the doorway, stood the colonel to greet me. I would not have recognized him from the photo which is the frontispiece to his unique literary work: *Across the Sahara and Back*. He had put on flesh through the years as a disguise; tricking himself out in snowy white hair down to his shoulders, a big curling mustache and a pointed goatee. Under his White Hunter's hat, he tried to look as much like a plump Buffalo Bill as he could, while wearing a fine white burnous and excessively shiny silver-rimmed glasses which made me distrust him on sight. I could see he liked the looks of me only too well.

Barigou disappeared into domestic shadow along with a slim, wild-looking boy of about fifteen, who had, I could see, nothing on under a short, torn tunic, belted by the thong of a slingshot such as nomad Chaamba shepherds tie around their waists. The colonel shouted after them: "Don't let Ahmed make the coffee, Barigou, or we'll all be poisoned again!" and, turning to me: "Come, I'll show you around my museum myself." I stumbled over my own feet with fatigue but I nodded and mumbled politely as the colonel guided me through his "collections," which looked like so much desert rubbish to me. As we went from one bare, dusty room to another, the boy Ahmed kept popping in and out opening doors, scowling at me from under his black curls. The last room of all was devoted to high moments of the colonel's career.

While still only a spruce captain, detailed to the desert after World War I, he became by a singular stroke of luck *Half the First Man across the Sahara,* all because a very white American, name of Hopkins from Boston, had suddenly started up from a 1925 cocktail party or a café table in Paris with a wild blue stare around, looking for the last white spaces left on the map of Earth. It might just as well have been the Arctic but someone suggested the Sahara, which was very much in vogue with the French at the time. Kissing Scotty and Zelda goodby, he had flown due south in his own Gypsy Moth, armed with a handful of letters to military types in the desert, provided by a French buddy-pilot left over from World War I. Landing at Algol, Hopkins blurted out to the super-dapper captain: "Will you take me across the Sahara?" The captain screwed in his monocle: "When I saw how that Amerlou threw out his stale socks instead of having them washed, I knew he was rich. I proposed: 'Half a million gold francs to cross the Sahara: you bring the trucks and equipment: I'll bring you back.' " They made it, discovered a prehistoric skull and brought out a book, badly printed, with maps. Captain became colonel with enough money put aside to buy the oasis and build Buffalo

Bordj. Houses are sepulchers for the living, the nomads say. It takes more than an Adept or two to set yourself up as an Old Man of the Sands.

I glanced with some amusement at fading photographs of Sudanese boys naked by a river with their cocks hanging down to their knees. That's what we're good for, I guess. Next to these hung a pre-World War I cabinet portrait photo, as I believe they were called, of the young officer in his first dress uniform, I judged. He wore pince-nez glasses and a sharp waxed mustache in those days. Beside this hung another from the same Parisian photographer showing him still with glasses and mustache but, astonishingly enough, dressed as a rich bourgeoise French lady of about 1910 in an evening gown with feathers and beads beneath a huge plumed hat. An armor-plated necklace covered his plunging décolleté. "My mother's jewels," the colonel breathed in my ear. I was taken aback to find he was pressing my hand. I snatched back my hand before he could kiss it as Ahmed Chaamba came in with the coffee. The colonel looked moved.

Barigou was clucking around the courtyard like a semi-insane African comedy version of an imported French wife; his body presumably occupied by the ghost of the colonel's mother, now playing Friday in the Sahara. We were served semi-French food in a curious underground room which had old Perrier bottles from France set into the low vaulted ceiling, pouring down on us a liquid green light. The Old Man expounded the rule of his house: "No eggs, no milk. I buy cheese from the nomads. I won't let a female animal enter my house!" I nodded in sympathy: "The rule of Mount Athos." I hate chickens, myself; cannot bear their cackle and feathers and get little enough pleasure out of smiling: *"Bismillah!"* while

53

slitting their throats. "My house is my fortress!" boasted the colonel: "Will you give me a kiss?" I begged him to excuse me and, as Ahmed Chaamba came back at that moment to clear the table away, I asked: "Could I just lie down for a few hours in his room, perhaps? I am terribly tired." I pulled out my pipe to turn on but the colonel snapped: "Please! Not in front of my Adepts!" Who the hell did he think he was, anyway?

Mister Barigou showed me into a bare little room with mud walls where I threw myself down on the iron army cot, rolling up in my own burnous. Barigou hung his black moon-face in the crack of the door, playing me his desert version of "Poor Mister Bones." I can hear that sound, so I slipped him a bill as I told him to close the rough plank door. I was in a hurry to light up and, as soon as I did, I began to pick up the Chaamba boy's low-frequency delta waves pulsing through the bed. The rhythms set up by such a young creature are just what I need. Here was a wild young postulant under a bad master who seemed to be learning the ropes by himself as any young Adept should. A bright shaft of sunlight fell through a chink in the door directly onto my closed lids. I fanned out my fingers, flickering them through the ray of light at something like the delta rate. Deep waves of migraine red, blue, purple and green pounded through my head in the heavy color-language in which Deltas talk to themselves.

My interior screen was swept by psychic static like a color 3-D TV screen in a blistering electrical storm. Some people, finding these visions as intolerable as real sandstorms in the desert, run screaming for a doctor at this point; for me, to know these wastes is to love them. Limitless bright pastures of light exploding on the never-to-be-numbered grains of sand

flashed through my skull until, somewhere out there on a great
burning beach, I picked up his tiny, cowering figure. Chaamba
nomad herdsmen call such barrens a pasture when one spindly,
rapidly-flowing plant every fifty paces springs up after a rain.
And it did rain across my screen; rain like driven shards of
glass under which the boy, Ahmed Chaamba, huddled against
the goats of his mother's tent. Then, as a tiny jeep raced like
a maddened mechanical beetle across the scoured and polished
floors of my visionary Sahara, the boy started up like a gazelle
but in less than a minute they ran him down with the jeep.
There he was, broken and panting; slung over the fender. Black
Mister Barigou and the colonel, all in white including his ten-
gallon hat, tied the boy up in a sack and threw him into the
back of the jeep. "Caught me another one live!" the colonel
exulted. I suppose these were the first words in French on the
boy's new sound track. That is the way I really like to see
them; when they bring one in fresh. I wish I had been there.
My ways are not this Old Man's ways, of course; nor, I expect,
are they yours.

There was a long period of mending and brooding in one
of the colonel's dark underground rooms. I thought I caught
a glimpse of the boy's astral pattern in the buzzing pinpoints
of light; his path in the stars, learned since childhood through
the seasonal migrations of his tent. When Mister Barigou pushed
him up the ladder to the colonel's iron army cot for the first
time, the boy Ahmed saw by a glance at the stars that his tent
had moved far away after fresh pastures, almost certainly
counting him dead. The Old Man took him there night after
night while he stared at the stars and, plotting the position of
his tent, bided his time. As the tent moved back toward Algol
with the returning season; nearer and nearer, from pasture to

pasture known only to the Chaamba nomads, he counted the nights until his escape. Yet, when the time came, and the False Southern Cross rode high overhead as he lay under the stars with the colonel, he could not raise a finger nor move a limb but lay there impaled while the voice of the Old Man rumbled in his ear like the voice of Ghoul himself: "I can see you, Ahmed Chaamba! I can see you from here on the top of my tower through my telescope. You run in the wind. . . . I can see where you run . . . I follow wherever you go. You may run, Ahmed Chaamba, and leap from dune to dune like the tender gazelle I bring down with one crack out of my rifle but, now, you are falling . . . panting and sliding down a whirlpool of sand. There is nothing in front of you, Ahmed. You are falling, falling, falling. . . ."

If I am yours, you are mine. The boy began stealing into his Master's head, now he saw how the thing was done. He lay there, taking it all in night after night as they linked under the stars. He slipped into a garden called *"Lafrance"*; garden after garden over the whole land with no Sahara between the gardens. He stole like a thief into cold rooms, schools, barracks and bars where Christians drank the forbidden Arab poison called *Al Cohol* in public while they stumbled about to music with their hands on almost naked women; held, unbelievably, to be their wives. He glided with a knowing smile through a world of shadows who pounce on boys in underground lavatories and shabby Parisian hotels where the dapper young captain ogled them through his pince-nez as in a series of old curling yellow photos which faded when he took them in his arms. The Old Man's life died as the Chaamba boy took it over. The Old Man's life will soon all be mine, he gloated: when I have the very last gasp of him in me, he will be dead.

56

He took the colonel with growing pleasure, starry night after starry night. I'll soon be the colonel and all this will be mine, he thought, but Black Mister Barigou still ran the house.

At that very moment, Mister Barigou was shaking me out of my torpor deeper than sleep to say that the colonel had a contraband truck waiting for me at the edge of the oasis. It was night and the sandstorm was screaming high in the air over the narrow, whitewashed court in which the colonel stood to bid me good-by. Barigou held up a blazing torch a pace behind him, leaving the Old Man's face in leaping shadow. His voice betrayed a very thin frosting of politeness, as he bade me: Adieu! Barigou led me out the main gate and down an avenue of wind-lashed palms to where a truck with its lights off throbbed in the crashing confusion of the dark. All of a sudden, the Chaamba boy reeled out of the night to throw himself like a parcel at my feet. The truck ground into gear as I picked him up, kissed him on top of the head and took a deep breath of his perfume before I climbed into the cabin, slamming the door as we moved off into the sandstorm. Thus, I took him with me while leaving him there; a neat trick.

One of the most popular perfumes in the Sahara comes in a bottle the size of your little finger with the picture of a naked Black girl on the label, which reads: *"Bint El Sudan"* in Roman letters. More correctly, it should read: *"Bint es Sudan,"* of course. In very small letters beneath the girl's feet, it says: *Hackney E.8,* I think. All the boys in the desert like to pour a whole bottle over their heads before they go out in the Sahara: they smell very nice.

Impossible to express my feelings when I climbed into that infernally hot metal truck-cabin to find I must share a single seat again and, this time, with a sour-smelling, wiry, old

Frenchwoman, wearing a White Hunter's hat. She was known on all desert trails as the Rock Scorpion. This scourge of the sands traveled everywhere for years under more or less official protection as the widow of one of the First of the Sahara. All winter long she sped from fort to fort, bordj to bordj, like a hornet with gossip, while posing, back in Paris, as a Dissident like the doctor in Tam. Her voice carried over the wind and the hammering diesel as she launched into the history and function of the bright orange *jupe-culotte* she wore; very visible from the air, she assured me, in case we got lost. It was a sort of combination skirt and shorts, very handy for doing *pi-pi* on the flat desert, she explained. "I am seventy-two; same age as the colonel!" she screamed: "I'll show you all!" I winced away from her but that meant I sat half on the diesel in a position so uncomfortable that the heat later peeled all the skin from my left buttock and thigh. Her dry little bones poked into me on the other side until she subsided in a heap as her metabolism, altered by the near-zero humidity, dried up her saliva along with the rest of her mucus.

She had drunk all her own water and began croaking to me for some of mine. Mr. Barigou had handed me up a *guerba* at the last minute: a whole skin flayed from a goat, used hairy side out with its sleeves tied, as it were, in which water is carried everywhere in the Sahara. I untied the neck and she drank greedily of this water which seems to have been excessively charged with magnesium. The colonel must have ordered it drawn from the most brackish of his wells. The old doll fell back on my shoulder, gurgling. I barely had time to push back the cabin window for her to be sick. She went on retching for hours, until we were all splattered with her vomit and the cabin was whirling with sand because she insisted on keeping the window open. She collapsed by dawn, giving me a little more space, but Black Greaser turned around, insisting: "That Roumia is dead!" They still use the word "Roman" for all of us Christians; even me. Greaser poked her into violent convulsions, during which she screamed that I had poisoned her. Poison is common enough among women, here in the Land of Dissent. She dug into her sack for an antidote, coming up with a *Eubyspasme* suppository. I turned away, preferring to lean on the red-hot diesel while she struggled to place it: apparently, her *jupe-culotte* was not so practical for that. When the *Eubyspasme* took hold, she dropped away into some other world, leaving us her old sack of bones between me and the window, where they took up almost no space at all. I breathed easier.

We sailed on blissfully all that next flaming morning over salt-pans as bright as mirrors, through a sandstorm blowing about like golden chaff in the wind. Driver steered by the compass, shoulders down at the wheel. The Old Girl next to me called out deliriously: *"Driver! Driver! Even though there's no road, you can't run away from me . . . !"* No one else opened his mouth. Greaser taught me to communicate glottally, with mouth closed to save saliva. Driver and he kept up an inane conversation in this engaging baby talk at which they were incredibly proficient until, finally, they began to sing together in a gurgled duet that old desert favorite:

> *Oh, I got a girl got so much gold*
> *She can't get 'round*
> *Get up gazelle, 'cause I'se you' guy!*

We'll swap you' gold for a taxi, love
I'll throw in my clutch an' never stop goin'
Oh, we'll cross the Sahara an' never turn back!

We drove on that afternoon, west south west, with the red sun in our eyes until it dropped out of the sky and we steered by the stars.

I woke with a start to find we had drawn up under the half-ruined arch of a formerly fortified refuge. This is the cara-vanserai at the shrine of Hassan-i-Sabbah, Old Man of the Mountain and Great Sandy Waste. A hair of his beard is said to be preserved here at the heart of the tons of desert cement which they have piled up and whitewashed, calling it his *koubba,* or tomb. Naturally, it is a refuge for Dissidents. Few travelers pass this way, ever. Our Old Girl was asleep and would never even know she had been here. I made an only half-humorous hypnotic pass over the old harridan, to knock out her subconscious recording system, as I climbed over her carcass to force my way out of the cabin. The truck was surrounded by a gang of hoarsely shouting desert-drifters and ragged riffraff of Broken Boys who swarmed over us like pirates taking a prize. A handsome, old, white-bearded man with a turban came out of a dark doorway carrying an iron-shod staff with which he cleared me the way. Driver agreed we would leave in an hour.

"You may not pass this way again in a lifetime," said my guide as he led me through a pitch-black passage. A great blaze of sudden light broke through the tall wooden doors which swung back at his touch to let us step into the narrow *Heart of the Diamond,* as the inner court of the sanctuary is called. *"Put off thy shoes from off thy feet!"* As I stooped to loosen my sandal, I stumbled for fear I might fall into the

intense hallucinatory patterns of the ceramic-tile floor. Each pattern exactly covers the grave of a Brother fortunate enough to lie buried here, just outside the Shrine of the Hair. The tombs are fitted to cover the ground, wall to wall, with a dazzling variety of geometric patterns in combinations of colors which seem to flutter and jump, playing back and forth with perspective and perception. These magic carpets in tile can catch up the soul into rapture for hours. They begin with mere optical illusion in which colors leap and swirl but the effect goes on developing to where pattern springs loose as you move into the picture you see. You step from this world into a garden and the garden is You.

I stood barefoot on a grid of electric-blue while, below me, revolved a firmament of candy-colored flowers through which flowed streams of incandescent stars. I stood on a glowing grid of red while a sea of flames boiled like a caldron of transparent naked bodies bobbing up and down in uncontrollable lust under my feet. I stood on a grid of budding vines, writhing like jeweled serpents whose eyes flashed with all the colors of the rainbow prism. I stood on a grid of melting gold while worlds fell away beneath my feet and I looked up. I lifted up my eyes to the golden honeycomb walls of the court and my heart welled up within me for each cell in the comb was the diamond-shaped pattern of Man as seen by da Vinci and each one set the Golden Number echoing out like a gong. In each identical cell burned a diamond-white *kinki* lamp set on the clean woven mat of pure gold where a Master sat gazing on the burnished face of his Adept and each Adept was someone I loved: Carlos, Costa, Andonai and Nico; Philippe and Giovanni; John, Mario, Robby, Mirko; Antonio, Juan, Alberto, Julio; Hamid, Targuisti, Ahmed Maati and Ahmed

61

Marrakshi; "Verigood," Franco, Francis, Benaïssa, Mustache and "The Prince." . . . Named and unnamed, they rose up tier upon tier; all the ones I ever had burned for. They truly sat there but they were not Flesh; they were Fire, the color of a burning rose. They sat cross-legged, smiling at me in absolute love and confidence, for they had no bodies but flame. They were not human images in the flesh but the Real Thing, which is Light. I looked up, higher and higher, as the honeycomb rose to the skies, where all the faces were One, melded together in one fiery river of light. I rode on the surge of the Fountain, straight up out of this sphere into the Other, from where I thought to take a good look at the Masters who all turned their backs on me when they gazed at their Adepts—and mine. With all the passion of my earthly mind, I sought to force them to turn and they turned: all of them turned with one familiar, identical smile, for all of the Masters were Black. All of them had chosen to put on the image of Me.

My guide coughed politely, touching my arm to lead me away down a dark corridor toward a big room full of smoke and the hoarse sound of men shouting; the bawdy laughter and coarse joking of the porters and desert-drifters who had swarmed over our truck at the gate. He just left me there, standing in the arched door of this vaulted room, awkwardly holding my rucksack, startled by the wild faces which gleamed up at me from around a small fire which the Broken Boys had lit in the middle of the room, on the floor. *"Salaam aleikoum,"* I mumbled, conscious that Muslims do not like to hear these holy words of greeting from other than Muslim lips. "Why doesn't the Merikani take a plane?" shouted one rough voice. "Because he is Black!" answered another. Roars of laughter. "The white Merikanis won't let him, so he has to travel like us!"

I took a deep breath and stepped boldly over some of these people, taking a place in the far corner where I got my Primus stove slowly out of my sack before I replied—giving myself time to say it correctly in Arabic: "This gentleman wished to give himself the pleasure of visiting the Great Sandy Wastes of the Sahara where he knew he would meet such distinguished travelers as yourselves." There was a general roar of applause and, before I could light my stove, someone had handed me a shot-glass of smoky desert tea and a pipe of keef. I smoked it and refilled it in turn with what I had left from Ketama and handed it back. More pipes were offered out of the dark and refilled.

Behind the circle of smokers, my eyes began to take in a whole squirming choir of husky young Tuareg, blue as the night. A dozen or more unmarried, veiled boys of fourteen to eighteen were scuffling and Indian-wrestling there in the dark with their face-masks bound tight. I could see that a good deal of this horseplay was put on for me. The Tuareg are a self-conscious people, not in the least effeminate but vain and coquettish as well as indifferent, lazy and cruel. They do not smoke keef but their matriarchs do chew tobacco. These boys were elaborately veiled in yards of purple-blue carbon-paper material so heavily dipped in indigo it comes off at the touch but all they wore was a single garment like a sort of shift simply made by doubling a length of material, cutting a hole for the head in the middle and tacking the ends together at the bottom with a couple of thorns. When they raised their arms to arrange their veils, they were naked. They giggled and nudged each other as they folded and refolded the little pleat of veiling over their noses; taking out tiny pocket mirrors the size of a playing-card, which they carry in leather pouches

63

around their necks, along with a stick slim as a match to paint black *kohl* around their eyes, preserving them from glaucoma borne by the flies. Even from where I was sitting, they smelled very good. Indigo has a musky perfume of its own.

"Who are they?" I asked of the man with a *gimbri* who had settled down to play a little tune beside me. "The Growlies!" I thought he said. *"The Growlies?"* It sounded like a wonderful name for a football team. "Dag Ralis; Tuareg vassals. They come with the queen of the Tuareg: you like?" In a tired, husky, dissolute voice like the sound of pebbles rolling around in a can, he began to sing:

> *Oh, I know an Old Man in Buffalo Bordj*
> *Stuffs his asshole with millions in gold*
> *He wanted to play but I said: No!*
> *What's this dirham for—coffee? Eh, gazelle?*
> *So I reamed him out with my bicycle-pump*
> *Scooped up the loot he had in his pad*
> *And, flagging a cruising taxi down,*
> *Oh, throw in your clutch—Go on, Go on!*
> *We'll cross the Sahara and never come back!*

The Tuareg boys got up and left with backward glances. Their leader had come to say the queen was waiting outside and wanted to see the Merikani. I followed them out in the dark where a tall, heavy-set, unveiled and unsmiling woman stood with a hurricane lamp at her feet. She looked as if she had been waiting a long time to see one like me. She gave me a real white-lady look and I was surprised to see just how white she was. She looked like a middle-aged Virgin Mary or a Roman matron in slightly soiled marble. Grinning out from the shadows beside her was the familiar toothy black face of her personal slave-woman; a skinny, little, hunched-over, bobbing sort of a Black woman who looked like she knew me all of my life and I sure Lord-God knew her. The queen allowed me almost a nod but said not a word as her slave-woman gave me the message: "The Roumia needs you in the truck." I bowed and said: "Queen, we are all here to serve the Romans."

I found the old Scourge of the Sands lying across her seat and mine, fluttering her eyelids. "Have we got to Timoun?" she quavered: "Take me straight to the captain of the fort! This Black Merikani has poisoned me." I suggested to Driver that we lay her out on the cargo on the back of the truck where Third-Class passengers snuggled down in the sacks under the snapping tarpaulin more comfortably than we rode in the cabin up front. I rolled her up in my burnous to carry her there. She was light as a feather; like carrying Mother to her grave. I rode out there with her to make sure she did not smother as we sped off with the canvas cracking in the wind, like a sail.

We were skirting a shoulder of the Great Sandy Erg so, as we ground up an *akba*, a rise in the ground, I peered out over the swelling pink ocean of sand, all blond, all dimpled and titted, and I laughed to myself: "Aha! so Ghoul the Ogre is a woman as well as a man, or: Is the desert all woman, the Great Howling Banshee?" When we got to Timoun about midday, this particular old woman jumped up like a fennec, that odd desert fox who hunts the jerboa, and she barked at a startled middle-aged Arab merchant to catch her as she swarmed over the side of the truck. I knew she was off to the fort to say I was there and had poisoned her.

Timoun is a beautiful African town whose bright red mud

walls, five times or more the height of a man and three times a man's length through at the base, rise from a scoured plain, white as a bone. Within the gates is a great sandy plaza broad enough to harbor a hundred rich caravans or an army of trucks—such things have been seen in the Sahara. Today, the arrival of even one truck in Timoun is an event from which other events can be dated. A single rusty gas pump stands in the middle of the plaza like a marine signal wrecked offshore from a crumbling reef of once-handsome arcades for shops, which run all around the vast open space. They say it is so hot here in summer that one cannot cross the square to the gas pump on foot. The town is the usual hard-packed maze of streets narrow as corridors but there are some fine buildings, too. Big family houses like forts whose thick windowless walls of sun-dried red mud are finely sculpted in elaborate geometrical designs of Sudanese origin, enclosing cool patios shaded with trees and running with water. Several broad avenues of white sand are lined by high walls over which one glimpses red mud domes and minarets of mosques stenciled with abstract designs in whitewash. Everywhere, inside and out, there is hard-packed white sand underfoot and, so, the softly hissing silence of the Sahara is heard. All lanes and alleys lead to the palm gardens; the tiered gardens of date palms which shade the blossoming fruit trees from the blazing sun, as they in turn spread their sheltering branches over the thick carpet of irrigated greens; bright with water, quick with singing birds.

All this playing with water and building with mud is old, very old; Mesopotamian in origin, surely, linking this desert with that other called Arabia Felix—not called Felix because it is happy but because it lies *al limine* (the Yemen), to the lucky right hand when you look back east across the Tigris and the Euphrates, east to the Gobi from whence all the pale-faced freaklinas of history have always swept down on us poor Africans. So, here I was, now, striking west and anxious to get the hell out of town. Somebody said a diesel was leaving and the skinny little Black boys who guided me around the oasis assured me this was, as they said: "An Occasion." So, remembering Hamid, who always tells me I don't know my own luck, I took it. We shoved off about midday with an electrical tail-wind crackling behind us, driving us, now and then, into little date-palm oases like ports on the Secret Sea where honey-faced boys came up to stroke the side of the truck as if they were touching a spaceship.

Hadrar, our next stop, turned out to be in the hands of the Water Police, as they chose to be called at that time to hide their real purpose. I turned myself in at the fort, reporting to the captain what had passed between me and the old She-fox of the Desert. He listened to me with a courteous smile and assured me again that I would not be allowed to go further south. I was free to wander about the town, stopping here and there to do some little color sketches in my notebook. This is an excellent way to get to the children who are all natural-born Dissidents and, therefore, possible allies. They crowded around me in absolute silence as I sketched the picturesque walls of Hadrar. I picked a young Adept to hold my water bottle and exchanged a word or two of pass before I interrogated him. He reported briefly: The fort was hollow; the captain straw. I began to understand the man's easy jocular courtesy: behind him was the real force, the Heavy Water Police who had made a great orange flash to the south. One day, there had been a great wind which swept away the tents of the nomads and a Pillar of Cloud had risen from the sands of

67

Reggan in the form of an immense mushroom, bigger than Ghoul. Many people were sick: no one was allowed to go south.

A one-armed lieutenant came up on us, cracking a whip to scatter the children. He bent over my notebook: "Nice little watercolors you do. My wife had the same talent. We have just seized your rucksack. Have you any raw opium on you? Balls about the size of your fist? . . ."

No, luckily not. I remembered how Singer had smiled when asked about that: "*Aphioun?* Why, yes; there *was* a ball around here, somewhere. . . . Now, where can it be?" He looked about smiling, helplessly stoned. That room of his was scoured clean as the Sahara: where could he hide anything? Under the fine white sand floor or up in the split-palm rafters, perhaps? Singer rustled around for quite a while in the flue of the fireplace but nothing showed up. A round ball of opium in the raw, about as big as your fist, would be the very best crop you could possibly draw from a patch of poor soil near a trickle of water out in the middle of nowhere. You sit by your poppy-patch a few feet square with a couple of goats to keep you alive while you wait for your poppy to blow. I can't wait that long. No, I do not have any O.

In the bar of the *Hotel Hadrar,* I heard one French colonial officer say to another: "As soon as we leave the Sahara, this bar will dry up." I was too shy to go over and ask him just what he meant. The other one laughed as he replied: "The day after we leave, the Sahara itself will be taken over entirely by Ghoul!" Just then, a jolly dissident captain of transport bought me a drink. He was bowling through on his way north to Bechar in a Dodge command car with a tall technical sergeant from the Legion to drive it. I told him of my plight.

"Come on!" cried the captain: "Come on, come on! We'll leave the Sahara and never look back!" We left together within the hour, tearing north through the night five times faster than the diesel could do it and we stopped to piss in the wind or make tea wherever we chose. Tech Sergeant crouched over his wheel as he sang:

> *Oh, I know a garage in Ghardaïa*
> *Got every model of taxi-girl*
> *I want to tarry but Madame says: No!*
> *You pay on the landing and not on the stairs*
> *Nothing's as good as a jeep, gazelle*
> *On any flat bed I'll ride you down*
> *I'll pump you so full of my lead, tonight*
> *That, when I've shot the bolt of my gun*
> *Oh, I'll leave the Sahara and never come back!*

We slept out and it was cold.

We drove rapidly north up the sand-drowned bed of a fossil river and, by the following dawn, had covered more ground than a camel does in a week. At sunset that day, we came to the oasis of Targ, where a troop of young soldiers on their way north for evacuation had gleefully cast off their khaki uniforms to bathe in the trickle of red water forming a pond under the palms in the *oued*. The boys were all right, with merry brown faces and half legs and arms tanned by the sun and the rest of their bodies snail-white, but the truth of it is that albino freaks are attractive only to their own kind. The soldiers were, also, mucking up the irrigation system for the gardens and in the Sahara water is money. The raggedy locals hung about under the palm trees, grumbling but not daring to

69

throw stones. My transport captain averted an incident by ordering the soldiers out of the water before we took off for El Bit, where we spent the night in the government guesthouse, a tumbledown place.

Late in the afternoon of the following day, we got to Bechar; last town on the Sahara going northwest toward Morocco. In Bechar, the news was official: the last of the French were to leave the Sahara by the end of next week. No one knew what was going to happen to the atomic center of Reggan and there was an armpit odor of panic in the air. I, too, wanted to get the hell out. From Bechar run the few miles of rail they were ever able to lay across the Sahara; from there to the shores of the Mediterranean, the Great Salt Lake, but no one knew when there would be a train. Nor was there a room to be had in the town. Every bed in Bechar was occupied by military advisers, atomic consultants, deep strata geologists, contractors, contacters, plain hustlers, three-card men, dingers, dippers and dead-ringers for all the pale-face freaklinas this side of Metropolitan France. Bechar was one wide-open and shut town. Water diviners dressed like tough Klondike sourdoughs tore through the unpaved streets in armored jeeps with shotguns over their knees. The entire oasis strangled in a bright cloud of sulphur-yellow dust. Armed patrols enforced a curfew at nine when all lights went off at once from the main switch, simultaneously plunging the town into darkness and setting off the barking of what sounded like thousands of dogs chained up in all the courtyards against night attack. Arab dogs, tied up in mud huts deep in the oasis, barked back antiphonal choruses of vainglorious boasts and insults to the dogs locked up in the grim, blacked-out, barricaded European houses of the New Town on the edge of the desert. As the moon came up, waves of hysterical threat and counter-threat rolled across the desert like a visible haze of hatred engulfing the town. Wild yellow dogs, more than half jackal, hunted in swift-padding packs through the sandy lanes. Everyone walked with a big stick in Bechar.

My captain offered me a driver's bed in the Legion garage, so I bought provisions and lived in the bare, cell-like room with only a single iron army cot on which I began to dream again.

On the third day, at noon, a little toy train stood on the bright bare sweep of the desert floor at the end of the line. There was neither station nor ticket office nor anyone to stop me from getting on the train. I slid into a seat at the far end of the only passenger car, huddling there under my burnous. An Arab conductor came by and poked me, thinking I was an Arab: "No baggage?" I drew a deep breath: "No, no baggage. This is the Way I came and this is the Way I shall return, *Inch'Allah!*" He was startled to hear the password from me, so I grinned at him broadly. *"Ya Sidi!"* he grinned in reply. I fumbled about in the dark under my stiff, crusty burnous, which wrapped me from head to foot like a cocoon, as I fitted together the two sections of my slim keef-pipe with a handsome brass band at the link. Around the link is engraved the cyclical, endless word of our *zikr*. As I took out my masterpiece matches, I rattled the box. *"Nam, Sidi;* I hear you," the conductor replied, smiling even more broadly.

At that moment, a group of French people bustled into the other end of our car, calling him: *"Here, boy!"* It took him some time to settle them in. They were very loud. "We have come to eat!" shouted a really big, middle-aged woman with a mustache, waving a hamper of food and a bottle of wine. "To eat, to eat!" they all shouted in chorus. Within a few minutes, they had a tremendous meal spread out on their knees in front of them. It was time to go. I leaned out the window to see a whirlwind whipping across the desert in our direction. An armored jeep tore straight up to the train. "The Heat!" I thought to myself, automatically breaking my pipe to hide it, as I patted my passport over my heart. Four sourdoughs dressed like the posse, yanked an elegantly costumed Arab out of the jeep; planted him there, jumped back in their jeep and tore off in a yellow cloud of dust. I let out my breath. The young sheik shook out his movie finery, flapped the dust out of his gold-embroidered cape and stepped aboard the train. Without any warning, we left that place.

You may not pass this way again in a lifetime. Our very modern train seemed to be suspended in air, as silent as a crystal box, while they pulled the Sahara out from under us. The dazzling desert sped past the big picture windows like the vanishing tail end of an enormous golden rug, now, more and more thickly embroidered with the snarled and yelping thickets of thorn and thistle which spring up like a catfight whenever they find a drop of water. I filled pipe after pipe of my good Ketama to share with my Brother the Conductor in his swaying broom-closet at my end of the train. "Who is that Muslim in the burnous covered with gold?" Conductor spat on the floor: "The Caïd of Bogdour, may he rot! Bogdour is a garrison town on the pass just ahead. The captains taught him to drink: to lie and steal he knew already. Beyond his town lies Oujda and the border. If you have no baggage, you can easily go around it. The World is a Market . . ." and he faltered politely as I had explained I was American. "The world is a Market for Muslims!" I finished it for him triumphantly as I passed him over the pipe.

The caïd, intrigued by our conversation, came staggering along the aisle looking for water, he said. He waved away a pipe and sighed like a man with a terrible hangover. He had very bad breath. He had gone to Bechar, it turned out, to do a little business and, there in Bechar, he had fallen in with some prospectors who taught him how blackjack differs from baccara. Their fee for this lesson had come very high. He had been carrying the entire budget of Bogdour with an eye to speculation on a big scale and he had nothing left. He tried to borrow a hundred francs from each one of us in turn. I listened to this dreary old tale with only one ear, for the fat French-woman at the other end of the train had burst into a richly detailed denunciation of Lourdes, where she had been the previous season. As the caïd's oyster eye fixed on the bottle she waved, he left us to insert himself into their group where they received him with condescension. The conductor beside me spat on the floor.

Now, we were speeding through the long, knotted fringe of the desert. Clumps of oleander bushes covered with candy-pink flowers, the color and odor of circus floss, and thorn trees unclipped by the grazing of camels, whipped past like burrs caught in the last torn shreds of desert running up into rising country until we stopped beneath an escarpment of rock which is the true rim of the desert. A battered tin sign on two posts announced Bogdour. The caïd stumbled down the length of the car to fall dead-drunk from the steps of the train into the deep white dust of a deserted trail which runs from the train track up to his town. Silently, the little train began to rock again as we picked up speed and as the Caïd of Bogdour, lying back there like a fallen vulture, was drawn away into the improbable past.

73

In Oujda, I slept with a Brother who was the night watchman of a filling station. He laughed as he bedded me down on the floor of his *"Shell Hotel."* In the morning, he took me to the house of a brother-in-law, where, by passing over a few adjoining roof-terraces, I crossed the frontier into Morocco. I slunk around to the railway station on the Moroccan side of Customs and bought a Fourth-Class ticket to Tanja. The wooden railway carriage was rather like an old-fashioned streetcar and there was nobody in it but three young Moroccan soldiers on the benches playing Ronda, a card game almost as simple as Snap! Filling my pipe with some crumbs of Ketama, I handed them over a smoke. They joined me in good spirit and, in no time at all, we were laughing together like lunatics. The youngest of these was a sturdy country lad from the very fairy-tale landscape near Taza through which we were running. He was so moved by the sight of the hills of home that he leaned dangerously far out of the window, shouting up at the mountains of Morocco. He spouted poetry until we had to hold him in by the legs. Then, he chanted bellicose verses from an old Berber epic called *The Love of War:*

> *See those oueds?*
> *Those dry stream beds?*
> *They flood*
> *With blood*
> *See the Laurel rose?*
> *It blows*
> *With Roman blood!*

Gravely, I filled him a pipe. "I love you!" he cried. "I love you like a brother! You are the first Roman I have ever loved." I replied as best I could with some doggerel picked up from Hamid:

> *I love these rills*
> *Whose ripple fills*
> *The Little Hills . . .*

Perfectly spherical tears popped into the round eyes of my new little friend. I saw the entire moment, flying landscape and all, mirrored for an instant in their trembling crystal.

"I am a soldier!" he cried, snapping to attention, "and soldiers have nothing to give but their lives. So, I give to you three days of my life! Here, take my dogtag. When I report in without it, my lieutenant will give me three days in jail. This is my gift to you."

I had to accept.

In the glare of the noonday sun on the railroad tracks, my soldier stands forever to attention where I left him on the platform of the station-yard in Fez, beneath a flowering cloud of magenta bougainvillea climbing into the enameled blue Moroccan sky through which the clouds go running to the Little Hills. In Morocco, it is spring and the hills wash in torrents of color, all the mountains patched out with vast tentings of flowers. One mountain is blue, the next mountain is red and the mountain behind is bright yellow with borders of purple. White valleys below are great lacy aprons of waterwort meadow, smelling even more hauntingly rotten-sweet than the orange-blossom odor of honey that sets my head spinning as it pours through this train.

Will Hamid be up in his village, Jajouka? Can I leap from

this train when we get to Kebir and run straight up into those blue Little Hills where Hamid and his uncles, the Master Musicians, loll about easy all dressed in white, practicing Pan music on their pipes as they always have done these last twenty centuries and more?

2

Yes, Jajouka is always itself; a secret garden on top of Owl Hill. Of all the green regions of earth, I know of none more beautiful than Hamid's leaping Little Hills but I had forgotten just how impossible it is in this pastoral place to be alone, ever, for more than a minute or two. To be left alone, strictly, is almost the supreme punishment up in Jajouka, so only the magic act of writing can excuse my eccentricity to my hill-village hosts. Hamid, however, has to know exactly what I am writing and why.

"Well, you might call it my desert diary, Hamid," I tell him. "It's my trip. It's my account of my trek from here to there and back again. That's part of the trouble, you see; you're not supposed to come back the way you went. This desert, you know, can take a lifetime to make it from one end to the other. I feel I only zipped in and zipped out again, like a panic-stricken American. I might as well have been AMERICAN EXPRESS. I only tasted the Sahara, Hamid."

"Who tastes knows," nodded Hamid. What makes him so wise?

"Oh, I got beyond Barbary thanks to your passport of keef but, when once you hear the Sahara, Hamid, when you're actually in it, why, the desert's in you! You know that song the Sahara is singing right now this minute, down there on its long windy flute? *'Oh, you'll cross the Sahara and never come back!'* it sings. But I did, Hamid! I came back and I still haven't seen what I seek: my Black Africa!"

"*Mektoub,*" he shrugs. Hamid could hardly care less about anything Black. "It was written," he drones in his pat Moslem way.

"The next time around, I'll write my own ticket!" I hotly reply. "The Sahara still owes me a lot. The next time that I'm down there, I'll take the place over from Ghoul! I'll whip over the desert in my jet and I'll piss on Ghoul's head from thirty thousand feet up!"

"*Inch'Allah!*" Hamid nags after me nervously: "If God wills."

Hamid is, after all, my Baba, my Bab, my little back door into Islam through which the hue of my hide helps me slip in disguise when once I slough off my American cultural color.

"I'm an accidental Occidental, Hamid," I assure him. "I'm an African: same-same, like you. You say so, yourself," I insist, slipping into the loose Arab robes I brought back from the desert. Naturally enough, I have never been able to pull my Occidental mind along inside Islam after me but Hamid knows that and makes all sorts of allowances. After all, it was he who first brought me up here into these gamboling Little Hills where I am both a trespasser and forever at home. I remember, I once asked the caïd up here just how far his authority runs and he swung me around the grand circle of mountain and valley with an expansive gesture of welcoming pride as he stated, quite simply:

"You see that line where it is very very blue?"

The Master Musicians, all dressed in immaculate white woolen jellabas with their hoods up over their turbans, are grazing their flocks on the green and gold mantle of the hills. They are playing their flutes and the crystal-clear current of piping runs in rills down into the lush valleys below, watering and fructifying the crops. Yet, however much I may love their music, the only windy tune I can hear them play is *"Over the hills and far away across the Sahara and back!"* Once found, the words run around in my head with all the maddening reproach of a needle caught in my memory-track. Hot green tears spurt into my eyes and, when I clench them, the desert burns forever on the back of my lowered lids. For one haunted moment, I bathe again in the great Sea of Solitude, for whose barren shores any man who has once not only sighted but surveyed them must sigh forevermore.

"I've got to go back to the Sahara again," I tell Hamid. "There's so much to see and so much to learn. That's why I've got to finish this copy of my Sahara notes and send all these papers off to the people in Switzerland who gave me the money to go on my trip. It's what they call a sort of report: where I went, what I saw. It wasn't my fault I couldn't break through the roadblock at Tam. Tam is a very magnetic, mysterious place. What you see there is one thing and what really goes on is another, You know very well what I mean. I seriously suspect Tam must be the enchanted castle of Ghoul. When the Foundation for Fundamental Findings gets wind of this, they'll send me more money, maybe, to make another trip."

"Thass good!" Hamid states firmly, instead of muttering: *"Inch'Allah."* He firmly approves of my having money when I spend so much of it with him. "Next time, I go too. No man should travel alone. Thass no good."

Hamid, happily, has not yet got a passport and passports are hard to get. So far, he travels only on the magic carpet woven of his imagination and mine. How many times have we sat here sharing his *sebsi,* his keef-pipe, sailing to the States in the ship of Hamid's head. Sure as shooting, that is one trip I am in no hurry to take in cold blood, so I tell Hamid I have no money.

"Thass all right!" he assures me. "You sell me to someone as soon as we get to New York. When you get the money from the bank, I run away and come back. I don't care: you can sell me whenever you like but I'll always come back."

"But you can't do that any more in the States," I weakly insist. "Slavery is dead."

" *'Burn baby burn!'* " quoted Hamid, lighting a *sebsi* of keef. "Thass what the matches say to the box."

The day after that, I went down to Tanja alone and took the ferry across the Straits of Gibraltar to Gib to send off my manuscript from there for security reasons. Right opposite Her Majesty's Post Office on Main Street, I saw in the window of an Indian shop just the very tape recorder I have been wanting all of my life—a UHER! An end to all this painstaking writing and rewriting of words. When the bearded Indian sage in the shop demonstrated to me how well the UHER both records and wipes out the words, my heart went out to the machine and I bought it with what was left out of my Fundamental funds. Now, I am never without my UHER wherever I go. Up in Jajouka, I sling my UHER over my shoulder like a mountaineer's purse. There is so much wild music running through Hamid's Little Hills that I am as anxious to tape it as a tripper is to slaughter wild flowers. Here, for example, I have a recording I made almost by accident on one of those occasions when Hamid, maudlin with keef, mumbled away as he does about how I am ruining or have already ruined his young life:

3

THOU

Thou art the crossroads of my life, Hassan Merikani!

You know what that means in the language we speak. We say about people like you: He can walk in the *souk* of my head, the marketplace all Arabs live in. More than that, you stepped into my head without even knocking or calling out: *"Trek!* Make way!"* and you made your home there like my head was your very own house where you walked up and down teaching me school without as much as taking off your big Nazarene shoes. Christian or not, you're an African, Hassan, belonging to us. American passport or not, we know people like you. I may be God's Little Burro or Allan's Ass, like I always say, and I may be a square-headed Berber just down from my own Little Hills, like they call me in Tanja but I was Hamid the King of the Train before I ever knew you. When I see a prize, I know how to take it. You never do.

I swung into Tanja one day about noon on the back of the train from Kebir and I dropped from the still-moving cars as we glided along by the beach before we got into the station:

no money, no ticket; I travel free! I tumbled head over heels six times in the sand and when I got to my feet, there were you. Playing Ping-pong with beachboys in the smallest bikini-slip ever seen on the beach, you were leaping about like a naked *Afreet,* one of King Solomon's magical Blacks. My flesh crawled at the sight of your flesh, the cool hue of your skin. "There goes my *Abid*—my slave!" I swore to myself. "I've bought me a Black." I was a newly ruined man of nearly sixteen who felt he had nothing to lose. How could I know you would cost me so much before we were through?

That midnight, alone, you sat drinking mint tea on the terrace of Fuente's café in the Socco and there, not a full arm's length away from your chair on the other side of the iron grill they took down more than ten years ago now—there hunkered Hamid, ex-King of the Train, hidden under the hood of his ragged jellaba. You slapped at your neck, like my black eye was a tickling fly, because I was trying to peer deep in your ear, drilling to see what you had inside of your head. Now, all these years later, I know. When I'll be dead, Hassan, I still will remember some things that you said. I always remember the first time you turned and your eyes caught in mine—so do you. You jumped up like something had bit you, calling the waiter as you dropped some loose change on the table, and ran up the Street of the Christians, heading for home. I chuckled and ducked through the shortcuts, just watching you dash up that flight of steep steps and into your house, double-bolting the doors without catching your breath. Were you spying on me from out of some little slit of a window high in the wall? Why didn't you turn on a light? I had nothing to do, so I could hang about all that night and all the next day and all the next night until you got over your fright and came out, or until I climbed into your house with you—somehow. I didn't know how.

I hung about easy down in the steep street below, under the arches and deep in the shadows, well out of sight. I slouched in an alley or I prowled in a lane, watching who toiled up the steep street of stairs or who drifted down to see Aissha the Whore in her neat little cupboard under the steps. A sailor crawled out on all fours with his buttons undone and his guide, who was waiting outside, collected commission from Aissha, who brazenly jangled all her gold bracelets right up to her shoulder to pay him his cut. Jimmy the Guide steered the sailor down the steps by the mosque and away out of sight. Then, the Barber Drunk with God, who used to have his barber chair in the middle of his one little room right under your house, where he dyed his own beard bright henna-red, shaved his own head and the heads of his customers, and rolled fancy turbans for his patrons on Fridays, strolled out of the mosque chanting night-prayers. He sang a long holy verse on one quavering tone as he slowly moved up from one broad step to the next of your street until, standing right under your window, he suddenly stopped, climbed into his little shop and he slept. That fat Soussi neighborhood grocer, who stayed open all night, slumped over his counter asleep on his vegetables with his head lolling out in the street. For an hour or so a chorus of cocks crowed on the flat roofs of all the houses in town but nobody passed. Then, at last, your new next-door neighbor and my old friend from the train, Si Mohamed, came staggering down from where a pirate-taxi had dropped him in Amrah, dead with sleep because it was the middle of the night, and

84

he was carrying a big roll of straw-matting to go all around the inside walls of his little house.

"Have you become a snail or are you some new kind of turtle, Si Mohamed?" I asked him politely as I bent down low under his load to look into his eyes. I knew he must have been smoking a lot. People who smoke are always out doing crazy things like that in the middle of night.

"Oh, so it's you!" grunted Si Mohamed. "Here, take the key to my house and open the door for me will you, Hamid, there's a good lad!"

Mektoub! It was written! Inside that one minute, I was inside the house next to yours, like a bee in the very next cell. Already, I knew exactly how I was going to get into your house. Si Mohamed set down his load and starting making the tea. I passed him a pipe of our great grass from the Little Hills and we passed an hour or so before pink summer dawn, talking about the people we both knew in smuggling who worked the train. Si Mohamed used to run chickens and contraband meat over the border from Kebir into Tanja, so we had all the same friends. I told him the tale of how I had just lost all of my smuggling capital down in Rabat. He could see I had been really cleaned out: he knew the girl. While he was pouring a fresh pot of tea, I said: "Nice little place you got here. Who's next door?"

Si Mohamed spat on the floor: "A Black Christian! Didja ever hear the likes before in your life! Why, I spoke to the man in the street, the day he moved in on a Friday. Just to look at the man, I thought him a Muslim, of course. I asked if he'd been to the baths, expecting to walk down the steps to the mosque with him, as the muezzin was calling the prayer and, d'you know what he says: I'm a Christian! he says. *Annah Nazrani!* And him Black, think of that! Says he wants to learn Arabic, too! Then, why can't he be a Muslim like everyone else in the world, tell me that? You can hear him moving around in there sometimes and I don't care if he hears *me!*''

I calmed down Si Mohamed and got him back onto the subject of matting, until he made me a fairly good price to fix it up on the wall with wood-stripping screwed into pegs in the plaster. I had two days to do it in, while he made his run to Kebir for his chickens and meat. Not one dirham in advance would he give me, and I half thought of selling his matting to eat when, all of a sudden, a much better idea popped into my head. Si Mohamed went out to borrow the tools because that was part of our contract. He was to get the plaster, wood-stripping and pegs and the screws and, above all, a big heavy hammer to knock holes in the walls for the pegs to hold up the mats. I just sat there and smoked while I thought out my plan.

About seven o'clock in the morning the pounding began, you remember? I knew it was waking you up. Si Mohamed hung around for a while, until he was almost late for the train, just to see me put in my first pegs in the thin wall with fresh plaster and, then, he went away satisfied I knew my job. I did and I do. I took that big old hammer in my two hands and, saying: *Bismillah!* I spat on its head before Si Mohamed was well down the steps. I wet both my hands with more spit that I slicked on its slippery shaft. Hard as that wall was, my hammer was harder! One two three and the wall came tumbling down! There you were like a hole in my picture. Were you really astonished when I came through the wall, right into your room? Really, really? Were you, really? What a *scandale!*

That same afternoon, we discovered together that cave on the beach all alone. Do you remember that day? The grapes! Do you remember the grapes we hung up for the little *djenoun?* What a day! Ah, but, of course, that was way back *then!*

The very next day, you turned purple and green when I wanted to borrow a suit. You Christians are all alike, every last one of you, white or Black. You're all always screaming: *"Don't take that! That's mine! I want it right back!"* Every last thing you lay your hands on is *My* this and *My* that! as if anything really belongs to you, here in this world, or really is real. I never could get into my head the way you all feel about things like a suit or a shirt or a life. I can feel that way for a moment, if a woman is mine, but you in American say: "Here's the keys to the car. Why don't you take out the wife?" That old yellow suit was the suit you had bought for a wedding, you screamed, and I screamed right back: "That's right! It's a wedding I'm going to!" So, I took it and went. Did you think that a wedding of ours is over and done in a couple of hours? Why, up in my village, Jajouka, a wedding lasts eight nights and eight days, a whole week!

Inside three days, I was back and I knocked on your door. When you came down the steps, you took one long look at me and you snapped: "You've been sick on my suit!" Somebody had, it was true. You know how it is nowadays at these modern weddings in town, some of the boys bring in a bottle or two that goes around as quiet as sin and as quick. Someone has got to be sick. You made me so mad, I bit blood in my lip as I turned away from your door, blazing with sorrow for you in my heart. I brought water into my eyes just to think how bad you must feel to be talking to me like that for so little. At that moment, I could have given you up. I raced back

87

to the *fondouk* where the smugglers stable their donkeys. In the room of a friend, I shucked off that suit and I put on my rags. I rolled that old suit in one bundle I took straight to Casa Luxy the Cleaners, on the far side of the Grand Market near the Cinema Rex—now called the Cinema Rif because it belongs to a big stiff from the Rif I used to know on the train. He never lost *his* capital and so much the better for him. Luxy wanted so much money to clean that suit that I took the ticket and sold it for a few francs more and bought an old seersucker suit out of the grab bag of rags the Americans used to send us to dress ourselves in. With my new clothes in my hand, I went to the hammam where who should I run into but my old friend from the train, Si Mohamed. Before he could say a word about the wall which I had fixed and repainted on your side but not his, I slapped him on the bare buttocks saying: "How's your Black Nazarene neighbor, these days?"

Every day for more than a week, your suit hung high on a perch in a tree above the Grand Market while I sat smoking over my tea in my little café from where I could see you walk right underneath it, five or six times a day. Every time you threaded your way through the streets of the town, down from your house in the casbah, down the Street of the Christians out into the Socco Chico where the cafés line the plaza and on up the Street of the Jewelers, out the old gate past the money-changers in their booths and across the Grand Market, the way it used to be before they cut down the trees in the middle all hung with cages of bright singing birds and goldfish in bowls to be sold by the flower-sellers who banked up their blossoms around the whitewashed boles of the trees against which they leaned smoking their pipes and smiling at any who

passed, up past the daily market for maids where the veiled
girls hang around to be hired by the day or the hour or even
less if they were pretty—well, if you *had* ever looked up,
you'd have seen your old suit cleaned and hanging high in the
air like a scarecrow of you. You really were sick. Your face
was as yellow as that old mangy suit when you marched through
the maids without even a glance and on up the street past the
Jewish Community building, right to the end where the traffic
cop stands, and not turning right to Dean's Bar—he's dead,
too bad—climbing on past the *Mingih Hotel* with a slow turn
to the left around the Cape of Good Hope for the hustling
guides and a quick glance up and down the rank of tables and
chairs on the terrace of the Café de Paris to see who's new,
rich and alive and, then, straight down the Boulevard to the
British Post Office. Who else remembers, today, in which
building it was? That's where your check was supposed to
come in and, according to you, it never did.

When I needed any money from you, it was always too
soon or too late. Us Moors can eat misery for breakfast, dinner
and supper and we get used to seeing a thick slice of it on our
plates but Hamid is a *hakim* for money. I can say: *presto!* and
make money come out of your nose. Who needs any more in
this life? You were the one who always was asking me questions like: "How old are you, Hamid?" and: "When were you
born?" How do I know! Was I there to ask them what time
it was when my mother was giving me birth? You think I pop
out of her belly to say: What day is this, please, I be born?
Do I know? I know only one thing: I am a ruined man. I who
was Hamid, King of the Train—I who played cards with the
Customs, letting them win—I who could bring anything in,

as big as the train, if I liked—can smuggle no more. How was I ruined? By a wicked woman, of course. How old was I then? Oh, maybe fifteen.

You never saw the old train the French made for us, here, hundreds of years ago, with open cars out on the back for us "natives"—Fourth-Class? That train brought me from Kebir to Tanja almost as soon as I could walk. My Pa had put me to school in Kebir in a room big enough for four donkeys or twenty small boys on the floor but the schoolmaster beat me over the head with my own wooden slate. When he found I drew pictures of him instead of my letters, he threw me out in the street. I was sitting in the middle of the road, drawing faces with my finger in the dust, when an old woman grabbed me by the arm. She said: "Little boy, help me carry my baskets to the station and I'll give you this penny for candy." What she smuggled to Tanja was mainly market-produce and our rations of sugar and oil which cost more down there. She brought back to Kebir things we really were needing, like bobby-socks, bubble gum, Lucky Strike cigarettes. When we got to the station, she tried to pull me up after her into the train so I struggled and cried but she promised the ride and one more penny in Tanja to carry her things from the station up to the Grand Socco Market—that's where the smugglers' traffic took place. Once I saw how that worked, I never had to ask anybody for a ride home.

I worked three years for that old woman and I learned how to smuggle and steal. Fourth-Class in the train carried nothing but smugglers, out in the open car on the back of the train. While we ran through our Little Hills between Kebir and the sea, we hid our merchandise all over the train, fighting each other for the best places and even crawling from one axle to the other underneath the cars. I knew every place. I knew every Customs man, too, and they all thought a lot of me because I gave them a tip every trip. Out of what I made stealing from the old woman and dealing, myself, I paid some to the Customs men and hid some away for my capital. It grew every trip.

One day the old woman came panting up to the station. "Carry me this and carry me that!" she cried. I told her: "Old woman, go carry yourself! I deal on my own from now on." The first time I ever went with a woman I found in the train, it was nice but nothing much happened. I had to wait another six months for that, so I must have been twelve or thirteen. By the end of that year, I had two women I kept—one at each end of the line all set up in a house to be nice to my friends from the Customs. I did the cooking, though. I don't trust the hand of any woman alive in the pot, not even my mother. Women put terrible things in your food, calling it love. Here in Tanja, any woman at all will use Borbor to turn a man into a donkey and do whatever she wills. In our Little Hills, all the Master Musicians cook their own food all their lives.

Inside three years, I was Hamid, King of the Train. I rode with the Customs, behind drawn blinds, playing Ronda with cards, pouring out wine which was mine. I kept all my merchandise in with me too, to be safe. The Customs men watched it for me while I checked out the train for them. I was rich for a boy of my age, so all the smuggler-women swarmed around me like flies. For them, I was a prize because they all had daughters to sell. I picked out a girl like an apple who was thirteen or twelve, still unveiled. When we fixed on her price with her father, I paid the down payment in front of the Cadi, our judge. Then, I took all my capital into my hand and set out for Rabat, where I'd never been before in my life, to buy all the things we were needing to make it a really grand wedding.

When I got to Rabat in the late afternoon, I saw just outside the station a boy I knew very well from the train and he was riding around on a brand-new bicycle, purple with trimmings of gold. One hundred francs in advance for every short ride from just here to the corner, that's what he wanted from me but, because I was rich, I paid for ride after ride after ride. The streetlights turned on while I was learning to ride like a bat, swooping out further afield until the boy called me back because he had to go home, so I followed him there, as blind as a lover. I completely forgot he had a well-known wicked sister who worked the train with only the merchandise she carried between her legs. She already had ruined many a man. That bicycle blinded me or I'd never have walked right into her house with my pockets bulging with money. Before I sat down, she had sent out for five cases of beer and, then, five cases more and, then, we sent out for ten. By the end of the week, we had filled up two rooms of a vacant house next door with beer bottles up to the ceilings and pouring out of the windows and doors.

That woman never would leave me alone. When we went out for a ride, she always ordered a carriage with two horses and she sat there beside me as decently veiled as a wife but, *"Ho!"* she would cry to the coachman whenever we passed in front of a shop. That woman was all the time needing some things. "You just wait for me here!" she would say as she disappeared into that shop for an hour until she called me to come in and pay for everything that she and her brother and I and the coachman could carry out in both arms. I paid and

I paid and I paid. I woke up one morning and saw her asleep on the pillow beside me, so I decided to slip on my pants while she slept. *Crinkle-crinkle! Rustle-rustle!* That crackling noise was my very last five thousand franc note in my pocket, whispering to me: *"Get out, get out!"* At that very moment a handful of coins fell out of my pocket to ring on the floor. "What!" she cried, bobbing up in the bed. "Where you going?"

"To the hammam to wash," I lamely replied as I kissed her.

"My brother goes with you!" she snapped. "Here, let me see that."

I gave up and gave her the works. When the last round was emptied, she threw me out on my ear. I went shambling slowly away down her alley, singing out at the top of my voice, so all the neighbors could hear:

> *Love is like a snake*
> *That glides between your thighs*
> *Before you feel it strike*
> *It has put out both your eyes!*

I was ruined and I knew I was ruined so I wandered along to the Street of the Women. That's gone, now too, like the little old train and all. Even the big iron door they used to have to keep the women inside doesn't hang any more in the arch of the gate. There, I saw a man with a ladder and pails, so I hailed him to say I was an expert whitewasher and painter out of a job. He and I walked together into the very first house on the right where we talked the Madrona into a price to get her whole place done up spick and span, inside and out. When they gave me the money for whitewash, I came back with

93

bright red, yellow, blue, brown and black to paint out a story of mine. Back in Tanja, I painted the walls of my house with girls in a jungle full of monkeys, devils and men, evil spirits and lions and birds but these walls in Rabat were *big!* I told the man I wanted no wages if he'd let me do all the work. I want what I want so, when he looked suspicious, I told the Madrona to spill him a beer, as I tickled her tired old tits.

When I laid my equipment out on a table, all the girls in the house came fluttering down like a covey of quail to see what I got. What I got is a lot, so I gave them all a peck on the cheek and a pinch on the ass as I pulled out and showed them my big magic brush. There were just seven girls in that house, I remember, so it took me a whole week to paint my way through. I could brush only one girl a night because they all thought it was such a treat to be in my picture that they wanted to take it in turns to be brushed by me. Before I got finished that first house of girls, there was talk of my brushwork all over the quarter and the girls in the very next house were yammering and lullilooing to get theirs done, too. They just couldn't wait for me to come over and do the whole house. In the end, I did the whole quarter. I got my big brush in there solid and got down to work but, first, I had to jerk my equipment away from the Madrona who'd seen what a job I'd done on her girls and wanted hers, too, right there behind the cash-box. I would sooner have stuck my fist in the till than her box but she gave me the gold ring I drew off her finger by force. I gave that ring, later, to a girl in a house at the far end of the street and, would you believe it, that almost started a war. Those girls *fight!* Any one of those girls could lay a man flat on the floor from one bang on the head with her bracelets.

When one house of girls got into a war with another house, they slashed each other with switchblades or bottles and glasses they broke on the bar. When I hear them breaking the glasses, I run! In one of those houses, a girl once cut off a guy's root at the root!

I was there a long time, painting houses and girls. Let me see: a girl a night times seven nights in a week is seven girls, isn't it? That's a week and the weeks in a month are four with some little scraps left over now and then, so I've got little scraps of girls to add up but that's hard. Like the fat Mina Smina I had on the steps when the Madrona screamed out that old song:

Oh, you pay on the landing and not on the stairs!

excepting she said: "You paint on the landing," because she saw I had my brush out. So, that makes about thirty a month. It is more? And how many months would there be in a year? Only twelve? Oh, there were a lot more houses than that in Rabat, in those days. I painted a lot. It was all one great big picture, you see. It began as soon as you walked in the door and there was the music and dancing and drinking and girls and my pictures under the light. There were thousands of soldiers and men swarming through there every night in the week, not to speak of the tradesmen, musicians, gamblers and pimps who lived in the place, which was like a small town. Now, it's gone. Now, it's all torn down or people are living in there who don't even know or could guess some of the things that went on in their rooms. Here and there, maybe, there might be a trace of my picture left in some dark corner under the stairs but, little by little, ever since Independa, they whitewashed it over until there isn't a trace of my brush in Rabat. I've heard French people saying that painting is French.

The old train that used to run back to Kebir has gone, as the Customs have gone; as the houses and the paintings and girls have gone, now, forever. At the Customs, they said: "Why, we heard you wuz dead! Ayesha bought a taxi with your capital and her brother can drive it. What you gonna do, now?" When they saw I had no more capital to start in the business again, they turned wicked and kicked me off the train in Kebir, where I went to the house of my mother: as a matter of fact, that house is mine, in my name. You've seen it often enough: you know how it is. It wasn't such a ruin, in those days.

That house was Grampa's house and he had only one boy, my Pa, to inherit his orchards and farms and a quarry of clay and the kilns to make bricks, besides all the other houses and gardens he owned. All of his wives had given him only daughters but the last wife of all gave him a son. All those other women were mad because my Pa would inherit it all, so they cursed him. When he grew up, he had no use for women at all. He spent all his money in cafés with musicians or in the barbershops and steam baths with boys. He promised a boy he would take him to Mecca on the pilgrimage to make him a Hadj. When Grampa heard this, he called in the lawyers to draw up the papers saying my Pa could not inherit one dirham until he had married and had a son and that firstborn son would be the owner of the house so my Pa could never gamble it or give it away, but you'll see, later, how he got around that.

Kebir is a town and the maidservants in our houses are girls who come down from the hill villages barefoot, looking for food. In our house, we had such a one who always was saying: "In *my* village this and in my village that," until you were sick of it. "In *my* village, Jajouka, we have a girl who's a pearl like no other. What a girl! No man who sees her wants to live one more minute without her! She's so lively and gay: she's so sharp and so bright. She's witty and clean: she can dance: she can sing: she can weave: she can spin. She's so sweet that she's sour. She can laugh but she weeps. She's tart like an apple, with a tongue like a thorn. She's all honey and amber and a wonderful cook. She's so quick and so light she never touches the ground. She married my cousin Mohand, the chief of the Master Musicians, up in Jajouka, and she's got him half-dead and half-alive. He can't live with her and he can't live without her. They're divorced and remarried two times, already, and if he does it again and still wants to re-marry, he'll have to go to Tetuan to get the permission from the big judge, the Cadi-in-chief."

That girl could get up to her village and back in a day. So, one evening at nightfall, she comes dashing back into our house, crying: "Here she is! She's here, she's here!" She got hold of my Pa and told him some sense: he should marry this girl. Why, even then, her first husband was toiling over the mountains to Tetuan to get the permission, mad to remarry her. Here was this pearl: what could he be waiting for? I suppose he went out and took a look at her; I don't know; I wasn't there, yet. That pearl was my Ma: you knew her well.

The day I was born, my Pa started spending the money. He made the pilgrimage twice from Kebir to Mecca and back, taking a friend with him, all expenses paid, both ways, each time. The first Hadj he set up in the wool market of Kebir where he sits to this day in his cupboard-sized shop stocked

97

high with hand-woven bolts of fine wool: he's still a good-looking man. My Pa's second friend demanded at least the same thing and he got it. He has an identical shop on the other side of the Souk. So, my Pa ate up all his orchards and farms and his quarry and kiln and one house after the other, buying Swiss watches and French racing-bicycles for good-looking boys. He divided our house with a wall through the middle of the courtyard and rented our rooms to get more money for keef and, later, for wine.

Pa rented out the little shop we call the *biblioteca,* which is built into the outside wall of our house, and a funny thing happened: it turned out he had rented it to a Soussi magician who had come looking for a treasure and the gold was hidden *inside our own house*. The Soussi had an old, very secret book like a registry of all the treasures in our Moroccan soil, guarded as they are by the little, invisible *djenoun* of the gold. The man lied, of course, telling us he was taking the shop to get the Kebir agency for Bebsi-Cola, which we didn't have, yet, in our zone of Morocco. He never did, of course, but he did start selling charcoal and kerosene to get friendly with the women who run out into the street for a penny-worth of this and a penny-worth of that, with only some kind of a rag to cover their shameless faces.

We found out he was really a magician because, one morning early, a poor little girl toddling down the gutter, too young almost to walk, asked him for water to drink. He was handing her down his earthenware mug, when the man from next door dashed out with a stick and he knocked the mug out of the little girl's hands to smash on the ground. He had looked through a crack in his door and he had seen the Soussi each morning eating his very own shit. To be a magician, you have to make yourself truly impure every day in order to put yourself outside the rest of the community who follow the Law which guards them from magic. You may need a magician for practical things but you don't have to drink out of his cup.

The Soussi magician made friends with a boy going blind. He's a man now, still feeling his way about town as he goes up and down hawking lottery tickets pinned to the front of his brown woolen jellaba. In those long-ago days, he was a very good-looking lad who played a music so sweet on his flute that he nearly landed in jail as a seducer of women—all the women in town! As he walked through the streets of Kebir with his hood pulled down over his head and only the flute and his hands sticking out, all the women and girls, whom he'd never seen and who never saw him, all fell sick of love inside their windowless houses. Some people said they just lay on the floor, kicking their heels. They pined away in their interior patios sniffing up jasmine and burning the meals in the houses, day after day. When the men of Kebir got together, they all agreed things could not go on that way; so, they jumped on the blind boy and carried him off to the Cadi, our judge who sits outside of his house on Friday at noon, sending people to jail. The cadi said: "Let *me* hear his flute!" To tell you the truth, we have no one in Jajouka who plays any better than this blind boy did then. The cadi lay back on his divan of justice to listen in rapture for hours. "Stop," he cried weakly, lifting his hand. "That's enough. You can't play this stuff any more in Kebir. Here, take these lottery tickets to sell and give me the flute." Turning aside to the men of the town, the cadi went on: "You have to extirpate this sort of thing by the root." What did he mean? Why, he took the boy's flute in both hands and he broke it over his knee. You see, that music was far too sweet to be heard in the streets of Kebir where the boy, now a man, is still selling lottery tickets up and down the alleys of town.

That boy, in those days, used to stop by the shop of the Soussi, who once dropped a hint that they had in the Soussi a magic for curing the eyes. It might be some use. He could send for it but it was expensive, of course, and it might take a long time to come. The boy stopped by every day, wanting and waiting to see, but the Soussi always would say that the magic pomade would be soon on its way. Then, one day, he said it had come. By that time, the boy was his slave and a slave is what the man needed. You see, his old Book of Treasures had told him there was a pot of gold which none of us knew about hidden in one of our rooms, and he wanted to get in there to snatch it while we were away. For this he needed a good blind assistant and he needed to get us all out of the house. That was easier when Pa went out of town. The magician bought us all tickets for a good Moroccan movie called *Charlie Chan*. Ma, scared stiff of what Pa would say, and knowing the neighbors didn't think it nice for a woman to go out in the street, tied our big iron house key around her neck with a rope and us kids led her off to see the movie through twice. What we found when we got home was not very nice. The Soussi had knocked a hole right through the back wall of his shop into our house and, in Grampa's room, there lay the blind boy like a dead man, alone. The Soussi was gone but his clothes and some money were still in his shop and the shop was still locked from inside. The blind boy almost died when we beat him some more but that way we got the whole story out of him.

The magician had twisted his head with the promise to

bring back his eyes. Magicians are doctors of lies but everything about money is always a little funny in Morocco. Here, the mice eat your money because it is sinful to put it in banks. When you look for the bundle of greasy bills you hid in the rafters last fall, all you find is some mouse-must, some colored confetti and shavings made out of what once was your savings! When you're rich, you buy gold and you bury it. Then, you call in a magician and pay him to weave you a spell to make your gold pieces look like a bag of old buttons until the day comes when you want your money back. Grampa had probably hidden his sack of gold in his room because he had so many wives he couldn't trust any of them. The magician who wove Grampa his spell had written down in a book the secret directions on how to find it, so this other Soussi knew where to look and he knew all the words of the spells but he needed the blind boy to help him unbind them.

He had made a big ball of magical gum—axle grease and incense from Mecca—to burn while he said the words to open the ground, but he needed someone around to hold it, burning and smoking, during all the time he went down in the crack in the ground to talk in a thundering voice to the spirits who guard the gold, while he took it back from them; dangerous work. When all us kids and our Ma passed by his shop on our way to the movies to thank him, we saw the blind boy in there with him, smoking keef. We had not got down the street before they shut themselves in there and started to hammer the hole into our house. They went straight to the room where my Grampa had died, set down a lighted candle in a saucer of water and quickly laid out a circle of flour on the floor. The Soussi then brought in a pot of live charcoal and threw salt in it until the flames came dancing up orange and blue. He drove

101

a short stake into his ball of gum, which he held over the fire to get it starting to smoke. He handed the stake to the boy, telling him this was no joke and to be sure to keep turning the stick and, no matter what happened, not to let go. When he said the words, there came a sound like the flapping of great wings in the room but the air did not stir although the wind could be heard, screaming by outside fast. The room rocked and trembled. The floor quivered and the tiles split open at their feet. "Hold onto that ball! Don't let it drop or I'm lost. Do you hear me, Mohamed?" cried the magician as he stepped down into that hole. When we got home it was done. The boy was lying like dead. When he dropped the ball in the pit, he almost went out of his head. He nearly fell in the hole, himself, before it closed up again without leaving a clue. The Soussi was gone, too.

I run up to my village, Jajouka, whenever I can and that's often. Whenever I want to touch earth, I go up there. No hills on earth are more blue than our own Little Hills and that's true. I was born up there under a hedge and I'm related to all of the village, the Master Musicians who never have done anything else in their lives but make music since the first man danced with his goats on the hills in the moonlight, a long time ago. Once a year, for eight nights, we go dancing in memory of him. My uncles stand fifty abreast in front of a wall on one side of our broad village green, blowing their oboe-like *raïtas* into the sky until sheet-lightning flashes and snaps in your head. My hundred young cousins in white drum out thunder like oak trees playing football with boulders and, up on the hill, the olive trees thrash their long silver hair like dance-crazy maidens who tear at their veils. In the middle of that, with the whole village leaping and howling, children bawling, dogs barking under the moon, leaps one single figure in goatskins, lashing about him with flails. *Bou Jeloud!* All the villagers, dressed in best white, swirl in great whorls and circles around one masked man. *Me!* I danced Bou Jeloud. Maybe, that's why I act a little crazy, sometimes. Up there in Jajouka, there is no wheeled traffic, no running water other than rills and no electricity. Electric light scares Bou Jeloud away and one day soon, when it gets to my village, it will.

Bou Jeloud is Fear and Fucking; running wild, chasing, beating, catching, biting, tearing and fucking; again and again and again. Bou Jeloud leaps high in the air with the music to fall out of the sky on top of the women, beating them with switches so they can go on having the kids. The women all scatter, like marabout birds in a pasture, to light in a huddle on top of a hillock in one quivering lump. Then, they throw back their pretty heads to the moon and let out a long *lulliloo!* They flutter their gullets, lolling their tongues around in their empty heads like the clapper rolls around in a bell. Hot, narrow black eyes brim over their veils, sparkling with dangerous baby. Every mouth is round-open, so, yodeling: *O!*

Bou Jeloud is after you, chasing you! You're run down, overrun, screaming with laughter and tears. You're trampling children while wild dogs snap at your heels. Everything, suddenly, is swirling around in a great ring-a-rosy, around and around and around. Go! Forever! Stop! Never! More! and: *No more!* and: *No!* . . . *More!* Pipes crack in your head and you can't hear a thing. You're deaf! Or, you're dead! Dead in cold moonlight, surrounded by madmen and ghosts. Bou Jeloud is on you . . . frisking you, fucking you . . . beating you, butting you . . . taking you, leaving you. Gone! The great wind drops out of your head and you begin to hear our heavenly pipes, again. Someone is whimpering, grizzling, laughing and sobbing right there beside you. Who is it? Why, my friend; that is You!

Who is Bou Jeloud? Who is he? My uncles killed two goats, saying: *"Bismillah,"* as they drew a knife over their throats and flayed them in a cave where they stripped me naked to sew me up in the reeking, hot skins. When they blackened my face, darkness swirled down like the beating of drums. As they put the flails in my hands and began to play our music, I fell to the ground. When Hamid fell, Bou Jeloud jumped into him. Even now, I'm afraid. Bou Jeloud is the Father of Fear: he is, also, the Father of Flocks. The Good Shepherd works for him. When the goats, gently grazing, brusquely frisk and skitter away, he is counting his herd. When you shiver like someone just walked on your grave, that's him! That's Pan, the Father of Skins. Did you almost jump out of your skin, just then, Hassan Merikani? I've still got you under my skin.

How did you like it up there? I know it got under your skin—and I don't mean the fleas. We let you sleep late, so breakfast was goat cheese and honey on fresh golden platters of bread from my sister's mud-oven out in the yard where our dinner, the rooster, was crowing to his last morning sun. My uncles, the Master Musicians, were lolling about in their big woolen jellabas and white turbans, sipping mint tea, their keef-pipes and their flutes. They never work in their lives so they loll about easy. They cop a tithe of one-tenth of the crops in the lush valley below. It's always been so. They're musicians and play for the king. Every sultan who ever lived in his palace in Fez, signed a *dahir* or order-in-council, giving us the full

power of our right to play to the king in the morning to wake
him and, on Fridays, to pipe him down from his throne to his
knees in the mosque. We have privileges, rights.

Late in August, each Master Musician slips away up to the
borders of Rif country, in the blue mountains miles up, over,
beyond and above our own Little Hills. High above those keef
meadows of Ketama, where I've never been, hangs the ruin
of an old fortified monastery from which, so they say, the Old
Man of the Mountain once ruled the world. His Adepts were
called the Assassins because of the hashish they smoke—
Hashishins were monks who ran naked in August, ran naked
and mad through the meadows of keef. When they fell in their
cells like a stone, the Old Man scraped off their skins with a
knife because their shaved bodies were covered with gum from
the keef flowers. *That* gum is hashish. They spread out the
gum on great marble slabs where they pressed it and cut it in
cubes which the Master sent out all over the world to Marseille
and to Hollywood, even. That trade is finished, now, too.

Now, we just run into the valley to snatch up a bundle of
grass to take home. We have privileges, rights but, yes, we're
afraid of that valley and glad in our hearts that the castle above
is a ruin and the Old Man is not there any more; for, they say,
he could point a long skinny finger like *that,* at any one Adept
of his standing sentry up there on the tower and that Adept
would leap, would throw himself down to smash on the rocks
in the valley below because he knew that his moment had
come. We don't like to be told. *Hamdullah!* we still have
plenty of keef.

There is so much keef smoked in my village you can see
it rise over the hedges of prickly pear and the thatched roofs
of our houses. You can see the keef smoke rising blue, like a

veil for the winds to catch up and drop back on this village of mine like a blessing. We're invisible, here in our hills. The music picks up like a current turned on and the kids are all out in the leafy green lanes, bawling:

> *Ha! Bou Jeloud!*
> *Bou Jeloud the Piper met Aissha Amoka!*
> *Ha! Bou Jeloud!*

My uncles, the Master Musicians, know all the music but our women know the words to tease Bou Jeloud. When night falls, they sit with their drums in some place apart from the men and they sing over the fire:

> *O Brother Bou Jeloud, come up in our hills*
> *As God is our guide, you can have all the girls*
> *Allah, allalai i lalli*
> *Allah, alla lai wai wa!*
>
> *O Brother Bou Jeloud, don't hide in the melons*
> *Eyes blacker than pips, false eyebrows like felons*
> *O Brother Bou Jeloud; good-by, good-by*
> *Your rotten straw hat cocked over one eye.*

Women tease Bou Jeloud just to make him run after them. That's all women want. Bou Jeloud wants Aissha Amoka; that means Crazy Aissha. He's crazy for Aissha. She drifts around after dark, cool and casual, near springs and running water with a silvery-blue face in the moonlight where she pulls back her veils like a wanton to show you her twinkling tits. Her face and her breasts are a beautiful blue, all starry with sparkling lights. She coos at you in the husky voice of a dove:

"Young man, can you tell me the time?" If you answer her one single word you are lost. From that day forever, you are her *slave!*

Women are wicked but she is the worst of them all: Aissha Kandisha, Aissha Amoka or that Macarena I saw with you, once, in the streets of Sevilla, she's the same. Beautiful, deadly but she can be tamed, if you're a brave enough man and quick. You jerk out your knife and you plunge it deep in the ground between her two feet. That makes her *your* slave. It is then you will see her legs are all hairy and they end in two cloven hooves instead of two feet—like Bou Jeloud. They are, really, the same kind of people. When you've got her pinned down by your knife, you can ask of her all that you will. I've met her and jumped her: I, Bou Jeloud. I'm not afraid but I don't want to meet her again. The first nights of our dancing we dance out that Fear. When our music catches you alone in the dark, you're choking with panic. All the people down there in the valley are shaking with fear so they fall into bed with their chattering teeth. *Ha, Bou Jeloud!* High up in the Rif, they can hear us and shiver. *Ha, Bou Jeloud!* The rest of the nights go by like a dream.

This is our play: Bou Jeloud leaps like a goat from a thicket, falling on Aissha, who's crazy enough to be out dancing around in the moonlight. When Bou Jeloud first came up to Owl Mountain—Jajouka—Aissha was already here. She's so big and so powerful, she has to be danced by a whole troupe of young boys dressed as girls who, all of them taken together, are Her. Our women don't dance to this music in public. Oh, no! That would be shameful. Our women are good. They run from Bou Jeloud. They sit on a hillock and throw him out one wriggling little boy-dancer they've dressed up as a girl. It's the women who teach them to dance when they're little, the real tiny kids who haven't been circumcised yet. They never made me. I never danced for the women, not me! When the time came for me to be cut, it was the Caïd of our village who held me in front of him on the silver-studded saddle of his horse and he cut the skin off my little *zib* with his very own knife. I never cried out: I was Bou Jeloud all of my life!

We have comic characters, too, like the Three Hadjis who dance with wobbling crowns on top of their turbans but one cannot hear, one cannot speak and one cannot see. Then, a man in big baggy pants comes on pretending he's pregnant, screaming for help. The Three Hadjis jump on his belly and pull a big monkey out of his pants but the monkey's a boy, naked and furry because we grease him and stick yellow wool all over his parts. The man leads his monkey around on a rope, beating him and screwing him for hours and, then, the monkey grabs the stick and beats the man, leading *him* around and screwing *him* for hours. It's crazy: it's fun!

When Bou Jeloud was, finally, married to Aissha that last night of dancing under full moon, I slipped away to Kebir with a boy of thirteen or ten who had been dancing for Aissha all of those nights. I needed a clever assistant if I ever was going to get back my spot on the train. He was a good-enough lad but he didn't have luck. In a day and a night, we walked down to Kebir, where I showed him how to get under the train. I could see he was scared. You have to get in there wedged tight and never look down at the wheels. When we got to the old border of Tanja, the train ground to a halt and the Customs got out to walk up and down and show us their legs. They never looked under the train except on market days, sometimes, when there were too many smugglers in there who

108

hadn't paid up. Then, all of a sudden, the train gave a jerk and my boy fell under the wheels. His hand and a piece of his arm flew up to hit me so hard in the eyes I nearly let go. His scream and the scream of the brakes stopped the train. People peered in trying to pull him out from under the car with his arm spurting blood like a fountain. A man tried to tie up his arm with his belt but nothing would stop it until someone in the back of the crowd started shouting: "Oil! Boiling oil!" It was some old thief who remembered the days when they cut off a hand for a theft, plunging the stump of the arm in boiling oil. *Moojood!* It was ready, the oil! Right there on the platform was sitting a man making doughnuts he looped in his fingers and dropped in his bubbling cauldron of oil. They picked up my boy gone white as a turban and ran dripping his blood right up to the man. Before he could stop them they'd plunged this boy's stump deep in along with the sizzling doughnuts. What a terrible smell, like burning kebabs! I thought for a moment my poor boy was screaming but he slumped there like dead. It was only the doughnut man screaming for money from someone, anyone, because they had spoiled all his trade.

It took us a week to walk back to Kebir. When we slept in the rain, my boy got the fever and caught a *djenoun*. It wasn't the boy's fault, because he was *amok,* but I could see his *djenoun* wanted only one thing, my knife and my life. I was so afraid for my throat that I slept with my eyes open. When we got to Kebir, I went to a blacksmith I know and I told him: "Make me an iron collar and chain for this boy or I'm a dead man." He could see he had to do it for me, with money or without. I'd looked after the boy like a doctor all day and all night for so long without sleep that I was half gone crazy, myself. I took him to Sidi Bou Galeb. You know, the shrine on the highway through town by the traffic lights where the tourists all want to stop with their cameras and one crazy Christian once tried to take photographs even inside. Only Muslims can go in there, of course. It's a holier place than a mosque. If you have a rich family they chain you to rings in the wall under the arcades near the tomb of the saint. There were so many crazy people chained up in there I was afraid. If you're poor, they attach you outside in the courtyard to trees. I began to feel so crazy, myself, I nearly fell on my knees when a guardian came up for a tip and asked with a leer: "Which one of you stays?" When I threw him the chain he laughed till he cried as I ran from that place. I sent word to our village for someone to go tell the boy's mother to bring him some food. She sold the tin roof over her head to buy the boy bread and pay his way out of that place. Now, they both live in the bushes, stealing eggs from nesting chickens and milk from strayed goats.

I went on down to Tanja and, there I found you.

Oh, now I know how you Nazarenes think about things! I know how you think about things like radios, suits! You never could forget that radio, either, now could you? I remember how it happened, perfectly well. One night about midnight—oh, long after the affair of the suit—you were toiling slowly up the stairs of your street, just as I—oh, quite accidentally—happened along down the steps. I could see you'd been drinking. You said: "Hi, Hamid!" and five minutes later we were both smoking keef and listening to Radio Cairo on the shortwave, inside of your house. In the morning, you loaned me the radio of your very own free will, I remember, and I swore on the head of my mother to bring it right back.

But, who can weigh his words in the face of the Unknown? A policeman I know, a very good friend of mine on the train, dropped into my room in the fondouk and he fell in love with that little radio as soon as he saw it. I swore on the head of my mother the radio belonged to an American friend who trusted me like a brother. "Why, then," sneered the policeman, "he'll buy you another." I shrugged and forgot it, right then and there. *"Mektoub,"* it was written: what else can I say? But you—you never forgot that radio, right down to this very day. That's the way all you Nazarenes are! You hold grudges for years where a Muslim forgives and forgets.

But I won't forget you, Hassan Merikani. Oh, no! not for a long time, yet. I gave you the Key and I taught you the Lock. I let you walk in without having to knock. I taught you to eat like a Muslim, putting none but your right hand in the dish and keeping the left hand for things counted unclean, like wiping yourself without paper because paper is sacred, a bit. When Nazarenes go to the closet, they don't wipe themselves with Holy Writ, now do they? Well, any scrap of paper *could* have the Name of Allah written on it, couldn't it? Even a newspaper might have, *"Allah"* in print, in a piece about politics, no? How do I know? I can't read, so I'm careful— I use the left hand God gave me and I know how to wash. I taught you how to wash yourself, too. I taught you to shave all your body-hair so I'd not be polluted by living with someone unclean. It was good you were circumcised because I could show you to Muslims and not be ashamed. Muslims like the alike. All Muslims are Brothers and, therefore, are Even, you see. But, God is Odd and loves the odd—that's why He loves me. You, too, are odd and that's why I never pressed you about God. Maybe, that's been my sin, this letting you in

111

without your submitting, but me, I'm a little wild man from the hills and I know what it is to be free.

When I told my uncles up in the hills, the Master Musicians, that you knew who Bou Jeloud was the first time you saw him, they said: "Bring your Black Merikani up here, so we can get a good look at him." When I was too small to remember, my uncles tucked me into the hollow of their knees under their tickling beards, as they smoked while they talked Holy Things. "Can't you remember?" you always were teasing me, filling a pipe the way I had taught you to fill it and light it for me. "Can't you remember the Secret Name? Say the Word!" you insisted. "Tell me just the beginning Word."

There you were, already inside of my head, so I laughed. Time passed. When I was ready, at last, you asked me to look a long time in the bright silver ball you hang on your key-chain. I saw nothing at all. "Look!" you insisted; "they're tiny, they're small. Can't you see the Master Musicians in there?" My eyes filled up a moment with water and, when it ran down my cheeks, I saw them. I saw them all sitting against a wall in Jajouka, talking. Now I understand television. "If that's television," you insisted, "you can hear what they're saying." Well, I listened a while and, I guess, I said what I said. I didn't drop dead. The skies didn't open up, even, or crack when I told the Secret Name we still know in the hills. You're the one who almost jumped out of his skin. "Why, that's Punic!" you cried, or something like that. "That's pre-Roman!" Did you take us for tourists, perhaps? We've been here forever, a very long time. Light me a pipe and I'll tell you some more but the Name, now that you have it, Hassan, you can't write. The Name, Burning Name—it would set the paper to flame!

112

"And Aissha," you'd ask me, "whose daughter is she?"
You find her by springs and by wells and by brooks but she
came from the sea. She's Aissha the Moon, who dances on
water. I never heard she was anyone's daughter. "Do she and
Bou Jeloud have any children?" Children from her? She's a
harlot who ruts with the ram in the sun. She's silver. He's
gold. Leave me alone, now, I'm cold. No! Don't bother me.
Get out of my head, Merikani! *Get out of my life!* These are
secrets you don't tell a wife!

What we both have in common is this: you and I, Hassan,
are *kaffirs*—Outsiders. That's the truth of it and I don't know
why. Maybe we both strayed too far from our houses, if ever
we had them. I don't know what sent you out from your home,
Hassan, but I was born under a bush. My mother ran out of
the big house in Kebir in the middle of the night when she felt
her pains coming on. She ran barefoot in the dust out of the
town of Kebir, on up through the gardens and the orchards in
the moonlight, through the blue valleys toward the Little Hills
and home. Beneath the giant blue cactus palisade around Jajouka, my mother fell and bore me in a herd of goats. I am
Bou Jeloud. I know all that and I know Tanja, too, because
Tanja was always my city-girl, lying down there on her rock
by the beach with her legs wide open to the sea. She's not
just a sailor's slut: she's been like a mother to me. From our
side, from the hills, we have always run down to the sea and
the city and back like a trail of ants with packs on our backs.
Time and time again, giants and generals and sultans have
tried stamping on us as we scurry along in our race to escape
all their taxes. My blood is hot every time I make a run into
Tanja to swarm up her old legs. I mount from the train at her
feet, up her knees to the Grand Socco Market, spread like the

113

belly of food on her lap. She used to wear a money-belt of booths where you could buy and sell cash all night and all day, as she dangled her other leg down the American Stairs by the port, enticing rich sailors to visit the girls. But all that, the girls and the money-changers and the money, have all gone since the day the whole city of Tanja was swallowed alive by the Whale.

I used to run that whole city by ear. I could sit in my favorite café, just sipping my mint tea and smoking my keef, and you may not believe it was true but I truly could hear almost every last thing that went on in the town. Not the Boulevard up on the hill in the New Town with its skyscrapers six-stories tall and its six hundred banks, but our Old Town inside its own walls was my house I had rented for life. When the maid breaks a plate out in the kitchen, don't you see, in a flash, just which plate it is? When you hear the taps in the bathroom, don't you know who's taking a bath? The World is a River. If a Fountain shoots up in a River, don't you know there's a Whale? Well, one day in Tanja when you were away in the Sahara, we caught a real Whale.

In my little café, I heard Radio Cairo saying our sultan was the prisoner, now, of Madamegascar. Through the keef in my head, I could see this Madame Gascar with her yellow hair and her little yapping white dog she had trained to bite Arabs. If any real French madame had passed through the market right then, I'd have spat on her. And at that very moment, I heard the Whale blow, down below in the Old Town. Oh, I can tell you that's a sound you know the first time you hear it! No other sound in the world but Bou Jeloud can match it for fright. Your short hairs crawl right up the back of your neck and, before you can breathe, your heels are

114

kicking your ass to get out of that place. The Whale gave a roar like a beast eating buildings, crunching up little houses in one single bite. A voice in my head said; "This Whale is the Whale that's going to eat Tanja!" And it did. It flushed up from the port, flooding into the Socco, our little plaza framed with cafés, where it began flailing the flukes of its tail in a spray of plate-glass. It tossed tables and chairs through the fronts of cafés and blew in the doors of the Indian bazaars every time it took a deep breath. The waiters and patrons were skidding inside as the owners slammed down their steel shutters; *Clang Clang Clang!* Jewelers were jumping inside their own safes when the Whale tasted blood. A Swiss tourist went down, his head bashed in with his camera. His blood and his brains washed over a shoal of Swiss watches that slid down the sidewalk like the guts of a shop streaming out in the gutter. The Whale, too wide for this steep narrow street up to the market, ripped down all the signs and the shutters on both sides as it came, sliding along on gold bracelets and rings rolling in rivulets under its centipede feet. If you stopped to pick up a thing, you were lost. Money-changers tossed their bills into baskets and were still scooping up change in their hats when they burst into flames from the blast from a hundred, a thousand! hot Arab faces all bellowing: *O!*

Two or three bare-faced girls of the kind they call "students," and the first we ever had seen, came screaming like Aissha Amoka out front with some half-naked boys who tore off their shirts, to make flags. People in rags and people in gowns were spewed up in one belch by the town and vomited out onto the broad Grand Market square right under the stare of two dozen policemen who pushed their way out of the commissariat with their buttons undone. They just stood there, rubbing their eyes with surprise. Those girls without veils and the half-naked boys with banners flew up toward the Boulevard with its six hundred banks. The policemen popped in and popped out again but, this time, with guns. Their captain screamed: *"Fire!"* In one minute, there were so many people kicking and twitching or dead on the ground that it looked like a movie. Up on the Boulevard, was there a panic! Rich Christians and Jews ran out of hotels with their hair in the air, screaming for taxis to take them out to the airport. Other men and even some women with pistols ran to the banks, backing up trucks, station-wagons, taxis, anything on wheels. They loaded the gold onto handcarts and pushcarts and go-carts and baby buggies, to run with it out to the airport where planes swarmed out of the skies like bees to suck all the honey from Tanja and never come back.

Up in the hills, my uncles the Master Magicians had only one thing to say to me: "Get your Merikani back!" I smoked a lot of keef for a week and I saw they were right. Night after night, we sat talking of you in the house of my Uncle Mohand, whose second wife can make you see what people are doing far away by looking into a tray covered with sand. We could see you in a truck crossing the tray and every day we saw you getting closer and closer to a red pebble where a captain in a white tunic was holding trouble for you in his hand. I was out there with you crossing the sands, every night for weeks. Once, we saw you were dead. Once we saw somebody we didn't know it was you because you had turned blue and there were two of you. When you reached the edge of the tray, the wife of Mohand would reach out with her hand to shake it like a sieve. When I leaned over the tray one night, it turned into a well and I saw you way down there beckoning to me from the far away bottom and I fell and I fell and I fell. I got well when they made me drink water in which they had washed out a spell written on paper with rust. You may not think they know anything much but my Uncle Mohand said: "That Merikani must come back soon!" And, isn't it true, Hassan Merikani, you were up here in Jajouka dancing with us under the next full moon!

It was written: *"Mektoub!"*

4

It was written, indeed! But does that mean I am supposed to believe on some level that Hamid actually brought me back from my trip, magically? I ought to be downright mad at him if he did it but, instead, I have spent all this time translating, transcribing and, yes, transposing the Hamid I captured on tape. When I read back what is written, I hear how very far it is from Hamid's real speech and I ponder on how much I betray him each time I correct or rewrite. Only this morning, I found myself switching still more of his so-called sentences around, trying to catch at some of the unconsciously rhyming effects he manages to ring from the voluble but wildly incorrect Spanish he still uses with me; although my own bed-and-kitchen Arabic is already good enough to get by. Fact is, the man in the marketplace here in North Africa takes me automatically for a fellow Moroccan as soon as I slip on a striped silk jellaba and slap a red tarboosh on my head. Everyone calls me Brother: *"Hai."*

Not up on the Boulevard in the New Town of Tanja, though, where I wear my American threads. When I sit out on the

118

terrace of the Café de Paris, every last hustler who ever guided an American gob still slobbers and hovers around but they keep their distance, these days. Not one of them would dare, any longer, to call me: American Joe. I guess I owe Hamid that, too. I am Hassan only with him up on his mountain or down below the Socco Chico in the underground keef cafés. Up on this Boulevard-level of town, Alcohol is King. It is not the cool thing to smoke pot in public; at least, not in a pipe. Instead, I take a deep drag on the Casa Sport cigarette I gutted and refilled with great grass I got from Hamid before I pulled my poor self together and struggled up here in the European town for a change of elevation and air. The tangle of traffic, out there in front of me somewhere in the Place de France, looks a bit distant and glassy, I have to admit, but everything is bright, bright, bright! Every last little dancing blob out there is all jazzy-bedazzled with candy-colored light. I adjust my shades with distinction, puffed up with pride at how well the taste of Tanja suits someone like me and, then, I carefully drop my eyes to the pen and paper on the table in front of me but my gaze never gets there because I break into a loud laugh. I laugh like a lunatic to think that a year of sea and sand has burned up behind me since I first dropped into Tanja for what I thought might be, at most, a couple of weeks.

Now, I think I have got Hamid safely tied up with his family and flocks on their Pan mountain and here I am back at the Crossroads again. *"Do something!"* I keep telling myself, but what, really, do I *want* to do? If I dared, I would ring my last dime on this marble-topped table and get on my feet and then . . . and then, with bowed head, just shuffle off into the crowd, known to no one, with the wind whistling behind me as I shuffle off into the Sahara again. If I had the nerve, I could launch myself like a leaf on that sea of life, flowing by me out there. If I really wanted to catch up with that tide, I could mutate into just one more mad marabout like the Marvelous Major of Merzouk who was both revered and kicked about by the natives for years until the day the Marines landed, when he threw off his rags and stood there revealed with, tattooed all over his white ass: CIA! *Nay!* Very well, then I will have to become a saint of the so-called absurd, a man without a country, wrapped in a pied cloak sewn of nothing but flags. I've seen some of those cats—Bouhali Brothers —and they really look great—like they really *have* got it made. There they go, their bare feet deep in the dust but their heads, man! their heads touch heaven: *loser take all!* Just the mere thought of that fate makes a shiver run through me. I feel my scalp tingle and tighten on the roof of my skull. My hairs stand on end, one by one; all frizzling out slowly in a fuzzy electric halo that comes down around my ears. My ears are becoming the ears of the fennec who hunts the jerboa; bristly antennae that pick up and tingle with the silky sound of the sand sighing across the Sahara. It crackles like static inside of my head. Grains of sand, more numerous than the stars, are slipping and sliding and I am startled to hear in the roar of traffic on the Place de France, abruptly, the rumbling voice of Ghoul! I could easily blast so much keef night and day I become a *bouhali;* a real-gone crazy, a holy untouchable madman unto whom everything is permitted, nothing is true.

I was thinking along these lines this morning, if you can call that thinking, as I sat at a round marble-topped table on the terrace of the Café de Paris, today about noon. It was hot and I wanted to be alone so I propped this Moroccan leather briefcase I have, full of this manuscript, on the chair beside me, reserving the seat. On the table in front of me, I had my pad of letter-paper over which my pen has been hanging fire, now, for over a month. I hate writing letters but, if I was going to go on, or so I told myself in order to whip my pen-hand into action: *"You better write this."* This was my letter to the Foundation, from whom I had heard nothing since I sent them a copy of my desert diary; pretty heavily varnished, I have to admit. I want my follow-up letter to be more business-like, maybe. After all, I have to brazen the whole thing out; my failure to cross the Sahara in less than a lifetime; my failure to find myself in Black Africa, floating down the bosom of its broad rivers through the jungle to the sea and, then, to return to the world around its hump. I mean to say to the Foundation: Frankly, I am fresh out of bread. In your service, O mighty Foundation, I have experienced extreme experience and been taken for an Adept along the Way. Extreme experience is, naturally, extremely expensive and so it should be. I have given of my person. I intended to add, rather insolently: "Now, pay me!" I considered enclosing a street photographer's shot of me taken in the thick of the Socco Chico crush and scrawling across it, perhaps: *"Which one is me?"* To a man who has little or nothing to lose, after all, everything is surely permitted when dealing with these powerful abstract entities like Fundamental, for whom, equally surely, after dealing with hordes of applicants like me, nothing is true.

My other less abstract application for re-entry into the Race would be to answer a want-ad I picked out of the Paris edition of the *Herald Trib*. The Independent American School in Algut needs an assistant headmaster. Do they want a Black one? The ad had been running for weeks. It looks mighty like nobody is hard-enough up to take a teaching job in Africa. Besides,

121

nobody wants to hear about Algut, the way things are going there, now. Yet, Algut is nearer the desert than Tanja, I was beginning to tell myself. Of course, I would have to teach a whole year there to get free. *"Are you out of your mind?"* I heard myself asking myself: *"You work? Work, you?"* I talk back so much all the time to that little voice in my head that anyone overhearing me might think I smoked too much keef. Which reminds me, I must have an all-out session with myself and my UHER, one day, just to see if I can make my little voice talk for the tape. I clench my eyes tight for one pico-second, just the time for one all-knowing blink, and I open them again.

All this bit just to show you how far I could be from consciously conjuring up this outrageous cat who had apparently curled himself up at my table totally unnoticed by me and was already deep in my briefcase, clawing into it like a real cat after fish, before I could snap: Scat! I blinked and here was this white fellow, already plumped down beside me, plunging into my manuscript totally unasked.

"Hey!" I shouted. "Get the hell out of my book!"

"Is that what you think you are writing?" he drawled, bathing me at the same time in a ten thousand watt Cheshire Cat grin. I started to splutter with rage but I ended by laughing at him; I just had to laugh. He was funny, hilarious even, to look at but he looked, also, very very rich in his regulation threads of camel, cashmere, vicuña and Thai silk. Quite a few years my junior, I judged with a glance at his bald head—or was it shaved? His straggly red beard was shaped Arab-style but on him it looked like a hopeless attempt at disguise. I continued to laugh. This whitey grinned back at me like a jack-o'-lantern with sunburn. "Good! That's better," he said.

"Laughter *is* refusal," he went on airily, "but, at least, it is in Present Time—the only real time there is. Snap into Present Time, Hanson," and he had the nerve to snap his fingers like a cheap magician, right under my nose. "Mankind sleeps in a nightmare called Life! Hassan, wake up! If what I see there on the table is your forever unfinished letter to the Foundation for Fundamental Findings, Professor Hanson, forget it; you hear me? Just throw all that letter-writing out of your mind. *We* are the Foundation, Professor: my wife Mya and I. The name is Thay Himmer but just call me Thay. Hakim is my Arab nickname as yours is Hassan. But let's forget about that, shall we? *Hmmm?*"

All this time, he is scanning me with his incandescent American dental work; feeling up my face. Ever since I was conscious in the cradle, I have hated this; hated all the slippery eyes that ever have flitted over my face like sticky-footed flies. I know what frail, hot-eyed Franz Fanon felt when he spat on himself: *"Ah, le beau nègre!"* I know the spleen Mohamed Ali feels when he proclaims himself, O how rightfully: the handsomest cat of them all. *I am beeeauuutiful!* I look down at my body, sometimes, and I say in despair: "It's this whole. *system* got me into this here and now." My current relief comes from living with Hamid, who never has looked at my looks. Monkey-faced Hamid thinks *he* is the beauty of the family and I like it that way. What am I going to do to counter the present blue-eyed attack?

This blue-eyes is bugging me with the offer of his freckled white hand. I find myself fumbling across my own chest, taking care not to upset my coffee with my elbow; unable to look at this character squarely, at least partly I realize, because he is so overwhelmingly white. His blue-veined, hairy fingers loaded

123

with rings wind painfully about mine with a grip like the Old Man of the Sea. I wince because I know who he is, of course: he has been cruising me, now, for a week. Everyone in Tanja knows Himmer from a photo they ran in the local Spanish-language paper, calling him: *El Unico Radja Americano*. Now, even the little bootblacks call him *El Unico,* as he sweeps around town, trailing his vicuña burnous. One good look at Thay Himmer, VII, last White Rajah-Bishop of the Farout Islands, is enough to tell you that he is more than a little bit mythological and, of course, quite unique.

His wife, the former Mya Strangleblood, is the Richest Creature in Creation. The title was worked out for her by an agency hired by her lawyers, who were anxious to avoid lit-igation with any of the old title-holders in the *Fortune* Poll of the Rich. As Suzy Scandal said in her syndicated society col-umn: "You can't have two Richest Girls in the World, after all, even though some of the old title-holders have refused to turn in their crowns when their fortunes faded or were spent. Princess Mya holds her title as long as she holds the Strangle-blood oil wells, pitchblende pits, uranium outcroppings and platinum lodes found on the tribal grounds of the Barefoot Indians in Northwest Canada. PP Strangleblood, her first hus-band, is still missing in Tibet. Her current consort, Thay Him-mer, VII, lost the family outpost in the Farouts and is not very well fixed but, as Mya's seventh husband, he was somewhat of a catch. Thay is fey but Mya is a Canadian Red Indian with both feet on the ground; said to be equally inscrutable at poker or in business, she has used her first good fortune as a spring-board to much greater wealth. Mya is said to have gotten out from under the dollar and does all her business in Basel."

"Of course," I ejaculated, finally; belatedly equating the

Foundation with Fundamental Funds. Suzy Scandal said that her Fund had made Mya so much richer that she had been voted *Hors Concours,* in all further *Fortune* Polls. When her money, finally, could no longer be counted because there was nothing higher than billions so far, Mya would gain the privilege of keeping out of print entirely. In the meantime, her husband is coming on to me so strong and so fast I can hardly keep up with the message.

"Be a rose among roses; a thorn among thorns." Who said that? Did he just say that or did I? Or, was that Hamid's voice? No, Hamid said:

"When I see a prize, I know how to take it. You never do."

Himmer is swinging his buggy blue eyes back and forth across my face like a lighthouse of brotherly love, and I sense, without any sense of shock, what a holy innocent he looks and probably is. "If I am thine, thou art mine," I say silently; taking him, I think, like a pawn. If I can believe my ears, this whitey is about to hand me over his wife and, maybe, his life.

"This is the Seal of the Sahara," he is saying as he flashes a big green stone. "It is carved out of an emerald and I have been instructed to give it to a man whose name is not Hassan. Mya and I believe that man to be you."

My ears are so tuned that I can hear the emerald crushing stray sugar crystals on the marble top of the table as he pushes it at me with long fingers, like a man making a move in a game. The scarab rolls toward me as relentlessly as a dung-beetle plowing its way over a dune.

"A beautiful bauble, Mr. Himmer," I admitted uneasily, hefting the bright green stone in the palm of my hand before pushing it back at him, "but I can't take your queen." I saw his big blue bug-eyes open even a little wider at that but I had

125

caught sight of a shoeshine boy stopped stock-still in the street, staring at the stone with coffee-cup eyes. "Have a coffee with me, Mr. Himmer," I offered him grandly while slapping away at the boy.

"Most gracious of you but, no; never!" Himmer protests. I am shocked to see just how flustered he is. "No stimulants ever," he grins. "I just don't need them, I guess."

"Oh, thass all right," I mumble, realizing with relief that his grin is a purely mechanical reflex of extreme oriental politeness. For a split second there, he looked almost Chinese: quite distinctly, I saw formalized orange and black flames of anguish licking his rictus.

"Welcome aboard," he is saying: "like a full-gown Dalai Lama found in the beauty of his age. In Present Time, it's your move, Hassan. You now hold the master-pawn which may well include some sort of claim on Mya herself, for all I know: but always remember that I am Mya's seventh husband and her last. I have no more to say—ever!—and, now, I must go."

"Am I supposed to give this jewel to your wife?" I asked, lamely.

"At your risk and peril!" he snapped. "She may try to cozen it out of you: in fact, she most certainly will, but if you give it to her—if you play it over to her, into her full power and possession, that's the end of that! The Emerald Seal, lawfully, is the Beginning and Ending of words. Having played the Green Beetle on you leaves me speechless. I mean that quite literally: I have only these few last words. Such has been the immutable rule since time immemorial when the Seal was first put on the Word. You can, I imagine, guess why. In Present Time, however, we must avail ourselves of the new knowledge, must we not? I have thought it wise, therefore—although it may not have been wise of me at all: it may have been downright criminally insane of me, who knows? to make you a tape! However, I have. Previously, the whole silly old Master-Adept game-situation had to be played out telepathically but Mya and I think that's so out of date, don't you? There's so much static about these days since electronics that most messages get hopelessly garbled. For Mya and me, the message is OUT! This, therefore, my dear Professor Ulys O. Hanson the Third, is our first conversation and our last. What you know, you know, and the rest of the garbage you'll get from my recorded Last Words when you play back this five-inch spool of magnetic tape on your UHER.''

With that, he handed me over a red, white and yellow box of ''SOUND MAGIC'' tape.

Then, he took a little white plastic bronchial inhalator out of his pocket and he opened his mouth round-open, so: like, O. My own so-called mind was working so slowly that, while I registered that Himmer had heavenly good breath, like flowering alpine pastures still half under snow—how rare! probably because his teeth were so wide apart he had no decay and he probably never smoked—no stimulants ever!—all this time, I was politely withdrawing my gaze from this wet open red mouth in order to drop my gaze and, yes, I remembered where I meant to look—at my UHER, still tightly gripped between my two feet.

''Damn!'' I sighed. ''I wasn't turned-on.''

When I raised my eyes from the ground, Himmer had inhaled his little puff of vapor and, without a further word, vanished; I suppose, into the noonday crowd on the Boulevard but who knows? I could hardly wait to play back his tape:

5

HE

He who tastes knows; so Mya and I have decided to give you a taste. Just to prove how serious we are, here is the text of the telex we sent to our operational headquarters in Africa; to "Malamut," the house Mya built way down south on Cape Noon: WITH HASSAN IN PRESENT TIME STOP CHANGE START OPERATION SCARAB PHASE FOUR SIGNED MYA AND THAY. You met Amos Africanus and Rolf Ritterolf in the *Hotel Saint Georges* in Algut. They manage our whole Stop Change Start device; of which Operation Scarab is, of course, only a part. Since your famous first interview with them, we have detailed them off to you as your personal staff. In Present Time, you are the Operator of Operation Scarab yourself. We hope you will be pleased with their work. They are two of our very best men in Africa or anywhere else, so, you see, we mean business. This is pretty big business even for Mya, who has irons in the fire all over Creation. What we mean to do is to snatch the Sahara right out from under that handful of prune-faced white bastards and their evil monopolistic double-criss-crossed corporations, who are already

128

crunching into the desert like crocodiles cutting up a live camel! We intend to save the Sahara and give it back to itself. Now, you have to admit, a woman can't be expected to swing a deal like this all alone, Hanson: Mya needs help.

One look in the mirror will tell you why Mya needs someone like you in Africa. The whole trouble with me is that I look just too damned white for Phase Four. I could make it in Mongolia, maybe, but we haven't got there yet. I dream of the Gobi desert, don't you? I can make the yellow scene somewhat, having been born out that way and, besides, I've been a Brahman as well as a Buddhist in my day but, hard as I've tried, I just can't make Black. *Go Black, Jack!* Well, short of massive melanin injections, I tried up in Harlem like everybody else in my day but I can't say it worked. I remember once being at somebody's piss-elegant Easter cocktail with canapés on Morningside where, from across the crowded room, I caught sight of one nasty pasty-white face. "How did that whitey get in here?" I asked indignantly. It was my own reflection in a mirror over the mantelpiece. Imagine campaigning to be "accepted" by the human race after that!

Well, I did try again, later, to get into some skin other than my own; right here in North Africa where the problem is not, essentially, color. Back in those days when Tanja was really Tanja, long before you ever came here, I was, in a way, "initiated" as you have been but much less successfully than you, of course. Perhaps because of my whiteness, I always stuck out like a cop. However, do let me tell you briefly who we really are and how we got onto your trail and saw your light rising like that of a Mahdi long before you ever turned up: the man whose name is not Hassan, yourself. When I tell you the story, you'll see why I feel it was "written," of course.

129

* * *

At the time I am speaking of, Mya and I were just jetting around Africa getting to know people. This African trip grew out of my therapy for Mya's very first husband; Peter Paul Strangeblood, the Richest Kid on Earth. Poor PP, he was only twenty-one but he'd had it: there wasn't really much anyone could really do for him except take all that money away from him and he knew this. It made him as nasty as hell. Mya had done all she could since she first picked him up but by the time she called me in professionally—I'm a Doctor of Grammatology as well as Hereditary Bishop in the First Farout Church—poor PP was already pretty well beyond help. We did our best to get him to respond to Africa but he merely shambled along after Mya and me until that day in the hotel in Bukavu when the big cardboard box caught up with us, dropped in by parachute: we were under siege in a terrible poured-concrete hotel at the time. Mya and I started ripping the box open like two kids at Christmas, hoping it was food. I'd been giving Strangleblood various occult exercises for his "havingness" and one exercise we'd almost forgotten about had been making him send to his bank for one million dollars U.S. in cash. When PP saw all that money spread out on the bed, he turned as green as the bills: he was all choked up. I felt very sorry for him because I suffer from asthma myself. He had to be flown out by the Swiss Red Cross, eventually; they called it an *"évacuation sanitaire."* Somehow, Mya and I lost sight of him until the divorce.

Eventually, Mya and I landed here in Tanja together but not as lovers; not yet. Mya wasn't ready for me: a great many things had to happen to both of us, first. I merrily went my own mad mystical way, which has led us at long last to you,

130

as you see. For a time, Mya went quite another way. Mya is no Lady Bluebeard, no matter what the papers may say. When she first flew in to consult me in New York, Mya still had a lot of the original starry-eyed cowgirl from Medicine Hat or some such awful place which I have never had to visit, being a native South Sea Islander myself, but I know all about it from Mya. Mya is part Indian on both sides of her family and she comes of an awe-inspiring matriarchy of potent old squaws who, for seven generations in one single century, have taken mates upon themselves as they pleased. These mates were French-Canuck trappers and rugged Scots Hudson Bay Company factors or, like Mya's own father, fifteen-year-old Tom Bear Foot, simply the hottest moccasin cousin at the time and the place. Mya was born with the aurora borealis dancing around her birch-bark crib and she is the Great Queen of the Crees in her own right. Mya can take on the whole white and the whole yellow race.

In Tanja, as I say, we went our own ways and, here in Tanja, Mya first tangled with Dr. Pio Labesse. Pio was what people used to call "a bad hat." They told me Mya was singeing her wings but I knew she was only burning the pin-feathers off her pinions to grow her own eagle spread. I let her have her head, naturally, and she got a lot, eventually, from even Labesse. They had their ups and downs, of course. At one time, Mya claimed Pio was poisoning her with pills and he did have that sort of reputation but she found a way to poison him back so they made it up. She's terribly clever at all that. Then, she decided to sue Strangleblood for divorce in Switzerland, in Basel where she'd first picked up her lawyer Rolf Ritterolf; he's Swiss. She separated PP, legally, from so much of that loot that he began to feel a lot better right away,

131

and left for Tibet. Mya, at loose ends and alone in Europe for a moment, absentmindedly married a prince. In First-Class on an airliner to Brussels, of all places, where she was going to pick up her new Lear jet, she was set upon by this dazzlingly handsome Himalayan, who was so persistent that Mya felt she owed it to herself to be swept away, just this once. Before she knew quite what was happening to her, she found herself marrying him in his embassy. In the air over Afghanistan, he explained the marriage customs of his country.

"Polyandry," he told her.

Mya was only nineteen at the time. She said: "I've had my Salk."

"No," he explained, "you are now married also to all my brothers who are Khans like me—you can translate that as prince."

She looked at the fuel gauge and she looked back at him. "How many brothers have you got?"

It turned out they were four and that wasn't so bad but they all had other wives, too. When she was left alone for a minute with the women, they all flew at her like harpies, beat her and stripped her of her money and her clothes. When they poisoned her, she got hold of some of the stuff they were using and smuggled it out to be analyzed back in Basel. Mya will tell you herself about her deep and abiding interest in pharmaceutical folklore. It was quite an adventure but, all in all, it took Mya less than a week, flying both ways in her own jet, of course. Back in Basel, Rolf was still so hot from the Strangleblood case that he got her divorces from the four princes through—I was going to say; in a trice. Divorcing four princes in one swell foop was quite a feat, don't you think? One permanent scar: Mya insists on being a princess ever since.

With me, she's a white-Ranee, if she wants to be, but she made Labesse, her fifth husband, build the base of an African empire for her and she wouldn't marry him until he managed to have himself made a pontifical prince.

Poor Prince Pio, the day he got a crown he lost his head. He began acting like the caliph of Cairo soon after he rammed through the deal, with the Spaniards who claimed it in those days, for Mya to buy up two million bare acres of sand in the Sahara, including Cape Noon and the ruin of the Portuguese fort they found on it. Out of that pile of rubble, Mya made "Malamut," which she built, as they say, in her own image and likeness and Mya thinks big. It was a draw, for a while; who could think bigger, she or Labesse. "Malamut" was meant to cost six million dollars but, so far, it's cost nearly twenty times that and it's not finished, yet. Can you imagine something between Mont Saint Michel and Gibraltar but set out on the blazing Atlantic coast of the Sahara right on the Tropic of Cancer, the one and only rock bigger than a pebble in thousands of miles of unmapped blue lagoons? Inland from "Malamut" is absolute desert, whose hard surface is stamped with giant moving dunes of amber-pink sand and each dune is carved by the wind into a perfect crescent with horns running due south. "Malamut" means megalomania to people like Pio and in that palace Prince Pio became a real prick.

But I'm running ahead of my own story because, all the time "Malamut" was a-building, I was down below the Socco Chico in Tanja, deeply involved with the Brotherhood of the Hamadchas, only coming up as far as the European Boulevard now and then for air. My encounter with the head-chopping Brotherhood was ordained by the fact that, from the first moment Mya and I drew breath in Tanja, we were under a spell.

We were so sick of those poured-concrete shells they call hotels all over modern Africa that we asked for an old-fashioned place and they took us to the *Hotel Africanus,* hanging over the port on the edge of the old Arab quarter. Amos Africanus, whose grandfather built it around the turn of the century, said the old man had designed the hotel to accommodate the pig-sticking trade from Gibraltar. It seems that Her Majesty's Lanc-ers, lacking a good gallop on the Rock, used to sail over for long weekends in International Tanja to hunt wild boar from horseback with spears in the Diplomatic Forest. If you've ever been in the place, you've seen their ghosts still lingering in the long lawn curtains of the old mirrored dining room and the leather-lined bar. If you've ever stayed there you know how enchanted we were with our vast suites of rooms with every last Edwardian tassel still hanging, the big brass beds with their mosquito-net canopies and the long shuttered win-dows down to the floor.

But, when you open those windows, what strange sneaky smells come crawling up from the surrounding streets! And what noise! I almost fell off my various iron balconies, leaning out to see where such a din could be coming from and, let me tell you, we were used to the African drums. I tried ringing down to the desk to complain but, of course, no one answered the phone, so I ventured into the long stuccoed halls and down the marble staircase covered with dusty red carpeting into the Moorish lounge: no one about. I rapped on the ground glass of a mahogany cubicle and out stepped a very tanned man with prematurely white hair, who said: "I am the management. Can I help you?" That was my very first meeting with Amos and you heard what he said: "I am the management." We have learned always to take people precisely at their word. Amos

Africanus is a big help, you'll see; he still manages things for us and he will, now, for you, Hassan, too.

When I asked him where all that weird racket of Arab music was coming from, he laughed: "Some American beat-niks next door, as a matter of fact. They've settled into an Arab house and become Adepts of one of the local ecstatic brotherhoods." I knew the sort of thing he meant because we have that in the Farout Islands where I was brought up. The servants all used to get psychic relief by chanting and dancing all night until they passed out. My amah, my nursemaid, took me to their secret services almost as soon as I could waddle and I became an initiate at a very early age. I introduced myself to Amos Africanus: "I'd like to contact the local mysteries," I said, offering him at the same time a grip which I thought he might know and he did, apparently, for he refused it with another laugh, saying: "I'll introduce you if you like, but I'll not go inside with you." I knew what he meant. The Sephardim are exceptionally careful, even coy, about the magic which surrounds them in North Africa although they have always been practically the only authorities open to us on the subject. Amos took me through the outer cubicle of his office into a vast old library built in ornate Moroccan style and filled with books on North Africa in six or seven languages. "This is the French section," he said; "added by me. I would have taken my degree in anthropology under Levy-Levant at the Sorbonne if the war hadn't interrupted all that."

"How about a little fieldwork next door?" I suggested.

"On Lenny and Lorna? Or on the Hamadcha they've called in to dance in their house? I'm afraid the Levines are getting in a little over their depth with the Brotherhood, as a matter of fact. The Hamadcha think they're just Americans and, what's

135

more, the Brotherhood wants to go on thinking the Levines are just Americans because of the money involved. Lenny plans to take a clutch of Hamadcha back to the States, to get people trance-dancing in the East Village basements before he takes over Madison Square Garden and the Fairgrounds and the West Coast, Gulf Coast and Canada; until he's got the whole continent dancing. Mexico, Central America, Honolulu, Japan. . . . They tell me that kind of fantasy comes from shooting amphetamine in the mainline or do they call it: 'mainlining amphetamine'? Well, anyway, Lorna comes here from time to time to confide to me that she's afraid in the house because everybody seems to be trying to poison them. Their Moroccan maid, who is not a Hamadcha and disapproves of having the Brotherhood dancing in the house at all, told them that the only antidote was to eat a bat's liver. So, they went out to the Caves of Hercules on the Atlantic beach about fifteen miles from here and paid a small boy to kill them two bats. They ate one of them fried.''

As Amos was telling me all this, he piloted me through a maze of dark corridors to the back door of the hotel, which opens, as you know, right onto the gate into the teeming Arab alley that leads to Dar Baroud. As I slid off the narrow step, I was almost sliced in two by a bicycle-boy flying past like a steel bat with a knife-edged tray of bread balanced on his head. Underfoot was slippery with veiled women and litters of nearly naked children everywhere even at midnight. I remember feeling that one false step might send me slithering into a roaring bake-oven fire, wide-open on one side of the narrow lane, or into a medieval urinal on the other. I looked up to see Amos was knocking on a handsomely studded door in the blank wall of a sordid cul de sac. A tall dark young man as handsome as a Hindu god in a nightshirt splashed us with light as he opened the door inviting us in. That was Lenny. Amos tried to wriggle away from the invitation, insisting he'd come only to introduce me but I could see he was fascinated by what the Levines were up to so, when Lorna came up behind Lenny in a flame-colored Moroccan caftan of silk, looking exactly like the beautiful Rebecca in *Ivanhoe,* we all went inside; almost pushed in, as a matter of fact, by the growing crowd of little snotty-nosed Arab kids in the street behind us.

The house itself was enchantment. Maybe you know the house I mean or have been in one like it: until then, I never had. The colored tiles in the patio and the lights and the flowers and, above all, the people in their gorgeous robes! People furnish a house in Morocco, I could see that at a glance. There were over fifty Moroccans present, including more than ten musicians in spotless white robes and turbans who sat apart on a golden straw mat to one side of the marble patio, looking peculiarly picturesque and what I call "historical"—as if they were floating there in some sort of golden jelly of the past through which one could really reach *into* the past and touch them. I guess some of the effect was produced by clouds of keef smoke and gum-Arabic incense, which they kept tossing into the pots of red charcoal over which the musicians warmed and tightened the skins of their drums.

Everyone was grinning at me as if I'd just come home. I grinned and bowed back at them as I took out my little asthma inhaler, my Bronchomister of isoprenaline, which I get from France. You'd think it was the trick of the century, the way they all reacted. Applause! "They think you've got *pranna* in there!" Amos hissed in my ear as he drew me aside to give me an extramural lecture on what the Paris school of social

137

anthropology led by his Professor Levy-Levant thinks of ecstatic practices. I know quite a lot about all that myself but
I'm always ready to listen if there isn't some simply great
music going on at the same time. When the beat picked up, I
began joggling and jiggling, much to the annoyance of Amos.
When they began swinging in earnest, four or five barefooted
men and one woman, whose long mane of black hair fell over
her eyes, began hopping and flapping their arms to the beat
of the drums, swaying and bowing to the long shuddery raucous
railing of the big bamboo flutes. I began jerking myself, losing
Amos completely except for the supercilious sneer on his face,
full of sheer disapproval. My elbows were thumping up into
my armpits while my calves began pumping something into
my knees to give them a little more jump. Before I knew what
was happening to me, I was up in the air and over the heads
of some fat Arab ladies all wrapped up in white on the floor
like a row of bundles of laundry and I was clearing them all.
I looked down at them from my orbit to catch their broad
smiles of approval as I hurtled past over their heads toward
the drums. When I landed, I landed in a new world: I was out
there front and center, leaping and twisting for the Hamadcha
music along with the best of them. A break eventually came
when someone beside me fell to the floor with froth on his
lips and had to be carried up close to the drummers for shock
treatment. I went back to slump down on the floor beside Amos
and the Levines. I could feel Amos beginning to bristle as
some old gink with one eye leaped up in the orchestra and
started apostrophizing us. When all the Moroccans began swaying
and bowing and chorusing back: *"AAAAAmen! Aaaaaamen!"*
I knew right where I was in the service, I'm a bishop after all,
so I brayed: *"AAAAAAmen!"* along with the rest of them. For,

did not the Prophet say: "He who does not cry *aamin* with the Sufi is recorded as one of the Heedless"?

Out of the corner of one eye, I did begin to notice that my hosts, who understood a good bit of Arabic, were looking less comfortable by the minute, while even my ear could catch an ominous edge on all these invocations of *"Allah!"* which swelled up in almost hysterical chorus around us. I got to my feet. They didn't have to urge me to edge along around the outside of the crowd along with them toward the door but before we got there the old gink in the long gown and turban fixed me with his one good eye and suddenly shot a long skinny finger right under my nose as he shouted or screamed rather: *"Ha houwa!* There he is!" You don't need the language to understand that: There he goes! That's the man! That's the one! and you expect the whole pack to be launched in full cry: "After him! After him! Don't let him go!" I just stood there with my shoes in my hands and a sickly white grin on my face as the old man pushed his way through the crowd to throw himself at my feet, calling me "Hakim!" When I caught his eye, Amos translated: "Hakim's a common name for a magician. Let's go!" A whole lot more people were suddenly slobbering over my hands and my feet, so I gave them my most solemn Episcopal blessing until I remembered I shouldn't be making the sign of the cross. Lenny and Lorna were delighted by the drama but Amos wanted to leave. Lenny insisted on walking us back to the hotel, pestering Amos all the way to tell us who Hakim was. "He must have looked just like Mr. Himmer, don't you think?"

"Well, he may have at that," Amos allowed. "Hakim was the caliph of Cairo about the time of Charlemagne and history says he was a blue-eyed Berber or, even, a descendant of

139

Vandals with red hair. Hakim was a ferocious puritan who slaughtered so many thousands of his subjects by his own righteous right hand that he is said to have reduced the population of Cairo by nearly nine-tenths. The survivors revered him, of course, swearing that Hakim was the embodiment of divine justice on earth: the caliph became a cult in his lifetime, inevitably one might say. In the end he got tired of it: simply walked out. He got so disgusted with all these spineless Cairoites that he walked away alone out of an empty street into the desert one moonlit night, dragging his cloak behind him to efface his footsteps as he went. He never was seen again from that day until, maybe, this.''

"Oh, no, Amos!" I cried. "I am not Hakim nor was meant to be. Maybe the first rajah-bishops of the Farouts behaved a bit like that with the early islanders but I've always thought of myself as someone out of Russian rather than Arab literature—Aloysha the bore or the idiot prince Myshkin.''

"You know what that means in Arabic, don't you?" laughed Amos. "*Meskeen* means 'poor thing.' ''

When we got back to the hotel we found that Mya had moved out in the middle of the night, leaving word that because the noise was too much for her she had gone bag and baggage up to the *Hotel Mingih,* on the Boulevard. Crawling up out of the Medina next day to get up there was like leaving one world for another. In her hotel, the desk sent me right up to her room without ringing and I found Mya in bed, with the doctor. She hadn't been feeling well so she told them to send up a doctor. Dr. Pio Labesse was this Catalan specialist who ran his clinic in the bar of the *Mingih* where he could keep a close tab on his drinking patients; among them, some of the richest women in Tanja until Mya blew in. Mya may still have been just a

140

backwoods Canadian girl in those days but she had a lot of other things besides several hundred million dollars and about thirty years on those other babes. Pio psyched Mya out immediately: in a way they were really twin souls. When Mya divorced PP, who had just turned twenty-one and come into his money, she walked out with everything he had in Africa, just for a start, and Pio knew exactly what to do with it. But that's Mya's tale and I know she expects to audit it all directly with you tonight at the picnic. By the way, I'll not be there in person.

So, I went back down to the *Hotel Africanus,* had two stiff whiskies, and told Amos I intended going through with this Hakim thing. When he saw I meant what I said, he agreed to go along with me as a guide. He just dropped his hotel like an old overcoat to show me the ropes in Morocco, so, at first, I offered to take over the whole hotel as our headquarters; but when the Hamadcha, looking much less magical and even a bit shady by daylight, came trooping in to claim me next day I could see That Look on Amos's face. When Arabs appear on his very-near horizon, Amos's faculties are inclined to fog over in front of your eyes. Amos sees all Arabs through a glass darkly or through the wrong end of the telescope down which he can snap at them in perfect Arabic if you ask him to translate but he doesn't necessarily hear what they say back; not real communication, you see. For example, I tried to find out from the Hamadcha about the old man who'd cried out: *"Ha houwa!"* at me, calling me Hakim. Nobody seemed to want to know what anyone else was talking about until I suddenly remembered the microphone dangling from the balcony. "Lenny must have a recording of his voice!" I cried. So we all went looping back over there to Lenny's house and banged

141

on his door. Lorna opened the door just a crack, fearfully at first, looking more beautiful than ever when she revealed herself dressed like one of those girls from Dogpatch in a pair of tight blue jeans sawed off at the knee. She was, obviously, not quite awake yet and the sight of us all in broad daylight seemed to paralyze her. "Lenny's not back from the port," she murmured in hopeless protest as we all swept inside. I thought she was going to faint at the mere mention of the microphone because it seems that they had been making a recording unbeknownst to the Hamadcha. "They're acting kind of funny on us," she muttered. "We thought maybe we should split." The upshot of that was that Lenny came in with two tickets for New York on a Yugoslav boat leaving immediately and somehow, in the shuffle, I found myself the new tenant of the house in Dar Baroud with a full company of Hamadcha Brothers ready to sit around eating and smoking and dancing until Lenny got back. I never did get hold of that tape, by the way, and it had some pretty potent words on it.

Anyhow, I plunged into my new life and, as my trance-dancing improved, my asthma cleared up. I thought it had disappeared entirely by itself, until one day the little old one-eyed man showed up wheezing at me about money so I accused him of stealing my asthma, gave him my inhalator and sent him away. I could see that such an act of authority on my part was much appreciated by the Hamadcha. As their hopes of Lenny coming back from America vaporized in less than forty-eight hours, the Hamadcha Brothers came to look on me more and more as their leader, proposing to make me meet the grand chiefs of various different brotherhoods in Morocco. I began to learn Arabic, counting out money: "Food for four is food for six is food for eight . . ." More than twenty people and sometimes as many as fifty sat down to food twice a day in my new house. Allah was providing in the person of Thay Himmer and as I was just as delighted with the arrangement as they were, there were no complaints in the household. Instead, there was music running like a river through the house all day and all night as the Hamadcha practiced their peculiar beat to which I danced like a doll on a string—not that I didn't know what I was doing all the time, of course, and loving every minute of it, too. I've been through every branch of Eastern mysticism, always finding it rather glum. I came to the conclusion, finally, that its meager telepathic fundament is only the result of centuries of overpopulation and overcrowding. Everyone knows just what everyone else is doing and thinking all the time, of course. Even as a child, I had felt suffocated by it. All the women in my family, for the last three generations in the Farouts at least, have been ardent Theosophists, followers of Madame Blavatsky and Annie Besant, in close contact with Swami Vivekenanda and Krishnamurti; aunts, great-aunts always talking about Gurdjieff, *"pranna,"* and the hallucinatory effects of superaeration— and all that sort of thing—or trailing around in trances at home. Even Grandfather, who was the last Rajah-Bishop to officiate in the Farouts, used to meditate in the lotus position wearing only a G-string. So you see, I knew both the practical and the theoretical side of the business, since childhood you might say, and in Eastern philosophy I found no hilarity. For a while, I almost let myself become interested in Saint Teresa of Avila because I heard she kicked up her heels and went into long peals of ecstatic laughter, but when I found out she took deep whiffs of the incense pot into which she had probably thrown a handful of hemp, I left her flat. My asthma had always turned

143

me against smoking but with the Hamadcha I ventured, now and then, to take a little whiff of a tiny pipe and after one particularly insane session I proclaimed to one and all that Morocco was the Wild West of the Spirit. I think that just about hits it on the head, don't you? Every day—every minute—we did something hilarious.

The Hamadcha saw to it that I danced until my feet were raw and every bone in my body so sore that when I finally fell in front of the flutes I thought I'd never get up again. But just let me hear one long sobbing tremolo blown hoarse and husky on the long bamboo *chebaba,* and my soul kindled, caught fire and leaped up in me to send me hopping and whirling out there again in front of the music. It was all pretty tiring, I have to admit, and I was very glad I had kept on my room at the *Hotel Africanus* to which I used to creep away when I could, to toss down a swift Scotch or two at the bar with Amos, who kept his back door locked in case the Brothers came calling after me. Amos was and is a real darling, you'll see; although he has a quite different world-view than we do, naturally. Deep down in his heart somewhere, he thinks we're just Tourists. He lectured me, gave me books to read, was helpful and kind but he always disapproved utterly of what I was doing. To study anthropology was one thing, to practice it quite another. But I was constantly calling him in to translate, so, sooner or later, he got mixed up in everything we're doing and he's really invaluable, you'll see! However, don't be fooled for a minute, Amos simply doesn't get the message that comes from Beyond—either he thinks it's sinful or just not practical and he honestly doesn't feel that he needs to make any spiritual progress other than that involved in protecting himself from the slings and arrows of outrageous fortune. Lest this sound

144

too harsh let me add that I, at least, think Amos can be brought to see a *bit* of Beyond. Mya denies it. Oddly enough, Amos dearly loves me, but Mya he admires, fears and respects.

She, by this time, had begun shacking up with Pio Labesse on the Boulevard. I phoned her up there from the depths of the Socco Chico, once or twice a day, to see how she was getting on, but it was such an almost unthinkable effort to haul myself out of that hole in the Medina that I didn't see much of her. Over the phone, Mya was a bit snippy about Amos, pretending to think I must be having an affair with him but nothing could have been further from my mind. I was all wrapped up in the Hamadcha, with whom I was advancing step by step into their labyrinth of initiation, or, so I thought. When I tried to tell Mya this, she said she was coming down to see for herself but I said No, I'd go up to her at the *Mingih*. When I got there, her room was still unmade but there was no sign of the cardboard box in which we'd been carrying PP's million dollars in greenbacks. We never gave it to the hotels to take care of because the box was too big for most vaults and besides nobody looking at it ever would think it was money because we had EXPLOSIVE written on it in big red letters with a big exploding pop-art bomb for people who can't read. It frightened the hell out of hall porters and Customs men, too. As I bent down to kiss Mya on the bed, the communicating door opened into the next suite and there was Labesse in a gold brocade Arab caftan down to the floor. In his room, I could see the box torn wide open with green bricks of hundred dollar bills spread like a mattress over the bed he'd been lying on. Somehow, before I knew it, just out of habit I guess, I'd invited them both to my party, which I hadn't known until that minute I was giving. It was a catastrophe, of course.

145

Labesse had a genius for enraging Arabs which a former French governor general might have envied. The sneer, with Labesse, was a scimitar with which he whittled all Arabs down to what he considered their proper elevation, grass-high. He reserved the other side of his blade to shave Americans, all rich Americans: North, Central and South. I've made quite a study of Dr. Labesse: we've got a huge Labesse archive down in "Malamut" which I hope you'll have a chance to consult when you get down to Cape Noon. It's all in audio so you can have it played to you while you're asleep, if you like: we have all the equipment. Amos, it turns out, is an electronic genius amongst other talents and he's seen to the wiring of "Malamut" under Mya's direction, although like most women she really hates sound unless she makes it herself. The house, as you'll see when you see it, is meant to amplify her. Mya built it with Pio while I was away on my stumbling spiritual quest so you'll hear the story of "Malamut" better from her lips.

Mya still thinks Labesse was a cross between Talleyrand and Machiavelli with a dash of the Borgias thrown in. It was that last dash she found irresistible. Her greatest childhood experience had been being poisoned by mushrooms out on the Canadian prairies, so when she got to college that took her into toxology and, eventually, genetic biochemistry before she married poor PP and got interested in money. As an Old Moroccan Hand, himself, the first story Labesse ever told her was about some mysterious substance which Moroccan women are said to give their husbands to make them complacent. You must have heard of it, of course; *"Borbor,"* it's called. You see, when Mya and PP first moved from Saskatoon, Saskatchewan, to Basel, it had been with the idea of studying with

146

Professor Forbach: you know, the man who discovered the hallucinatory principle of all the new drugs.

Actually, in the end Forbach threw Mya out of his laboratory when he learned that she had launched a mutual fund scheme from Basel. You've heard of Fundamental Funds, haven't you? Well that's Mya's baby or was in those days when Professor Forbach dismissed her because he could no longer consider her a "seriously dedicated scientist" if she insisted on making millions or hundreds of millions of dollars like that on the side. So she offered to buy him out from his pharmaceutical combine, which paid him only some annuity, but that was a mistake, waving her dollars around. Professor Forbach was furious, naturally! She called him a "kept chemist!" and swept out to the sounds of breaking glass test-tubes, slamming the door.

Mya was running a North African fever that first night with Labesse and it must have been wild, something like the mating of a basilisk and a gryphon. Afterward, she's always sworn to me that it was by pure feminine intuition that she dug Pio for a poisoner but, of course, it had been in all the papers when it happened. She still swears she hadn't read a thing about it and didn't even know who he was when he got into bed with her. When I tried to tell her, she snapped at me: "That's just the type of nasty tale people in Tanja are forever telling about each other and, besides, I never even heard of Lindissima Reuther either . . . until last night!" I'd been foolish enough to advise her to watch out because everyone including Amos Africanus lost no time in telling me how Dr. Labesse had spent ten months in jail in Barcelona, accused of poisoning or trying to poison Lindissima's adopted son for her.

One word out of me and Mya always does just as she pleases, naturally. As soon as they got the Pio thing settled between them, the ladies went into business together; mines in the Sahara—for the next couple of years. You can imagine how popular *I* was with everybody concerned! I simply made myself scarce for a very long while as I went on about my own business of spiritual progress: which includes learning how to button one's lip, of course.

I guess the way Lindissima Reuther first figured it was, she could afford to spare Labesse as long as Mya would put up the cash to help her get her Saharan mines into operation. Both girls thought they knew all about mines, concessions and subsoils rights; things *I* know nothing about, heaven knows! Mya got this from her oil-well childhood in western Canada and Lindissima from her young if not tender years in South America, where she is said to have burned down two Latino presidents and their republics along with them. As I said, everyone in Tanja was only too ready to fill me in on the legendary aspects of Lindissima's lurid past even before she'd married this Reuther, who was, as she always said, a clean old man, half-Swiss and half-Spanish, who'd spent years of his life wandering around the Sahara before anyone else got there in a helicopter. He'd lived like a nomad and became a Muslim, buying up subsoil rights from local desert sheiks under binding Coranic contracts which any Arab government would be bound to observe. Reuther got the Spanish government to ratify all this at a time when the really big boys in Madrid and Barcelona hadn't even got the smell of oil and phosphates in their nostrils yet. Reuther passed for a very rich man during those years that cash was so hard to come by in Spain and, besides, he lived the life of the mysterious recluse who doesn't

like to spend it. He must have been over seventy when Lindissima hit Madrid hard, flying in from an overextended tour
of the Middle East, where she had cleaned up quite a bit of
loot, including some gorgeous jewels from grateful oil sheiks,
which hid the fact she was slipping from everyone but herself.
In Madrid she had herself quite a fling with some major movie
star for a while and a couple of fairly expensive young bull-
fighters before Reuther met her and invited her down to the
desert to show her his mining concessions by helicopter. Lindissima fell in love on first sight with the Sahara; so much so
that she wanted to own it. She married Reuther and went into
business with him, handing him over her stash, which amounted
to almost one million dollars, at that time; all she had including
the jewels. Her money set them up in one of the last big palaces
on the Castellana, about a hundred yards from the Hilton,
where she started entertaining the right people, whoever *they*
may be in Madrid.

Anyhow, everything was going along fine when the old
man died on her, plunging her into the usual hassle with lawyers and even that was working out not too badly when some
idiot Spanish boy of nineteen was arrested for pimping on the
Gran Via in the middle of Madrid. From jail, he started screaming that he was Reuther's natural son who was being gypped
out of his inheritance and the whole thing with this girl could
be explained. He was innocent and even suggested that he had
been framed. One of the newspapers, since suppressed by the
censor, got hold of the story and printed it to the delight of
whatever other interests hoped to pick up Reuther's fortune.
Lindissima went to see the boy in jail, managed to get him
out of jail, moved him into the big house on the Castellana
and, eventually, legally adopted him. She'd have done a lot

better to marry him and be done with it, the hell with the thirty years' age difference between them, but she didn't. Her basic mistake was her vanity. She thought she could hold the boy as a lover and lord it over him as a mother at the same time. It turned the boy very nasty. When she caught him fiddling around with her medicines in her bathroom one day, she didn't say a word but made the basic decision—*snap!*—just like that.

They were invited out in the country to some Spanish duke's estate on a hunt with over a hundred guns and twice as many beaters, the old-fashioned kind of slaughter of birds piled up in the courtyard of the castle. Lindissima knew some desperate young captain whose debts she was ready to pick up if it worked out. But the boy, the adopted son and lover, was too quick for them or simply by accident he tripped at the right moment, throwing himself flat on his face on the ground. He got only a little lead in his backside but, duke or no duke, they had the police in and the captain began to talk. The first thing they did was to arrest the boy, naturally, in the hospital. A high police official visited Lindissima and found her most charming. Lindissima was still a striking-looking woman even when Labesse left her for Mya. Labesse was her doctor who certified she was far too nervous to answer any further questions except in bed. The result of all that was the boy came back to floods of tears on all sides; a typical Spanish denouement, I'm told. Lindissima persuaded everybody including herself that the stupid captain had done it for love of her fine eyes, as they say in Spanish, and, for a while, that was that.

But the boy kept slipping away to the girl on the Gran Via, who by this time really was a whore even if she hadn't been in the beginning. Lindissima got so nervous that she had Doctor Labesse in day and night. Labesse apparently gave her something to keep the young man at home. To keep up appearances that he was really living in his own wing of the big house on the Castellana and not with the girl, the boy showed up for very grand candlelit dinners served by butlers and footmen in white gloves. Almost right away he began to suspect that they were putting something in his food so, in a sort of slow-motion yawning scene, he began to denounce them as poisoners at the dinner table. Then, he dragged himself slowly out of the house like a snail, leaving a trail of vomit behind him. They let him go, because in front of the servants they were afraid to stop him and anyway as Labesse guessed correctly, the boy went not to the police but to the girl. There they had him arrested in her bed for proxenetism, pimping, living off the immoral earnings of, etc.; throwing the book at him. The thing was already much too public, someone had to hear his squeals from inside even one of those Spanish jails. Labesse was arrested and held in Barcelona where he'd been foolish enough to flee but it may not have been as foolish as all that because inside ten months he was out again scot-free and the whole thing forgotten. The boy's still in jail, of course, and while I've never met him, I send him some money now and then— conscience money, I suppose—because Mya plucked the Reuther concessions off Lindissima one by one during the following years—Labesse aiding, of course.

Lindissima and Pio had come down to Tanja to get near some fresh capital, not guessing, poor innocents, that there hasn't been any fresh capital in Tanya for eons! When the *Mingih* manager mumbled that Madame Strangleblood needed a doctor, you can imagine how they both jumped. You see, I got to know this crowd when I managed to crawl up from the Medina, leaving the Hamadcha still jumping down in my Arab house with Amos Africanus standing by to keep an uneasy eye on his neighbors. Living between two worlds, as I did, I got provoked by Mya into doing the one thing one should never do—introduce one world to the other. That's how this famous party of mine happened. Before I knew it, the whole crowd from the *Hotel Mingih* bar on the Boulevard were suddenly standing out there in the open sewer of my Medina street in their minks and their diamonds, being pelted with fish heads by the Arab urchins. I simply had to let them in to the house to save their lives. Actually, I'd absolutely forgotten that I'd invited them because I'd been dancing that evening with a big black sailor's belt someone had given me.

I'd begun by giving myself a few little slaps with my new belt as I danced to the music and it felt so tingling good, like a shot in the arm to my dancing, that I gave myself quite a few more belts when I found that I liked it. *"Belt! Belt! Belt!"* the drums kept belting out, so I gave myself quite a belting until the blood came before all the guests arrived. I just pulled somebody's shirt on so as not to catch cold when I went to the front door to greet them. Their entry stopped all the music dead in its *tracks,* of course, but when I turned around to get the musicians to play again as if nothing had happened, a couple of *Mingih* barflies began to shriek at the sight of the blood oozing out of my shirt in the back, it seems. I was quite unaware of it. Dr. Labesse, like an officious medical fool, insisted on putting a dressing on my back right then and there so I was made to feel an idiot; badly humiliated, they put me to bed. Mya insisted on staying to nurse me but when I explained to her that I needed quite a big sum of money for my initiation in the mountains which the Hamadcha had promised me, I caught her exchanging such a look with Labesse over my prostrate body that I knew right away that Mya was going to be stuffy about money from now on out. I was so furious I never mentioned the word "money" again until the day we got married, years later this spring. Then, I made over all of *my* money to Mya and that's the way it still stands, today. I don't want to have anything to do with money any more than PP did. Just counting One Two Three used to make *him* nervous. I began by shutting up about money and my next move is going to be shut up about everything else.

But back to the Brotherhood! You may know that in those days their political situation was so unstable that they had to draw in their horns a bit and be careful about public demonstrations. All that was of interest mainly to Muslims and I found that I'd gotten in deep with the Hamadcha before it really dawned on me that all my new Moroccan friends took it for granted that I was a Muslim or was about to become one. As I once said to Amos Africanus, the Himmers always were pantheists—it made no difference to me. When someone intoned slowly for me to repeat after him: *"There is no God but Allah and Mohamed is His Prophet,"* I said it, why not? One great-aunt of mine actually became the abbess of a Shinto convent in Japan after the war. My next goal was Moulay Youniss, the holy city where no Christian or Jew had ever slept until I did. The millennial ban was lifted by the late king I believe, but the town has no hotel and none of the inhabitants would think of socializing enough with non-Muslims to invite them into their houses to spend the night. I'd stopped drinking alcohol entirely and gotten quite handy at Moroccan manners and ways but as I didn't speak Arabic and still don't, really, I didn't say much. My feet were killing me but my asthma didn't come back even when I traveled along with the Brothers

153

on foot through Morocco in harvesttime. We were climbing up to Moulay Youniss to spend the night before going on to the Hamadcha feast at Sidi Hassan on the other side of the mountain.

It was one of those celestial African days in June when you could look back down the steep ravines full of spiky cactus candelabra shooting up as high as telephone poles from the acid-green aloes. The ruined marble columns of Roman Volubilis stood higher still on the tremendous sweep of the green-golden plain far below. The whitewashed cube-houses of Moulay Youniss hung over us, capping the hilltop. Quite apart from the celestial beauty of the spot there was the thrill of climbing up into a forbidden city on foot. We were quite a woolly-looking little group with only one pack-donkey for twenty or thirty of us as we scrambled along, but when we caught our breath, our drummer picked up and our wild wailing music skirled out under the big green silk banners of the Hamadcha flying in the crystal clear air. We stormed into town hopping and howling in a pack with me in the middle, quite unnoticed. I was looking as wild as any poor postulant could be expected to look, barefoot, with my head shaved, bone-thin and hollow-eyed from our practices, hung about with some picturesque Arab rags I'd bought very dear from a Brother. The townsmen received us with honor, leading us off to one of the most imposing houses in town, which the late Cadi had built to hang out over the chasm so that he could see from his deep-set windows everything that was going on in the town. The Brothers, with me last as a postulant, filed into the big cool square room which had been the Cadi's judgment hall and sat down quietly all around the floor against the walls. It was very like being inside a giant lantern into which the fierce

154

Moroccan light bounced back up from the white terraces of the surrounding houses where the volubilis-purple morning-glories cascaded over the trellises of cane. While the Brothers muttered their long litanies, I leaned back exhausted, gazing up at the marquetry-maze of the inlaid rafters which fitted together like a giant wheeling Indian mandala overhead, holding up the high hollow pyramid of the roof.

At that point, an intense young man bristling with hostility plumped himself down beside me in a synthetic city suit. "Never in one thousand years, no Christian except a slave ever spend one night here in Moulay Youniss holy city." I looked him straight in the eye, pronouncing in Arabic as well as I could: *"There is no God but Allah and Mohamed is His prophet."* He went away sulky but apparently satisfied and, in a short time, they brought us in food which we ate where we lay on the floor—at least, I did: the others sat up around little low tables and dug in with their hands. During dinner, our host, a young man under thirty in slick city clothes who did not eat with us but surveyed the service, came over and sat beside me, feeding me little choice bits by hand. I was really exhausted but, gradually, I picked up when he told me that his grandfather had built this room hanging out over the precipice at such an angle that he could predict what was going to happen in town. You can imagine how I drank in that kind of talk! He said: "Oh, it was all very easy in those days! Until less than ten years ago, now, time simply stood all but perfectly still, here, for more than one thousand years. When Grandfather saw a man coming down one street with a knife in his hand and another man coming down another street carrying a club, he knew they were going to meet and to fight and, that in less than half an hour the whole affair would be brought

155

here to him for him to mete out our justice. He knew everything: past, present and future, you see."

True enough, there in Moulay Youniss for a momentless moment I saw life in the simplest terms of a man with a knife and a man with a club, inevitably bound to meet in the marketplace, but I saw no one around, not even my host, on whom the old cadi's mantle might have fittingly fallen. They were all rather city-soiled young men in ready-made suits and plastic sandals. Yet, I had to argue back with myself that, if they had not been, they would never have let me in here at all. The old man with the beard, whose enlarged hand-tinted photograph still dominated the hall, would never have seen fit to receive me, I was sure, but the last of the patriarchs had been killed off by the change into Modern Times. That night I slept in the spruce little whitewashed house of one of the young married men of the holy family of saints of the place. He lived down a long crooked lane hugging the inside of the old walls of the sanctified city but his tiny upper windows, mere peepholes like eyes, looked out over the battlements, down another plunging gorge choked with all the greens of myrtle, olive and aloes down to the distantly burnished newly-harvested plain. The moon came up, turning it all into one great silver tray before I could sleep because all the dogs of Moulay Younis were insanely barking the incredible news down to the astonished dogs in the faraway farms that someone who smelled like a Christian was spending a night in a house. *"Ha houwa"* they barked in hysterical choruses: *"Ha houwa! Ha ha! Ha ha!"*

When we got up just after dawn, one could look out over the holy city and see the heat already beginning to make the rosy-golden air tremble over the flesh-pink hills set out with gray-green olive trees. We sipped tall glasses of rather choco-

latey-tasting coffee with milk and ate some leathery fried
doughnuts still dripping with hot oil. All of these things were
carried in to us by a solemn sloe-eyed toddling child who
teetered in with a tray from the unseen part of the house where
the women lurked. Only our hosts, the husband and his infant
son, could freely go back and forth. We left without ever
setting eyes on the women of the household but with that
common uncomfortable feeling one always has of having been
spied on in every detail of our persons by them.

Even as we started out up the dusty lane, my left sandal
began biting into my foot. It needed a cobbler but it was much
too early to find one already by his bench in his shop, and no
question of waiting for the heat of the day to come up, so I
had to set out bravely trying a little mental manipulation on
my foot. We crossed through the silent streets of the whitewashed town as the cocks crowed and the gray and white doves
took to the air, looping stupidly under the unwavering eye of
an earlier hawk still higher up. Preoccupied as I was by my
effort to ward off the pain in my foot, which I was busy
switching from extreme heat to extreme cold, I was startled
to look down at least one hundred and fifty feet into a gorge
right under our path, gazing down for another timeless second
onto what I learned later was the original Roman hot spring,
a circular stone bath which is still in operation. A man entirely
naked was somehow suspended there directly below me in
exactly the pose of Michelangelo's Adam creating God and
the World, fainting back in the bath at the effort as he reached
out to touch Nature and make the world Be. All that lacked
was to hear him speak the Word but, of course, we were much
too far away, so I just hung there like the hawk hung above
me, not knowing whether I looked down on him or whether

157

I was back in some other life looking up at a painted ceiling through my binoculars. For that momentless moment, I was suddenly *everywhere* at once. My man slowly lifted an earthen jar of water and poured it over his own glistening head, in the very act of creating himself. I stumbled over my own sandal, almost falling, but was pushed on ahead rather roughly by one of my Hamadcha Brothers. I held my picture of that man firmly in my mind all the time we were crossing the mountain in the gathering heat of the day.

We toiled on up a long dusty path through the fragrant pines and under the olives and cork-oaks until we came to the heights of the bare ridge covered with thyme. The heat all around us hammered hard on the stones. Suddenly from the summit, the plateau of Meknes spread out a good many miles in length below the ridge we had crossed. The sky rippled over the plain like a pale blue silk tent but the floor of the valley seethed. The jumbled blocks of Meknes' houses and factories burned white-hot on the distant horizon hazed over with heat. A green gorge, gashed into the brick-red earth, split the mountain right under our feet. Sidi Hassan lies there in his white-washed tomb at the bottom of this ravine, which reminded me later of the cleft the Hamadcha make in their heads with an ax. Directly below us was a steep slanting meadow where the thousands of pilgrims had strung up their tents, tying torn sheets and old ragged rugs together with pieces of string, pinning them down with rocks or spinning them onto twisted trees and scrub, until the whole camp covering them and their women looked as light and as strong as cobwebs in the sun. Hobbled pack animals and sheep slated for slaughter; all wide-eyed, all nervously nibbling down their last useless meal, all jumped at once and skittered away as a wild pack of Black drummers padded up the path in scarlet silk tunics and black cone-shaped hats covered with cowrie shells, pounding on big-voiced African drums. The Black Brotherhood of the G'naoua gathered a group of Adepts in a minute but we came slithering and sliding right down on top of their crowd with our hysterical pipes blowing full blast. I just slumped down under an old wrecked cedar tree and collapsed.

A child offered me water in an earthenware cup but just as I was going to put my lips to its rim, the mother dashed the cup out of my hands, smashing it on the ground. I never did figure out why but I thought at the time that it must have been because she sniffed the Christian in me through my disguise. A cold shiver ran through me because I could see things were beginning to really hot up. A group of Aissaoua had begun to dance in a circle beside me: beside me, I say, but there they were almost on top of me, trampling me. As you know, they claim the Aissaoua once ate a Swiss tourist right after Independence; I don't know if it's true. Others say he was a German photographer who was filming them from the ledge of a crumbling wall when he fell into their whirling circle at the moment they usually throw a live sheep up in the air to catch it on their thumbs. Then, they tear it to pieces to eat it up raw before the sheep touches the ground. They ate the poor man, camera and all one supposes. Do you think that could really be true? Well, I did at that moment and I was even more scared when I saw that six or seven of them were brandishing live snakes in both hands as they flung off their turbans to let their long locks writhe about like a headful of hissing serpents.

The Aissaoua were hissing and kissing their snakes on the snout when a woman broke into their circle with a couple of live frogs or toads in her grip. She waved the poor things

159

wildly about by their legs, showing them off to the crowd before she crammed one into her mouth and half-swallowed it, gagging on it a while. One long-fingered webbed-foot still kicked, trailing out of the corner of her mouth. With another big gulp she got the thing down but the frog in her stomach set her jumping and screaming more than ever before. While trying to cram the second frog down, she vomited up the first one and was ignominiously dismissed as a charlatan. For a moment I thought they might tear *her* to pieces for wasting their time. I watched her trying to fight her way back into the circle of trance-dancers but her place was taken by some other wild women with eyes revulsed back into their skulls. Their long wild black hair was lengthened by ankle-length pony-tails of braided black wool, which whipped the faces of nearby spectators who began clapping along in unison to the hysterical beat of the music. When this whirlwind moved on away from the foot of the tree against which I was resting, I noticed crowds of young country yokels and boys a few feet away, packed tight around several pitchmen under rusty umbrellas running three-card games or the old shell and pea game on flimsy little portable tables which they could collapse and clear out when their lookout man called the Arab equivalent of "Hey Rube!" But, of course, at this sort of a feast there were no policemen about and no trouble. The locals apparently loved to be robbed for they threw their poor pennies away with more frenzy than I ever have seen around the expensive green tables of Monte. I got up painfully and staggered over to look closer at what they were playing. The charlatan running the deal squinted up with a grin: "Hi, Hakim!" he wheezed.

It was the same little old geezer with one eye to whom I had passed on my asthma. I began to show him my teeth as politeness and self-preservation demanded but before I could gasp out: "Isoprenaline Bronchomister Inhalator," he picked up the board made of a worm-eaten plank over two thousand years old as dated later by carbon 14 at Cambridge in England and cracked it over my head. I would like to claim I had satori at this point but I don't remember a thing until I woke up under my tree again with my half the board still firmly in my grip. A half dozen Hamadcha Brothers were intently watching me as they hunkered down in a circle a few safe paces away. I realized I was still under my blasted cedar tree looking out over the factories of distant Meknes. When I put up my hand to my head, my hand came away from my shaved skull covered with blood. My scalp had been split open as the first step of the initiation demands.

The Brothers got to their feet, picking up our silk banners whose tall gold-knobbed poles were leaning against my tree. Other Brothers helped me to my feet, making me totter over to join in the pilgrim crowd. Adepts all over were beginning to jump to our music as the Hamadcha cut loose. Groups formed on the narrow paved causeway leading down the worn stone steps cut into the side of the gorge; leading further down into the tomb of the saint. Somehow, I knew just what to do without being told but my feet hurt so much that it took me some time to get swinging along with the gang. The honky-tonk side of the fair had picked up and was going full blast under the temporary tents which were a straggling line of ragged restaurants belching out greasy smoke from the lamb kebabs roasting over open fires. Smoke trailed through the wailing music. The Adepts swirled about their drummers, hopping and whirling as they moved slowly down the narrow defile. The air thickened and apostolic fires sprang from the tops of our poor broken polls, I could swear it. Wide-eyed youngsters lined the walls, dangling their feet over our bloody heads. Now and then, apparently tranquil people who had been merely milling about in the crowd, simply sailed into trance as suddenly as if they had not expected to be swept up in it. We wound down the causeway past a battery of young Arab candy-butchers who were crying: *"Grass Green! Paris Green! Pluperfect Pink* and *Ultra Mellow Yellow!"* They were hawking bright-colored country candy from trays swarming with mountain bees out after quick honey. Rather like me with my Instant Enlightenment, I thought wryly, as I flapped even harder to beat off the bees.

Dancers around me began splitting their heads with big earthen pots which they broke on their skulls with a sound like coconuts cracking. One spinning woman kept wheeling until her long hair stood out like spokes stiff with blood, splashing everyone around like a lawn-sprinkler. We kept leaping and whirling, jumping to the music as we made it down two or three broad steps every hour. It took us from just before sunset until well after midnight to get down to the tomb illuminated by flaming torches. I had long lost all contact with my feet; they were just bloody stumps by that time. I started slipping in and out of my body to cut down the pain but I went on hopping more madly than ever. Suddenly, someone dressed in white seemed to step out of the stone wall right beside me. A glow of light blazed up behind him. His eye caught in mine and I felt that my soul had been grabbed in its gut by a longshoreman's steel hook. No need to tell me that this was the Living Saint of the place, the descendant of Sidi Hassan buried below. He materialized in the arch of a shrine halfway down the stone conduit, as if he'd stepped out to inspect me. He glanced sharply at my bloody board with which I'd been beating my brains out and shot me a look of approval. I was so sure I had heard him say to me: "Later!" that I hopped away beating it out on my brain with my board. *"Later, later! Initiator!"* I banged away on my head.

A big woman, whose broad face was all wrapped and wimpled up like some medieval nun's, abruptly shot me a keen look over the Initiator's shoulder. I tagged her for the head of the local Ladies Auxiliary but, for a long second it was Mya who looked at me out of her eyes. As it turned out later, Mya and Pio Labesse at that very moment were already steaming around the mountain in Mya's new Bentley, determined to rescue me from myself. By that time I was practically out of my skull from bashing my brains with my board and then— *Whoosh!*—and I was really out of my skull but just for the pico-second it took me to slide into what seemed to be quite another skull. I was now sitting quite calmly, high on the hillside with a group of young Moroccan students who were telling me about their exams in faulty French. Ordinarily, I don't know French well enough to tell the difference. We were so precariously seated on a pinnacle of rock overhanging the ravine that I looked down about a hundred feet and fifty, directly onto the cortege of torch-waving, howling and hopping Adepts cascading down to the tomb of the saint right below me. The courtyard of the tomb was lying brightly lit and open to the night sky, like a box of rubies between my knees. A skinny brown cow as agile as any mountain goat suddenly crashed out of a thicket and crossed over in front of me, blocking my view and nearly smothering me in her soft smell of sweet grass and manure. I almost pushed her down the precipice in my frenzy not to lose sight of the dancers below.

163

"Dancing is only for people who don't know any better," one of the Moroccan students was assuring me. "None of us ever dances. No. Of course not."

Lights twinkled and torches were flashing red and green amongst the branches in the dark canyon below me. For some seconds of super-sensibility, I felt I could read the message written in the landscape, spelled out in every little nervure and veining of every last leaf breathing beside me. My very own juices were pouring in torrents through the infinite hydraulic maze of green life-tubes linking the vines over the valley, tying down the dusty red-brown face of the earth. The dancers below me were running down the stone stairs into the sanctuary like a rope of ants which I confused with a migration of "real" ants apparently scurrying hurriedly somewhere under my feet. I was aware that the young students were bored with the scene and anxious to distract me away from it by inviting me into the big whitewashed windowless block of a house immediately behind us on top of the rock. They were practically dragging me away by force. Regretfully, over my shoulder, I caught a last glimpse of Sidi Hassan down below me, looking like a bright box full of tiny toys come magically to life.

I had the dreamlike impression that the fortress-style house had turned on a pivot to greet us rather than that we had gone around it to get in. There was all the usual lengthy Arab palaver about getting into a house; the knockings, the callings back and forth and the delays and even the mutterings as we crossed a fierce-browed old man with a white beard and turban who glared balefully down at my shoes. I looked down, too, to find myself dressed in a European suit and a pair of brown suede shoes which I felt sure I had never owned. We went through a dog-leg entrance into a big dimly-lit square patio with marble pillars looming up on all sides. A bright light blazed out from the far side as two tall doors swung back to let all the women of the house troop out and disappear grumbling into the dark again, vacating the principal salon for us men. A quick clatter of wooden clogs on marble paving, the crackling cackle of catty laughter, a derisive snort in the darkness and the women were gone again, trailing the scorched smell of resentment through the hot summer air. The desirable drawing-room was the usual Arab affair; long and narrow, lined with divans on both sides like a subway car in the Bagdad of the Arabian nights. My new friends were a self-conscious lot; stiff in their slick city clothes, sitting facing each other with their shoes on in order to be thoroughly "modern." As I stared at them in fixed fascination, something gradually went wrong with the focus of my eyes. Boyish faces shriveled and faded slowly away into starving old men pinned to the walls. I made signs I would suffocate unless I got to the only tiny window at the far end of the room where I clung to the grating, gasping not only for air but for a view of the dancing down below.

I learned later from Mya that this was the window through which she caught her first distant glimpse of our dance. There was a forged-iron grill across the casement in order to keep everyday robbers out but the curly calligraphic design included a magic inscription from the Koran to keep demons out as well and, in this particular case anyway, also to keep them in. Gritting my teeth and crossing my fingers in a way I know how, I plunged through the screen and plummeted directly down into the candlelit court of the shrine where thousands of packed people were wallowing in a conglomerate puddle of trance. The beautiful stuff really was running like a river. It

165

swept me in and swirled me seven times around the shrine before the little low door opened for me in the wall behind the tomb. My cell-brothers were already in there, stooped under the low vaulted ceiling as they strained to flatten themselves back against the curved walls. They were stripped to their skivvies and I noted that one wore homemade drawers from a flour sack still stenciled with *Gift of the American People*. I wanted to laugh and reject the whole thing but, Hassan, I really was scared.

"Later" was Now. The Brothers were all pinned to the walls by long kebab skewers thrust right through the gut and hammered on into the wall. With my hands at my back, I felt for the door but there was only smooth wall behind me waiting for my nail. I caught the sharp smell of fear from my own armpits and crotch. Under the eye of Initiator burning at me over a candle flame, I dropped off my bloody rags and stood there in my boxer shorts, hiding my rising erection. As Initiator put down the candle and stepped over it to thrust a long icy-cold finger into my abdomen, finding the place, everything went black and I woke up in a clinic on the outskirts of Tanja.

What had happened was that Amos told Mya that I'd gone off to the mountains to sink an ax in my head with the Hamadcha and she'd asked Labesse if he thought it was serious. They'd just bought a new Bentley with bread from the cardboard box and, besides, the car had to be broken in anyway so they decided to drive it about thirty-five miles an hour around Morocco, stopping in to see the feast at Sidi Hassan on the way. It was pretty late when they got there and they fell in with a group of young Moroccan students who invited them to a big house on the hill overlooking the saint's tomb. There, they had been overwhelmed by Moroccan hospitality, lots of sweet mint tea and sticky cakes, but no mention at all of the frantic festival going on right below. They could catch, now and then, the wild ecstatic music as it came swirling up from the ravine but it was effectively drowned out by not one but two transistor radios blasting and battering them with two simultaneous cacophonous programs of plastic Egyptian music from Radio Cairo. Mya insisted on being allowed to sit at the far end of the room where, through a small grilled window, she could catch a glimpse of what was going on below. Labesse had brought along a new pair of very fine night-glasses, which he had bought for the new yacht they were getting. Through the glasses, Mya caught sight of me as I disappeared, all bloody, swallowed up by the shrine. She simply raised hell until their hosts went down and rescued me. Pio went with them and, on the way down, he ruined a new pair of fine suede shoes.

I came to, days later, in a run-down clinic on the outskirts of Tanja, out beyond the foundering bullring which hasn't been used since Independa when most of the Spaniards left. The clinic was in a collapsing villa belonging to Dr. Estoque, a colleague of Pio Labesse. Dr. Manuel Estoque y San Roque was a bullfight doctor and, therefore, just the sort of man I needed for my peculiar wound but Estoque was inclined to let himself go like an *espontáneo,* wild with excitement to throw himself into the ring. He would enter my room whirling a bright saffron-yellow bullfighter's cape lined with magenta. Whipping out his scalpel, he would make a pass over my bed as he spun around, his steely black eyes glittering as he launched into staccato Spanish of which I caught only the general drift. He dressed all in black, with no shirt over his hairy belly and

167

chest but candy-pink silk socks and bullfighter's ballet slippers on his feet. Tossing his flat Córdoban hat on my bed, he would launch into a lengthy account of every move in some bullfight which had brought him a client, always taking the side of the bull. A few words of English would spurt out of him as he lunged at my bed: "*Cornada,* right up his rectum!" he'd scream. Then he'd grab up one of those wickerwork bull's heads they use for practice and he'd ram it down over his ears as he charged up and down around my bed, snorting like a bull. Every time he passed me, Dr. Estoque would toss up his horns at my bedclothes and me like a fresh bull sniffs at the mattress padding alongside the picador's horse. As he swept over the night-table with a clatter of broken glass, I reached over and cracked him across the horns with my board. When I saw him laid out on the floor, I knew I was getting better but the noise brought in the night watchman.

The night watchman turned out to be my Initiator down from the mountain. He put his fingers to his lips and, with the aid of the Moroccan male nurse, carried the doctor away for good. He wasn't much loss, for the only thing Dr. Estoque knew how to do was to give people shots of morphine with hairy fat fingers wearing gold rings. He was an old professional sidekick of Pio's but I must say one thing for Pio: he did come around to check up on me. Mya, herself, was terribly busy those days, out getting together the things for their first trip south together to the Spanish Sahara—still a difficult place to get to and almost impossible in those days. "Mya wants to buy a sort of headquarters," Labesse told me: "A big place for all of us!" Labesse seemed to think Estoque's exit quite normal and told me I'd be all right with the night watchman to look after me. He'd spoken to him at the gate, he said. I've always wondered about that. Did he know who the watchman was? Pio was a deep one: I never found out.

There was no more electricity in the clinic and the house began to crack apart in earnest. One day, while I was lying there looking at the ceiling, a plant poked its head in through a crevice and unfurled a green leaf. I thought it might be time to leave the clinic before the plants took over but my nurse, the night watchman, merely shook his head: No. By day, he took me for walks through the overgrown jungle of the garden or I would lie for hours in his little bamboo hut while he cooked delicious food for us both over charcoal. It was quite an idyllic time because we never had to speak a word. There was the language-barrier between us, that's true, but we didn't need words. At night, he sat at the foot of my bed with a candle at which he made me stare until I saw visions like a few feet of film, flickering on and off. One I kept getting showed me a vision of myself getting on a plane for Cairo, I didn't know why. Finally, because he was so persistent, I realized that I was supposed to go there and bring something back for him. These people always want presents, you know. Frankly, he ended up by being as much of a pest with his visions as a shoeshine boy is with his shoeshine box on the Boulevard.

Mya and Pio came back from their first trip to the Sahara looking tanned and fit. They were still flying that old DC-4 that poor PP had picked up off the airport in Basel, the day we first set out for Africa. When I began to get around again, I managed to catch Mya in the bar of the *Mingih*. I let her persuade me that I needed a short trip to Cairo to catch up on myself. She cashed a check for me, passing me a packet of money just before they took off for Villa Cisneros on the Tropic

BRION GYSIN

of Cancer, where they had an eye on this extraordinary piece of property they could buy on Cape Noon. That was—or is —"Malamut." Strangely enough, it was Amos Africanus who gave it the name.

To get to Egypt, I had to take Air France by Madrid, Rome, Athens before I got hung up for six hours in the airport in Beirut along with Mr. Moise Tshombe, who never did have much luck with planes. I sank into deep meditation, staring at him through a hole in my newspaper from where I sat in a very comfortable airport lounge chair. This bugged him so much he got up and ordered a taxi to drive him around the city until plane-time. I sat on there awhile, savoring my little triumph as I said to myself: "No! That's not the man!" Finally, I was picked up by the local Lebanese postal clerk in the airport who came sidling up talking of hashish, in which I'm less interested than you, dear Hassan! I couldn't care less! You can imagine my utterly unfeigned boredom when I realized he thought he was leading me on, if you please, with his tales of postal sacks full of hashish in cubes, spilled out on the floor behind his high desk everytime there was a police seizure in a plane. Then he began expounding on the utter ineptitude of all Egyptian pilots when I told him I was flying United Arab Airlines to Cairo. The plane was finally called long after midnight and we got into Cairo airport about 4 A.M.

I managed to knife my way through their panicky, practically wartime customs, grab the only cab into town and check in at the old *Hotel Semiramis* down on the Nile by dawn. That creaky old caravanserai is on its last legs. When I threw back the fitted mahogany shutters of my non-air-conditioned room in which Lawrence of Arabia might have caught forty winks between missions, I was hit by an eyeful of pharaonic Horus

170

hawks swimming like tea leaves in an amber sky through which scudded little gold and mauve, turd-turreted clouds like scrambled eggs with ketchup which kept spilling over the old British Embassy down on the banks of the gray-green greasy Nile. In my young days there, Cairo was the Garden of Allah with a coating of Turkish Delight but what I looked out on now was, apart from the Embassy, whose front lawns to the water had been sliced away by a very necessary new boulevard, simply a stack of new skyscraper-slums standing like a wall to cut off the Nile breeze from the city. I could barely bring myself to look at the new streamlined Shepheard's next door. I slammed back my shutters to get a few more hours of sleep before I shaved, showered and slid down the old marble staircase into the lobby as I had first done when I was thirteen years old. Anyway, the old elevator in the form of an Ancient Egyptian sarcophagus still hangs out its sign in seven languages: *Out of Order*. The lobby looked like a stripped tomb in which a couple of very old and creaky Greeks were still shuffling around waiting to be buried. I tiptoed across the marble floor, feeling like a ghost of myself, too. Then I braced myself just inside the curtained swinging door beyond which I knew was the blazing street and the raging rabble of dragomen, the all-too-famous Cairo guides.

Pausing to button down my inside pocket over my passport and my *Express* checks, I put one paw on my wad of Egyptian pounds in my left pants pocket and pushed through the door. I fully expected to be overwhelmed, as always; simply bowled over by a howling pack of the most ferocious guides on earth. Nothing happened: nothing at all. A few fine old men, their deeply-lined faces refined by the wisdom which comes from having manhandled many a generation of tourists, were quietly sitting or standing against the wall, looking like magnificently well-costumed and made-up extras from Central Casting waiting for their cue. Some of them even nodded almost like old friends, as if they remembered me only too well from the old days. Hailing a taxi out of the rank and not one of those tourist-trap limousines, they just let me slip through their clutches but, as I got into the cab, a little man not much bigger than a wizened fourteen-year-old, with a toothpick mustache, opened the opposite door and slid in with me. In two seconds flat, as I gave the street address of the Arab Museum in Arabic, I guessed he was the Little Man the Austerity Egypt regime details off to foreigners these days. He and I got talking, and, in the time it took us to get across Cairo, he was well launched into the story of his life with a wife whom he had divorced when he got home one day to find she had clipped all his twenty-four suits into scraps with a pair of nail-scissors. He was still with this tale when I led him into the Arab Museum, which, I felt sure, was the one place in Cairo where he had never been before. I was right: I managed to lose him in the Fatimid fretwork. Pretending I had to go take a leak behind one of the screens, I slipped out through the side door into Nasrudin Street, where I hopped onto the running-board of a crowded tram bound for the Citadel section, feeling just like James Bond. I had one person to see in Austerity Cairo and that was my old Ismaïli Imsak instructor. I meant to make that visit alone.

My mother first pricked up her ears at the mere mention of *Imsak* when she heard Aly's mother talking about it years ago, in the old days at teatime on the terrace of the *Hotel Semiramis* when I was still in short pants. Aly's mother said that Aly's father had sent him to a venerable old sheik who ran a school near the Citadel of Cairo, where he taught *Imsak*. She said the word meant "withholding" and my mother thought that meant continence, which it has nothing to do with, and asked if I could be sent. Now, *Imsak* is the art of love as an art and, eventually, a spiritual exercise for getting out of the body, right past the possessive demon of the flesh. At that age, the demon between my legs did not have to be provoked or, even, evoked. With training, this demon can be forged into a precision tool to satisty every last woman on earth. Love as lust can be icy-cool or used cruelly, eventually destroying the lover himself. The great Don Juans, like Casanova or my friend who could take a woman in a carriage or a taxi while running between two other dates, have been the matter of much re-flection in Western society whose verdict, apart from dissen-sions, has been that theirs is not an entirely enviable fate. Their trouble is that they, the Don Juans, all left before the end of the course and, because of the war, so had I. I felt I simply had to go back and attain the degree of the Permanent Peak. We hope to be able to arrange a full course for you one day, Hassan, although after twenty it is usually thought to be too late.

I may tell you, my old Master was more aghast than agog-gle to see me. I thought it very decent of him both as a man and as a magician to admit that I was the very last person he had expected to see. Anyone else I have ever come across in that line of business would have said solemnly: "I've been waiting for you, son." Not he: we got down to business at once. Because of Austerity, he no longer had his charming young assistants on hand—they had been drafted—so he took me through into the next degree of *Imsak* himself; poor old man. I'm afraid I can't tell you anything useful about that, not

173

at the moment, but I must tell you what happened when we were through. When I asked him if he wanted his money in dollars, he said: "No, dollars are dangerous!" so I handed him over all the gold I was wearing around my neck. Then, the most extraordinary thing happened for, of course, the Master must not ever give the Adept anything but his instruction: it is quite against the rules, but the old man solemnly handed me over the huge emerald you now hold. He hastened to add: "This is not for you. You must give the Seal of the Sahara to a man *whose name is not Hassan!* When you meet him, you'll know."

I got nothing more out of him except that he drew my horoscope for me rapidly with a long bony finger in the sand and, before he wiped it out again, he peered at it a moment and said: "With your new degree of ability, you will become the seventh husband of a princess." I'd already made my mind up about Mya but he didn't know that. "The seventh husband," he said with a sigh, "and the last!" He was most anxious I get out of Cairo immediately with the Emerald because he didn't want it to fall into the hands of the colonels. Every real ruler of the past has held the Seal of the Sahara at one time or other. Frankly, I cut out of Cairo with the Green Bug—for safekeeping from Customs—shoved right up my ass!

BOAC gave me tea—English nursery tea out of a thermos and wet jam sandwiches—over Aphrodite's island of Cyprus; let me down for several hot hours in Glyfada near Athens, where I caught Alitalia for Rome. There, I switched planes for Tunis. In Tunis, some anonymous nervous airline lifted me gingerly after a lot of chatter in Arabic about my American passport and dropped me into Algiers. In Algiers, I was expected: the sharklike young cop in a plastic trench-coat had my name on his list. There was an official government car to meet me, sent out to the airport by the Ministry of National Guidance. I was invited, you see, by the twin sister of Amos Africanus; Affrica Fard. She is called Freeky by everyone but her famous husband the Black Doctor, at that time still Minister of Culture: Dr. Francis-X. Fard. He always gave her her full name: "My wife, Affrica!" or, "Affrica, my wife!"

You know who I mean; Fard the Father of Fardism, as he's called throughout the Third World. Fardism is Black Power pressure applied to all those who, up until now, have always liked to think of themselves as ranging only from delicate old ivory to delicious cinnamon brown. It's hot stuff. Brother-in-law Francis is from Guadaloupe originally and culturally French but he became nationalized in order to take a portfolio in the First Revolutionary Government—what they call, now, the First Wave—right after their National War. Because he was already a world-famous psychiatrist and the internationally Prize-winning author of *Paleface and Ebony Mask,* Fard was a natural for Minister of Culture and National Guidance, too, except he wasn't a Muslim and still isn't, yet. His marriage to Freeky on top of that and the fact that there is, or he always says there is, color prejudice working against him there as much as anywhere else, including Black Africa where they find him too white. "My father sold your father!" It has given him a complex, poor man.

I've always steered clear of the psychoanalysts myself, and what I looked into of the good doctor's works has left me gasping for air. In *Islands of Night,* his memoirs of a tormented West Indian childhood during which the sun seems not to have shone even once, he has a page-long footnote on transvestites

175

in Trinidad whom, he solemnly assures us, cannot be queer because no so-called Negroes ever are. I wish I could quote it to you verbatim: it's the most preposterously and absurdly unscientific statement I have ever read in my life. One must presume, therefore, that Francis is a great deal less bright than he looks. As a man, he's a maniac. At fifty, he's still outstandingly handsome on the outside but, on the inside, he's a molten mass of scar tissue stitched together with raw nerve: a matted maze of contradictions, in fact.

"And when is the genuine Egyptian revolution about to take place?" That was the first thing he threw at me. "Are the Fellaheen ready to rise and throw their white Arab oppressors out of Egypt, yet? In all the time you were in Egypt did you ever see a black or even an aubergine-colored Egyptian driving anything but a donkey? Did you ever go into a government office and see any true Egyptian with any job better than sweeper? Cairo has a color bar higher than American Alabama!" I was taken aback. I've been going to Egypt since the family first took me there for my asthma when I was a kid and I've never looked at it that way, I guess, but I had to admit there was a lot of truth in what he said. "Even in Africa," Fard insisted, "the real Africans haven't stood up yet for their names to be called and their numbers to be numbered. There are great peoples, great nations, all over Africa and millions strong, of whom newspaper history has not yet heard even the name, the bare name! But they will! These great peoples, they who have been nothing, they will one day be all! At a cultural conference in Dakar, I met the UN ambassador from Lake Chad who tells me he can read the rock paintings in the Tibesti like a comic strip. Malraux once showed him some enormous facsimiles made at great expense for the Louvre and His Excellency had laughed. You understand, don't you? What is *pre*-history for you whites, sure enough, is plain *History,* now, for us Blacks!''

Francis is an ancient African orator. If you remember that, you'll know how to use him, I think.

"In the Beginning was the Word, say the white Semites, but the Word was *ours;* not yours or theirs. Dates prove it: the words written on the rock walls of the Sahara are admitted to be ten, fifteen, twenty thousand years old. The thickness of the desert patina over them is the measurable proof. Perhaps all that Biblical babble does recount the short shabby story of six thousand years of *White* man on earth but all the recent discoveries of genetic chemistry spell out the fact that Man with undamaged genes and chromosomes is a Black Man. All you whites and yellows and browns are genetic freaks!''

I wondered how that kind of talk went down with his government because, at the time of my visit, the Fards were still living in an official government residence, a confiscated villa overlooking the harbor with presumably socialized servants doing the housework, leaving Freeky with nothing to do at all all day but entertain me. Supremely comfortable guest rooms, good food and, besides, Freeky and I got along right away like a house on fire: I could see poor Fard's point of view. You come home from that day at the office to find your wife all flushed and glowing as she confides her life-story to some intimate stranger.

In this case, me, with my new degree of *Imsak* under my belt. The poor thing needed comforting. Freeky's tale was a sad sibling story which had hatched in a overly comfortable cocoon of Moroccan-Jewish middle-class life that simply doesn't exist in the Magreb any more. Behind the imposing façade of

177

the Villa Africanus in Anfah, the elegant Casablanca suburb down by the sea, two girls and their brother were being brought up by traditionally doting parents. Amos and Affrica are identical twins and that was hard enough already on Freeky, who at twenty-four must have looked like Diana the Huntress, good at golf and tennis, a bit of a blue-stocking intellectual and not much interested in the boys. But Mister Right did come along at last and was highly approved by the family. The complex engagement and wedding arrangements were solemnly and joyfully got under way. Launching that kind of a marriage takes months, of course, so the young man was around the Villa Africanus like one of the family for the best part of a year. He was on good terms with everybody; even difficult little sister Ana Lyse, who was only fourteen, precocious and pretty as a young cat. In an old-fashioned family like that, young girls were considered to be still of nursery age until they actually "came out as young ladies," at debutante balls. Dinner in those houses was still served at Spanish hours like ten or eleven at night so, after a drink or two of an early evening, the young man often dropped up to the nursery to kid a while with young Ana Lyse because all the others were running around about something to do with the wedding.

On the great night, when the engagement was to be publicly announced to all the foregathered families and friends, young Ana Lyse was supposed, as usual, to be up there in bed. At a couple of minutes to twelve midnight, the fiancé perchance was nowhere to be found. Everyone set about looking for him everywhere, calling his name all over the house. Someone ran up to look in the nursery but Ana Lyse had slipped out of bed and run down into the garden, spying on the party from the dark. Did he see her? Did she signal to him? That one doesn't know, but Freeky—followed by a bevy of darting maidens, alas! who screamed, spreading the news—Freeky found them both in an arbor of jasmine; Ana Lyse on her knees in a nightie, giving the fiancé a blow-job. Freeky shrieked and was carried to bed where she managed to stay for the best part of the ensuing seven years, insisting she couldn't get up because her legs were made of glass; imperiously demanding that her whole room be made pink and nothing but pink down to the very last object she could bear to have in her sight. Even all the food she ate had to be pink or tinted pink with cochineal before she would look at it on a pink tray. "Freeky analyzes all the analysts and baffles the doctors!" her mother would proudly explain to the other ladies for years.

Ana Lyse grew up utterly devoted to Freeky. For weeks at a time, Freeky would allow no one in her room but Ana Lyse and one Moroccan servant all dressed in pink caftans down to the floor and a big pink bandanna handkerchief bound around her head. Ana Lyse had a photographer's developing tray in which she dipped all the newspapers in pink cochineal solution every morning and then ironed them out dry. Freeky always read *Le Monde* flown down from Paris, the London *Financial Times* because it prints on pink paper, the old *Herald Trib* from Paris and all the local papers, of course, like *España* from Tangier; *La Vigie Marocaine, Le Petit Marocain* and the little semi-legal flyers that used to float around in those days before Independence. Ana Lyse got Freeky passionately involved in nationalist politics, psychoanalysis and all the fashionable paraphernalia of the day. She even dragged in some young Moroccan student rebels, who, like all visitors including members of the family, had to sit behind a pink silk folding-screen because Freeky insisted she was too old and ugly to be

179

seen. They gave her Fard's books, which she took like sac-
raments administered directly to her: *Awake Mother Africa!*
Obviously she thought he meant her. Then she read, *Fate and
Fetishism* and, of course, *Paleface and Ebony Mask* with Fard's
famous analysis of the Othello legend: *The Moor and the
Maiden*. That was pure Freeky, too. I don't know whether the
books were dyed pink for her or not but she found it such
heady stuff she started writing to Dr. Francis-Xavier Fard, care
of Gallimard, his publisher in Paris.

I'll leave it to Freeky to tell you one day how she eventually
got him, because, in those days, he couldn't have been further
away from her world. Dr. Fard had an ultra-fashionable practice in Paris as permanent psychiatrist to a group of dazzling
celebrities, who all called him God; *Docteur Dieu*. The fact
he was Black had everything going all for him in *that* milieu
and besides he was so overwhelmingly good-looking that it
hurt. Over the years, he had a series of seven icy-blond wives,
many of them quite well-known women: a Danish countess,
a Polish woman writer, a French bombshell-type movie star,
the racing-pilot daughter of a well-known political figure and
a couple of other wives I seem to forget. And throughout all
the wives, he had a Black mistress called Catherine de Saint
Kitt, whom a lot of people claimed was really his sister or
half-sister from Guadaloupe. People said, too, they slept three
in a bed. I don't know about that: never saw it, myself. Catherine ran a dance group called *"La Chapelle de Sainte Catherine,"* giving Black Mass cocktails in the garden of Fard's
hotel particulier in Neuilly; absolutely the most chic thing in
Paris. Everybody was there. Authentic voodoo initiation ceremonies were performed for the fashionable ethnologists and
the social anthropologists and all their publishers who came

with the literary lions of the day and their ladies. There were always lots of well-dressed women about and plenty of starlets ready to drop all their threads as soon as the fashionable beat-niks present led the way into the fray with the members of Sainte Catherine's choir. Even middle-aged intellectual French Protestant pederasts plunged into the fun. Photographers were barred. Dr. Fard, always dressed all in white, moved through this scene like the Master with his current cool blond wife on his arm. Fard could whip it up, freeze the action or cool it all into slow motion with just one nod to Kitty de Saint Kitt, who stood there black and bare-assed in the bushes with a knife in her hand ready to sacrifice a kid or a cock.

Fard picked up a lot of politically powerful friends at his parties or got through to them through their wives on the analytic couch. Right from the start, he gave it to them straight and he gave it to them hard: *"Pour Voir Noir!"* "To See Black!" and a cunning pun on Black Power! They loved it. That was the title of his long poem he read to Malraux and the rest of them when he won his first prize. Along with Senghor and Césaire, Fard is certainly one of the Nabobs of Negritude. Aragon has him in his anthology—had to have him in there because Francis won the prize, too, from his old pal Chou En-lai in the East. His psychiatric practice took him all over the French-speaking world; consulted by a sterile empress in one Moslem land, he was immediately called to handle an outbreak of hysteria in the harems right after premature polit-ical emancipation in another. Contacts made that way even-tually took him to the Casablanca Conference, where Ana Lyse waylaid him in the lobby of the *Anfah Hotel,* begging him to cross the street with her to the Villa Africanus, where Freeky was lying, after seven long years still in bed. Dr. Fard was on his way to the airport where he was to enplane with Ben Baraka and the other members of the First Revolutionary Government in Exile but he remembered her letters forwarded to him by Gallimard, so he agreed to see her for a few minutes. As they tell it, Francis simply walked in kicking over the pink silk folding-screen and snapped his fingers at Freeky to get out of bed. She would have followed him to the airplane if he'd let her, still wrapped up in her pink sheets.

You remember what happened to that plane? How it got off course over the International airlanes over the Mediterranean and was scouted into Algiers by French military planes? 'Way back in the fifties I'm talking of. Well, that was his first contact with the boys he eventually threw in his lot with politically. After the revolution, he became naturalized in order to enter the government; what they now call the First Wave. He was still a First Wave minister when I first knew him. Both he and Freeky were trying to persuade me to fly down to Tam to stay with the younger Africanus sister, Ana Lyse, who was down there married at the time to a young Polish deep-strata geologist on contract to the government to look into their subsoil for them. He would provide transportation to take me to see Pigeon Gorge, the name the French had given to the great canyon that splits the Tibesti.

Pigeon Gorge is a cleft running nearly one hundred and fifty miles through the mountains, entirely covered on both sides of the rock face with prehistoric paintings infinitely bigger than any billboard in America; hundreds of feet high; advertising the Foulba Way of Life: pastoral, peaceful and moderately prolific for the past ten, fifteen or twenty thousand years. The Foulbas first got the Word. Needless to say, this is news to the Foulba, at this point. After all, the last Foulba of the day pulled out of there at least a couple or more thousand years ago, as the Sahara dried up behind them. Few Foulba, if any, have even ventured back there ever since. Nor would they ever have dreamed of claiming it back, as they do, or demanding precedence in the UN, even, as the First on Earth with the Word, if Fard hadn't put them up to it first. Fard first demanded the limits of pre-history be moved back to accommodate them: that's Fardism at work.

"Black Man," preaches Francis-X. Fard, "must sweep away forever that white man's fable of Genesis and all the curt, brutish history of the last six millennia. All that rubbish may, indeed, be the history of a sub-race of white freaks first produced by genetic mutation about six thousand years ago but that is of no concern to us. In the Beginning was the Word? *Right!* Word came, therefore, before Light. *Ergo:* the Word was Black!

"Go take a look at what's written all over our mountains down beyond Tam. I'll have my girls at the office make you a copy of the material I've gotten together on this, along with a preface I'm writing for the first book to come out on the subject in French."

I clearly remember, Freeky looked frightened and said something like: "Don't you think I should type it, dear; here at home?" Francis simply snapped back "No!" and that was that. Some spy in his office ran off a Xerox for the eyes of the colonels who were already preparing their coup. That was part of the evidence used against Fard when they overthrew the First Wave government and arrested him, too. Jailing the ex-ministers was simple but, for reasons of international cultural prestige, even the junta jibed at Francis. In the end, they sent them all down to Tam and put them in prison but with Dr. Fard nominally, at least, in charge of the place. The fort is new since you were down there; a military marvel delivered by the Chinese and assembled in a star-shape of stainless-steel sheets designed to bounce back the rays of the sun: I don't know that it works. The joke of it all is that Fort Tam was ordered by the very same First Wave ministers who find themselves prisoners there in Present Time. Francis is a prisoner, too, really; although his title is splendid enough: Doctor in Charge of the Desert and Civilian Governor of Tam. The fort is now named Tam Psychiatric, but everyone calls it Star Citadel. The junta colonels announced to the world press: "Our revolution does not devour its children: it sends them to hospital!"

We've seen this hospital, from thirty thousand feet up; before we were warned off by their radar. It was very clear and we got some good pictures. In them, the fort looks more like a crinkled pop-bottle top at the bottom of the ocean than it does like the Chinese twenty-four pointed star. It can look, if the light hits it right, like a gem on a spar of black glass set out on a tray of fine sand in a jeweler's window. Due west of there lies Reggan, the atomic center set up by the French. Beyond that, even as the jet flies in a couple of long hours over nothing but idle desert, you begin to see the blue wash of the Atlantic where it separates out from the blue of the sky. Below it, the endless gold bar of the beach bends over a whole arc of the earth and, in the middle of that like a stone set in a ring, stands "Malamut," alone. Hassan, that's heaven: that's home! You'll see what we'll do together down there; we'll start a new world.

184

Now, what we want to do with you is . . . or, rather: what we want *you* to do with us is . . .

Thaaay!

Yes, Mya; I'm out here recording . . .

Sorry, Hassan, but that was Mya for *Imsak,* again; it's a regular ritual with us like prayer. We like to sustain at least an hour of Ultimate Orgasm several times a day, every day, you see. Or, rather, you don't! No need at all to put on a show, is there; my dear man whose name is not Hassan? It's perfectly simple: I won't. You'll have to work out your own ratio with Mya when you meet her: I can only tell you again that I am her seventh husband and last. You can see, can't you, how easily life itself could become just one more fretful fantasy for Mya, as it often has done for many a girl a lot less rich. Mya packs so much power herself that the trick is to keep making it real. What is real can be real only in Present Time, you'll admit, and that—I'm sure you follow me—is what *Imsak* is about. The consort "withholds" the Queen "Be" in Perpetual Present Time on the prong of his prick. Without her phallic plungings several times a day into real reality and beyond, she could not be what she is. I'm not her Pygmalion: I don't claim to have created her deep-strata geology but I have staked it all out. If she should start singing you siren songs about becoming Sultan of the Sahara or some such, just throw it out of your mind: steer clear of that reef. Mya will not, indeed cannot, remarry unless she comes across a man higher in *Imsak* than I am and I am about to take the Fourth Degree, now.

We are, all of us, about to enter Phase Four, as our cable to "Malamut" ordered today; but each one of us, naturally, has his or her own move to make in the game. I abhor the word and hate having to use it to refer in any way to our activities, but Mya, being a woman, has to be "played with," of course. Do not make the mistake of playing the Seal over to her; no matter what she may do to try and get it away from you, under any pretext. The moment Mya is in full possession of the Seal of the Sahara, she'll drop you and it so fast that she'll shatter both of you: you'll think the whole thing never happened at all. *Imsak,* call it "Withholding," if you like, that is the only control. Withhold the ultimate object from Mya or you are lost. Mya's ambitions are, like Mya herself, potentially limitless. It would not be good for her or for anybody else if she became what she wants to be: the Ace of Space!

As the man who first uncocked this power-release in Mya by thrusting Present Time perpetually into her, my own next move can be accomplished only in silence—utter and absolute silence. I mean this quite literally, Hanson; don't laugh. I am about to become as mum as a monk. Time is running out and so is this side of the tape. I have little more to say beyond what I feel I owe you as a fellow-male who has been drawn abruptly into this tale of ours. *Mektoub:* It was written! The rest is up to you. Be as cautious as you can, of course, for you know that as soon as you have anything like a kingdom, enchanters and conjurers will always drop in from all over Creation to take it away from you, naturally enough. The Saharan Scarab you hold in your hand is the pre-hieroglyphic Emerald Beginning and Ending of Word. So, spin out the rest of the story with Mya. She will be only too glad to give you a glimpse of what our common future holds in store for us all in the Sahara.

186

One thing. If it should ever become too much for you, Hanson, and you really want out, I'll tell you one thing you really should keep to yourself: the World is contained in that Word. If you have understood, there is no other mystery. The Way Out is to permutate the *zikr:* *"Rub out the Word . . ."*

6

The next thing I knew was the telephone ringing outside the door of my room in the old run-down *Hotel Duende,* where I was staying: down in the Socco Chico, sure enough. As I woke and reached out automatically for my keef and my pipe, my ear caught the insistent flicking of a dry end of Thay's tape still whisking around and around on the UHER beside my bed. I rolled over to switch it off and checked on the battery. It hadn't run down too far so I couldn't have been out all that long. I pulled out the bedside lamp and plugged the UHER in to recharge. My watch had stopped but I could tell more or less what time it must be by the roar of voices coming up through my shutters from the little closed square of the Socco below. The telephone went on ringing out in the hall. In the Duende, they usually let it ring on like that until it rings off by itself. I was surprised to hear somebody answering it: *"Halloo Yass Halloo!"* It sounded oddly like Hamid and, when I peered out, so it was: Hamid in an elegant new white on white striped-silk jellaba; short because he is short, the jellaba swung on the ground. "Yass, the Merikani," he was

188

saying as he handed me over the phone. I was wondering where he'd got that very expensive jellaba from as, over his shoulder, I saluted a little group of his cousins the Master Musicians in the dimly lit hotel hall. They had shucked off their bright yellow leather slippers and hunkered down against the cold tiled wall with their white woolen hoods up over their heads. They gave me quite a shock, looking so countrified.

"Hello," I said into the receiver, automatically imitating Hamid: "Yes, hello."

Hamid was hopping up and down in front of me making mad monkey-faces; wild gestures apparently meant to intimate something about the caller, I couldn't tell what.

"Yes! Hello, Hassan," said the voice on the phone, so deep I thought for a flash it was a man's: "You *are* very quick!"

"Glugh!" was all I could answer to that.

"Good, Hassan! Quite right! Now go back to your keef-pipe until twelve o'clock midnight but don't overdo it. I just phoned to say that Thay won't be able to make it, tonight, but our plan for the picnic still holds good. I'll pick you up in my car in the Socco at twelve on the dot."

"Picnic lady!" Hamid was hissing at me as she rang off. Hamid was kissing my shoulder, hugging my arm as he jumped up and down: "Picnic lady very good. Very big. Very rich!"

Being the sort of hotel it is, we all went back into my room to blow some more keef. Master Musicians smoke all the time: they've always got either a flute or a sebsi of keef in their mouths. We all beamed and embraced each other like brothers going through all the salaams and salutations like we hadn't seen each other for a week of Moslem Fridays. Then, they all settled themselves comfortably on the floor while I climbed

back into my sagging brass bed with Hamid hopping up alongside me holding a big bag of grass. A pair of pipes shuttled
back and forth between us as we went through the ceremonies:
I needed some time to get all my buttons done up and work
on this plot. Now, that crazy white cat called Thay: him washing out like that right away! That was no good for openers:
what did he mean: *"Rub out the word"?* His tale was done,
I could see that and I was glad I had it on tape. And that other
voice: that was Milady Mya, was it? Well, that wasn't the first
time I'd heard that transatlantic tone. But: "What's all this
pack of pied pipers of yours doing down off their mountain?"
I asked Hamid point-blank. At the same time, it ran through
my head that this grimy group could well be my bodyguard;
safety in numbers. And: "Hamid! How the hell do *you* hook
up with the Himmers? Tell me that!"

One of the Master Musicians produced a special holiday
pipe out of his wicker picnic hamper; a primitive clay water-
pipe smoked, as a rule, only during the holy month of Ramadan
and at night. Time out for distraction: this particular Master
was thrown into paroxysms of gurgling delight at being able
to fill his water-pipe from my tap. The mere idea of water
leaking out of a wall like that instead of being caught spilling
out of rocks or having to be drawn from a well tickled him
all to hell. The Masters had all come tumbling down from
their village to see me in town and, besides, the big city is
full of thrilling adventure, as everyone knows. While Hamid
was herding them through the Grand Socco market this afternoon, a lady stepped out of a very big car and hired them to
play their Pan pipes at a picnic, tonight, in a cave up the coast.
It seemed not at all far-fetched to them that this was a picnic

190

being given for me. "Well, Hamid," I said between pipes, "and what does she look like?"

Hamid rolled his eyes around in his head, making a globular gesture like: "Big!" High praise in Africa and, besides, Hamid's not huge. A lady of leisure about Tanja was once heard to say that Hamid would have been a much taller man if so much of him hadn't been turned up in cock—his famous big brush. Just as I was going to ask him if he'd ever heard of *Imsak,* he bounced off the bed and shot over to the window; having heard, as we all had, a roar like a riot in the Socco Chico below. As Hamid threw back the shutters, the breath of the beast in the crowd came in like a blast of hot air. My first thought was a lynching but I left that lay in Louisiana and, translating myself into Present Time, I said, getting up out of bed: "What is it, Hamid: the Whale?"

My window in the *Duende Hotel* was like a loge in an old Venetian theatre from which I could look straight down onto the paved stage of the Socco Chico, where absurd theatre has been going on in dozens of languages, right around the clock every day since forever, perhaps. Visible tale-ends of old-fashioned Arab plots torn alive out of the Thousand Nights and One Night shuttle back and forth under your eyes like bright threads running through a gloomy loom of out-of-work cats slapped into uniform Levis. More up-to-date, highly colored plastic plots tend to pass through after midnight and the bell was tolling, now. There was standing room only down there where a thick throng of extras was boiling about a gigantic old Rolls Royce touring-car which had beached center stage. The crescendo of circus-noise died away like the tide rolling boulders out to sea as a very large lady I took to be the Queen

191

of the Tuareg got out of her car. She stood on the running-board in a hell of a hairdo of beads braided onto her head, clanking her barbaric jewelry and flapping her long desert-blue robes. My first guess was: She's selling something like a magical embrocation of ostrich eggs, for example; so I turned away, saying: "Don't look at it, Hamid; it's on television. Some new kinda 3-D TV!"

Then, I squealed like a stuck Christian pig when Hamid suddenly made a dive past me and scuttled across the room to unplug my UHER from the wall: he is strictly forbidden ever to touch a machine of mine. He pulled out the jack to the charger, checked to see the tape was properly threaded before he packed the UHER expertly into its traveling case, me still protesting, and, slinging the holster-strap around my neck like a halter, dragged me out of the room, trailed by the Master Musicians. One of them threw my black burnous from the Sanara over my shoulders while we slid down the stairs. As we hit the Socco, a general yelp went up from the crowd when the lady flung up her arms melodramatically, and all the men fell back one sudden step, heels hard on each other's toes. A child wailed out: *"Cinema!"* as Hamid, my handler, hurried me forward like a punchy old prize-fighter being hustled against his better judgment into the ring. I had the impression the lights went up full and, because it seemed to be expected of me, I kissed the lady's hand to a round of applause from the mob. She got back into her car and gave it the gun. Dogs and children ran yapping as old graybeards with turbans waved the young riffraff out of our way when we followed her into the car and drove off to the cheers of fools who knew no more than we did what it was all about.

Now that I remember it, all that she said was "Get in!"

I suppose I didn't dare look at her: anyway, my eyes were glued to her neat square bare blue feet planted on the pedals of the Rolls. As we were spinning so silently up steep Siaghine Street, I ventured to break into the ticking of the clock with some mumbled remark about the car. "Yes," she said, "it's a Rolls I picked up cheap out of an old novel by Lawrence Durrell." What the hell kinda talk is that? I thought to myself and shut up. Our big leather seats were set apart like two thrones in the front of the car but I could smell that the lady had drenched herself in a bottle of *Bint El Sudan* before leaving her tent. I remarked that all the little knobs on the fittings of the car had fat little closed crowns on them over the letter F. She laughed and confessed that she had bought the old bus at the King Farouk sale in Cairo, years ago now. "It's all solid gold," she admitted, "and the biggest one Rolls ever built. Even the Nizam of Hyderabad . . . you know, the rich one in India . . . never had the horsepower or the head-room that I've got."

We barely skinned through a narrow alley and swirled out around the Grand Socco, nearly taking a strolling policeman with us as we went. We chopped like a great golden hatchet through the secondhand-clothes market where they sort out the bundles of rags from America. My Master Musicians were bunched up in the back of the car like five live white teddy-bears in their rough woolen jellabas. I leaned around to snuff up their good country smell: lanolin from lambs' wool, wood-smoke, spicy Moroccan cooking and keef. I saw Hamid had found a handy little folding "jump seat" in front of the built-in bar and was helping himself to a mixture of drinks. Knowing only too well how he can be with alcohol in him, I reached around to stop him but he batted back my paw, proudly point-

193

ing to the crown on his glass, as if that gave him royal permission to drink. Then, he unbuckled his prizewinning chuckle as he gave the back of my hand a wet kiss, saying fondly: "Who is whose guru? Fuck off!" It sounded more like: *Hooz hooz gooroo foo koff!"*

"So," said the lady, "you speak Arabic together."

We were shooting through "Suicide Village"; so called by all the rich foreign villa-dwellers on the Old Mountain, who sail through it all the time at top speed. This narrow paved alley swarms like a market all day and all night. We were cutting through traffic like a hot gold butter knife through butter, until that Diving Diana out there on what the English call the "bonnet" of the Rolls, stuck her golden nose right up a camel's ass. Pandemonium broke loose in the street. Moors who know me and know Hamid were squashing their noses against the glass with their hands over their eyes, popping their eyes at me, the lady and the car. The lady gave a blast of her great golden hunting-horns and we swept on, scattering man and beast in our wake. We whipped around the Third Commissariat of Police at Jews' River on two wheels and flashed on out past the Catholic cemetery at Boubana; then, turning sharp right, we flew up the New Mountain Road through the night on this slightly worn magic carpet of hers. There could be no doubt, either, that this was really her car; the way she drove that pile.

My musicians passed me up a slim pipe and, taking the regulation three drags, I spat out the live coal very neatly in a solid-gold ashtray set into what must be called the "instrument panel."

194

"Do you have to smoke that stuff all the time?" the lady asked.

We whirled past the governor's mansion and Caca Culo castle in the dark and other big estates with their private parks to the right and the left of the road until we came to a spot where she changed gear and we turned off the pavement into a trail down under the trees. I had always intended to explore these big wooded properties running down from the crest of Old Mountain Road to the high cliffs hanging over the Straits of Gibraltar, but I certainly hadn't figured to do it at night. We were bumping down a water-worn lane under lacy acacia trees until the headlights picked up a dark grove of cedar, practically hanging over the cliff. "It's no worse on the car, really," the lady was saying as she ground the back axle over a rock, "than the road from Cairo to Alex."

She flipped on her lights, blinking them twice, and an old crooked Arab fairy-tale crone, with a pointy straw hat like a cone on top of her red and white striped veils and long raggedy cloak, stepped out of a thicket with a lantern in hand, waving us on. "That's Calypso, my caretaker," the lady said. "When I took over this property, I found her already installed in my cave. As if I didn't know the place was magic enough . . . some doddery old English don has been writing to tell me it is . . . actually and historically according to him . . . Calypso's Cave. I thought calypso was a steel band from the Barbados until he sent me this book to curry my culture. I can't think how he got my address . . . probably figures I'll invite him out here to explore it but he's got another think coming, I guess. . . . Since we've found you, Hassan . . . and the dollar has . . . has gone . . . well, wobbly. . . . I've wiped

195

out my Foundation. The Fundamental has been found. No! . . .
let *them* carry the baskets, Hassan. Get out of the car . . .
from here on you walk.''

The loony old woman with the lantern was leading us down
a path around the face of the cliff while Hamid and five little
musicians trailed us fearfully in the dark, toting their instruments and the wicker picnic hampers full of food and drink
which had been packed in the "boot" of the Rolls. We stumbled around a big shoulder of rock and came into a nice little
nook, looking bright Paris-green in the white light of our gasoline lamp. A spring of clear water, ringed with dwarf fern
and moss, seeped out of the rock close by the entrance to a
big dry cave in which a little fire was dancing away by itself.
Below us and so far below that the distance looked dizzy, a
highway metaled with moonlight ran twenty miles or more
across water to the Rock of Gibraltar swimming away in veils
of blue night. The old Arab witch gave a sharp cackle to her
half-wild pack of flat-headed yellow dogs, from whom Hamid
and the musicians cringed away, reaching for clubs. Madame
Mya stood in the mouth of her cave with her back to the
firelight, flapping her veils as if she were about to take off as
she intoned:

"Ulysses of Ithaca, welcome back home!"

Then, in a voice so different it might have come out of
another woman, she said:

"You know, Hassan . . . you and I must be the two most
American Americans who ever stepped into this enchanted
cave. After all . . . I'm Pocahontas and you're Uncle Tom!''

Wow! Wait a minute, lady! Uncle Tom! That's a hell of
a thing to be tagged at this point in the game: where did she
pick up on a story like that? But, then, I reflect on how very

easy I am to research: Professor Ulys O. Hanson, III, of Ithaca, N.Y. So, after all, I shrug. There may be a little Tom in the best of us, may there not? And, in my own case, casting about in the darkest corner of my mind, I do recall some cousins in Canada, spell their name different, who admit—just admit, mind you—to descent from the runaway slave turned Black preacher Underground conductor and agricultural colonist in Canada with a side show at the Crystal Palace where he was presented to Queen Victoria and was lost. Poor man had nothing but troubles from then on in: trouble with John Brown at his congress before Harpers Ferry, trouble with the Abolitionist Boston bankers and preacher-trustees of his colony, trouble with the white folks down to the end. Poor Tom! How much can he owe to H. B. Stowe and how much does he owe to himself? He billed himself for half a lifetime as The Real Uncle Tom, because he gave her world rights to his not so exclusive story in exchange for a nice hot dinner under the kitchen sink. White folks! I was thinking as I turned on my UHER and started recording Mya while she pinched out some pennies for poor old Calypso, who slunk off after her dogs:

7

SHE

She just took her money and went away, didn't she . . . not
one word out of her, did you notice? Typical . . . isn't it?
That old Berber witch . . . or whatever she is . . . seems to
think this is *her* cave and *I'm* paying *her* rent for it. Well,
never mind . . . one pays for being an American, I suppose
. . . and we *do* screw them in so many other ways . . . all the
time, don't we? *Calypso's Cave!* You can feel this really *is*
Calypso's old cave, can't you? To Homer this was the end of
the world where his little wine-dark sea ran away through these
straits into nothingness . . . *the Maelstrom* . . . *America!* That
fabulous coastline of southern Spain, strung out over there
through the blue, must have looked just about the same . . .
except for the lights, I suppose, that frame it . . . and this
same big yellow balloon of a moon sailed up there between
Gibraltar and Ceuta, the Pillars of Hercules. Funny, isn't it,
to think that our dollar sign comes from a snake wound around
those two pillars . . . the serpent Baby Hercules strangled in
his cradle. That's a really *mad* image for money . . . now,

isn't it? What does it *mean*, Hassan . . . or don't you care, really?

What *do* you care about, Hassan-Ulysses . . . only your keef and young dancing boys? Well, don't fret . . . we have more and better of all that down in "Malamut" than even the Old Man of the Mountain ever dreamed a hashish-dream about. Why, all this cool green and blue country north of the Tropic of Cancer is *nothing* compared with what I've got going down south. You know it, yourself . . . the Sahara's pure gold! You've heard of a people called the Foulba, of course . . . the Peuls . . . the most beautiful boys in the world, bar none. You must, *at least,* have seen books of photographs of their ritual beauty contests for which the young men begin preparing at puberty . . . when they're first allowed to wear makeup and start earning their jewelry. Along with huge Floradora Girl ostrich-feather hats and a little leather apron they take off for the contest . . . that's all they *do* wear . . . their jewels. Well, they'll be holding their finals this month . . . and guess where! . . . in the courtyard of *my* castle down there. You see, Cape Noon is their capital rock and on *that* rock *I* built my house: "Malamut" . . . where the Tropic of Cancer cuts out across the Atlantic on the map. The Foulba first got there about the time anyone's worm-white ancestors . . . and I'm afraid we've both *got* them Hassan . . . by the time those whites were first grubbing their way up out of the caves, the Foulba had written their own lengthy literature on several hundred long miles of mountain before the Sahara began to dry up all around them. Driving their lyre-horned cattle ahead of them, the Foulba went west . . . and wandered on out of history. When they *did* find the water they were looking for, it stopped them . . . the sea . . . the Atlantic. On the low, level shore they saw my big rock sticking up in that landscape as sudden as Mont Saint Michel on its tidelands. The Foulba say "Malamut's" head touches heaven. Cape Noon, they call: Heaven Rock. "Malamut" is *my* secret garden. "Malamut" and the Foulba, today . . . nearly two million in all of them . . . belong solely to *me,* Hassan: I own not only the Foulba . . . we're *absorbing* new ethnic groups of previously nameless nomads in the southwestern Sahara every day. How many of them could you possibly *have* in a lifetime Hassan . . . or would you prefer to possess what's left of your old enemies, the Blue Men? I'm telling you, Hassan . . . in Present Time, *I* am the most powerful woman in Africa!

The Word, Hassan! All you have to say is the Word . . . when you know it . . . and *you* can be Emperor of Africa! Emperor Hassan the First! You *do* understand . . . don't you, the move Thay has made . . . was *obliged* to make only today at noon? You *must,* after all, because Thay laid his last words on *you,* my dear . . . not on *me.* That *transfer* of the Saharan Seal to you *could* make *you* the Master of Words when you know what to *do* with it . . . and no one on earth can tell you but *you,* you know. Thay calls it the Roller, rolling out all the words in the world over and over, again and again, since the first Word was spoken. What you hold in your hand is the emerald Beginning and Ending of Words, Hassan . . . as a woman, naturally I *fear* you! As a woman, too, all I can tell you is what *not* to do. . . . That's my nature. *Don't* . . . for example . . . don't press the Seal into wax or putty or anything soft . . . you haven't tried doing that, have you? *Don't* do anything silly and artistic like inking the Seal and running it onto paper. Just *don't,* that's all . . . don't! That's printing,

200

you see . . . rolling out replicas. We'll go into that later. In Present Time, down on Cape Noon, we're fed up with replica Foulbas, you see. They've bred true-blue for so long that they're *all* practically *identically* beautiful! The one perfect specimen multiplied to infinity . . . and why *not?* . . . in some sort of biological barbershop mirror. Dr. Francis-X. Fard has produced a little prose-poem pamphlet praising the Foulba for being the one people we know in the world who have come up with not *one single* object of culture in all their lone history . . . not even a knot, let alone the cord to tie one in . . . not even a *pot!* They boil things by dropping a red-hot rock in a leather sack of water or milk. The Foulba have known exactly how *not* to let them themselves be tied down by *things!* They're innocent . . . beautiful . . . *pure!* Until I laid hands on them, they'd always been as free as the wind. Long, long ago they gave up their writing . . . except just for fun and to teach the young ones . . . they write in the dust where the wind will be sure to erase it. So much for the Word. The one big problem with them is the one you can guess . . . *overweening* vanity! That's how I was able to grab them up cheap . . . the whole lot. When *I* buy, it's *always* in lots . . . things come so much cheaper . . . and the *cheapest* one can get something for in this life, after all, is for *nothing,* don't you think? That's what I like to pay, really . . . nothing at all. You see, I have my *own* little ways of getting what *I* want in life. I have a trick or six I picked up right here in Africa.

This particular, ah, product . . . I owe to Dr. Pio Labesse, an Old African Hand who was . . . well, *really* . . . my second husband and *not* the sixth as the newspapers always say. I'm his widow . . . or *was*. I'm sure Thay has painted you the worst *possible* picture of Pio but, truly, I owe him a lot . . .

poor Pio. He had all the lore of North Africa at his fingertips,
literally . . . but he lost it. He left it where he is, now . . . in
the Past. This one, ah, product . . . is something I've gone
into scientifically . . . chemically . . . and refined it out of all
recognition, you see, but . . . perhaps, *essentially* . . . it *is*
the same thing the original Calypso brewed up when that *other*
Ulysses dropped in. What I've done is bring the whole thing
up the time-scale to bring it in line with Present Time, so . . .
Hassan-Ulysses . . . in *Present Time* . . . *Look!*

The lady who owns this cave is a nymph . . . a very *wise*
nymph who knows not just a thing or two but . . . at *least* . . .
a thing or sixteen! There are also thirty-second degree nymphs
and she may *well* be one of these . . . or she might be of even
higher rank, who knows? For the moment, that doesn't matter
because she's . . . well, how shall I put it? . . . a fairly *simple*
provincial nymph, in her own way. She doesn't have a villa
with a swimming pool on Capri, like Circe, but she's doing
all right . . . right here in Africa. There's a full moon . . . it
is night. Straight down there . . . right down where those
Arabs are night-fishing . . . there, you see it? . . . a boat. She
sits here, perfectly still on this rock, interviewing the moon
as it crawls on its knees across the floor of her cave to her
feet. Down there . . . rooting around in the brush under this
cliff, she hears what might be a boar . . . a wild boar or an
even more dangerous animal . . . *Man!* Nothing happens for
quite a while and then . . . abruptly . . . there *is* a real man
peering over that ledge!

"I am the nymph Calypso," she says, drawing herself up.
"Who are you?" The intruder is somewhat taken aback. He
gulps and gives her what sounds like a phony title: "The king

of Ithaca,'' he mumbles . . . taking a good look around. When he spies all the edible goodies she has stored up in the back of her cave, he calls up his men to share in a good hot supper at her expense . . . with champagne! *Charles Heidsieck* champagne, as a matter of fact. Here, Hassan . . . just let *me* pour some more of my wine. . . . *So!* She takes out a vial and pulls out the stopper with her teeth . . . like this . . . and drops three drops of a magical elixir into his glass. ''Here, drink this up, my Lord Emperor of Africa!'' she says. Here, Hassan . . . cheers . . . drink up!

Nothing happens for quite a while, of course . . . the stuff doesn't take effect immediately, naturally. He wipes his lips and hands his half-empty cup on to his second-in-command, who drinks deep and passes it on around the circle of men, who finish it up. Calypso looks wise. I don't suppose we could get your magicians . . . I mean, your musicians to share this champagne with us right now, could we? . . . or I'd show you what I can *do* with this stuff. This is *Borbor,* Hassan . . . and you've just *taken* a dose. No, don't worry . . . so have *I,* so I'll be along on the trip with you. Wait! Nothing at all happens to Ulysses, Hassan . . . *that* is the trick! Borbor makes *him* more than ever what he *really* is . . . every *inch* a king! His followers, now . . . well, that's something else again. My sister Circe used to turn them into what they *are* . . . into pigs, for example. My caretaker . . . Calypso, here . . . might have more mangy dogs to feed and fend off if we gave your musicians some *Borbor,* tonight. On that *other* occasion . . . or so I am told by my potty professor from Oxford . . . Ulysses threw back his big black burnous and, under it, he was wearing . . . not a UHER tape recorder . . . my dear . . . but a breastplate looted from Troy, made of purest soft-solid gold.

203

In Present Time, I propose you hang this Order of the Golden
Fleece over the microphone around your neck. This chain was
made by Benvenuto Cellini for the Habsburg Emperor Charles
whose Spanish grandmother, Queen Isabella, had been far-
sighted enough to pick up the Americas for him . . . quite
cheap . . . he lost them, of course. This valuable bauble once
belonged, too, to the Rothschilds, who wore it to fancy-dress
parties in Paris. You might attach the Emerald Seal to it with
a thread or a fine thong. Don't use a gold chain . . . it would
cut into the stone.

What happens . . . *Now?* why . . . in his case, that *first*
Ulysses took seven long years . . . so the story goes . . . to
find out who he *really* was . . . not the lady's husband at *all!*
Now, Thay Himmer the Seventh, last White Rajah-Bishop of
the Farout Isles, and I . . . although we've known each other
for seven years . . . have been married just *seven weeks!* That
leaves me an American Ranee . . . if I *want* to be! But, shucks,
that ain't nuttin', no more! Ranee of a long-lost kingdom the
size of a coral atoll on the other side of the world, lost in the
middle of the Pacific? Thanks very much but no *thanks!* I
mean, I simply *adore* Thay . . . who wouldn't? . . . He *is*
such a *child* . . . besides, it's very handy in Present Time to
be a U.S. citizen BUT . . . I have my eye on *much* bigger
game right here in Africa. Africa, today, is where it *really* can
happen. . . . *Watch me!* On the other hand, I wouldn't *dream*
of divorcing poor Thay . . . he's an absolute *elf! And,* he's
quite right: It's going to suit me to have a husband who never
talks. . . . Poor Thay, he's so helpless. . . .

Thay Himmer was brought up helpless, like royalty . . .
until Japan overran the Farouts when Thay was just six. The
Himmers had founded the Farouts when the first Bishop Him-

mer of Hyannisport, Mass., got himself there first on a
Clipper . . . and waded ashore with his Bible and his wife.
I'm sure you think you know the rest of the story. . . . "Stop
the music, stop the dancing, wear Mother Hubbards and get
down to work. . . ." but, *no!* The Himmers were different.
In the next generation, the family went native to conform with
some local prophecy which allowed them to crown themselves
rajahs with full native pomp. They introduced sugar-planting,
built a refinery . . . a bakery, a brewery . . . and grew *very*
rich. Always under the American flag, of course, and . . .
while they married no native girls . . . the Himmers were
always *very much* of the East. They shopped in Singapore
instead of San Francisco, for example . . . things like that.
Black sheep of the family, like Thay's queer Uncle Willy, fled
to Hong Kong and Macao before settling down on a remittance
in some super-civilized place like Peking. Girls of the family
were rather more spartan. They ran away to spin in an ashram
in India with Gandhi . . . or took vows as Buddhist nuns at
the court of the Queen of Siam. Thay found himself in the
ashram of Sri Auribindo in Pondicherry with his grandmother,
the old Ranee, when the war broke out. He had to burn the
old lady with his own hands, eventually, on a funeral pyre by
the banks of the Ganges . . . very bad for his asthma, he said.

Thay's mother, the young Ranee, was prisoner for a couple
of years in Japan and then . . . after V-J Day . . . Thay joined
her at a Brain-breathing establishment in Carmel, California,
where she was killed by a hitchhiker, eventually. Thay was
terribly upset. He was *madly* in love, at the time, with a middle-
aged Hindu Swami . . . in a purely *spiritual* sense. I never
laid eyes on his guru, myself. . . . *But* I've seen photos in
which the Swami seems to be smiling sardonically at some

sinister private joke as he chews away on the end of his own long hooked nose. You can picture him selling you . . . and for a whole *lot* of money! . . . a *very wrong* rug. After some silly old stock-market crash swept away the Swami's first fortune, the Swami snapped: "Money talks! *I* don't *need* to talk!" Whereupon he took a vow of total silence which he's kept to this day. I think that's influenced Thay, too. From his Shrine of Silence, the Swami launched his "Ten Million Dollar Nirvana Fund" . . . which was to "Build the Invisible Temple of Love in Everybody's Heart." Thay tried to give his entire inheritance to the Swami but his brother-in-law, Renfrew . . . he's a big lawyer in San Francisco and one of Thay's trustees . . . called in the cops. Thay fought them tooth and nail on it but the family finally got the Swami deported before they actually had to fork over any property. *Thereupon,* Thay refused to have anything more to do with the family *or* his money and took off alone for New York . . . on his *own* for the first time in his life.

Wandering about New York the first day, like a tourist from another planet, you can imagine! . . . Thay thought he heard the . . . to *him* . . . all too familiar droning of monks mumbling mantras on the corner of Fifty-sixth Street and Madison Avenue. Like a man in a trance, Thay made straight for this old rotten building . . . 563 Madison, I think it was . . . it's since been torn down. What Thay *really* was hearing was the first murmurings of GRAMMA. You've heard of them . . . No? Well, if Thay Himmer and I hadn't put a spoke in their prayer wheel, GRAMMA might have swept the U.S. with its simple techniques for creating human ability out of . . . so to speak . . . nothing, nothing at all. *Any* two humans you put into communication can *create* this increased ability to a *mea-*

206

surable extent! Human ability could put the atom back in its place . . . if we harness it . . . and the fact that GRAMMA techniques really *do* work. I'll have occasion to show you, Hassan, GRAMMA really had something going . . . so I *took* it from them. That's one of the power factors I'm depending on right now in Africa. Empires are taken . . . not given. Nobody ever *gives* you or even *sells* you power or special knowledge in *this* world . . . or the next, I suspect. You have to *take* it . . . *steal* it to make it your own. That's how the Masters play the Game. Real Players don't *need* any Guides. You grab what you want in the Big Bazaar: if you're feeling good you toss out a buck, saying: "Keep the change, my good man! Keep the change." Thay didn't do that: instead he *joined up* with GRAMMA and was playing *their* game, until I came along and snatched him up out of there . . . out of the marketplace of Madison Avenue where Thay Himmer the Seventh simply didn't *belong!*

GRAMMA was a splinter-group of something called "Logosophy" . . . a do-it-yourself psychology system put together by a group of more or less anonymous professors working for the Ford Foundation . . . who later disowned it. Essentially, it was . . . *is,* rather . . . a compilation of simple-sounding communication techniques which can be exercised by any two people willing to play. You can do "Gramma-calls" . . . reciprocal word combinations batted back and forth, even over the telephone, for hours. You can do "Gramma-rubs" . . . two people touching each other in turn . . . at home or *even* in the office. As a weapon of wordsmanship, too, Gramma is *great!* You can "grammatize" people in business . . . at home in your family . . . or out at the beach. GRAMMA founded itself as an organization when a group of go-getters on Madison

Avenue read the book. They tried the techniques out on each
other . . . and were absolutely *overwhelmed* . . . as I was to
be later in Switzerland where I first came across it. In New
York, they rented this condemned building and . . . by the
time Thay Himmer happened along . . . they had the entire
office-space humming like a Tibetan lamasery. They needed
competent new operators to handle the hundreds of people who
came in at fifty dollars a head for a twenty-minute half hour
of chanting back and forth at each other: "Hello Yes Hello!"

It's so simple, it sounds almost simpleminded but "Hello
Yes Hello" is the ineluctable law of *all* verbal communication
which most people fumble just as your Moroccan did with me
on the phone, tonight: "Halloo Yass Halloo!" . . . he said it
so loud and so often he couldn't hear *one* single word *I* was
saying. Just think how often that happens! Haven't you noticed
how often the people you talk to don't even hear a *word* that
you're saying . . . *really* hear you: take it *in?* People just rattle
on about themselves like squirrels in a cage . . . and you *know*
it. Most people communicate very imperfectly and some not
at all . . . like my first husband, Peter Paul Strangleblood.
How do you *get* them into communication? Well, it's so simple, it's almost . . . *sinister!* No . . . I'm only joking. You
do it like this:

First, I say to you, "Hello" . . . that's to initiate this
particular communication. What I do is I *offer* to communicate.

Now, you must answer back to me: "Yes" . . . a signal
which shows you've accepted my offer. This move . . . in *our*
discipline, Hassan . . . constitutes the first *half* of a Link.

Then, you say back to me: "Hello" . . . to show me you

are *willing* to communicate . . . to go on communicating with *me*.

Therefore, I accept your fine offer very positively with: "Yes." The First Link, Hassan, has been made in a chain a lot longer than from here into any next week. All Eastern philosophies are hung up on the Word . . . "In the Beginning was the Word." Well . . . *I'll* tell you the Word, Emperor Hassan! The Word which created the world is *Hello!*

GRAMMA initiates . . . and I use the verb very *thought-fully . . . initiates* anybody and everybody into an area where communication is clear . . . and very often for the very first *time* in their lives. The results are usually spectacular yet it's really quite simple:

You sit like this . . . face to face, toe to toe . . . no creaky old Freudian couch in the corner . . . I ask you to situate yourself spatially . . . to look around and see just *where* you are sitting right now. You've done that? Good! Now make yourself aware of the two corners of the cave above and behind your head. Take a look around, if you like. You've got them? *Good!* Now, we start in with "Hello Yes Hello," and we'll run it back and forth for the next twenty minutes . . . half an hour. When I first tried this on Peter Paul Strangleblood, he screamed right away: "I can't *take* this! I can't *take* any more of this! Stop!" Now, just from reading the book, I realized Peter Paul had coughed up one of his "ingrams" . . . the ingrown word-clots which made it impossible for him to *take* anything out of life . . . and, partly, because he put so little *into* it, he was simply not in *communication* with life at all. That therapeutical side of the business is what first got GRAMMA in trouble with the AMA . . . and then they had a rumble from

Internal Revenue so they incorporated as a church: The First Grammatic Church, practicing Grammatology. That's when Thay walked in. He saw right away what brand of word-magic they were up to . . . and he laughed. He laughed to himself just like one Farout magician laughs when he meets another Farout magician coming down the Farout jungle path. They both sit down . . . facing each other . . . and have a contest to see which one can make the more horrible scary face. When Thay began showing them their own business at GRAMMA, they sat back simply stunned. It was like a bunch of businessmen watching someone spread out a million-dollar invention with no possible patent protection. Thay assured them he couldn't teach them to walk on water in a week but he *could* and *would* teach anyone in Grammatology who wanted to know, how to walk over *fire* . . . they did it all the time in the Farouts as the very *first lap* of any initiation, he said.

GRAMMA was claiming to create human ability? Well, fire-walking and faith-healing and a few other things he knew how to do might qualify as *unusual* human abilities. They agreed to see fire-walking first. Their publisher had a place down on Long Island . . . Locust Valley, I think . . . and they all moved down there for a weekend with lots more people to follow on Sunday afternoon . . . to lay on the media. Thay went to work or, rather, Thay had a gang of workmen he'd found . . . all handsome brutes, I'm sure . . . who moved onto the poor publisher's lawn like a butch ballet or some nightmare machine which hewed a hole . . . a long trench . . . right through his croquet lawn! Thay filled in the trench with I don't know how many hundreds of little bags of barbecue charcoal which he laid down in a bed and sprinkled with gasoline. Then he set it off with one tremendous great *whoosh* which nearly set fire to the publisher's home. By the time the crowd had assembled, Thay tells me, he had a nice stretch of satiny braze about fifty feet long. He'd been soaking his feet in a bucket of alum as he sat in a deck chair ordering his workmen about. He says it doesn't help much. He put back on his running-shoes over heavy woolen socks and ran a bit to get up a good protective sweat, then he went barefoot to meet the press. Everything went off just fine. There were pictures in the papers . . . all that sort of thing. Thay's full identity came out, of course. He might no longer be a white rajah but he still was a *bishop!* Neither the Japanese invasion nor the new Farout Federal State could take his hereditary bishopric away. The very idea made GRAMMA greedy. In the peculiar branch of the game they got themselves into when they incorporated as a church, only a *bishop* can roll you out replicas in order to make you more bishops. The Grammatological Church had it *made* . . . if Thay would only start smearing them with his chrism and his unction and I don't know what all! At that point, *I* dropped out of the sky crying: "No! Don't do it, Thay! *NO!*" . . . and I swept him off to Switzerland with me to treat my poor husband, PP. Thus, at one single swoop, by snatching their bishop I won the whole GRAMMA game in my very first move. . . . Are you following me?

I got onto Grammatology, first, by attempting to absorb their sacred best-seller in Switzerland. The book's as thick as a pillow, I might as well warn you . . . and just about as digestible. It's got *kapok* in there instead of prose! It was first thrust upon me with almost psychotic intensity by a slightly psychic Swiss *fraulein* stenographer I had in the house in Basel . . . doing some tri-lingual work for me. "You'll find it worthwhile, Madame," she kept insisting. . . . and, believe me, I *did!* In the end, I simply *devoured* this dreary word-paste because it was the only book in the house in English . . . if that's English it's written in. I was living in Basel with my first husband, Peter Paul Strangleblood. We'd been married less than a year . . . straight out of college . . . but PP and I weren't even on *speaking* terms, at that point in the game. PP was suffering from an acute case of what I call "Dollar Disease." In his case, it came from too many oil wells, too early in childhood. PP had oil wells like other people have boils. What communication there *had* been between us had *completely* dried up over money. I *knew* Peter Paul was so sick on the subject that the mere mention of the word "money" could make him actually throw up, *so* . . . I went out without saying a word and started making a few million dollars of my own with something called mutual funds.

Oh, I didn't *invest* in one. No . . . I started a fund of my own . . . *Fundamental Funds* . . . and the money rolled in at our good Swiss address. I'd taken this magnificent old house overhanging the Rhine with big grounds all around it . . . we were living in style! A young Swiss lawyer named Rolf Ritterolf came by our house one day, selling mutual funds. That drove PP out of the raftered room right away but I held onto Rolf . . . picking his brains. He's still with me, today. . . . In the end, I hired him to run my own fund. In the meantime, if you please, PP had gone down to the banks of the River Rhine with his air rifle . . . taking pot shots at the plastic sacks Swiss workers from Basel stuff their clothes in as . . . swimming in groups . . . they drift down the Rhine-current, home from work. *Daily,* I had to fear scandal from PP . . . and just at a moment when I needed some respectable Swiss names on my Board of Directors! I had some trouble about that. Without securing his *written* permission, I put down my own Herr Professor, Dr. Karl Forbach . . . you know: the LSD, DMT, STP and mushroom-man . . . with whom I was working on the structure of hallucinogenic alkaloids in his lab on the outskirts of Basel. I'm a very cunning chemist, *too,* you realize . . . that's why I was there. I could see Dr. Forbach needed the money . . . he was building a house in the country. When I told him more or less what I was doing one day in the lab, he said: "Go right ahead, my dear . . . anything you say!" He'd had quite a crush on me until this money thing came up *but* . . . and I'm not *trying* to be vulgar . . . when I walked into the lab that day with those shares all printed up and bearing his name on the Board of Directors . . . why, the shit . . . as the vulgar *really* say . . . hit the fan. For the first time I understood what the Freudians meant with their equation: money equals *merde!* Here, I was giving the man money and he was giving me back *merde!* I realized that my communication with *everybody* was completely fouled up!

That's when I really got onto GRAMMA. I'd suspected that even Peter Paul had picked up the book and was fumbling through it when I wasn't around . . . "Hello Yes Hello" might be just the right way to get back into communication with *him.* I was hardly surprised when he agreed. Yes, he'd try a little, "Hello Yes Hello." He'd been trying to do it with the gardener's boy but it hadn't worked out. When the two of *us* tried it . . . golly . . . it *really* worked! In a minute or two . . . it couldn't have been more . . . Peter Paul broke out with: "I can't *take* it! I can't *take* any more of this shit!" I caught his "ingram" . . . the operative word was *take!* I decided to run that word "take" on Peter Paul, again and again . . . as the book suggested, thus: I pushed him gently back into position with a big friendly smile, saying firmly: "Good, Peter Paul; *good!* Now, what *can* you take from this room?" and PP . . . of course . . . snapped back automatically: "Nothing!" I pressed on gently but firmly with "Good! and what *else* can you take from this room?" For a long time, he made nothing but neg- ative noises but . . . finally . . . as I went on softly insisting: "Good! Peter Paul; *good.* And what *else* can you take from this room?" . . . thus running his "havingness" over and over again . . . he admitted . . . he *had* to admit that even his "Nothing" was very much *something* . . . a *thing!* That flipped Peter Paul . . . he literally, *flipped!* Before even I realized what it was doing to him, there he was flat on the floor . . . in some kind of a fit! It was two o'clock in the morning, besides, so I called in a Swiss doctor who gave him a sup- pository, natch! Those European doctors! Well, maybe it's not exactly lady-like of me to joke about it but . . . poor PP *could* be a bit of a pain . . . in the ass!

You see, PP turned out to be suffering from *money- poisoning,* in just about the worst way there is! He had *money- mold* growing all over him, that boy. I noted it the very first time I ever laid eyes on him on the campus of the University of Saskatchewan in Saskatoon, Sask., but I didn't know what ailed him, at first. I guess I thought it was just dirt. . . . PPS Blood, as he called himself there, was disguised as a beatnik in *those* days. He had a hangdog look and I saw at a glance he was Indian so I felt sorry for him . . . you know, Hassan, what I *mean.* PP *looks* like a Redskin while people take me for, oh, just about anything . . . Italian, Greek, Arab, any- thing . . . any nationality at all. PP's features are . . . well, rather marked. *His* people were Athabasca Barter Indians in the Northwest Territories, who were just stubborn enough never to sign any *treaties* with *anybody*. They just stayed out of sight in the wilds throughout the first half of the twentieth century, *so* . . . when their *time* came, right after the war, they found they still owned *all* their subsoil and mineral rights which all *other* Indians . . . like *my* people . . . had long since signed away! Overnight, the Athabascan Bloods became as rich as Croesus on pitchblende, petroleum, platinum, uranium . . . the *works!* It didn't do them much good. By the time he was six . . . picked up by the red-coated Mounties, half-starving and covered with lice . . . PP was the *only* member of his tribe left alive. All the rest of the Bloods had frozen to death in their cabins . . . been eaten by their own sled-dogs . . . mangled by their own bear traps . . . or they killed each other with axes as Peter Paul's parents did, over a bottle of whisky in a motel.

You simply *must* have seen somewhere a picture of wee Peter Paul when they found him. It's been trotted out for reproduction time and again . . . every time they do a story on him. There is this pathetic little pot-bellied wolf-child in rags on the prairies, with the subtitle: *Peter Paul Strangleblood, the Richest Little Boy in the World*. Poor little tyke, he lost even his *name* in the deal . . . it still makes him sick. His *real* name was Strange Blood but it became Strangleblood by somebody's typographical error somewhere along the line and that's how it went into the books and the courts where he was declared a public ward. Peter Paul . . . as *they* called him . . . was put into what looked to him like a series of gilded jails . . . with guardians named by the court to administer his almost incalculable fortune. When Peter Paul was fifteen, he had an allowance of one dollar and twenty-five cents a week! "Home" was a huge big old house and garden where he simply skulked around in the basement or drew himself up through a trapdoor in a bathroom ceiling . . . into the empty attic where he spent most of his days . . . doing *nothing,* he claims. In my day, as I said, he turned up at Saskatchewan U. disguised as a beatnik by the name of PPS Blood. All you could see of him . . . winter or summer . . . was an old red-and-black-checked Mackinaw with the collar turned up so that only a tall bristle of shiny black hair showed above it. When you got a good look at his face you were actually sorry he smiled . . . *when* he smiled. The whole campus called him: "Coyote" because he had a full *double* set of *much* too-white teeth. I've seen lots of other Indian boys with maybe six or eight extra teeth like that . . . or even just four upper canines instead of two . . . but Peter Paul looked much better when I persuaded him to have the one set pulled out. He looked actually quite handsome, then . . . but no one else in Saskatoon thought PPS Blood was a *catch!*

You see . . . *my* people were *Bounty* Indians who had signed away everything forever . . . about the year my youngest great-grandmother was born . . . *all* in exchange for one bright red Hudson Bay blanket a year and two one-hundred-pound bags of flour. We had to scramble for the rest . . . a houseful of women without men, living in Edmonton, Alberta . . . on the Flats! We used to make money by wandering along the banks of the Saskatchewan River picking wild berries to sell. Clear bright-red chokecherry jelly and plump-purple ripe Saskatoons! We could put them up only if we already had money for sugar and Mason jars. One old granny of mine and I used to toddle out in our moccasins culling herbs which she taught me. With my *eldest* granny nearing ninety, I went hunting mushrooms and edible puff-balls we sliced to fry in butter.

You had to be *sure* to be right about *them* . . . and even more sure about the *other* mushrooms we took home and dried and made into a tea which we drank on an empty stomach . . . all of us generations of women . . . on late Saturday afternoons. No one else but us ever came to our house . . . I found out when I grew up that the neighbors all called us witches and it's true, in a way. In winter, it could be sixty degrees below zero . . . Fahrenheit, of course . . . and we'd all sit in the kitchen in front of the fire . . . all my grannies and me . . . and we'd wait for the mushroom tea to work and, when it did, why, it was *true!* . . . we used simply *fly* away to another land that all those poor white people outside . . . those palefaces, never knew. As I sat on the worn rag rug like an island in a sea of cold linoleum, looking into the eye of the fire with my head on a granny's knee . . . a pair of hands as soft as old doeskin would reach around to pick up the reins of my eyes and gentle me easy down along a long trail that all young Redskin-Indian ponies should know. . . . Oh, I've been on *trips* in my childhood . . . such *trips!*

I was "other-directed," I think . . . from the start. Thay thinks I was poisoned once by some mushrooms and I've let him go on believing that story because he's really rather hostile to drugs . . . did you notice? . . . Right from the start of high school, when I first took chemistry, I knew at *once* that chemistry would always be my love! I had a hard time in school . . . oh, I don't mean scholastically: I was brilliant . . . I mean with the kids. My maiden name was Jackie Mae Bear Foot. That became Barefoot and . . . on the way from school . . . Jackie Mae Bare-ass! You can imagine! I was always a *big* girl and grew breasts before anyone else did, *so* . . . when all the boys ran after me . . . I became the Bad Girl of the neighborhood, I guess. I'd have been asked to leave school if my grades hadn't been good . . . always the *best!* Home was another world. We were seven generations of women . . . believe it or not . . . the night my daughter was born and died, the summer I was twelve and passed out of Grade Eight . . . I didn't lose a day of school, either. My mother had me when *she* was thirteen and my first grandmother was only fifteen years older than her . . . about forty . . . and there were three *more* generations of great-grannies in the kitchen, going back to the oldest gallant old gal of them all . . . going on ninety and not seeing so well. There were no men of *any* kind around our house . . . *ever.* Greatest Granny, as I called her, insisted that men were bad for the mushrooms . . . and she knew *all* about *them.* Dream-mushrooms always came up out of the ground when she called them by name, she said. She called them. . . . I picked them. I learned about mushrooms from her but later I learned their lovely Latin names. . . . *Candida Albicans,* for example . . . wouldn't that be a lovely name for the heroine of a novel? I learned Latin at school and I tracked down the mushrooms in the Carnegie Free Public Library in Edmonton but I never read anything in those days that told about the Great Dance of the Mushrooms . . . constellations of dancing mushrooms filling the whole interior universe. As a mere *child,* I'd already seen that . . . before I was into my *teens!*

When I won a scholarship to Saskatchewan U., my majors were Chemistry and Cybernetic Psych. There in Saskatoon, a young Psych prof was the first to use mescaline to show his class what he thought schizophrenia might be like. "If that's what it's like to be crazy, what are we all waiting for?" I remember somebody saying. Our chem lab was churning out mescaline to such an extent that reports of our experiments attracted figures of international renown who were floating around Saskatoon on supervised mescaline experiences . . . people like Aldous Huxley. Huxley added *tone* to our trips by suggesting that we be given *cultural* stimulation, as well. As a part of *my* experience, I was taken to a concert given by Gieseking playing the Brahms Second Piano Concerto . . . and did I *ever* have a strange *contact* with *him!* Years later, I read a profile on the pianist which quoted him as saying that, in any concert, he always looked around first for his *"receiver"* as soon as he walked out on stage. He went out of his way to say that he sincerely believed in magnetic emanations . . . ESP, mediums . . . *all* of it. Once he found his *"receiver,"* he played all the rest of the concert to that person . . . while the rest of the audience simply assisted. And was I *ever* his *"receiver"* that night!

Gieseking hopped out of the wings . . . smartly flipping and smoothing his tails as he flitted through the twittering orchestra perched on the edge of their chairs. Applause . . . a sudden sharp *hail* of applause crashed down so hard on my head that I thought all these blackbirds were rising to flap away offstage as they got to their feet to greet the maestro. A great billowing *gale* of applause . . . a wavelike ovation rolling up, nearly *lifted* me out of my seat in the balcony. Gieseking bowed . . . cocking his head as quick as a cockatoo and his brilliant black eye caught in mine. I felt like the Early Worm . . . practically *plucked* out of the sea of seats and people surrounding me . . . caught by the gills right away. If he'd pulled in his psychic line, right then and there I'd have flown over the heads of the audience to flounder flat on the stage in front of him at his feet. When he turned to the coffin-like grand piano,

219

I noticed his hair was gray feathers fluttering about his head. The maestro was a *bird!*

Gieseking, the world-famous piano player, was a simply *shameless* gray cockatoo as big as a man dressed in a loose-fitting frock coat. When he flipped up his tails to sit down in front of the keyboard, it looked like a feeding-trough or a giant corncob of white and black pearls. Under his coattails, I caught a flash of his tail feathers . . . gray and bright red! When he *did* hit the keys, he didn't play music . . . he *talked*. Gieseking began talking about a mile a minute without punctuation . . . and he was talking to *me!* He rambled on about his early childhood . . . all those hours of practicing, beginning at three . . . his debut at seven . . . his international triumphs at twelve . . . a worldwide celebrity before he was twenty-one and how very *bad* it all went on him, after . . . critics, audiences, himself with himself and the music. He was talking so much that I heard not *one* note he was playing until I noticed that the orchestra had disappeared. In its place, the maestro was conducting an atomic pile of precision machinery packed into the proscenium arch about and above him. "They downgraded me once for not playing all the notes!" he tossed at me over his shoulder as he prodded and pushed the machine into shape. I believe he went back to school . . . after *fifty*, I think he said . . . "and I taught myself to play it like *THIS!*" He whammed the piano . . . plunging on into Brahms.

The great pianist and the orchestra receded a long way away from me . . . down the wrong end of the telescope. I had an exquisitely jeweled mechanical toy in my sights . . . a musical carousel . . . a pie-dish of platinum from which crystal canaries were escaping. The whole scene was darkening as the orchestra swelled up and burst like volcanoes in a land of lagoons, dissolving into puddles of power through which the fiddles sent up swarming clouds of golden bees. The bees were all numbered, flying to their appointed dots in a screen that was run through and rent by great golden pistons of fire every time the brasses rolled over in unison. Somehow, it came to an end. When Gieseking . . . still a gray cockatoo in elegant Italian tails . . . briskly hopped out in front to take his bow, there was a little old lady, all dressed in rusty-black with a Victorian widow's bonnet on her head, who bobbed up and down under his elbow . . . his wing . . . for less than the sixtieth part of a second . . . for a mere *n* microseconds, sharing the applause. "I thank you!" he bowed deeply. "*We* thank you! My old mother . . . I practiced for *her!*" And, with that, he shot us all a real old show-business look . . . a long liquid-eyed look like Svengali . . . or Paganini . . . counting the house.

Aldous Huxley himself was next on my list of *"stimulations"* . . . and, with him, I got off on what looked at first like a very wrong foot by trying to tell him about what had just happened to me with Gieseking. I'm aggressive, I guess. I hadn't learned yet that you don't . . . simply *don't* . . . talk about one *"star"* to another. Mr. Huxley looked at me blandly and blindly as he asked in his *most* English voice: "Do we really *need* mescaline?" I learned later that he had four hundred and fifty milligrams in him that night, himself. In the Saskatoon sitting room, the Northern Lights were playing about Mr. Huxley's head. I gulped back a little wave of nausea and . . . when I looked again . . . he was my oldest great-granny . . . the mushroom one. She looked just as she used to look long ago by the campfire on Hog's-back Ravine back home. There in the leaping shadows behind her was our old torn tepee sheltering our pine-bough beds. I caught the smell of earth through the sharper smell of the pine as I said: "No, Mr. Huxley . . . *not* if we've got *mushrooms, instead!*"

That shot him down, right out of his tree . . . that old British bear! As a matter of fact, he carried it off jolly well . . . when you consider that up until then he was sure that almost nobody else in the world knew about the Sacred Mushrooms, but him. A banker friend's Russian wife had assured him that Siberian nomads partook of a hallucinatory mushroom as a part of their shamanistic religion. He had just received their first private report on the mushrooms in Mexico. I tried to come on . . . of course . . . like I was reading his mind. I told him a thing or two he *never* had heard about! How to *make* a Shaman . . . for example . . . that's a woman's secret, all right. Of *course* there was mushroom-magic, I assured him . . . right all the way across the North American steppe. He asked me to write him a paper on it and I did . . . for only *his* eyes: *Sight Without Glasses* you know . . . he practiced it but that meant he had to put my paper right up to his nose, poor man . . . but he did have *another* kind of sight, like my grandmother had. Later, he asked my permission to send on my report to another old friend of his: Dr. Forbach of Basel, the biggest chemical man in the game. LSD, you know . . . DMT, STP, BRB . . . that's my *Borbor* in a very unsophisticated form. I've been all the way up to BRB 144, I think . . . or *more!* Permutations of the formula I first worked on with Dr. Forbach in Basel during my post-graduate year. That was all thanks to Huxley, I guess . . . and thanks to him, too, I suppose that I got a fat letter one day just before graduation . . . air mail from Basel, Switzerland . . . a rather business-looking envelope printed with the name of a famous pharmaceutical firm. There was no letter inside but a flat packet of very tiny pink pills marked: PSYLOCIBIN. I'd picked up a paper on *psylocibin* in the lab . . . *"extract of mushrooms."* It had been a long time. I could hardly wait to try them to see if *theirs* were as good as my old granny's and mine.

At the time, I was living in an off-campus rooming house run by a terrible old woman who called herself Mrs. Murphy. Whatever she was, she wasn't Irish. . . . I've always thought she must have been a fence. She lurked in her kitchen like a fat old spider with crippled legs, brewing coffee in a blue enamel pot day and night because she slept in her chair . . . from where she could reach the key in the back door and the key in the door to the basement. People came in and out down there all night. She never got up to my room and that just suited me fine. . . . I liked it that way. Up there, I knew I always could be alone. I had the place pretty shipshape. . . . I've always liked building. I'd made all the shelves and the work surfaces on weekends myself. I had my own little world up there and no one had even the right to come knocking on my door except Peter Paul . . . who wasn't even attending classes any more but just darting in and out. When the reporters came around, after PP and I got married, Mrs. Murphy told them that I'd always been known as "Hamburger Mary," because I slung hash in a hamburger joint . . . an absolute lie! *Nobody* ever called me that. Thay Himmer first called me Maya and I changed it to spell it *my* way: M Y A . . . but in all those damned newspapers, that dreadful nickname *has* stuck to me: "Hamburger Mary," well . . .

Automatically, I took off my dress to put on my work shirt and work pants. Sitting in front of my broad black desk, I stared at the tiny pink mushroom pills . . . as tiny as seeds.

223

There was no posology . . . no dose prescribed . . . the whole
packet must be the dose. By accident . . . by some *very* strange
accident except that there *aren't* any accidents . . . the pharmaceutical firm in faraway Switzerland seemed to have du-
plicated the dose. I mean . . . the first envelope came air mail,
unopened by Customs . . . no letter attached, as I've said . . .
it looked as though they were merely filling an order at someone's request . . . it didn't say who. *But,* on the following
day, another identical letter had come. I had the two packets
of pretty pink pills in front of me on the top of my black-
painted desk. What did I *do?* I decided to change my clothes,
first . . . put on something more suited to mushrooms, a gown.
I picked up one single tiny pill . . . touched it with glue and
stuck it on a card on which I wrote: "I've taken this. In case
of trouble, the phone number of the maker in Basel is on the
envelope. Call them collect." I know my mushrooms, I thought.
I took the rest . . . the other twenty-three milligram pills at
one gulp. I put out a tube of barbiturates as a possible antidote
and turned to make some herb tea I always had with me from
home. A knock on the door: *One One-Two!* Peter Paul the
Coyote in his old rotten Mackinaw was already inside of the
room. "Whzzat?" he asked, pointing to the pills. I told him.
He picked up the other full packet and pinched them. "Can I
take some? How many d'ja take?"

I was already so far gone by that time that I merely waved
permissively at the *psylocibin* as I lay back on my bed and
just *floated* away. With his coyote cunning, Peter Paul took
just six pills the first time. . . . *That* was the proper dose as
it turned out later. As soon as he'd dropped the pills, he cut
out the door and out of my mind for the next couple of light-
years through which I took off. As I went, I noticed that all

the familiar fixtures of the mushroom world were flying past me much faster than I'd ever remembered them from childhood. I reached out through space for the notebook on my night-table to mark something down and I never got there because so many other things were happening simultaneously that got in the way. I wasn't able to make much of my notes, later . . . after all, I'd taken *four* times the maximum dose, as it turned out. That thrust me quickly into a very tricky world of prickly magic . . . magic-tricksters . . . mountebanks . . . Roger Bacon, Cagliostro . . . I saw them *all* and they all *wanted* something from me . . . maybe only my approbation, perhaps. I saw coffins and candles . . . I was in a crystal coffin with a sharp stake held to my heart . . . but no one was holding it there in the dark and, at once, the lights flashed up as monumental doors of polished black granite soundlessly turned on invisible pivots and whirled . . . twirling. They were trying to frighten me . . . trying to *win* me . . . to scare or to *buy* me with a pageant of paltry magical tricks! So I ran from them . . . whoever *They* were . . . down endless corridors of some old hotel whose wallpaper pattern of leaves was swaying and rustling an arm's length away . . . while from behind every identical leaf was peering an eye . . . an *identical* eye to *infinity* spying on *me*. I ran on through the hotel hallway screaming: "The Management! I want to see the Management, right here and *now!*" I wasn't afraid . . . I was *furious!* Besides, I could see They were worried back there . . . behind the scenery. There was rustling . . . anxious whispering in the wings. The houselights went down . . . the audience sat like a jury on the edge of its seats. I heard three loud thumps of wood onto wood flooring . . . the Divine Sarah stamping the stage with her famous peg leg. I almost saw her! The curtain was just about to go up . . . parting and lifting . . . when Peter Paul Strangleblood came bursting in through my door, which I'd forgotten to lock.

Peter Paul was as naked as an Ancient Egyptian wearing the jackal's head of Anubis. "I'm down off my head . . . my high, I mean," he said. He snatched six more *psylocibin* pills and ran out again. I got up without any difficulty although my bedclothes were on fire and the room had turned into a tank full of green and purple algae. I wobbled through them toward my gas ring . . . intending to boil some water in order to put out the fire but the whole scene changed in an instant . . . the moment I cracked a match and lit that little blue flame, I realized all my grannies were sitting around me in a circle so big that, in the brilliant blue starlight, our circle reached out until we might have been *all* the women in the world . . . ever! . . . guardians of the fireside . . . tenders of the flame. I was standing on a silver sickle of moon. A snake slid from my hand. The women were putting out bowls of blue milk for my snake. I looked up-out and over their crowd of bowed heads to where I saw the rounding horizon of Earth as a satellite sees it . . . all Earth seen as great muskeg of water and land . . . a few rocks in relief but all the rest steppe . . . prairie . . . desert . . . until suddenly *everywhere* a pattern of pinpoints of light began to sparkle up through the dark that had dropped again . . . whole constellations . . . a firmament of tiny lights toward which I hurtled out with no effort at all to a point where I could see that each little light was a fireside where a woman was offering a blue bowl of milk to a man turning his back on me. I reached out to tap at the back of his head . . . psychically . . . and the man turned around. He turned around, Hassan . . . with one identical lift of the chin and a flutter of nostrils, Hassan . . . I knew it the moment I laid eyes on you, Hassan: All those men turned around simultaneously, Hassan . . . and *all* of those men were the image of *you!*

All around and beyond you . . . *all* of you . . . was prairie or desert, I couldn't really tell which . . . a primeval desert of stones like the Sahara, perhaps, with a skyful of stars tied down tight like a tent, to fit the rounding horizon. Campfires were extinguished . . . blotted out by a great storm of mushrooms blowing up like sudsy detergent . . . or a hail of pale pumice stones hurting me horribly as they hurtled through me. Nameless nomads went streaming past on the edge of the dark . . . starving. They flapped by like rags in the wind smeared over with blurry vague features which ran in the rain of mushrooms bleeding like ink. Doll-like dead pot-bellied children blew past like overripe puff-balls whose spores exploded in dust. Survivors struggled up to collapse at my feet like a muttering pile of old rotten sacks. The air was so sudsy and thick with transparent mushrooms dancing like jellyfish that it was getting harder to breathe. I sniffed the back of my own hand and . . . with horror, my armpits. My flesh was *raw* mushroom! When I tried to spew out the smell I saw I was *all* mushroom . . . even my lungs. I reeked from *inside!* In despair, I threw myself down on a bed of moss . . . mossy muskeg of North Manitoba . . . I was all sewn up in sour-smelling furs. I had all the flat places of Earth in my memory . . . snow fields behind me . . . Asian steppe . . . chains of deserts ringing the planet all the way to the south Saharan sands. From as far away as all that, a jackal came loping straight at me like a mistimed missile . . . from a long way off still, I knew who it was . . . Peter Paul. It took him so long just crossing that steppe that he had the time to grow up before he could get to me. You could see he was *destined* for me. He was lost out there, the last of his tribe but coming on fast . . . determined to hang onto life by all of his teeth . . . so deprived in his singular struggle to survive that it was costing him quite literally *everything* to get there! I was *all* for him . . . he had *no* other choice . . . but *I* did, I thought. There he was scrambling up that last cliff on which I was standing and, as I thought for a minute of kicking his head in, like a "punkin," he suddenly came sliding down cascades of mirrors at me . . . *on* me . . . something was breaking. . . . We were together in bed.

Are you feeling the *Borbor,* at all? Or do you go on smoking your keef as an antidote, Hassan? Nothing will help you now, Hassan . . . you simply *have* to listen to the rest of my tale. Don't yawn! Don't you *ever* take off those dark glasses of yours?

Well, right after graduation, PP and I got very quietly married in Saskatoon . . . under the not *quite* legally correct names of Peter S. Blood and Mary B. Foote. I added that "e" to be fancy and it cost me a lot of legal pain later . . . when we came to divorce. I didn't know a damn thing about PP, *really,* when I married him. After the mushroom-event I had an even later menstrual period than usual so I guess I mumbled something *dark* to him about marriage and PP just said: "Sure. OK. Why not?" I didn't know, then, that his father had chopped up his mother with an ax in the shower of a motel near Medicine Hat and been mowed down by the Mounties. He said both his parents were dead, "in an accident," so I guessed from that and some things he did that he *must* have *some* money . . . but I had *no* idea how *much!* In all the time I'd known him

228

I'd never seen PP pull *one* single penny out of his pocket . . . *never,* under any circumstances did he touch money. We didn't go Dutch: *I* paid for everything . . . *everything!* . . . out of my scholarship money or money from working weekends and nights. At the mere mention of *money,* Peter Paul used to pull out a switchblade he always carried on him, mumbling about how he was "going to take care of his guardians" . . . so naturally, I thought someone was keeping him short. That "someone," I soon realized after I married him, was PP *himself* . . . and, after all, I didn't really know who *he was!*

That came out when we went to apply for our passports and were told by some little local official in the capital city, Regina, that Blood Indians and their spouses were not *eligible* for passports at *all!* We were members . . . and in Peter Paul's case the very *last* one . . . of an independent but unrecognized nation which had never signed treaties of reciprocity with the Canadian government. *We had no status at all.* "Are you trying to tell me I don't exist!" I menaced the man. "Oh, no, Madame," he protested. "You can have bank accounts, driving licenses, dog and hunting licenses but no liquor license, nor even a permit to drink liquor at any time; neither vanilla extract for cooking nor after-shave lotion are you permitted to buy or consume, nor wood alcohol nor anti-freeze may be sold to a Bounty Indian but you can get onto public relief at a pinch, since you're residents, or so I think. Here, let me just look that up in the book a minute. In any case—and I'm quite sure of that—passports, no!" Peter Paul was so cowed, he didn't even want to go to the papers with this. He was ready to call off the whole trip to Basel . . . my post-graduate year of fellowship study with Dr. Forbach, imagine! . . . not *me!* I simply sailed into the offices of the *Saskatoon Sketch* with the

229

story and it hit the front page. It hit the front page not only locally but all over the world as the wire services got hold of it. *Peter Paul Strangleblood, the Richest Little Boy in the World Denied Passport. Deny Passport to Red Indian Oil Heir* . . . and on and on . . . ever since.

At least I knew who I was *married* to . . . at *last!* It's sort of funny . . . now that I come to think about it. . . . I've often enough in my life found myself in quite *deep* with a man before I even found out who he was . . . really. The next one . . . a little over a year later . . . was Thay. I've told you how *that* happened: I simply flew over to New York to look into GRAMMA after I'd knocked poor PP flat on the floor with it . . . him and his lack of *"havingness!"* . . . and I swooped back with Thay Himmer to get him to *"grammatize"* my husband into some *money sense*. I felt at the time that he had to be cured even if it meant taking *all* of his money *off* of him. . . . It wasn't doing *him* . . . or anybody *else* . . . any *good* . . . and I told Thay as much. Thay, as you know by now, loves to come on as a magician and . . . I *must* admit . . . he does pretty well. Can't you just hear him saying: "A magician? I *am!*" He took hold of our household in Basel . . . but quick! Thay was "running" PP four to six hours a day on his "havingness" and he "ran" everybody else in the house: Rolf Ritterolf, my Swiss lawyer running Fundamental Funds; Fraulein Freulich, my Swiss tri-lingual typist: even the cook. When he got to me, he soon turned up the fact that I wasn't in contact with Dr. Forbach . . . *badly* out of communication, in fact. Thay Himmer got Dr. Forbach to come over to tea and . . . like a good Swiss grandfather, come to make peace. . . . The professor brought along his unfortunate

230

granddaughter whom Peter Paul had once slapped around in a rage . . . for making fun of his money, *he* thought.

Well, it couldn't have turned out better . . . or *worse*. This time, the child got *burnt!* We were all having tea in our fabulous house on the Rhine and I had some nice things including a big silver samovar which Peter Paul somehow managed to overturn *over* the child. It got her one arm from the wrist to her shoulder. . . . The howling child was *very* badly burned. Thay jumped on her right away . . . slapping her face to get her attention. *"Good!"* he shouted at her to get her into communication: "Does it hurt *here?"* The surprised and suffering child shook her ringlets: "No." Then Thay slapped her hand . . . passing right over the burn. *"Good! Does it hurt here?"* Again, she had to say "No." Thay went on like that with her relentlessly . . . passing back and forth over the burn; making *her,* each time, *negate* the pain, you see. I hope you won't ever have the occasion to *try* it but . . . I swear to you I've seen Thay *do* it . . . and it *works!* In the end, we sent the little girl home quite exhausted but with only a little redness on her arm. . . . *Faith Healing!* . . . It took Thay nearly an hour of utterly intense work to *do* it . . . but we'd all thought that poor child was going to be disfigured for life!

After that, Thay could do *anything* with Peter Paul that he liked. We were all driving to Freiburg im Breisgau one day, I remember, with PP at the wheel of our Mercedes-Benz. "Where do I turn?" PP asked vaguely and Thay, who meant a perfectly visible crossroads a few yards ahead, said: "Right here." Instinctively and without one second's reflection, Peter Paul swung over the wheel, turning us all over into a ditch. Luckily, we weren't going very fast so no one was hurt *but* . . .

it just goes to show you how *blindly* PP was following Thay. That night, Thay brought out of his luggage a Ouija Board which he and I had picked up at Hammacher Schlemmer's in New York as we tore through buying silly Christmas presents on the way to the airport. I knew how it worked so . . . when Thay and I both put our forefingers on the planchette, the first thing it spelled out was *SCRAM!* "Do you mean we should all leave Basel, dear Ouija Board?" That was Thay talking to it. The planchette shot off under my reluctant forefinger to "YES." "And where should we *go,* dear Ouija?" asked Thay. TAMANRASSET. The board painfully and laboriously spelled it out—and that's your "Tam," isn't it? We all were ready to swear that none of us, Thay included, had ever even *heard* of the place. "And when, dear Ouija Board, when?" Thay insisted. ANTEXMAS, the ouija board said. That happened just three days before Christmas and . . . in three *hours* . . . we were off! Thay found where the place was on the atlas and Thay it was who simply dragged us out to the airport in Basel where he simply *made* PP Strangleblood write out a check for our own private plane. . . . We were off!

Just before leaving the house, I grabbed up a handful of mail to go through in the plane. . . . I had things to sign so, luckily, I took along my Swiss lawyer, Rolf Ritterolf, with the idea of sending him back from Algut. He carries around a dispatch case like a cabinet minister with a portfolio of all my affairs. Among other things was a letter from you to the Fundamental Foundation saying you were on your way to Algut. I had really . . . excuse me, it was true . . . I *had* picked you because of your photograph. It and your project: "The Future of Slavery," both pleased me . . . but nothing was official, yet, nor had the Foundation informed *you* of

anything. I happen to *know!* As I say . . . I laughed. I remember, Thay looked up from a crossword puzzle and remarked: "Laughter is refusal." But I shook my head. . . .
"Not in this case," I said, and told Rolf to meet you in the
Hotel Saint Georges and give you the money for your trip. He
and the American Vice-Consul Knoblock met you, I know, or
we wouldn't . . . would we? . . . be here.

I've heard poor Thay tell such a *different* version . . . at
times . . . of everything that went on after that! I won't bore
you with *my* version . . . except, perhaps, to insist that it was
no fault of mine that your mission failed. Thay . . . he's a
darling but *most* unreliable, really, and at times an absolute
liar . . . he'll admit as much to you himself. Except . . . I
forgot . . . Thay is not going to talk any more! I wonder how
long *that's* going to last? He's gone through *dozens* of other
self-imposed disciplines before. Well, Thay . . . who is quite
capable of telling you that *his* Amos Africanus . . . and mine,
too, don't get me wrong . . . but Amos was never in Algut
in his life as far as I know. We didn't even meet him until
much later on in our trip. We had hoped to meet *you* somewhere
along the way but you took so long crawling across the Sahara
just to get to Tam . . . that our plane had long ago left. What
did happen . . . *most* unfortunate, really, for you . . . is that
Thay interfered when he had really no right to . . . telling the
captains in Tam to look out for you. As you saw, it had quite
the *opposite* effect from what was intended . . . at least, so I
hope . . . by Thay.

So. . . . really to make this up to you . . . we would both
be happy if you would accept to come with us to "Malamut" . . . where we have some great plans under way . . .
for Africa . . . for the world . . . for you. We feel you fit in.

Thay . . . always excessive . . . says that you were heaven-
sent. I always go along with his games. Besides, we're a team
and together we hold . . . as they say . . . a handful of trumps.
When we get down there . . . let's say we get down there
tomorrow afternoon for a late Spanish lunch . . . I'll have Rolf
Ritterolf run through the whole portfolio with you and explain
all the things we are up to. Hassan, you'll come, won't you?
You have only to say it . . . you know . . . the *word!*

8

Man, what a wild change of scene: last night in Tanja town and here we are back in the Sahara again! I guess I must have said: "Hello," all right, to the lady; how could I resist? "Hello Yes Hello," in fact. Here I have in my hand a big green carved stone, obviously ancient and said to be an emerald unless it's jadite or glass. I have, also, a gold chain of linked letter H's, presumably for Hapsburg, but it could be for Hassan, why not? The man whose name is not Hassan, I certainly am. So, what should I have said to the lady: "Good-by No Good-by"? Hamid says he always knows how to take a prize when he sees one but I never do. This time, we'll see. I'm writing this painfully by candlelight in the big electronic library of "Malamut"—"my brain," she calls it—surrounded by the consoles of the computers and the wired stacks of the communications system through which she intends to run this whole African scene of hers. Tonight, the generators are out of order, they tell me: for the moment, none of this works. The flickering light of my candle is lost in the shadows which race around this round room whose dome, high above me, represents Mya's head on the top of the bulk of this building when you see this whole block of rocks on Cape Noon from a distance. As big as the Capitol building, Mya sits on the immense sweep of the Saharan coast of the Atlantic on the big bulge of Africa; massive, unique and alone.

Very impressive, I guess, but my first sight of all this from the air simply sickened me and might have killed all of us. Mya's seven-passenger, two-million-dollar Lear jet nearly blew inside out, right overhead here luckily, but at thirty thousand feet up! Mya was sitting in her cockpit, like a throne under the plastic sky-dome, looking so luminous; looking so enormous; looking so like a whole galaxy of goddesses that I knew I was still under the effects of her Borbor, you bet! The Victory of Samothrace flying her jet with her classic bare blue feet set square on the pedals; solid marble arms reaching out for the power controls. Then, for a millionth of a second, she just flipped into the cabin; into Mya and out again, so quick I don't suppose I was supposed to see her at all: a Medusa with a head full of snakes. Everything I looked at had a bright fuzzy halo around it; orange to indigo but dimmer than the prism you catch in the bevel of good-grade plate glass.

Wow! I said to myself: Someone is fucking my everyday clean-cut, crystal-clear keef-connection with the visible world and, also, my go-ahead-green perception of same. What is more, all this bamboozle is being laid on me by means of a paltry veil of illusion drawn over my eyes; and, drawn *chemically,* no less! I also reckon that this glassy veil is producing prismatic effects because it is imperfectly adjusted, or else— and worse!—the product has been adulterated along the way. *Wow!* So, the lady can commit a fault, can she! That's all I

236

needed to know but, like it or not, I have to go along with the ride.

I wouldn't take a Nembie on a trip if the hostess forced one down my throat. Besides, I sit looking down on the desert I love from nearly a satellite's point of view and I see, I can clearly perceive that the Sahara is Man, all Man. How could I ever have thought anything else! The sand is his shimmering silicone shirt stamped in a uniform pattern of dunes like the scales on a suit of chain mail worn by Ghoul. Ghoul lies down to rest on his desert as polished and bare as a shield, and he slumbers until he hears the hammering of the white north wind on the doors of his desert and, then, he stirs; he rumbles, he raises his voice. A sinister sound like the gritting and grinding of all the grains of sand in the Sahara furls out over the idle desert in a great wave, like a command to arise. A tremor runs under the sands and, then, the whole Sahara stands to attention for one breathless moment before it throws itself like a great sea of sand on the foe.

Ghoul, Defender of Africa, I hear your clarion call! In one pico-second I parachute down thirty thousand feet and I am back, living again in the guerrilla conditions I know. I know them for sure: *Them or Us*. My comrades-in-arms, Terror and Hunger and Cold, shuffle along like Shakespearean supers or huddle over the fire I made, first, of my arrows and, then, of my bow. Terror, forever behind me, drags Hunger along by a knot in his gut but that coward, Cold, has deserted us, gliding away like the vipers who dance on these black fields of clinkers, white-hot in the sun. The air melts to liquid. It ripples and runs like the seething of water when it roils to a boil. I flounder on through the swell of the sand with the rags of my black burnous for a sail. Know that I am the Captain of Patience whose heart is the heart of the hyena, whose sandals are shod with flint!

At that point, the Medusa head in the cabin snapped at me: "As far as Mother is concerned, every trek is a trick!"

I refused to let myself be turned into stone. When you are as high as that in the stratosphere, it is always a beautiful day—until something pops. In the back of the cabin, Hamid was giving Thay Himmer an expensive lesson in how to play Ronda; slapping his cards down on the table like firecrackers and probably taking Thay's peach-colored Sulka underdrawers as well as his Sulka shirt. Thay grinned away goofily as he lost trick after trick. Hamid kept snapping: "Mine . . . mine . . . mine . . ." as he took them all and I was boozily amused to catch Mya with my other ear, singing exactly the same song to me as she swept us over this particular stretch of planet Earth: "Mine . . . mine . . . mine . . . ! I own two million, nine hundred and fifty-six thousand, two hundred and forty-seven hectares of this . . . not God's little acres, Hassan . . . hectares!"

The landscape I looked down on was so lunar and I was feeling so completely lunatic, myself, that all I had to do was to let the words "Lady Moon," form in my head and there she was in the plane, beside me under the plastic sky-dome: Princess Mya at her Lear jet cabin controls. That must have been about the time the *Borbor* hit its peak: just at thirty thousand feet, I happened to notice. At that point, she throttled her engines and we would have glided peacefully, uneventfully into "Malamut"—if Ghoul had not intervened.

"You won't believe it," she smiled, as "Malamut" swam up out of the great circle of sand and sea but, when I saw what

238

she was pointing out, my heart sank. All her bloody *Borbor* drained right out of my tank. I could believe it only too well. After all: I, too, have been to Southern California to see a six-story-high hot-dog-stand in the form of a giant Saint Bernard dog, makes you sick just to have to look at it on the skyline. Well, "Malamut" is Mya sitting in the lotus position with an Olympic-sized swimming pool on her knees. There she floats on the fringes of the Sahara and the Atlantic, like a giant broody Buddha with a two-thousand-mile strip of bare beach under her broad beam. It was crossing my mind that she hadn't been wise to turn her back on the Sahara and Ghoul, when she screamed in my ear:

"That's Heaven Rock, Hassan: that's *Me!*"

Pop! Pop! went my ears like a double thunderclap inside of my head! I looked up past Mya and saw the plastic sky-dome had gone; grabbed off by Ghoul. Mya sucked at her oxygen in time to pull the plane out of its spin. We were all shaken up but Thay was worst hurt. They've got him in some other part of this palace I haven't seen yet. I guess Hamid's there, too. I really don't know about this Thay Himmer cat; looks like he's conjuring himself out of the picture real quick. I'm told that, as soon as he shut off his word-line, his old asthma has hit him so bad we got to get him into an iron lung. I would have thought Dakar would be nearest but:

"Not at all!" snaps Madame Mya. "We must all take off for Tam . . . and tonight!"

Well, this is the way I came—with nothing but my black suit of skin and my recording system. I'll go anywhere, I guess; any time the lady says. Moreover, may I add, there is nothing to eat in this goddamn place. I have found nothing but a storeroom full of cases of chunky peanut butter, and that's all!

239

There are no servants on tap in this tomb because all of those faggotty Foulba have flitted off to the mainland to sew bead-fringe and ostrich feathers on their shepherdess hats for the beauty contest. They give me the creeps. Trust a woman to imagine I might be interested in the likes of them! Mya brought them down a present of five hundred gross of cheap blue cotton shirts from Hong Kong but, because they never wore shirts before in their lives, they hoisted them on little crossed sticks, over their heads, and tore off to their camp; looking like an army of *"men whose heads do grow beneath their shoulders."*

The Himmer's Swiss lawyer came in and I recorded him. Funny, I had to turn the tape over to record him on top of Thay, wiping Thay's words as I went. I wonder if that sort of cannibalism is what Himmer meant by: "Rub out the word"?

9

IT

"IT!" poor Amos always cries when I bring him in this portfolio of headaches; Princess Mya's affairs. "Please don't tag me with all that again, Rolf!" he begs me. "I'm It, already," he says. And, now, that's quite literally true since he has been taken prisoner and tortured, we have word tonight, by the captains in Tam. An emergency, a most unfortunate emergency arose abruptly during those hours we were out of communication with the Himmers; most disturbing, the first time it's happened, ever. As Amos saw it, there was nothing for him to do but risk a night flight to Tam to try and save his twin sister, Freeky Fard, who is one of our Players, of course. As I now understand it from the Princess herself, this unique break in the very communication on which all our success depends was entirely due to the events surrounding your, ah, contact by means of the Saharan Seal. While the Seal is suspended there are no available words; or so I am led to believe. Well. It is interesting, I suppose, to see the way in which Mr. Himmer's unorthodox, ah, methods work out. However, Amos and I have prognosticated your arrival or the arrival of someone

just, ah, like you at any rate, long before we became cognizant of Mr. Himmer's, ah, game. Nevertheless, let us, for a moment, call it just that: a game.

Well, what has happened in game-terms: what have we here? Here we have the newly-made king in "Malamut," beyond a doubt, but one of his Towers of, ah, Strength has been taken by Tam. That is Amos Africanus. This other, ah, Tower of Strength, here; i.e., myself, must move off to Basel immediately because Basel is Banking, you know. A great deal is involved. There is a plane waiting for me out on the field, ready to take off as soon as we have lights, so I must be very brief. To go on with the game: the consort, while making a king, has been overtaken; first, by a voluntary abstinence from words and, then, an acute shortage of breath. That is Thay. Thay Himmer needs immediate medical attention, we agree on that, but: is Francis-X. Fard a competent medical practitioner? That I cannot answer. Nonetheless, it has been decided that the next move will be to transport Thay to Tam tonight in the other Lear jet: that's what the princess flies best. You will be seven aboard: the plane's maximum load. There will be several Players on hand to help. Olav Pesonius, a Finnish friend, whom Mr. Himmer calls his Little White Reindeer, was brought into "Malamut" today by the Foulba, along with the younger Africanus sister, Ana Lyse, and a rather unfortunate American newspaperwoman called Mag Media, I am afraid. Here, by the way, is Olav's journal of his trip down here overland; it might amuse you to run through it before you take your plane, tonight or early tomorrow morning before dawn. The Princess Mya has done really very little night flying: you might insist on a dawn flight, if you can. I say advisedly, if you can, because the king merely modifies moves: he cannot initiate any move until he has been crowned. The king is simply a Champion, you see, until he has been shown to his people—in this case, the Foulba, first. There will be no tiresome parades or risky public appearances. Don't worry—none of that! We will project you on television when it is feasible—the Sahara has been widely transistorized, you realize—but we expect to do an inaugural fly-over while the Foulba bards and court poets are acclaiming you on international shortwave bands. However, before this can take place, you must first reclaim and rescue your other Tower of Strength from, ah, Tam. That is Amos, naturally, on whom a great deal depends.

Now, how can this best be done? A frontal attack on Tam would be absurd. The only way for a restricted number of people to take an impregnable fortress is from inside. You will, therefore, gain admittance to the Steel Star by flying in and declaring yourselves a medical emergency. *Voilà!* International law obliges Tam to allow you to land. The hypocrite colonels do have an iron lung in there because they call it a hospital. *Ergo!* You do a judo on them and play Thay the Consort into the Trojan Lung. Princess Mya must follow with her *Borbor* in hand, which she will instill into the drinking water of, at least, Captain Mohamed. The captain, from all I hear, may well turn out to be some other color of horse in Thay Himmer's psychic sweepstakes, but the princess herself is running this race, as you know. What she wants out of it, first and foremost, is freedom: she'll tell you so herself. ''I want all the freedom in the world!'' She says so every day. Freedom, first of all, for Amos and the Fards because they are, if you like, full-fledged Players. Then, freedom for the entire cabinet of First Wave ex-ministers who are being held prisoner in Tam. Once their considerable, ah, human ability has been increased by GRAMMA and they have been properly, ah, secured by Mya's Borbor, they will form an ideal super-government for Africa; for the world.

All that postulates Phase Five and Phase Five will link "Malamut" on the Atlantic to Tam in the center of the Sahara, its very umbilicus. This will be done through the atomic center—which very conveniently for us, lies abandoned by the French at Reggan, exactly midway between here and Tam. Since they pulled their rods out of the pile, the entire installation has been in the hands of the famous Belgian physicist Dr. Henri Feldzahler, who is an old friend of the Africanus family and a Player, too, in his way. Our contact with him has been through Amos's sister, Freeky Fard: you see her importance, of course. We need Dr. Feldzahler and his atomic artifact to blow out a harbor right here below "Malamut." The obstruction, here, is the famous offshore reef, the natural bar which has cut off this bump of Africa forever from outside contact and left this whole section of the Sahara so, ah, sensitive to our approach. We shall, ah, inherit this part of the earth. From Basel, I fly to New York to arrange with the UN our plebiscite, which we will hold here for the Foulba, who will be voting for the first time in their long cultural life. The necessary documents are in the hands of Dr. Fard, so you see why we must get to him right away. The Foulba will vote in a phalanx which we can airlift back and forth to wherever voting is to be set up. They are very mobile by, ah, nature— being nomads—and they have all been, ah, grammatized: "Hello Yes Hello." They will vote as a man, of course, for you.

The Board has often discussed your, ah, image and I must say you fit it very, ah, adequately, indeed. I am completely, ah, cognizant of Mya's judgment in men, having lived through all of her seven husbands, after all. You, on the other hand, are something quite else again. You were found by the Foundation for Fundamental Findings—you will recall our original interview in the *Hotel Saint Georges* of Algut. At the time, it was not possible to speak to you frankly in front of that man Knoblock, who represented the CIA. They were trying to infiltrate the Foundation. You can imagine how hopeless to offer *us* mere money but we needed them for the time being. We were casting for a man in a million; someone as unique as you yourself; someone, if you will excuse me, someone *odd*. Then, we had to garner, microfilm and destroy—utterly wipe out any documentary proof of that person's previous existence. We needed the, ah, special services to get into the files in Albany, N.Y., for example. Beginning with your birth certificate, we have erased Ulys O. Hanson, III, "Hassan Merikani," etc.; the infant, the child, the boy and the man.

In Present Time, you are the great-grandson of Ma el Ainin, the mahdi or miraculous leader who stirred up the Sahara a couple of generations ago. In his time of triumphs, your great-grandfather sent your grandfather to America to meet Marcus Garvey and the man called Elijah, a predestined name. In the time of his troubles, your father was smuggled out of the country to the States as a babe and the, ah, dynasty died out —or seemed to have done. You will not be asked to preach but your great-grandfather, old Ma el Ainin, was a fiery preacher, fulminating at the Foulba about what he called a "Desert Democracy," with him as sole chief of state and, ah, immortal, of course. He turned out not to be, but, as no one dared prod him, and everyone around him was blind, they didn't even know it until long after he was dead. In the heat of the desert, he dried up into a leathery mummy under which they staggered around and around through the sand with it on a palanquin, carrying it around on their shoulders for years. Your great-grandfather was called Ma el Ainin, which means: "Watery Eyes," because he had very highly contagious trachoma all of his life. He could always manage to see out of one eye until the day that he died but he blinded everybody around him by sticking his dirty fingers into *their* eyes. You know the phrase: "*Le borgne est roi!* In the country of the blind, the one-eyed man is king!" It was a very efficient way to govern these people. It ensured him the utmost in love and fearful respect that the Sahara enjoys. Prince Pio would have liked to, ah, pull something like this but he was not a man of such caliber. The Sahara is a harsh and scurvy place, is it not?

Before I begin to go into what we envisage as your role in all this, let me break out this bottle of American Borbor—ah, excuse me: I meant American Bourbon, of course. Alas, we have nothing glamorous to offer you with it, like ice. No one around here seems to be able to keep the generator going . . . well, cheers! Now, the Board originally intended to have Mr. Himmer teach you faith-healing, as being more in the line of what the UN approves these days but, now that Thay has fallen silent, I really don't know. The Board felt very strongly that your official title should be released immediately to the world press—a scoop for this Media woman, perhaps, but it may be more than she deserves. We'll see. In any case, there is still the question of your title itself. The Board felt it should incorporate all the singular strength of the Sahara. If you do not object to the word; its Soul. The natives all tell us that the spirit of the Sahara is named Ghoul. The Africans fear and respect Ghoul. Therefore, one suggestion was Great Ghoul or

Grand Ghoul. Both voted down. You can imagine, perhaps, whose suggestion it was that, in order to impress the impact of immortality on your people, you should be called The Ghost of Ghoul. It has been decided that it will have the greatest possible impact everywhere and, above all, in the American States where the, ah, television culture and the Garveyite heritage of Black Power must be considered, if you were to be known quite simply as: The Ghoul. How does that strike you: powerful, is it not? I need hardly give you a detailed exposé of the latitude this title allows you. Everything is permitted to Ghoul, they say, and nothing is true. Nothing . . . well . . .

Ah, yes! Now, where was I? Living down here in the Sahara on this blank page of history, I have become a little mystical myself. Mysticals are much more common than you might think, in our Switzerland; despite our republican sentiments. My first mystical meeting was with Princess Mya— Madame PP Strangleblood, as she was then. I was utterly "grammatized" the minute she laid eyes on me. Then, later, "Hello Yes Hello," gave me the ability to communicate with people like the naked Foulba out there where you see the lights of their camp-city; with your primary friend, Hamid; with you. I am a very down to earth Swiss person of business who can begin to grasp the amplitude of Madame Mya's magnificent design. Madame knows how to take things: that's Swiss! Quite apart from her stupendous advantages of beauty, intelligence, power, culture and wealth, she holds the final inestimable trump. "I am yellow!" she can proclaim, as she did to the huge Chinese delegation we received here and sent on their way. The Chinese offered to build her a solar-powered water-distillation chain-project to be strung right across the Sahara from "Malamut" to the Red Sea, but Mya just thanked them sweetly and said: "I am a poor Asiatic colonial victim of the whites." Now, who else could say that and mean it; I ask you? The woman is colossal, immense!

Just let me brief you on some of the, ah, shape of our projects; going through them alphabetically.

A: stands for: *Ability, the Creation of* (*see GRAMMA*), then: *Affrica, Mrs. Francis-Xavier Fard* (*see AFRICANUS, family*). All the headings in capital letters refer you to the very complete electronic library we have here; those panels over there and that screen. Alas, as I have already said, the generator . . .

B: stands for: *BIO-KEY*. Bio-Key is the name of our pharmaceutical combine based on Mexico, producing steroids for the Pill. Fundamental Funds won the patents to the thirty-two-stage process for extracting steroids from the Mexican giant yam. Weight for weight, steroids are worth about seventeen times the value of gold; some ninety-one million pre-devaluation dollars a ton. Today? Pull any figure you like out of the air. Right here directly below us, Madame Mya is sitting on the biggest steroid bank in the world. Unfortunately, steroids have to be refrigerated. Every time I become aware that our generator is not pounding away, I shudder to think of our steroid stock. After all, that's a good many yams. Mya is always complaining, too, that changes in temperature are not good for her *Charles Heidsieck* champagne.

There is no file for Borbor, you will notice: maybe she keeps the bubbles of that in her head.

C: stands for: *Chemicals:* (*Private File*). This file contains all her work on the hallucinogens in Basel. You might find the *Borbor* formula in here but only Mya knows which one it is.

D: stands for: *DOMINGUEZ* (*Lindissima Reuther y Dominguez, deceased*). Poor Lindissima, she was really a very foolish woman. "All attraction and then no traction," Mya once said of her. It was a bit cruel because Lindissima was no match for her. This file contains all the transfers, the property transfers by which this little corner of the hump of Africa became ours. There is a rumor, put out by the Spaniards, that Mya did away with Lindissima but that is as absurd as the story that she killed Prince Pio, Dr. Labesse. La Reuther had a terrible barbiturate problem and she tried to keep up with Mya, drink for drink. She was found on the floor with a broken glass in her hand. Pio died from sheer megalomania: he thought he was Hakim, Caliph of Bagdad, and walked off in the desert alone; trailing his gold encrusted burnous to wipe out his footsteps. He shouted: "I'll be back in no time!" as he disappeared over a dune. Mya ran him down in her jeep but he died in her arms, whispering: *"Assassinate everybody!"*

This little file must not fall into the hands of the Spanish authorities, who claim that the entire ex-Reuther estate, including Cape Noon and "Malamut" is still under their authority and jurisdiction. The UN has still not yet set a date for the last of the Spaniards to leave but we are asking for a plebiscite, the day that they do.

E: stands for: *Emerald Seal*. That is, the so-called Scarab of the Sahara which is now in your possession. The name was given to this artifact by Mr. Himmer, who likes to live under the impression that he got it for nothing. Here are the documents. This is the result of the assay done at Hatton Gardens in London: *Green stone: 45.7 carats. Specific gravity, 2.70: emerald.* Here we have the report from the British Museum: *"No ancient artifact of Egyptian provenance was made out of emerald.''* And, here, you have a record of the sum paid by our agent to a certain Mohamed Imsak of Cairo: quite staggering, as you can see.

F: stands for: *1. FARD (see files). 2. Farout Islands (Himmer estate).* As he may have told you, Mr. Himmer chooses to own nothing; nothing at all. What little money he had when they married—it could not have come to a million pre-devaluation dollars, at the most—he handed over to the Board. This file, therefore, is empty. That brings us to: *3. FUNDA-MENTAL FUNDS,* my own particular preoccupation and, then: *4. FOULBA,* which will be yours. Here are some pictures of the boys during one of their annual orgies. I am not entirely in sympathy with these people. In fact, I think it might be said that we have had an, ah, floop with the Foulba. The Himmers may like to think they got them for nothing but the Foulba cost us a fortune, daily, in fodder alone. Just to keep them and their cows on this idle desert around "Malamut" means that we fly tons of hay in from Switzerland, three times a week. We call it the "Milk Run" and that is what I will be catching to Basel, tonight, if we ever get any lights on the field.

As you may know, the Foulba have lived for many a millennia in a state approaching symbiosis with their lovely lyre-horned cattle. As a Swiss, I love cows and of all cows these antique animals are the most beautiful. When we introduced the Foulba to "Hello Yes Hello," it swept the Sahara as soon as we had paired off a few. Previously, there had been no real communication between them: "Never trust a fellow Foulba," they say about themselves, ingenuously. A Foulba's best friends were always his four-footed ones into whose soft furry ears the Foulba used to confide their infantile fantasies.

250

They lived off their cattle without ever killing them, drinking their milk and enough of their salty blood for both man and beast to keep going together. Now, they have suddenly stopped; now, for the first time in their long history, they have become Assassins to their animals, killers of cows, cannibals. I don't mean that they slaughter them; if only they did! Out there where you see the flickering lights of their campfires on the mainland, even now, they are feasting on raw, still-living beef. They hack quivering steaks out of the flanks of their bellowing, bleeding animals, who stumble and stagger away to die in the dark while their former lovers, the Foulba, cram their mouths with the meat. I have been a vegetarian all my life: I cannot pretend to judge these people, but I do know *why* it happened. They cut into their cattle, you understand, when the cattle could not communicate. "Hello Yes Hello," said into a long silky ear got only: "Moo!" in reply and that is why those cattle are dying so atrociously out there tonight that you can hear their pitiful bellowing over the cry of the sea when the wind is right. For me, the lesson has been that we must communicate that the other may not devour us, but the Himmers insist there is much more to it than that and, no doubt, they are right.

Now, we come to the letter, H.

H: stands for: *HANSON, Ulys Othello of Ithaca, New York*. I think you will be amazed by our documentation on this person. If ever they get the generator going, you must project all the material on the screen over there. As I said, the original documents have been destroyed and all this file will be demagnetized and, ah, disintegrated the day you actually become the Ghoul.

H: also stands for: *HORMONE* (*see BIO-KEY*). You may

find this horrid or endlessly, ah, fascinating. Some of the ramifications are, at present, quite distasteful; such as our dealings with Brazilian sources through Recife, where we have managed to tap a pituitary supply in the Amazonian jungle which looks as though it may be drying up. Amos has been concerned with the, ah, practical aspects of this business. It grew out of Mya's determination to get her money out of, ah, money; long before the dollar was devaluated, as a matter of fact. Mya, today, is the world's richest woman because she holds the key to the future in hormones: she's got a grip on the Life Force, itself. The financing of "Malamut" has devolved on me. The, ah, philosophic, ah, theory, behind "Malamut," we owe to Thay in his role as Bishop Himmer when he proposes the stockpiling of human pituitary glands as a sort of, ah, religious principle of, ah, Eternal Life. All our problems may be said to be genetic: it all depends who you like to have around. Race, color, creed, crime, cramps in the belly and death can be controlled only by hormones and hormones are horribly hard to come by. Each one of us has only one pituitary so, to prepare a thimble-sized stockpile of these hormones, we need five thousand cadavers. Your pituitary is a gland the size of a pea; right here at the base of your skull.

Now, if we are not merely to fulfill but surpass our, ah, purpose here on this planet, we need every single one of those pituitaries out there existing in Present Time. To begin with, the hormone content of that entire Foulba nation out there, nearly two million of them hacking apart their live cows, could be carried around in a briefcase. . . .

10

Happily, Hamid broke in at that point as he bobbed up from the lower depths of the house; the big rooms below being Mya's bosom, I suppose. Hamid was sharp in nifty new threads; a Highland-heather purple-green Harris-tweed jacket, white yachting flannels and a cream-colored silk shirt with a black and pink striped bow tie that looked like the misplaced smile on a stuffed cat. Over this he wore his shimmering striped-silk jellaba down to the ground. I thought the first scene between Hamid and the Swiss lawyer Rolf Ritterolf might be a bit rough but they had already met and sized each other up like Dignity and Impudence; a Saint Bernard and plush monkey, perhaps. Talking right over Hamid's head, Ritterolf said: "At first I thought that this one was an absolute primitive until I heard him explaining the Roman Lupercalia to Mya. Most extraordinary! Did you teach him all this?" Hamid was bouncing up and down, clapping his hands like a small sultan cracking the whip on his slaves and, inside two minutes, he had swept Ritterolf off to his plane; promising lights on the field as if he had everything in "Malamut" already under control and was really running the place. I saw Ritterolf go with the slightly sinking feeling that this stout Swiss was my last link with sanity. When Hamid starts running things, anything can happen and does.

I once made up a fable about this part of the world to match the fairy tale about the frog prince on whom the princess had only to drop three drops of her magic elixir to turn poor Froggy back into a man; some kind of Borbor, no doubt. Anyway, in all the backcountry of Africa, of all the world; in from the desert, out of the bush and down from the hills, millions of young princes in rags are marching forever toward town with their shoes in their hands. City lights dazzle their eyes as they march up to a jukebox. Neon flickers, music rocks and as three bottles of Caca-Culo are poured into them, they turn into toads. So, when I caught that sourly familiar apple odor off Hamid's breath as he came back and threw his arms around me to give me a boozy wet kiss on the mouth, I knew Mya must have poured three bottles of champagne into *him*.

"You've made it with Mya," I said, disengaging myself. "You've been showing Mya the handle of your big old brush."

Hamid threw his arms around the elephantine air with his most diabolical grin, like saying: "Mya's one big girl!"

"I thought you said you knew how to turn on the lights," I went on, accusingly.

"I fix her generator! Ha! Ha! Ha!"

Hamid collapsed on a cushion howling with glee and, then, suddenly shot into the air again to bumble around the dark domed room like an angry bee in his hive; pushing back panels, throwing in switches and punching buttons I was sure he knew nothing about. The Moroccan approach to machines is the same as that used for directing a djinn, and a good many Moroccans have a highly developed genius for this. Most Moroccans can stop a watch or, even, a can-opener simply by taking one penetrating look at it but other Moroccans can repair a carburetor in the Sahara with a few half-chewed dates. In any case, I clutched my UHER, looking around for some safe hiding place to keep it out of Hamid's reach. From far away and below, someplace, came the hard hammering of the generator and, a few minutes later, the hum of a departing plane dwindling overhead. As Hamid hopped about like a mad monkey in the gloom, various machines sputtered, sparked and blinked into life. The entire electronic library began to light up.

I saw they had installed much the same sort of setup I was familiar with at Hampton Institute, or was it at Howard? I sat down in front of the screen and punched the letter H; waited for the signal to wink and dialed: HANSON. There in front of me, sure enough, was my birth certificate. I was pained to see that my parents' papers were attached but I realized they were bound to go, too, if I was really going to succeed in what I had always thought of doing—changing my skin but from the inside out, as it were. I was, at last, going to become myself by becoming somebody else. As I was savoring this abstruse search for a self, Hamid broke in with the mention of food. Even food could not tear my eyes away from a page of magnified microfilm which had appeared on my screen.

It was a page from a copybook I'd owned at the age of eight, in which I once wrote in block letters what I thought at the time was my final farewell epistle to my mother. I ran away into the park for what turned out to be a long, boring afternoon and an evening until hunger drove me back home. Luckily, Mother was still out so I ate and went to bed, completely forgetting the letter which my mother found and refused to return to me, ever. She must have read it aloud one thousand times to everybody, anybody; white people, even. She declared it was one of her lifelong treasures and here this masterpiece was again, flickering in front of my eyes.

> *Dear Pig*
> *I am run away for good.*
> *Your son Ulys.*

There was an annotation in my mother's hand:

> *These first travels of Ulys did not take him far. His trek downtown was little more than a trick to get out of his homework, I reckon.*

That gave me a chill; nearly turned me to stone for a second, as a matter of fact, but there was worse to come as I went on pushing the buttons. Their next item was a typed manuscript of my prize-winning essay which won me the I AM AN AMERICAN DAY CONTEST, in high school. It runs: *"This is my own, my native land . . ."* So help me, my mother wrote most of that and it won me a ten-dollar gold piece. Took that old gold piece and the letter that said the principal should present it to me in front of the assembled school and he looked at that letter and he looked at me and he handed me both of them back. I remember, that gold piece went on the rent and I thought my mother should have it made into a brooch for herself or a stickpin for me for my tie. I flipped on through the electronic record of my life with growing embarrassment.

Here was a paper of mine, written at Hampton for a course in Afro-American Lit. This thing was entitled: "Negro Renaissance Poets before Langston Hughes,'' and included lots of excerpts of verse. Now, who the hell wrote what I quote? Oh boy!

"You are the gilded pride of Day
And I the sable pride of Night."

Yeah! I was still stirring these faintly fruity lines around in my head when Hamid showed up with a cold lobster and some champagne but no glasses.

"What, Hamid!" I cried, "no keef? You know champagne gives me bubbles in the appendix. If I drink that stuff, I'll die of peritonitis out here in the Sahara."

"Thass all right," Hamid said and sped off. I set to on the lobster with my hands. On the table beside me was the grubby notebook left me by Rolf Ritterolf. On the cover was written: "O. Pesonius: His Journal." When I saw that the Little White Reindeer had written in English, I began flipping over the pages with greasy fingers and read:

11

WE

We are all so close in our Sleep & Dream Clinic here in Helsinki that when I told them, today, that I was going back to the Sahara to join my old friend Thay Himmer the Seventh in his castle called "Malamut," on Cape Noon, all the other initiates in the office suddenly broke out singing:

> *Olav, you are crazy! Olav you are mad!*
> *Why do you want to go back with that man*
> *Who treated you so bad!*

That may be because they have had to file so many of my dreams about the time Thay hit me over the head with a pail in a sauna: some of them still think I should have called the police. It was a big local scandal at the time because I am not altogether unknown in my little Finland as an artist and, certainly, Thay Himmer the Seventh, White Rajah-Bishop of the Farout Isles, was the most exotic celebrity anyone in Finland had ever brought back from his travels. (Like a tourist trophy: was I still that naïve? Perhaps.) Only Ingating understood and

258

she understood perfectly. Ingating is very intelligent for a Finnish girl because she has read special books. "Did you experience satori when Mr. Himmer hit you in the hot room," Ingating asked me, "like the adepts of a Japanese master of Zen?" She is a very good girl but I was still under sedation or I would never have blabbed out to her that I am, now and forever, Himmer's Little White Reindeer. I must say for her that she did not blink a blond eyelash. She kept comimg back to the clinic to see me and, when my head healed, offered to let me move in with her when I was released because, she said, we could all live very well on her state allowance as the unmarried mother of twins. That's Finnish finesse, for you. She was informing me delicately that I had lost my state-studio over the Himmer scandal and had no place to live. Luckily, the clinic has a Sleep & Dream Research Lab. run by our great oneirologist, Doktor Erno Aalto. He became so interested in my Saharan desert dreams that he invited me to sleep-in at the clinic, five nights a week, and offered me a big bare white room facing north as a studio. Weekends all last year, I slept over at Ingating's and, when she had twins again this last summer, I simply stayed on in the clinic but, on weekends, I treated myself to a slumber without attaching the old electroencephalograph or the loop for penis-erectile control which is wired to the videometer all other nights of the week. I am going to miss that.

Finland is a little country but in some ways we are well advanced. Actually, Finland is a country without too much excitement because the weather is no good for it. The arrival of someone like Thay Himmer in Helsinki can change the lives of many people in Finland. There were pictures of him in all the papers and magazines, waving at the camera. Only I in all of Finland knew that Thay was warding off image-spells with counter-spells from the Farout Islands. Wearing his funny cut fringe of red Arab beard and his big bright blue eyes, he became a popular figure in Finland. He always smiled at everybody with his more than American teeth and they loved him, at first. When I took him up north with me to see the herds, the whole Finnish nation followed him on television. Thay Himmer grinned out of the screen in every home in Finland like a jack-o'-lantern in a fur parka. While he was standing beside our Finnish President judging the reindeer races, a disgraceful technical accident occurred on the television but, as Thay always said: there are no accidents. Everyone knows who would do a filthy thing in Finland! A ghostly pair of antlers appeared behind Thay's head for several minutes on all the screens in the land and pictures like that ran in the newspapers, too. I was terribly ashamed as a Finn. However, although it may have been meant as a joke in very poor taste, state television pollsters announced that many country people in outlying districts had identified Bishop Himmer as the Norse hunting god.

It is true: Thay can look almost supernatural at times to very provincial people. Also, he did go around talking in a slightly eerie way about anything from astrology to Grammatology, whether they understood all that much English or not. Rumors ran around that he was the head of a new sect or a secret religion: other tongues clacked that he was an agent. "An agent for what?" I once had the occasion to storm at one fellow Finn, who was just flustered enough to blurt back: "International, I suppose." I had to laugh back into that Finn's face for not having the courage to say what he really thought: *"Interplanetary! of course."* That is the only possible word for Thay Himmer. Ingating saw right away how interplanetary

Mr. Himmer was, so, when I told her I was his Little White Reindeer, she just sighed and replied: "Yes, Olav, I know. If there's something afoot, you must put your foot in it and you're always pawing away at the clouds." Ingating is twenty-two months older than I am and very wise for her age.

When Thay's cable came, Ingating agreed at once that I should leave for Cape Noon as soon as we found out where it was on my map of Africa, published by *Kummerly & Frey; scale: 1/12,000,000, printed in Berne.* But, at the clinic this morning, Doktor Aalto drew me aside: "Do I understand you correctly, Olav? Are you really so brave and so brash as to be dashing off to some place in the Sahara which is calling itself, brazenly: 'Malamut'? You know what it means, of course: Hassan-i-Sabbah, the Grand Assassin and Old Man of the Mountain, called *his* castle: 'Alamut'! Is this something *worse?* Malamut means: The Bad Way, the Way of no Return. Are you ready to risk that, Olav? Are you properly prepared? I hope you have your return fare, Olav. We shall all miss you here at Sleep & Dreams. By the way, I thought your friend Thay, Bishop Himmer, came from the Pacific, the Farout Islands. You met him in the Sahara, I believe: can't he go home? What is he doing in still another part of the desert? Is this place 'Malamut' what he calls his *home?*"

"I understand it's a castle built by his wife."

"His *wife,* Olav? In the picture *we* have of *him* in *our* dream files, built up out of *your* dreams, Olav, there is no *trace* of a wife!"

"Here's a picture I cut out of a magazine; taken at Orly airport, right after their marriage. It says here she was previously married to the richest boy in the world. She looks bigger than Thay but maybe she was standing on a step."

261

"I knew there must be someone behind him; a woman, of course. Olav, I warn you: 'Malamut' is a challenge. By giving this name to their house, the Himmers unfurl a banner by far more cynical than any pirate's Skull and Crossbones. I am utterly taken aback by such audacity. They flaunt an attachment to old heresies kept alive in dark corners of the world, hidden out of the way of modern communication systems so successfully that they might well one day prove to be the springs of human nature if they were revived in a modern form by utterly unscrupulous people. Is that what your friends are up to, Olav?" Professor Aalto sounded me, his glasses glittering: "Keep in touch." And I will call him, too, every night. We have our dream-code. Dear old Dr. Aalto, he's such a well-known anti-feminist alarmist, but I guess I had better watch my step.

Helsinki, Nov. 3

The banks were open today but no money came through for me. Why does one always have to wait for money? Ingating is more nervous than I am but she will calm down.

Helsinki, Nov. 4

Still no money but I did find out about airlines and visas. No one here ever heard of Cape Noon, let alone how to get down there but, when I show them where it is on the big bump of Africa, they suggest flying to Casablanca or Dakar. All Thay's cable says is: JOIN US IN MALAMUT ON CAPE

NOON IMMEDIATELY MONEY FORTHCOMING LOVE
THAY but it is dated Tanja so I'll think I'll fly there. No
luggage: this is the way I came and this is the way I shall
return. Life is too soft in Finland, I can't wait to get back to
the desert. Ingating understands.

Tanja, Nov. 6

No one here in Tanja has ever even heard of the Himmers.
I have tried everywhere: consulates, banks, hotels and I've
even asked some of the more reputable-looking guides. Tanja
must be a very spiritual city because it simply swarms with
guides but not all of us are ready for them. I feel safer inside
the Café de Paris, where I am writing this, than I would on
the terrace with all this money in my pocket. Money makes
me nervous, anyway. I hate not to have money and yet I never
know what to do with it when traveling. Americans abroad,
I've noticed, always touch the talisman of AMERICAN EXPRESS
once a day, at least, but I am going where travelers' checks
don't travel. My spirit is already far away ahead of my body;
already down in the desert, but Tanja persists in taking me
still for a tourist. When I stride around Tanja with my eyes
up to the lovely tumbling skies, beyond which I know rises
the winter dome over the desert, swarms of shoeshine boys
cluster around my feet, tripping me up: "Soo-sine? Soo-sine,
buddy?" When I say: "No, go away, not today," they answer:
"Fuck-you, Jack! Fuck off!" I have been playing Pied Piper
to all the guides, too, who sidle up according to hierarchy;
each offering his wares until the right one finally gets through
to me. "Englishman, wanna get fucked?" When I ask any

263

one of the guides if they have ever heard of the Himmers, they all answer at once: "Sure, Johnny!" and lead me into yet another Arab bazaar.

Tanja, Nov. 7

Terrible hangover, today. I was still sitting in that Café de Paris at seven o'clock last night when a middle-aged American woman with big yellow teeth and stringy gray hair pulled back into an untidy but girlish psyche-knot at the back of her head, leaned over from the next table, gave me a rather revolting yellow smile, and she said: "Having the all-too-typical Tanja troubles?" It was a good enough gambit I guess. I ended up by paying for her coffee as well as my own and, then, she led me off to an American bar called the Exit, where everyone seemed to know her only too well. The very tall barman with a mustache and a pompadour leaned over her at her in an almost threatening way as he asked her:

"Well, what'll it be tonight, Mag?"

She went all kittenish, rubbing herself up against me, gurgling: "I want you to meet everybody's favorite barman, Billy Beachnut. Whad'ja say your name was, Mac?"

I think she must have taken me for a fellow-American, at first: "Olav Pesonius," I replied.

"Latin, eh?" cracked Beachnut. "Well, Olav, this little lady's got you in tow is Mrs. Mag Media, the newspaperwoman: She talks Latin, too."

"Not Missus! Miss!" She twitched herself onto a barstool, letting her old gray coat fall back off her shoulders.

"A miss that's still good for many a mile, eh, Mag? What'll you folks be drinking, tonight?"

My head is splitting and there she is, singing in the bathroom, right now! Last night she drank me—a Finn!—under the table and, when she fished me out to pay for the outrageous bill at the Exit, I guess I must have felt I couldn't afford to pay for a hotel room on top of all that so I ended up here and I feel simply awful.

Later

Things looking up slightly. Mag not only insists she knows the Himmers and how to get to them—"After all, I'm a newspaperwoman!"—but says she can get in touch with a girl in Casablanca whose brother, Amos Africanus, is general manager for the Himmers, down on Cape Noon. Ana Lyse Africanus will know how to get down to "Malamut." Unfortunately, Ana Lyse seems not to be on the phone so Mag and I will have to go to Casa together in Mag's old car to find her. I'll pay for the gas.

Casablanca, Nov. 8

I knew it. We got here so late that Mag insisted on taking a double room with a bath in this expensive hotel. She's in the bathroom right now, singing. We no sooner got settled in here last night than Ana Lyse herself phoned up saying she was coming right on over. I may be a dumb Finn but I did

265

raise an eyebrow at that. "I sent her a telegram saying I'd be at this hotel. I'm surprised she's coming over at this hour, though." I thought the hotel might be surprised also but, no; they sent her right on up. You might just be able to get away with one woman in your hotel room in Helsinki but never with two in the middle of one night! Actually, we sat up all night plotting our trip south. Ana Lyse is petite but she's the same sort of girl Ingating is; I felt it immediately. You just know she would know how to cook a good meal over an open fire. Poor thing, she has just heard that her brother, Amos Africanus, has been kidnaped down there in the desert and she doesn't know where he is. She has tried everything including telepathy but she can't get in touch with the Himmers, so she is as anxious as I am to get down there. The plan is to drive down as far as we can in Mag Media's old car and then see what we can do from there on. Ana Lyse speaks Arabic and insists that it is useless to try anything official because officials will only stop us.

Tiznit, Nov. 9

This is the first place south that looks like the desert but the sun doesn't shine much on this red-walled town because of the mile-high mist-bank formed by the Portuguese Current flowing south offshore a few miles away past this western end of the great beach of the Sahara. Seawater, swift and cold, condenses the hot air from the desert into fog. For all the sun there is this morning, one might as well be back in Finland. At the last minute this morning, I had to buy four new tires for Mag's car before we headed south with Ana Lyse in the front seat beside Mag and me in the back with her huge Great Dane puppy called Karl Barx. I've been treated like a spare tire in the back seat, wrestling with the dog as we swung around all the loops and bends of a superb road hugging the coastline. Luckily, Karl Barx is friendly.

Tomorrow, we ought to get to Goulmimime or Goulimine or Goulmina or Ghoul Mime—anyway, for lunch. Then, on to Tam-tam if the road is in good enough repair after these early rains. It is strangely solacing to be back on the verge of baby country, again: in the Sahara, so many places and people have baby names. There is Ta-ta and Tan-tan and Tam-tam and Da-da and Ba-ba and so many more. At each stop, the hotel gets more primitive and the food worse since the French left this part of the world, except in some cases where a long-gone Madame's former native "boy" still runs the place. Last night the food was so good I was convinced that some French Madame's ghost was still out in the kitchen making the omelets.

Tam-tam, Nov. 10

When we got here, we were arrested, right off. The road here from Goulimine has, indeed, been washed out in many places where the water must come across like a wall when it rains. Luckily, it was the long flat "easy" stretches of the road surface which had been wrecked, while hairpin bends over ridges of rock are still in good shape. All this road is new, too, since the Spaniards withdrew further south. At last, we came over a pass to see Tam-tam set out like a tiny, crenellated white toy fort in the middle of a vast sandy plain over which ran a road as straight as an arrow. When we got to the end of it, we found that road barred by a gate out in the middle of nowhere outside of town. Two sentries stopped us at the point of a gun. One of them kept us covered while the other got in touch with the fort through his walkie-talkie. Then, we were ordered to drive straight on in and report. Karl Barx very nearly bit one of those men.

We are now living the sequel to an old Beau Geste movie in which the Arabs have won the fort and are running the show, dressed in classic khaki uniforms, looking more or less like soldiers anywhere these days. The second-in-command here met us out in the sandy street in which we stopped. He was unsmiling but perfectly polite as we showed him our papers. Mag Media was out front with her press card at which he looked dubiously because the photo was so much better than what he saw in front of him. Mag was already wiggling and ogling him; up to all of her tricks. The short surly captain came out to inspect us and then, rather than call us officiously into his office, he invited us into his own poured-concrete villa, which stood out like an eyesore in the landscape of pure white-washed cube-houses surrounded by sand. Inside, Mag pulled out her press card again and went into her act. The captain, who seemed not to understand her French, was completely cowed.

We have all been quartered in the Officers' Mess, which was obviously built back in colonial days. Nearby, another unlikely relic lies awash in the sands. It is a long building in concrete built in the form of a transatlantic tanker and is said to have been a brothel whose rooms were the cabins in the superstructure. There was a bar on the captain's bridge. The well-deck was a swimming pool surrounded by walls like the prow of the ship. Today, this astonishing structure has the Cuban flag painted on its side. The mystery man around here is the major, who seems to be quartered there by himself. The captain has not come over here once from his fort or his villa but the major is in the bar here, right now. In the bar of the Officers' Club they serve only mint tea and soft drinks these days, but Mag and Ana Lyse are in there now with the major. He wears a full beard, a Castro cap and very elegantly tailored raw-silk khaki fatigues. He is so much more outlandish-looking here than we are that they will give us no trouble, I think. Our story is we want to take a look at Tarik, the next stop south and the border. It would be unwise to admit we hope to go further and we won't. The girls are good liars, I think.

Tarik, Nov. 11

Twenty hours in a caravan of trucks to get here, luckily on top of a cargo of mattresses. We are in the newly ruined Spanish capital city which must once have been shining white; perhaps, only a year ago. Unless someone catches this place pretty quick, it is going to go back to the desert. Only the barracks are well kept, while private houses and the hotel have been boarded up or have already fallen into ruin since they were broken into and looted. A few Arab fishermen in anonymous rags slouch through the streets and along the abandoned *avenidas* of shut shops. I noticed them hanging their nets from the marquee of a dilapidated movie house down by the beach. There is no proper harbor. Small boats come in over the pounding surf from ships standing a mile or more offshore in deeper water. There is fresh meat other than sheep only when a boat

269

from the Canaries pitches a few head of cattle overboard and they swim ashore to be slaughtered. This is in the very best tradition of this coastline; it's what was always done here throughout history to all shipwrecked mariners and in the pioneer days of aviation, downed pilots had their throats cut or were held to ransom less than a generation ago. I am delighted to find this part of the Sahara is exactly like the other part of the desert I know: silky, sordid and suspicious. How to explain its infinite attraction to anyone who has not sensed its silences? Only the Sahara and our own pure northern tundra are wordless wastes.

Now, for all my loose talk about words, we have been stuffing the poor officers here with nothing but lies. Mag took care of all that; preening herself and ogling the officers during the lunch they gave us in their mess. I think they have decided we are a thankless lot, just odd enough to be harmless and let alone. The border we have to cross without asking their permission is invisible, of course, but it lies just out beyond the outskirts of town, on the far side of the *oued* bed where we can see camels grazing near a few nomad fires. In the mad Arab scramble of our arrival here at high noon, Ana Lyse caught a ragged little nomad girl trying to pick our pockets as she slunk up to our truck, pretending to beg. Ana Lyse caught the child by the louse-ridden plaits of her hair and was trying to keep the brat from sinking her teeth in her arms as she panted to me: "Here, Olav, quick! Give me a ten thousand franc note: I've got to impress this child."

As I fumbled for the money, Media butted in with: "You're not going to give that kid all that cash!"

The kid caught on quicker than she did to what this move was about. Any random observer would have thought, of course, that it was just one of those casual tourist attacks on a native child but Ana Lyse knows her Morocco. She twisted the ears of the urchin as she gave her the money and then, without letting go of her pigtails, she gave her a good sound slap as she whispered something fierce in Arabic into her ear. There's more money than this where this came from; she was saying, of course. We want three camels and a man to guide us south. The big sum of money was to impress someone we haven't seen yet but hope that we will after we've taken our siestas. We hope to meet him walking down by the *oued*. I hope no lovelorn lieutenant takes it in his head to follow the girls with a jeep.

near Elayoun

Saharan security seems to have been magically suspended for us, as if we were the Three Wise Kings traveling through the night. In the gray-green light of pre-dawn at this halt, we look more like three tourists who have been taken on too long a ride by some rascally guide. Indeed, here he is with us: Mohamed, looking as picturesque and unreliable as anyone could wish. We have never seen anything of him but his shifty, narrow eyes but Mag Media says he is, "cute." Right now, she is singing snatches of the old "Desert Song," as she ties up her gray hair with a ribbon and tries to get the guide to let down his veil. She was begging Ana Lyse to help her in this game with a few Arab phrases when the guide said most unexpectedly: *"Soy hijo de España."* When I asked what that meant, Mag informed me acidly that everyone in the world speaks Spanish. I understand less Spanish even than Arabic,

271

although what little I picked up last year in Tam was quite another dialect, I am told. At least, our guide now seems a little less sinister than he did, even if he will not unveil for what he says rather alarmingly are *"political reasons"!*

Later

We are traveling fast and light to avoid meeting anyone on the trail and that means, of course, that we take the long inland route although, because of the mirage, the sea seems never far away. Tonight, Ana Lyse can hardly open her eyes because they are all puffed up by infection. Mag Media says she has become quite deaf, probably from the sound of her own voice. The desert makes people very disagreeable. We are all suffering from thirst, sunburn and bites. I begin to wonder how I let myself be swept away by these two determined females but, of course, Thay is somewhere down here ahead, waiting for me. All this afternoon, we trudged on through mirage which surrounded us like shimmering seawater with the quicksilver habit of suddenly sliding off like some science fiction cloud of intelligence or a huge soluble fish which can slither over land, suddenly deciding to surge up from one depression and slide down into another. We were plodding across an ancient lava flow, porous and crumbling, full of potholes and even giant caves filled with stalagmites over which we passed on sounding stone arches. Some potholes in the black rock were filled with bleached bones, making them look like huge nests blanched with birdlime. We rode sidesaddle on our camels, our backs to the sun, but we are sadly unprepared for such a journey. I wonder how long we can go on like this? The air smells, tastes of ozone, leaving an iodine taste in the back of my throat which reminds me of childhood delirium and intense anxiety. I am almost too tired to sleep or I would try and contact Doktor Aalto.

In the Middle of Nowhere

Ah, this is much better! We are sailing in an air-conditioned Landrover over ground so level that I can write in this hard-backed notebook on my knees. I would never have dreamed Doktor Aalto could be so severe with me. "Olav!" he snapped as soon as he appeared on my dream-screen. "Don't you even know when you're in the wrong dream!" He screamed at me so loud I almost woke up. "Who do you think you are, Olav—Stanley looking for Livingstone? That happened a lot further south and a long time ago. Are you reliving some French adolescent colonial nightmare, or what! Snap out of that dream, Olav, or you are lost! Of course, I cannot imagine why you have insisted on dragging those two females along with you but I can tell you one sure thing from here: Madame Himmer won't like it a bit! Nevertheless, you must get yourself out of there at once. Haven't you noticed that your Sahara has been transistorized since you were there last? Haven't you noticed that your veiled guide is wearing a Rolex? Dying of thirst on three camels, indeed, Olav! Why, the man owns a fleet of brand-new air-conditioned Landrovers. Stop dreaming: get with it!"

Doktor Aalto's voice came across with an almost feminine cackle at times but I put that down to my own poor reception.

"Malamut" looms in sight, swimming in the air like a

273

castle of mirage which we cannot approach by the heat of day.
I am writing this under a tarpaulin I begged from our blue-
veiled guide before he drove off and abandoned us here. I
think he must have had some trouble with the Himmers because
he said: "From here on you walk or you pay me fi' ten fitteen
thousand dollars apiece for the car." The girls argued and I
argued that the Himmers would undoubtedly pay him anything
within reason to deliver us at their door but he picked up a
whip that leapt into his land like a snake. Even Karl Barx,
who is panting in the intolerable heat, here beside us, cringed
and slunk out of the Landrover. Mohamed was out of range
before Ana Lyse thought to pull out of her corsage a little
pearl-handled revolver. It is a mere .22 caliber but I will handle
it from now on.

"Malamut" floats out there on the perfectly round milky
horizon like a mother-of-pearl Buddha on a tray of quicksilver.
Ana Lyse assures me that what we see is the rock of Cape
Noon, Heaven Rock, blasted with dynamite and rebuilt into
an immense statue of Princess Mya, turning her back on us.
All we have to drink is a hairy guerba, a goatskin of water
tasting of goat and tar. Even Karl Barx refused it until we
poured some down his throat. This is no place for a dog.

12

Hamid bounced back, having organized everything for our departure, as if "Malamut" had belonged in the palm of his hands for years.

"I am berry sorry, my dear," he announced, "but in this place is no keef."

"Hamid, I will not go another round of this unvarnished tale without I get some keef."

"Take some more Borbor the lady fix herself. Berry good Borbor, same-same all Arab womens give their mens."

"Hamid, I know that whole Borbor bit perfectly well and will you stop talking that awful pidgin you picked up in the port. I put you down here speaking almost perfect English. Besides, I know how Borbor feels, if anyone does. I am full of her Borbor: I'm under her spell, right now. I should be as mad as hell at her for slipping me the stuff—but I am and I'm not. Or, am I? Let's see. . . . You say no keef? *Walloo?* No keef at all? You've turned out the seams of your pockets?"

"I have just this one Casa Sport cigarette left over from

Tanja I empty out and am filling with keef. Together, we smoke."

"But, Hamid, you know how wasteful that is! Haven't you got a pipe?"

"And we drink some champagne," he grinned, pulling out an already broached jeroboam from under the skirts of his jellaba.

"You know I don't drink warm champagne if I can help it. Besides, if Mya opened that bottle, it's probably borborized."

"But, of course! There is Borbor in every little thing here, my dear. There is plenty Borbor even in me and I like it. It feels berry good. *Borbor kif walloo!* Like nuttin! How many Berber girls give me Borbor, before? Borbor is no more bad than Bebsi-Cola, unless the woman say the Words."

"What words, Hamid?"

"The donkey words. One Arab man buy one berry good Arab girl guarantee birgin he see the first time that night. Old women already tell that girl what she do: You put this Borbor in his chow and you treat him good, berry good. When that man slob on on you, you push him away and you say: *Rrrrrah!* like you say to one donkey to drive him. Next thing, you wind your legs around his neck and you make him carry you piggy-back. When that woman is up on that man's back, she use the donkey words. That man, he finish: he through. He can carry that woman from the bed to the bucket the rest of their days. When a man marry, he got only one thing to do and when he do it he say to his wife: 'I'll kill you if I ever catch you using those words.' "

"But, Hamid, what words?"

276

"Like I telly you: *Giddy-ap! Gee! Haw! Whoa, there!* and, *Whoa!*"

"But Mya can't use words like that on me! Besides, she's much too heavy for me to carry around on my back."

"You juss keep your ears open, you!"

"I'll be growing long asses' ears, Hamid: *Hee-Haw!*"

"Halloo Yass Halloo!" he bawled; jumping up and pulling my ears, to yank me back into Present Time, I suppose.

In Present Time, we are installed inside the stainless-steel shell of Star Citadel. It is rather like a projected installation on the far side of the moon but it is a Chinese moon. I find it very disturbing to be locked in these stainless-steel cells. The military mind, and the Chinese military mind at that, has, quite simply, added another dimension of terror to the Sahara I know. Violence, as they like to say, marked our arrival on this scene. That dumb dog belonging to Ana Lyse Africanus sparked it off. She is one of those compact frizzy blondes, dark at the roots, with big boobs, no neck and shoe-button eyes. I can see what Hamid sees in her, all right. She is a bit better than the newspaperwoman, who is as gray and grainy as repulped newsprint. We flew in at night, so I saw nothing of the Sahara and too much of them and I am getting bum kicks from the *Borbor,* all this time.

The daily sun came up like a big orange bomb as we touched down at Tam. Olav opened the door of the plane as soon as we landed and out bounded Karl Barx, as big as a young calf. He made straight for Captain Mohamed, who was waiting for us on the field. Not unnaturally afraid for his life, the captain yanked out a Luger and blasted Karl Barx in the head. Whereupon, the Little White Reindeer let loose with a

277

volley from a toy pistol belonging to Ana Lyse with which he managed to wound the captain in the elbow. Mya flew to the rescue to give him first aid: three little drops of Borbor, of course. "Hello Yes Hello and How are you feeling, Mohamed?" That's all there was to it. Like that, we were In.

Mya immediately took command of the fort and started snapping out orders. Thay was disposed of in the iron lung, with the help of everybody but me. I was just wandering off to look for the Communications center—where else?—when Mya spotted me.

"Whoa, there!" she cried. "And where do you think you are going with that UHER? Just hand that over, please. . . . I'll be needing that. Hanson, I want you to jump on that electric typewriter, over there. . . . I'll be wanting some transcripts made of what I record on this."

Mya had stabled me in this cellular underground air-conditioned office just big enough for one ass. I am chained, at least figuratively, to this twitching monster of a machine. The dam electric typewriter shies away at my lightest touch and balks like a mule when I lay hands on it. I'm learning to ride it. Right this minute, my UHER is recording under the bed in which his twin sister, Freeky Fard, is nursing the famous Amos. "I demand to see the Management!" I cry, but I have not laid eyes on him, yet. I begin to suspect, therefore, that all this lot of people I do see, here, are just Players and Amos-Soma may be the director of this operation. Certainly, he threw himself in here first. Mya must be wanting to keep an eye or an ear on her employees. She can't just be wanting to know what it felt like to be tortured by Captain Mohamed, last night.

The gallant captain, by the way, insists Dr. Fard operate on him without any anesthetic: that's his problem, I guess.

Mohamed became even more of a hero in his own eyes when he saw his arm in a sling. He went around braying with asinine laughter every time Mya gave an order around here. In the end, she detailed him off to Mag Media, who fell around his neck like a mangy old lioness goes in for the arts, all jangling with bracelets and beads. He better get in his kicks while he can, is all I can say. Some sort of awful reaction has begun to set in on me. If I could only get hold of some keef.

The generator here, if you please, does not produce enough juice to run both the iron lung and the air-conditioning at the same time. Five times a day, Thay must be removed from the lung in order to perform his *Imsak* with Mya. He uses a portable oxygen-outfit off the plane with a mask, to accomplish the act. Hamid and Olav have to help him in and out. While that goes on, the rest of us can cool off. Then, Mya emerges and spurts around with more authority than ever, while the rest of us wilt away again. Mya is in the Rally Room, right now, running all the ex-First Wave ex-ministers on: "Hello Yes Hello!" When I flick on the intercom, I can hear them droning away in there as if Mya was playing them at slow speed. Even Mya can't snap those cats into Present Time in this heat. You can hear that they'd sooner be back in their cells, playing Ronda. Naturally, Mya has given those cats doses of Brobro Borbro Bobrob Robrob dammit! BORBOR. I keep getting my fingers caught in these letters. I can hardly make my fingers punch out that bloody word on this mothering machine.

Filthy stuff! It can give a man a hangover last him a lifetime. Never again! I really must pull myself together if I am going to transcribe correctly the next tape of the conversation between Freeky and Amos Africanus, the twins.

13

YOU (FEM.)

You yourself were the one who first pointed out to Mya, if not to Thay Himmer, that immortality was the one and only proposition worth pushing, weren't you? Well, how do you feel about that since torture, Amos? Although, I suppose, an eternity of torture would be very much like an eternity of anything else, wouldn't it; just a terrible bore in the end? And, as for hellfire, we have it all around us out here in the Sahara, whether the Muslims believe in the eternity of Gehenna or not. Funny, I was talking that over with Mohamed only the other evening before our terrible trouble came up. *No, don't try to talk!* How that brute could have attached an electrode to your tongue and your penis! What villains they are! I mean, men.

You know what I mean about men, even if you are a man, too; or, are you entirely? Surely, half of you at least, must be me. I'm your sister, your twin, your other you in yourself whether you like it or not and, it's true, Amos; you do! Your poor peeling penis can't make all that much difference, can it? Is that reason enough to be other than I am and not think as I think? But, I suppose you're a man for other reasons, too, besides this bit of festering flesh that you have and I don't. Oh, don't worry, we're going to save it. Mohamed seems to have circumcised you a second time with fire but, apart from having to leave in the catheter, Francis says it looks good. The burns under your tongue aren't so bad, either, that they'll destroy your centers of speech. We're not going to leave you tongue-tied like Thay. I do think it's odd that two of Mya's merry men should be speechless at a time like this. *No, don't try to talk!*

I know what time it is: Present Time, indeed! I thought we were supposed to be on top of it and, here, Present Time is all over us like a great hairy blanket; the Sahara, itself. I never intended to play it like this and I still count on you to get us out of here. There, in the clinic, is my husband whom I love and respect, inside there trying to dig Olav's bullet out of my lover's arm: that murderous Mohamed, who would have killed me if you hadn't flown to my defense. Francis was no use at all: I owe you my very life, Amos, I really do. Mohamed's a maniac, isn't he? Imagine him killing poor Karl Barx but, then, all Arabs panic with dogs and dogs don't like them, either. I don't know that I like dogs all that much myself. I must say, I thought that very typical of our darling little sister, Ana Lyse, to bring such a big dog along with her and call him Karl Barx. And that woman; that newspaperwoman! Do you want to know where she is right now? No?

She's right in there alongside Dr. Fard in Mohamed's quarters, playing nurse and knowing full well—Francis is famous for it—that the doctor can never resist taking the nearest nurse every time he sees blood. That's how I first got Francis myself. We had a badly wounded guerrilla fighter in the surgery, dying on a slippery couch. As the man was apparently passing away,

281

Dr. Fard got more and more visibly excited and I did, too, I must admit; it's a very natural reaction to life coming and going, after all isn't it? We were both breathing hard as Francis motioned me to help put the man on the floor and then ordered me to get up on the couch in his place. Francis was all over me in a second; that's always his trouble the first time around. While he was washing his cock in the laboratory sink, I thought I heard the patient stirring under the couch; so I swung around, leaning over to see. Well, Francis, catching sight of my bare white bum in the air, I suppose, simply bounded back without wiping his hands of the soap and breached me brutally from behind for the first time in my life. It was, well, tremendous. The trouble was that when we got married it never happened again quite like that. Francis is getting on, you know, and he's had a hard life. We don't have seconds and thirds any more; that's out! I caught him once giving himself a series of hormones but nothing much came of it. I wish Miss Media luck but if Mohamed came up on her, now, that would be another story, indeed! Mohamed has positively seismic orgasms: he comes like an earthquake. *No, don't even try to talk!*

You didn't see Mohamed at his best: or, maybe, you did! Aren't you the least little bit masochistic, just like me? If you like being penetrated, you really must be. You must have been almost tickled to death when he turned his juice into you, Amos; confess! Ooh, I can feel it, almost. You know, Amos, it's true; I really can feel what you feel. I'm you. It's nice having you all naked here in my bed where I can soothe you and care for you and torture you just a little bit, too, to keep you alive until the next act of all this nonsense the Himmers have wrought. Mya's been using you like a tool, Amos! I know what she wants. She wants the Sahara and the Sahara itself is Police! Oh. There; I'm so terribly sorry, did I hurt your poor tool? I'm changing this catheter; *don't try to talk!*

You cannot imagine how boring it's been out here in this stainless-steel fortress, waiting for all this to take place. Practically the only regular visitor we have is old Professor Feldzahler, who comes whizzing over here in his helicopter from his atomic center in Reggan, looking more and more, talking more and more and acting more and more like the prophet Elijah, coming in his fiery chariot when he comes. You remember what an absentminded professor he used to be; well, it's all gone now. He can frighten the stuffings out of even Captain Mohamed with his apocalyptic atomic talk. While he was haranguing Francis, the two of us used to slip away into the flowering oleander bushes down by the *oued*. Mohamed's very well built. Things got more complicated around here when the Queen of the Tuareg blew in one day in a sandstorm. The sentinel at the gate who first found her would have raped her and robbed her, naturally, if Captain Mohamed hadn't just happened along on a tour of inspection: he's a terrible snoop. He's forever turning the poor political prisoners out for a bed-check after midnight, as if he thought any of us would be mad enough to throw ourselves away in the Sahara. The Sahara, itself, is our jail. We depend on this fortress for our lives, after all. What makes you think Mya can keep it running for even a single day more, tell me that! *No. No, don't try to talk!*

Nobody loves Sister Cassandra, I know. That's what Francis and I have been calling the queen, as a matter of fact. That poor queen! She has nothing at all but those tattered blue robes she's wearing; while she was unconscious, I went through her things. We found her clutching a roll of red rawhide, which was all that was left of the right royal leather tent around which the Tuareg used to assemble from all over the Sahara to the sound of the royal drum. When we took her in here we had no place for her, really, but a corner of the kitchen which we divided by hanging up her redskin curtains on the clothesline to give her some privacy. However, we both have to do our cooking in there so it's gotten to be more than a bit of a strain on the both of us. I thought Francis might have eyes for the queen but have you noticed the goat-smell of untanned leather in here? That's it. It ought to be nice to keep a queen in the kitchen but not when her leatherwork stinks!

Then, we had this odd English couple, mother and son, who came through here on foot. We called them Senior and Junior because they both had exactly the same name: Windfred Something-Something, I think. Senior knows every last blasted plant in the Sahara by name in both Latin and Arabic: the British used to train their people really well, didn't they? I feel sure she was sent to track down something like Mya's Borbor, don't you? Junior is a man in his middle fifties; so Senior must be getting on for eighty, at least, but she's as spry as a cricket and keeps the accounts. Junior, with a medical certificate from Medina and Mecca and a very sharp straight razor, does antiseptic circumcisions for money in the villages along the way. They get to places where the circumciser hasn't made his rounds in years. By the time they come along, so she tells me, there are often large groups to be circumcised, including boys grown so big they get an erection at the sight of the knife and ejaculate all over your hands; sperm and blood. Would you like a job like that? *No, don't try to talk!*

I became so impressed by the old woman's knowledge of plants that I wrote this in my journal after the Windfreds left. May I read it to you?

284

Maybe I would get out of myself more if I knew something about botany. As it is, the Sahara is here at my throat. Sometimes I almost go crazy inside this place that wears as thin as a sheet of paper in the whine of the wind while that very real monster, Ghoul, growls around right outside, forbidding me to open up. He's forever snuffling along the windowsill behind me or crawling along the crack under the door. I know, if I open up, he'll be bounding around in the room like a fist. My refuge is here in this journal between whose pages I cower as though I were between the covers of a cardboard castle and I try to lie as flat as ink on the paper or, at most, bodied out no more than the dried desert flowers I press between these same pages.

There, isn't that rather good? By the way, I think it a very bad magic for the Himmers to call their ruler Ghoul. That's really tempting the desert itself, don't you think? I say that's going too far. Well, listen to this:

When I can get out of this starfish fortress, this hospital-jail, this loony-bin which the clever Chinese anchored down to this rock of the Hoggar, I go botanizing. I don't learn much, naturally, not knowing enough to begin. It's as simple as that, but, at the same time, I feel sure that no botany book anywhere reproduces these ferociously ambitious plants I come across out in the Sahara. I observe them from a safe distance on some of my walks. These plants are at war, both with the Sahara, the sand and each other but, also, they are on the eternal lookout for any intruder who happens to put one foot out in front of the other through the desert.

There are plants out here with spined tendrils like elaborate steel traps and humanoid plants like silently screaming witches

285

BRION GYSIN

staked into the ground. I wouldn't trust the plants out here with as little as one drop of water. It's as plain as the Sahara itself that they don't mean *us* any good; any more than Captain Mohamed does the last gazelles he guns down from his jeep. If the plants had their way, they would tear us to shreds and butcher every last one of us for casual manure if they could. If you take this ten-power reading glass of mine to get a closer look at these so-called plants, you will see that they are out there adding hook to handle; one saber joint to the next and all that on top of sawteeth, prickles, darts, barbs and every angle of thorn. The wind is their ally and is always behind them to give a push in order to slash at each other or you or any intruder; animal, human or plant. They would contend, I suppose, that they fight for water but I see their innate hostility as just one more example of the extreme nature of the Sahara; of the world.

You see what I'm getting at, don't you? We are, all of us here, today and every day, in an extreme situation—between birth and death; you agree? Is there some still more extreme situation in which we can imagine ourselves? Yes; the extreme situation of leaving here willingly; do you follow me? Can you follow me if we go? Just nod your head: you don't have to talk. I don't mean just silly old Death, either; I mean sneaking past him. Oh, I don't mean necessarily bodily but maybe so; maybe even physically; maybe as if we were just thinking-crystals in some other state, imagine. Well, it's a lot less unthinkable since Space, isn't it? Anyway, our Dr. Feldzahler says: "There is no Place in Space!" No hope of heaven or home out there, either, but, maybe, a hope of my I being You everywhere, do you see? Otherwise, a rather grim prospect for us space creatures, isn't it; caught like astronauts dependent on their bodies like Thay inside his iron lung? *No, don't talk!*

Francis and I were out in the jeep with the top down one day. We drove over to a place called Tit where there is what might be a Roman ruin and, on the way back, a sudden curtain of sand blew up and encircled us with the oddest green light. On the inside of this funnel, Francis and I saw huge but hardly distorted images of ourselves hanging there, hovering ahead of us, upside down. When we got back, the Queen told us the Tuareg say that is the last vision of those about to drown in the sand. Typical rubbish, isn't it; how would she know? I do know, of course, as does anyone else whose name has been writ in sand, that the Sahara could breathe and cover us all forever like a book, closing on us, right now, but I wasn't frightened when I saw my vision. I threw out my arms to throw them around myself but I faded in front of myself as I went. Wasn't that sad? I'd like to walk into my own image as if it was you. Just imagine, you and I are on opposite sides of some shiny surface like a two-way mirror but thinner than paper; dividing two mirror-identical worlds, yours and mine. We stand as naked as you are now on my bed but without the bandages, of course. It's so hot in here without the air-conditioning, I wish Thay would go back to his *Imsak* with Mya. So, I strip off all my clothes: like this! There, light flickers and ripples equally over my naked body and yours; shimmering between us. Light rushes up like a curtain or drops like a guillotine, pulsing between your side of the mirror and mine. Now, I am the bold one, of course, with nothing to lose and a penis to gain, so I leap to embrace the image of me which is, brother, you! And, brother, that's what I really want;

to be with the boys. I want to be able to turn over—*Click!*—
the switch that made me a woman and you a man. I want to
be both of us, Amos! *No, don't even try to talk back!*

There, do you hear it? The air-conditioning is going again.
That means Thay is at *Imsak* with Mya. Do you want to know,
Amos; that makes my flesh creep! That woman's an addict;
no, don't attempt to talk! I know she has been giving all of
you her Borbor, for years. I know the whole lot of you have
been borborized over and over again by her until all your value-
judgments have been wiped out. I've had Borbor from Mya's
hands, too; don't forget, she really sprinkles it around. Borbor
has no effect on women except to make them a little lascivious;
that's the whole point. I'm not against vice, heaven forbid!
and, besides, who am I to throw the first little stone? I used
to make Mohamed take me "botanizing in his military jeep
because it excited me so to think of what he might do to me
when he machine-gunned down the gazelles. He's a horrible
racist, of course, but not as far as women are concerned.

He even stopped passing remarks about Professor Feldzahler when the old man showed up here with his new assistant
over there in Reggan. She claims her name is Chungalorn
Patticheki and she's a Loatian who studied physics in France
but I'd swear she was some sort of Chinese. No point in
warning the professor, though. He calls her his "Pattycake,"
and he's a completely changed man. She comes on like a
Dragon Lady in a black leather flying jacket and handles his
helicopter like a man. I wonder where Thay Himmer would
fit her into the game. That Thay Himmer, his games will be
the death of all of us, yet. Well, that's not entirely fair, I admit:
the professor's problems are equally apocalyptic, I suppose.
He's been having terrible troubles over there on his atomic

pile, facing outright revolt on the part of his young crew of mercenary mathematicians with long bristly hair standing straight up all over their heads. They're all in their twenties and pretty pent-up in the middle of nowhere, you bet! With nothing better to do, a gang of them have been feeding the computers with a calculation designed to predict when the next terrestrial magnetic-switch will take place; when the North Pole becomes the South Pole—*click!*—just like that!

The maddest of all these mathematicians worked on Telstar before he came out here and he insists on using a Chinese method called the Shortest Path. He claims to have already come up with an approximate calculation which practically throws the switch into Present Time—now! He goes around with a button he made for himself, reading: BOMB NOW, pinned to his atomic smock. Feldzahler insists the whole thing be double-checked, of course, just to give them something to do, but even he has to admit that the very calculations in which they are engaged are a danger in themselves. The Shortest Path, he claims, cuts swathes like cycles of light-years through the sea, the electro-magnetic sea which surrounds us. These very calculations are capable of pushing time further back than Fardism ever dreamed of and, therefore, they are building up an electronic tidal wave capable of sweeping down and over-whelming the lot of us; switching our current. What happens then? The professor, in his role of Elijah, suggests that all floods have their Ararat and, therefore, this time, because of the peculiar magnetic fields which are swirling around us, here right now, the Hoggar may prove to be it. Of all those in Present Time, we alone may be saved. *No, don't say a word!*

That's what I said: there's no point in trying to leave here right now. We might just as well, for the moment, sit back

and wait for the end of the world. We're all waiting for someone or something, always, so why not wait for that? In the
meantime, just let me read you something I wrote:

Professor Feldzahler says that, from his helicopter, he can
see new sorts of erosion eating into the Sahara surrounding us;
much more every trip. We notice it, too. Great gashes have
sliced themselves into the hills between here and Tit, making
crevasses which have cut off the road north. Feldzahler says
that, from the air, he can see that all the trails which lead up
to the Hoggar, here, have been broken off as if the Sahara
were ebbing away from us, loosening the sand which took so
long, so many eons, to gather in this volcanic cup. Those
tremendous flash floods which sweep over the Sahara like a
great floor mop, drowning countries bigger than France in an
hour, are pulling the Sahara out from underneath us. Enormous
flying dunes as big as provinces have suddenly marched out
of the Great Sandy Erg to "colonize" broad expanses of flat
reg over which trucks used to run. Professor Feldzahler saw
with his own eyes a stretch of hammada cliff many miles long
abruptly declare itself crystalline under some invisible stress.
The whole red range stretching off into the endless horizon,
suddenly shattered and fell like a curtain. A serpentine cloud
of dust as long as a frontier slowly rose in the air like a dragon
who had just laid a glittering trail of smashed polygonal spars,
each one as tall as a fallen cathedral spire. . . .

That's what I was writing when the professor called on the
shortwave to say; we still don't know what. You see, he and
I had agreed to discuss things over the air in the language we
both knew which was the least likely to be understood. It so
happens that we both speak Swiss Romanch; me from the years

I spent in that school in Rikon in Switzerland when I was interned there during the war. I don't know where he picked up his but that's what tore it. That evil eavesdropping spy, Mohamed, how would he know? He was sure it was Hebrew, of course. I barely had time to put a call in to you at "Malamut" before he was after me, waving a pistol. The key was open: you heard what he called me: "Jezebel! Spy! Bitch!" It was wonderful of you to come to the rescue like that. We simply couldn't have survived another day in this place together but you had to pay so dearly for the help you brought me; you poor thing. *No, don't try to talk!*

Just listen to the Sahara out there for a moment. You know how they always say they are going to the Sahara even when they just take a step out of doors? Mohamed does. Well, there it is whining to be let in; the Sahara, do you hear it? I swear, if you could look out and see it, it would be lying out there with its chin in its hands, grinning. Sometimes, when I am alone, reading or writing and not paying any attention to it, why, it's suddenly there; here alongside of me or, even, inside of me, breathing along with me but just out of time until, in a moment, I'm breathless; the Sahara is smothering me. I've been lying there where you are, Amos, when it has come down on me like a lover trying to get into me and I panic like a fish with its mouth open so, like: O!

Then, at other times, I know the desert's a void like the thin air outside of the cabin at thirty thousand feet up and we're all ready to explode out into it when, suddenly, there is this babble of voices outside like a whole tribe of Arabs riding by in the night. The wind marches right up and knocks on the door like a master proclaiming his right to get in. When you don't open up, the wind takes a few paces back and runs at the door, knocking more loudly again. Then, it gives up with a whoop and goes swooping away just to fool you. All the time, it's right out there waiting for you. Intent as a cat, it tries to push one silky sand-paw under the door to catch at some one little thing in the room, as a cat will; chasing it around in one tight little swirl while all the rest of the room watches, perfectly still. The Sahara is out there, always, pleading and teasing to please be let in. When it does get in and I fight with it, it snarls back at me until I pick it up by the scruff of the neck and throw it back outdoors. Through this very window, sometimes, I can see the Sahara march off with its great bushy tail stiff in the air as it strides down the dead-end avenues of the star-shaped fort where the barbed-wire thickens in the sand.

Here's a note I wrote on one of those days:

Spoons rasp horribly over the bottoms of our soup plates. Impossible to keep the sand out of the food. Chewing, one fears for one's teeth. Sand seems to sift through concrete walls and to abrade the surfaces of even stainless steel. Sand hangs glittering in the dry air; glassy, metallic and dangerous. I am afraid to breathe for fear of tearing my lungs. No filter is fine enough to keep the sand out because, diamond cut diamond, the sand crystals are filing each other down into scarcely palpable dust. My pen squeals over this paper. Behind the gritty whisper of the sand, I hear a rasping silence like white-sound feedback.

There, Amos, you see; it would take words ground into gravel to get that down. These aren't just my fantasies, either. Professor Feldzahler has seen from his helicopter an entire geological skin of the earth peeling off like a scab around the base of this volcanic carbuncle we live on. The bare cheek of the Sahara on this side of the planet is getting some sort of solar burn. Every day, you can notice, you can feel the sand slipping away from under our feet, ever-so slowly, a grain at a time, as it drains out of this big basalt cup our particular spar of stone stands in. Those Chinese geomancers knew what they were doing when they pinned Star Citadel here. They picked out spots like this all over Africa as if they were playing a game. Everyone, everywhere, feels that the game is just about up. We feel it even more hauntingly here. Present Time is draining away from this point like the sand in an hourglass.

There, how is that catheter, dear? Amos, just let me take a look at your dressings.

14

At this point, Amos exploded. *There is a noise on the tape unlike words; impossible to transcribe. The varnish peeled off the tape at one point.*

Presuming this to be the voice of Amos Africanus, I have given it a separate section. I hope this is all right with you. UOH.

15

YOU (MASC.)

You! Woman! Mother, Madame! Sister, Nurse! Get your paws off my penis and out of my mouth! Let me up, let me out of here! Elijah Feldzahler, the Burning Bush! Of course, he is right. Let me go get the Emerald. I have a date with a Chinese Dissident leader. *"Seek knowledge even as far as China!"* The Great Work!

(There is a good deal of noise like this. Amos seemed not to be in full command of his words. I have done what I can with all this. UOH.)

Of course the sands of Present Time are running out from under our feet. And why not? The Great Conundrum: "What are we here for?" is all that ever held us here in the first place. Fear. The answer to the Riddle of the Ages has actually been out in the street since the First Step in Space. Who runs may read but few people run fast enough. What are we here for? Does the great metaphysical nut revolve around that? Well, I'll crack it for you, right now. What are we here for? *We are here to go!*

So, what are we waiting for, sister soul? Pack up your

emeralds, Freeky: you and I have a date out beyond Deadline and we've got it together, as you said very well. This is Gemini, taking off! This is the way we came, you and I; one soul split into two bodies of compatible sexes and this is the way we shall go, taking them with us! Mya Himmer's Ace in Space is Love-All. It still takes a pair to beat old terrestrial Death and roll out replicas all over the universe. Let it be the perfect pair. Who could reproduce accurate replicas better than Pharaonic twins! Come, Cleopatra, all we need is the Emerald and the Emerald is not Egyptian at all but Chinese!

(*At this point, Amos let out a terrible shrill wavering yell that turned into a strangled cough, a hysterical laugh and, then, a chuckle. UOH.*)

So, laughter is refusal, eh? Well, maybe so. I was just trying to see if I could yodel again the way I did for the captain when he hit me with the high voltage. I find I can't. While he was torturing me, I could hear myself very well: it sounded like a dog taking a long time to die after being hit by a car. On and on the dog trills: won't he ever stop? This dying dog is shocking all the other well-fed dogs in the universe who are barking abruptly and clearing their throats, as much as to say: Why won't he stop? Why won't he die and get done with it? We don't like to hear that. I didn't either and, then, I was horrified to see that the bastard was burning my body but, strangely enough, when I took a good look at him, I saw that Mohamed was as deeply involved in the torture as I. What does he think he is doing? I said to myself. That's what saved me: I was no longer just one person but two. I was you, if you like; perhaps, your sort of Universal YOU.

Well, from that point of view, I was watching an Egyptian priest preparing a mummy into whose fist he slipped the Emerald to send the prone man off on his trip. The mummy was then set spinning, in order to wrap it in an infinite length of magnetized tape on which had been recorded the words, all the words. Current pulsed through the bundle to plate it. The mummy glowed and became perfectly transparent, white-hot. In the green and purple shallows, shimmered a white body which was both you and was me. I thought, at first, that the left-hand side was you and the right-hand me but we kept slipping in and out of each other, changing place.

What a fool that Thay Himmer has been. *"The answer to the existence of a fool is silence."* No one ever told him to play the Emerald onto Black. Mya knows better than that; or she should. But the Himmers are tourists, not to be trusted. There can be no question whatever of taking this whole menagerie into Space. I have a date with the Chinese Dissident Delegate, Mr. Lee. Mr. Lee knows what to do with the Emerald. Thay Himmer foolishly showed it around like a watch fob at a party we gave the China Committee when they came through "Malamut." I caught Mr. Lee taking a print of it on a paper napkin. Back in Pekin, they know how to read. They know, now, what we have. They have the ship but we have the chart. Where are we going? We are going OUT.

The Emerald seal prints in reverse an astral conjuncture, a cosmic crack which opens only once every so many millennia. That is the Way Out through which it is possible to slip in and out of the universe; just as I was slipping in and out of my body under torture, today. This stainless-steel star in which we are sitting, crimped down onto the basalt base, is not, as everyone knows, a psychiatric hospital, at all. But, neither is it a fort! Star Citadel is the base for a rocket and capsule, built in China and delivered by satellite, which can and will be fired from here to Eternity, today or tomorrow. You and I will be fired on a trajectory that knows no return unless the Traveler holds the Emerald as a map in Space and Time to get back.

Now, my pal Mr. Lee knows as well as you and I do that he who leaves an open door behind him, when he goes off on a trip, invites burglars and squatters into his house. When Mr. Lee's hordes of young Chinese technicians with bats' ears and bristly hair standing up all over their heads arrive, any minute now, to fit the capsule into place above us, you must be ready to leave. You won't need any baggage. So that there will be no squatters solidly ensconced in our property when we come back, Mister Lee intends to burn down the Old Homestead of Earth behind us as we take off.

I forgot to tell you that we have to take Lee along. We'll be shipping nobody else. You see, on this sort of flight, one man must steer by the Emerald while his co-pilot keeps an eye on the chart made from a reverse print. It's because of the symmetry, you see. The Universe is spinning and what spins must appear symmetrical whether it is or not. That is the essential illusion but we are symmetrical, ourselves; ambivalent, too. This is a split universe, run between the Image and the Real Thing; one is the mirror-image of the other but the point is to tell which is which. You see that, of course; or, rather, you don't.

Now, Freeky, what you must do is get hold of the Emerald for me, at once. If Mya lays her hands on that Emerald, we've had it: Mya is the one who will be leaving with Mr. Lee. The other great danger is that Black American of theirs. *"I am Black and I am Wise."* If he knows what to do with his UHER, we could all be rubbed out!

298

16

THEY

They can all be rubbed out by the *zikr,* of course! *Wow!* The minute I typed those last words to YOU, I knew what had to be done: *Wow! Anything* to get myself out of that trap in Tam. I paid the lady gladly; the Emerald for my UHER, cheap at any price. It was a simple matter, then, to record the *zikr* on a loop of spliced tape; playing endlessly over and over, again and again and again.

I press the old button to give it a whirl; double speed and, then, double that:

> *Rub out the word . . . Out-word rub Thee . . . The Rub-out word . . . Word out-rub Thee . . . Word rub Thee out . . . Out the Rub-word . . . Rub out the Word . . .*

Such is the process.

The word-process in reverse sounds less like blank verse than it does like a garbage-disposal unit built into a kitchen sink. Be as careful about inserting your finger in the running loop of words as you would be about plunging your finger

down your own throat. Abrupt word-withdrawal can be a shattering experience. Taken cold-turkey, it can cramp you with
chills of panic as the seasick words swirl around in a long
ring-a-rosy like a vomit of alphabet soup. The nymph Nausea
grabs you by the gullet, throwing you into severe anti-orgasmic
spasm while Pan, the dumb little brute-god, attacks you along
with his goats:

> . . . *frisking you, fucking you* . . . *biting you, butting
> you* . . . *taking you, leaving you.* . . . *Gone!*

I clench my eyes tight for one pico-second, just the time
for one all-knowing blink, and I open them again. They are . . .
gone! Gone, leaving me speechless! What a relief to be back
again at my own station in life. After all, I and only I; Ulys
O. Hanson, III, of Ithaca, N.Y.—or whoever this is that I
am—I am the sole captain of this super-stoned subway-system
called Patience which burrows under the sands of the Sahara
and—man! this subway sails only on keef. *Borbor?* What a
bore! What a mothering bore! One thing I can tell you, I have
come a long way but I'm back. I am not about to sign any
more of that crew on again, ever! I learned my lesson with
those characters. I have changed and, I think, progressed.

Could that be the clatter of my coffee cup crashing?
I am about thirty thousand feet high this morning so I have
to parachute down from my crown to take a better look at
those twin mountains I see down there, looking like loaves of
brown bread cast in bronze. They are—if I can believe anything any more—my own feet. From between them, a dark
brown *oued* is crawling across the Sahara paved with cement.

300

Higher up, on the marble plateau of the table in front of me, the flash flood of coffee spreads slowly but inexorably across my still unfinished letter to the Fundamental Foundation, blotting it out. I crumple up the soiled page, not forgetting that I still have that other letter to write; my letter of application to the Independent School of Algut. I must remember to ask them if they want their new assistant headmaster to be both a pot-smoker and Black.

Out there in the heat on the Place de France, I can feel the tangle of midday traffic on the Boulevard thickening and tightening around me like a web. When I peer at the scene over the tops of my shades, Tanja appears a bit peaky but I have to admire that every last detail is bright, bright, bright! Dazzled by all the candy-colored little blobs of light frantically jazzing each other out there, I pull down my shades to take a reading on my watch. It is just a few minutes past noon and here I am back on the terrace of the Café de Paris up on the Boulevard, penniless on that very corner Hamid once called the Cape of Good Hope. Slightly shaken to find myself still shipwrecked here, I take out my last white handkerchief to wave it, unconsciously, around like a flag. Forgetting for a moment what I took it out for, I decide not to mop up the coffee with it and break into a lunatic laugh.

I laugh at the very idea of letters. How can mere words get me across half a lifetime in the Sahara and back again in a matter of minutes! The thought of it makes a shiver run through me like someone just walked on my grave. My scalp tingles and tightens like a drumhead over the open roof of my skull. My hairs uncurl stiffly, one by one; all frizzling out in an electronic halo that buzzes around my ears like an alarm. My ears swell and stand up in total erection like the ears of

the jerboa when he hears the fennec hunting him down. Tin-
tinnabulating choirs of lullilooing women ululate like a limitless pasture of bluebells, one bluebell to every square mile,
ringing out over the Sahara after any short season of rain. A
sudden squeal of brakes on the Boulevard in Tanja cuts through
the heavy hum of the traffic on the Place de France like the
jerboa's dying scream. I nearly jump out of my skin.

I sat there feeling as if I had been turned into stone. Slowly,
I swiveled my eyes around like a periscope until I caught the
glint off the glass on a big old British car pulled up right in
front of me. Trust any White Hunter to spot me as soon as I
show the white flag! Slowly and stiffly, I brought the full power
of my blackest Black Look to bear on the bold blank face of
a white woman, obviously American, despite the desert drag
she had on. The cheap blue cotton sari she had pulled over
her head made her look dissolute rather than decent; like the
defrocked mother superior of some lay order of barefoot working nuns. She hung one mottled-blue arm out of the side of
the car nearest me like a slab of bad veal and put her other
hand up to shade her eyes from the burning sun as she trailed
her big tits back and forth over the steering wheel of her rented
Rolls Royce, with its GBZ plates from Gibraltar. In a flash,
I dug her essential indifference to all experience and association. That placid stupidity overlaid evident cunning: that soft
firmness, her motherly look, was a cover for cruelty. Yet,
there she sat projecting all this bundle like a challenge no man
could afford to dismiss and, at the moment, she shone for no
one but me. Instinctively, I jerked up, stripped naked, lathered
myself all over with soap, waved my big cock at her, rinsed
myself off, dressed and sat down like a good old boy; a real

spade stud. She did not blink. The striped awning flapped over my head as a red-hot gust of the gaïla, the noon wind, grabbed at my breath and—who should bounce out of the back of that old British pile but Hamid; my Moroccan mock-guru himself!

I thought sure I had left Hamid safely tied down with his family and flocks on his Pan mountain but trust Hamid to come up with any eerie American couple rolling around Morocco, on the loose in a Rolls Royce. After all, the world is Hamid's parish and all such, ah, "spiritual" chores of this caliber are part of his diocesan duties as a self-imposed "guide." From the back of this rusty old Rolls, a youngish billiard-bald whitey with buck-teeth and bug-eyes, obviously the husband, bobbed his head and grinned out at me; giving me the greedies, too, if you please. I could see at a glance that Hamid had this one firmly fixed on his big hook. Somehow, from even fifteen good feet away, these people embarrassed me: they looked too eager and too shoddily disguised. My first guess was that Hamid had hustled them in a hurry through some "cheap bazaar belong to a friend," where these buffoons come out the other end after great expense, masquerading as ersatz Arabs.

In fact, it turned out that Hamid had found them already dressed like this when he waved them down on the open road, on their way back from their first trip to the Sahara. Hamid was born to be a highwayman rustling Christian captives. All he has to do is to squirt them one look with his watermelon-pip eyes and promise to show them the Rope trick. They loop his lasso around their own necks. When they stumble after him into his Moroccan corral, he paints them in his own colors and rigs them as "Ringers" before he hawks them about in the world. I guessed that the woman took to Hamid's high-

303

handed treatment less well than the husband. She seemed a shade sullen and resentful; the white American look. Hamid bustled up to my table, cunning as a koala bear in his wooly jellaba, coming on strong to me like the spurious pusher of slaves. Hamid always has a bargain but, as they said of a man more after my own hue, Othello: "These Moors are changeable in their wills." So, when you deal in this kinda merchandise on the hoof, you don't shilly-shally around in the marketplace, do you? One single well-chosen word from Hamid, *"Food!"* and he had me on my feet. I was on! I rang down my last dirham on the marble-topped table and the two of us, arm in arm, *à pas de loup,* hungrily stalked our prey in their car.

"Him 'n' Her," as Hamid always called them, were dying to take us to lunch in their cool colonial villa out on the Old Mountain Road, overlooking the Straits of Gibraltar, in the middle of a garden set out with one hundred and sixty varieties of flowering mimosa planted by the brother-in-law of an English lord over a hundred years ago, now, at the end of a delicious ten-minute drive. In Tanja, the past is that close to hand. I am getting all this load from Her, up in front. Back there with Hamid, there is not word one out of Him although I can feel Him practically panting like an Irish setter down the back of my neck. I thought, maybe the language difficulty made for the silence between Him and Hamid but I was wrong. When I got it from Her, as we sailed through "Suicide Village," that they were missionaries from Champagne, Illinois, I felt like peeling right out of the car.

The Hymners, as I decided to call them, had rented a big old house it would take about ten servants to run and there was not one single servant in sight. The Hymners, in fact, kept a pretty seedy house. Piles of old magazines and tracts slithered about underfoot or slid from stacks, high in the halls through which they led us straight to the kitchen. You could see the Hymners liked that room the best. They had modernized it, as she said, with paint, plastics and appliances. Hymner got down to his chores without saying a word. Like a wizard, he whipped indented metal-foil trays of nameless foodstuffs out of a deep-freeze as big as a bank. Then, like a flash, he slid these through an infra-red ray oven on the wall and slapped them on the kitchen table in front of us piping hot but, before we could get down on all fours to gobble up this great chow, we had to say grace.

That is, Mrs. Hymner—call me Maya; like the Great Mother, she said, coming right out with it—Maya Hymner said grace wrapped in the endless yards of carbon-paper indigo-dipped blue material it takes to make a dress for a dancing girl in the desert. Some of those Guedra girls get so big they have to do their dance sitting down. Maya's gown swathed her like a tent but, when I squinted up my eyes at her, she looked like a giant bluebell to me. She had blue donkey-beads and cowrie shells braided into a sort of wild Saharan hairdo she allowed it had taken three women a week to plait on her head, but she wore no jewelry at all and strictly no makeup; except she was all smudgy-blue around the edges from the indigo dip. Somehow, despite this disguise, Maya managed to look one hundred per-cent corn-fed, barefoot, big old American girl with enlarged pores and gray skin. I shot this good look at her as she bowed her veiled head in prayer, spilling out a long flowery oriental-type grace over the plastic-topped table. To my astonishment, if ever I can be astonished by Hamid, I heard him gabbling along after her in his best hobbled English. Hymner just stood there agape, wordlessly gazing on Hamid with the liquid look

305

of a novice-master glowing over his latest Adept but there was still no word out of Him. I raised a tall eyebrow as Maya went on pouring out an entire seed catalogue of heavily scented flowers, endless bushel baskets of rare jewel-stones and piles of precious metals that clinked out of her like a jackpot of more than oriental confusion. At least, I knew where we were at: my mother once had a brush with Bahaï. Lest I be recorded as one of the heedless, when she finished I joined in: *"Amen!"*

All this time, Hamid is piously wig-wagging me to take off my shades. I can see how Hamid might ride right down the line with this Islamic splinter-group but I know it is too late in the day for me. I shake my head sadly at Hamid as I listen to Maya's thick thighs slap-slapping together under her robe as she paddles over to get a bottle of boiled water out of the frig. No stimulants, ever, eh? OK. I adjust my shades with distinction, indicating that I am not about to take them off to look on the likes of this great bargain of his. I can feel that my stiffness excites him. I know my Hamid, after all; what odd commodities have we two not bought and sold? Here he is trying to sell me his Hymners: what is my price? I figure Hamid cannot possibly know what the real deal is about: I don't know, yet, myself. I can see that reconnaissance conversation is not going to be easy. Unless we babble on about Bahaï, it is all going to be: "Have you read that book, whats-itcalled: *The Confessions of Denmark Vesey?*" and guff such as that.

In some ways, Hamid's take-over of the Hymner household was hellishly handy—and I mean it just like that. The Hymners were our meal ticket of the moment, feeding us both on their embalmed American food. Categorically, I refused to move in with them out there on the Old Mountain. I knew better

even if Hamid did not. Anyway, he was used to living like a
gypsy in seven different houses at once: they could never pin
Hamid down the way they could me. I stayed on holed-up in
my room at the *Hotel Duende,* letting Hamid break it to the
Hymners just how much I owed in back rent. The going was
not all that easy. That old meal ticket had to be punched and
punched regular; a lot harder, too, than I had at first been ready
to reckon. Happily, the local electricity went on the bum for
a few days, during which time the Hymner's endless stacks
of nameless frozen foods melted and died in their silent food-
safe. Hamid took over the cooking and it became really worthwhile to drag my ass out there to eat. Their old bus was pretty
much always at our beck and call to cart us around wherever
we wanted to go: Maya Hymner always heavy behind the wheel
of the Rolls, Him always silent in back. Hamid perched back
there, too, on the very edge of his seat, straining his ear and
his English to make out what she was saying to me; as, with
her eyes fixed on the road ahead, she slurred their lurid life-
story at me out of the side of her mouth.

This colorless couple from Champagne, Illinois, were living out a drama which they, at least, thought would yet shake
the world. Her people were from Canada, originally, and the
least said about that the better, I gathered. Was she "Colored,"
I wondered? I took a squint at her hair and threw that thought
out of my mind. The Hymners "had money." They had once
owned a sawmill someplace out West. "Him 'n' Her," had
met at the home of some Bahaïs in Illinois: met, married and
settled down in Champagne, as she said. They were both
Adepts who hoped to be accepted into the Faith but a couple
of things had gone wrong. She told me this when we were
back at their villa in Tanja but I swear I could hear the old

skeletons rattling in Maya's voice, all the way from the great Middle-West. Hymner was grinning and nodding, eager to corroborate every word Maya said. Well, it seems that Maya, at the very instant of conception, when his diamond-headed sperm-adder pierced the delicate membrane of her egg, Maya knew—she just *knew!* She was shy, she said, to tell even Him, at first but, eventually, all their circle in Champagne, Illinois, knew, too: Maya was chosen to give birth to the Babe!

Now, not everyone in Champagne swallowed this tale and, when the day came for her to face her, well, her Trouble; why, she found herself absolutely alone. Everyone failed her; especially Him. Hymner, it seems, took advantage of her pregnancy to get himself picked up by an electronic eye in a public toilet, like a Presidential aide at the YMCA. When Maya turned on, tuned in and heard all about it over the local network, she went into the kitchen of their ultra-modern home and aborted herself with a fork. Two cops in blue brought Him to Her in the hospital and, there on her hospital bed, she forgave Him. She got out and got home before he did. When he got out, she took Him back. But—and that was a hell of a But! he could never become the father of the Babe, now, could he? He had to shake his head: obviously not. So, she sent Him to the hospital to have himself sterilized and the operation so affected Him that he lost all his hair and his voice. Naturally, they had to get out of Champagne overnight and that brought them to Tanja, where else? In Tanja, at least, no one put all your business out in the street; now, did they? He nodded and grinned, content as a capon, confirming all this.

They had now decided, she went on relentlessly, that the Babe should be Black. It was on the tip of my tongue to tell her that would be quite a trick, when I bit the words off with my teeth. So, a spot of my sperm was the price! One diamond-headed sperm-adder of mine was to puncture her egg and plunge on into the Stream of Life; was that it? And did he think he was going to get to watch this? Maya stood there like a sibyl beside the kitchen sink. This child was to be a Mahdi, it was promised: Emperor of Africa. "Togetherness," I thought I heard her say: "You will all assist at the birth." *Great Ghoul!* There was a silence, as pregnant as you wish.

I began to get that old wound-up, wordy feeling and found myself talking too fast and too much. To put them at their ease, if you please! I launched into a largely fictitious tale about my mother, a very big powerful woman she was, too, who had much the same trouble with Ulys O. Hanson, Jr., her husband my father, who had taken off with her best black lace and her add-a-pearl Tecla necklace to go to the Beaux Arts Ball at the old Savoy Ballroom, years ago, and neither hide nor hair has ever been seen of him from that day to this. I could see that the Hymners were profoundly shocked. Panic-stricken, I began to blurt out yet another story; the story, I claimed, of how I had first ever heard about Bahaï. I felt their faces stiffen in apprehension but it was already too late. My technique is to overwhelm one enormity with another, so:

There I am back in Carnegie Hall with my mother, right after the war and still in high school. Up on the stage, Mrs. Roosevelt is sitting side by side with our own Great Educator, Mrs. Mary McLeod Bethune. This duo of dainty dinosaurs is perched on two rickety little old gold chairs pulled up by a skinny-legged gold table on which the girls are munching away at the "Star-Spangled Banner" like sisters until, all of a sudden, Miss Mary lets out a holler like someone just stuck her under the table with a fork. Looking blacker than Granmaw

309

in a pastel-pink potato sack and a hat made of ice-cream cake like Schraffts' melting on top of her meringue of fuzzy white hair, Bethune grabs the mike from the First Lady to bawl at us:

"I want all of you all out there to know that every last one of us here is descended from the Black Kings of Africa!"

Hamid, who had been sitting cross-legged on the floor, biting his nails as he listened intently up to this point, let out a loud snort; got up and left.

Too late! Carnegie Hall is rocked by applause like a mortar barrage. The Hansons, mother and handsome adolescent son, are beaming in the middle of a parterre of one hundred and seventy-seven handsome young Black Kings of Africa from Nigeria; all students at Lincoln University in Pennsylvania. The young kings have been obliged to leave their crowns with the white hat-check girl at the cloakroom, who insists that, made out of gold or not, what you wear on your head is a hat. The kings of Black Africa proudly sweep the streets of New York with their trailing robes gorgeously embroidered in silver and gold. Ergo, not all Black men are slaves or descended from such. Thank you very much! We who have been nothing, can become Black Kings, every one! Mrs. Roosevelt has skill-fully fielded the mike and is making her eloquent speech: "Not having had your advantages in adversity . . ." she seems to be saying.

Mother was a speech therapist so, at that point, she had to give me a big nudge: "She takes Voice!" she whispered delightedly. Eleanor was all too soon over for her and Miss Beryl Brown was announced. I could feel Mother stiffen when Beryl pranced out on stage, wound up in a little strip of leather torn off the skin of Life, like a lady-wrestler with nothing much on but a patch here and a patch there. Miss Brown announced, in a voice Mother could have done something with, that she was about to go into a Magic dance she picked up in Africa on her Fulbright. It was a dance of Initiation but she did not say who was going to get initiated into what. Then, Brown rolled out a big African drum, about as big across as a washtub, and she began to jump up and down on it like a trampoliner. That was all she did but, at every drum-jump— *Boom!*—and she pumped herself up just one more big puff. For a while, it hardly seemed to make all that much difference, she's such a big girl, but, when the drums began pounding into your head, Beryl began blooming and booming and looming so big she could have floated away over Macy's. Before she could explode the proscenium arch with her expanding naked brown-skinned flesh, they eclipsed her just in time with the big golden curtain before she could become what she was about to become, the great matriarchal myth-figure: Mother Maya Herself!

Hamid came back into the room and threw me a look of disgust. I could see that my elaborations had fallen rather flat. I had forgotten to add that, on leaving Carnegie Hall, my mother and I had decided to mark the occasion by venturing into the Russian Tea Room, which we understood was Restricted and, there, Mother had met up with a very nice woman from Larchmont in a mink coat, who told her all about Bahaï and offered her a job as . . . I could feel myself floating away into another one of my stories but I managed to stop. Simulating a sudden attack of brain-fever to the stony-faced Hymners, I rushed back to the *Hotel Duende* in the clamorous Socco Chico and dashed off that letter to the Independent American

School of Algut. By return of mail, they wrote back to say
that, what with the dollar and one thing and another, the school
was facing hard times, financial difficulties and blah blah blah.
They were dreadfully contrite to carry on like this with a man
of my caliber but they simply could not pay for transportation
at this point because, what with border controls and currency
restrictions and blah, more blah, but it was a deal: I was on.

All I had to do was to go out to the Hymners and hit them
up for the bread, I told myself. It was a lot less easily done
than said. One of the worst things at their house was that no
one could smoke because Maya suffered from asthma and other
allergies. Her asthma was aggravated by overweight and her
overweight was accentuated daily by Hamid's great cooking
with which he had, finally, hooked her. That girl was a greedy-
gut; never stopped eating crunchy peanut-butter snacks between meals. Who ever told her she could play Desdemona?
One night, we all dined out of doors by the light of candles
in Moorish lanterns, tearing chickens apart with our hands
under Hamid's orders, lying around Moroccan-style on cush-
ions and rugs. For a change, there was no Levant-wind blasting
through Tanja. The sticky-sweet, night-blooming flowers like
dama de noche, datura and jasmine, seemed not to bother Maya
for once. When the candles guttered out, Hamid and I even
dared light up a sebsi of keef on which we took turns in the
dark. The night was lousy with stars and that old pregnant
silence again from Him 'n' Her. When Hamid got up and went
inside to clean up the kitchen, Maya began to talk.

"Hanson," she said, perverting it into: "Handsome," I
thought I heard her; "when you say the Word, the Word will
be made Flesh."

"Of course!" I ejaculated, trying to pass it off as a cough. I was on! Coughing in earnest all of a sudden, spluttering and laughing, I got up and stumbled away through the dark garden.

Nothing daunted, Maya was down at the *Hotel Duende*, bright and early next morning, sitting on the foot of my brass bed. My Moroccan maids out in the hall made like they were scandalized; knocking and laughing, bumping their mops and pails against my door. I opened one blazing eye as I rapidly pulled on my black suit of human skin under the covers before I sat up and let Maya have it hard and straight. I told her I wanted no son of mine to be mooted about as a midget Messiah. I want no son of mine to preach *or* to teach and, besides— Yes, *besides!* I want no son of mine to be even one drop lighter than me. If I make a son, he has got to be *Black, Black, Black;* a real spade, see! Does she figure to raise this child with a white mother and a white father and him fitting into no skin at all? And what if it turns out to be a girl? If she really feels she needs an African for this deal, Hamid is an eager African. Delicately, I indicated something flattering about his painting technique and the size of his brush. As for me, I am only a poor old, retired, spade performer; just shoveling along, dig? Now, would she please be a good girl and go order me a *café au lait* and a *croissant* on the terrace of the café in the Socco Chico below. In the meantime, I would shave my beautiful black puss and be with her in no time flat. I meant that: no time at all. That was it. When I did get down there about half an hour later, she was nowhere in sight.

Within the hour, Hamid came trotting up with a sealed envelope addressed to me. I must have laid it on her, too, about needing that bread. Quite obviously, the letter contained cash and Hamid, who still cannot read, tried to shove it playfully into my ear; "making it talk."

"Here is the price of the Hymners," I told hin. "I have sold you to Her for this. I'm sorry, I know it's not near enough."

Hamid knew what I meant and he wept. I embraced him and told him how broken-up I was to be leaving him but there was just enough bread, there on the bed where I threw it, to take care of the *Hotel Duende* and buy me a solo ticket to Algut where the term at Independent is starting this week. Hamid was so emotional, he could hardly count his cut of the take through his tears.

"The train is standing in the station, Hamid. This may not be the way I came but this is the way I must go. See; no baggage, Hamid. I must return to the World."

"Here, take all the days of my life!" cried Hamid, much moved. "All I have to give is my brush and I'll do *anything* with it for you. I'll paint this lady from head to toe, if that's what you want. I'll give her my life!"

I do hope Hamid's words are not prophetic, because a very nasty scene took place, just now back in the station, as we pulled out of Tanja under the first autumn downpour. The Hymners did not come down to see me off, naturally, and I have not one dirham left. She even had the nerve to suggest that I sell my UHER and, somehow, between the hotel and the train, the UHER has just gotten lost. Hamid blamed it on her black magic, of course, but he was frantic and made a terrible scene with everyone in the station. My last vision of Hamid was a glimpse from the already moving train. He was practically throwing himself over the barrier, weeping and waving

good-by when, all of a sudden, two tall men who were obviously plainclothes police, swooped down on poor Hamid
like vultures and bore him aloft, backward over the crowd;
astonished and terrified. Hamid was bawling like a calf at the
killing until the rumble of the moving train drowned him out
and he was drawn away into the mysterious past. What was
all that about? What did that mean? Hamid is far too cool a
character ever to be busted for keef; what else could he have
been up to? Someone's revenge? Beware the fury of a woman
scorned and all that but: Would she have taken it out on Hamid?
No. I hope not. No. I sat down somewhat gingerly on the
brown plastic seat of the train leaving Tanja station at just the
right speed. I sat awkwardly because of the sheep's bladder
of keef Hamid scored for me as usual, at the very last minute
and for a very hurry-up price. I had stuffed what I scored into
the Y-front of my jockey-shorts, from which the hard-packed
poke of keef had slipped down and bulged like a baseball bat
between my thighs. I needed something to steady my nerves,
so I was prying into my own zipper like a pickpocket to pull
out the precious packet, when a uniformed cop on his beat
bumped past my compartment blindly, happily without bust-
ing in.

Suddenly, as I stood there swaying in and out of my mind
on the last few farewell pipes shared with Hamid, it struck me
like a blow between the eyes: I had forgotten to tell Hamid
one thing. I had forgotten to tell him why the Hymners had
no servants, no servants other than us; no hired servants at all
in their house. The Hymners feared local servants might inform
on them to the police. In theocratic countries, Bahaï has been
considered a heresy tantamount to treason and the penalty for

315

treason is death. Oh, well; are we not all condemned? I wouldn't put it past old Hamid to dodge even Death. However, I do recall what he said:

"Hamid, Consul of Keef, renews this green passport for you in the name of the Old Man of the Mountain, King of Keef. Long live the Assassins! On your Way, you are bound to run into some fellow-Assassins, you know."

"But I'm not an Assassin, at all!" I laughed. "I'm purely a potted professor. I insist."

"We are all of us Assassins," he gravely replied as he gave me the grass.

I find myself sitting back in the train leaving Tanja, gliding around the curve of the beach. I note sourly that they have truncated the beach once again to put in the new port installation and the enlarged railway yard. The necessary new mole has changed the profile of the beach for the worse by deflecting the wind-driven currents to pile up seawrack, refuse and oil slick on the sand. A minute back, we passed a man-made jungle of rusted iron girders, the skeleton of some long-forgotten fun fair, followed by a chain of leprous bathing establishments with: *Tea Like Mother Make,* scrawled everywhere to attract the vanished British tourist. Jumping up from my seat, I go lurching off down the corridor of my continental coach to the toilet. The cop comes out, still buttoning up. Having satisfied himself that there is nothing contraband lurking in there, he is not likely to come back this way soon.

I stagger into the swaying water-closet, lock myself in and carefully hang my jacket over the doorknob and the keyhole behind me. Above the immovable frosted-glass window, I turn a flanged air-vent to OPEN, before unzipping my fly. I pull out my business and pick out the body-hot bladder of keef to hug it between my knees while I redress. The old train is picking up speed, *clickety-clix,* as I fish into my passport-pocket to pull out my sebsi in its slim leather case. I fit the two sections together with a handsome brass band at the link. Placing a finger over my tiny flesh-colored clay pipe head, I try the pipe like a trumpet; airtight, good! A masterpiece match-box the size of a big postage stamp leaps into the overturned bowl of my left hand and I laugh.

I laugh because this whole business is, of course, just a trap well-enough woven of words—or so I must hope—for the meaning, if any, to show through like a lining of silk. What was it the matches used to say before they learned the latest: *"Burn, baby, burn"?* When I bend an ear to listen, the train is already rattling it out: *"Kaulakaulakaulakaulakau-lakau . . ."* I grasp the match firmly and strike it, exploding its head. Before it burst into flame, its head was a heavenly blue. I apply its red hair to the green bush of keef I have packed in my pipe and I suck it all up in one single toke. Exhaling, I breathe: "That's the truth!" blowing it all out the air-vent marked OPEN, from which it trails after the train to plane out over Tanja like a plume. Expertly, I spit the red comet of keef-coal into the open thunderbowl beneath whose open trap I can catch a patch of planet Earth spinning between our magnetic rails. Everything spinning must appear symmetrical: is that what it's all about? I turn back to the frosted window, standing on tiptoe to catch my last glimpse of the blue Leaping Hills through the air-vent; but night has already fallen in cold curtains of rain. I content myself with repeating the saw: "As no two people see the world the same way, all trips from here to there are imaginary; all truth is a tale I am telling myself."

So: there are no blue Little Hills and none of the rest is true, either. I condemn the whole thing. Then, like the governor before the execution, I want to wash my hands but, on this man's train, there is no water forthcoming. No matter what plunger I push: HOT or COLD, nothing flows out of the rocking walls at my once-magical touch. Fortified by a few more pipes, I replace my poke in my pants where it hangs like a blackjack. Pushing my face into the mirror over the basin, I say, I breathe to whoever is in there: "Human problems remain insoluble on purely human terms." Whoever it is I see in there nods in agreement with me. I light up a Player's to cover the keef before I boldly throw open the door to face a mob of Middle East refugees lined up six-deep, all twisting their legs. Then, when I plunge both through them and the swinging glass door in a panic, I see I am right back on that same old circular subway, suddenly; going nowhere again but fast. A handsome old white-bearded Arab loon, all dressed in white, bursts out of a blazing broom-closet, barring my way with an iron-tipped staff.

"You may not pass this way again in a lifetime," he says.

All the people I ever have seen in this lifetime are melded and jelled into some sort of red-hot honeycomb the old cat keeps in his closet. Outraged that we should all find ourselves, still, on this subway under the Great Desert called Life, I explode with all the conviction of a man who has found himself, finally:

"Let me in there again, goddammit!" I cry. "Whether I like it or not, I guess, I'm a Teacher and it's just because all you donkeys are so goddammed dumb that a Teacher has to go over the same old lesson, again and again and again. So, one lifetime isn't enough, eh? Well, give me more! No! More!"

The windows are streaming with gold. I look out to see we are spinning through the Sahara faster than the speed of light, escaping the clutch of the great hairy magnet of the Sun. From behind my back, this little old gink with one eye is asking me:

"Why were you in such a hurry to get here, when the desert gets us all in the end?"

Campoamor
Tanger, Morocco
1965–1968

They have all spoken.

As the dervishes desired, I have set down first the voice of one and, then, the voice of the others. In this book, I have not set down my own point of view because I am a man and a man does not know everything. In any case, it is not fitting for him to say everything he knows nor to write everything he says. Of one hundred thousand men, there may be one who knows and, of a hundred thousand things he knows, there may be one he should utter. Of the one hundred thousand things he utters there may be one he should write. If my own opinion had been set down in this book, both friend and foe might learn of it; both the competent and the incompetent might read it.

In other days, the initiate confided their secrets only to those they considered competent; swearing them to the secret. The incompetent, happily, are unable to pierce the thoughts of the initiate who, since the time of Adam, have obtained their knowledge of the essence of things through personal association with those who knew. Therefore, he who seeks the mysteries and the realities, must seek out someone who knows for, from the book alone, nothing emerges.

> *"The Unveiling of Realities."*
> Kashf Ul-Haqa'iq,
> Persia, 13th century.

THE CASE OF SERGEANT GRISCHA by Arnold Zweig   1-58567-335-8

"Some experiences in literature are unforgettable and this is one novel that culminates in an overwhelming effect of power and protest and irony and pathos of human fate."
—*The New York Times*

THE SORROW OF BELGIUM by Hugo Claus   1-58567-238-6

"With biting wit, gorgeous language and graphic imagery, Hugo Claus rushes the reader back in time as if by magic . . . This immense autobiographical novel is clearly Claus' masterwork."
—DANIELLE ROTER, *The Los Angeles Times*

PAST CONTINUOUS by Yaakov Shabtai   1-58567-339-0

"I cannot recall having encountered a new work of fiction that has engaged me as sharply as *Past Continuous*, both for its brilliant, formal inventiveness and for its relentless, truth-seeking scrutiny of moral life."   —IRVING HOWE, *The New York Review of Books*

MOUNT ANALOGUE by René Daumal   1-58567-342-0

"One of the most intriguing poetic reveries of contemporary literature."
—ROBERT MALLET, *Le Figaro Littéraire*

A NIGHT OF SERIOUS DRINKING by René Daumal   1-58567-399-4

"The book is Daumal at his witty, satirical, parabolic best. It demolishes all ordinary human concepts and then, in a final redemptive gesture, sends its protagonists out into the resulting chaos to 'pursue the business of living.'"   —P.L. TRAVERS

LE CONTRE-CIEL by René Daumal   1-58567-401-X

"In all of Daumal's writing, the world of concrete objects carries its full common sense of pleasure and hardship, of beauty and blight. At the same time, his philosophical turn of mind involves him in a real struggle of ideas . . . His is a startlingly clear voice in the din."   —ROGER SHATTUCK

GREEN HENRY by Gottfried Keller   1-58567-427-3

"In no literary works of the nineteenth century do the lines of development that to this day determine our lives become so clear to us as in those of Gottfried Keller. . . . His prose is unconditionally loyal to every living thing."   —W.G. SEBALD

Check our website for new titles

THE OVERLOOK PRESS
WOODSTOCK & NEW YORK
www.overlookpress.com